Praise for the previous novels in Rebecca Bradley's compelling series . . .

Scion's Lady

"A seamless story of deception, duplicity and evil . . . It is a taut, exhilarating yet poignant portrait of characters involved in circumstances not of their making."

—*SF Site*

"Well-written and engaging." —*SFX Magazine*

"Bradley's tone is an adroit mixture of wry humor and seriousness. Her plot moves quickly, and her characters, especially Tig and his catlike bride, are lively."

—*Starburst*

Lady in Gil

"Enthralling . . . [Bradley] tells her story clearly, with great pace, and a vivid and subtle imagination."

—*The Times* (London)

"Rebecca Bradley is a born storyteller who deftly advances the plot and sketches in her characters with lucid prose. . . . *Lady in Gil* is first-rate fantasy which doesn't require you to leave your brain at home. Read and enjoy, and perhaps weep a little." —*Vector*

"Rebecca Bradley has done a remarkable job in conjuring up fresh characters, vibrant plotting, and marvelous settings." —*SF Site*

LADY PAIN

Rebecca Bradley

ACE BOOKS, NEW YORK

LADY PAIN

An Ace Book / published by arrangement with
Orion Publishing Group, Ltd.

PRINTING HISTORY
Victor Gollancz hardcover edition / 1998
Ace mass-market edition / June 2001

The Penguin Putnam Inc. World Wide Web site address is
www.penguinputnam.com

ISBN: 0-441-00871-2

ACE®
Ace Books are published by The Berkley Publishing Group,
a division of Penguin Putnam Inc.,
375 Hudson Street, New York, New York 10014.
The name "ACE" and the "A" logo
are trademarks belonging to Penguin Putnam Inc.

PRINTED IN THE UNITED STATES OF AMERICA

10 9 8 7 6 5 4 3 2 1

With fond thanks to Christine Bernard and Jo Fletcher; to Jack Robertson for some entertaining suggestions; to Robin and Owen Thelwall for bearing with me; and especially to Katherine Thelwall, who read this book as fast as I could write it.

PART ONE

The Known World

. . . then shall the innocent, the brave and the righteously angry among the seed of the Naar be yielded up, and in turn yield up the Harashil, and be consumed; but Naar shall live for ever . . .

Naarhil text fragment, 'Khamanthana'; copy in the Archives of the College of the Second Coming

That Naarhil fragment Tig translated yesterday got me into trouble with Calla. I said I thought it was a little obscure. Calla said, don't be stupid, Chasco, it's not obscure at all, it's a prophetic reference to Tig – innocent, brave, righteously angry. I said Tig wouldn't agree he was innocent, not since the sinking of Sher; bravery hardly applied since the Pain had made him invulnerable; and I hadn't seen him get more than righteously annoyed in years. Tig said I was absolutely right, but Calla wouldn't speak to me all evening.

Excerpt from Chasco's Journal Vol. 4, 'Khamanthana', in the Archives of the College of the Second Coming

1

We had just decided to split up and look for him when Shree stopped and squinted across the torchlit market square.

'Never mind, there he is.'

I squinted across the square too, but there was no sign of him at first, nothing but a knot of people gathering in front of the shrine of the Shining Ansatz, a crowd where the shoulders seemed a little tenser, the fists a little tighter, the faces a little angrier . . .

'You're right.'

We reached the shrine just behind a patrol of the local constabulary and pushed in their wake to the centre of the storm. He was still not visible, but we could hear him speaking in his clear, reasonable voice, the one he used for explaining things. We groaned and pushed harder.

'In point of fact,' he was saying, 'your Ansatz-worship, though interesting in its own right, is historically a debased offshoot of an ancient cult found in Canzitar, the roots of which can be traced to—'

His voice was smothered under a roar of outrage, a rising roar. I could see him by then, half a head shorter than anybody else, smiling up at a pig-ugly giant in a black cloak who was probably, given our luck, the chief lawgiver in this benighted place. It would be just like him, I thought, to get noticed by somebody who could really make life difficult.

I reached out, being almost within touching distance, but Shree got to him first, grabbed his head in an armlock and clapped one hand tightly over his mouth.

'So sorry,' he said to the looming lawgiver, 'but as you can see, this unfortunate young man is touched in the head.'

'He doesn't know what he's saying,' I added sorrowfully, latching on to his wrists from behind.

The oversized person in the black cloak thrust his face into Shree's. 'He blasphemed the Shining Ansatz.'

'No, no,' Shree insisted, 'I tell you, the poor youth is mad.' He raised his voice to cover the commentary trying to issue from behind his hand.

The lawgiver glowered, but I managed to find his mailed glove and pressed a small bag into the palm. The scowl became thoughtful without ceasing to be a scowl.

'Ah well,' he said, 'the Shining Ansatz, in their mercy, have a tender spot for madmen.' He shifted his gaze from Shree to the mob, which abruptly transformed into a casual aggregation of good citizens who had paused out of concern for the stranger in their midst but were now ready to go about their business – fast. When nobody was left but ourselves and the patrol, the lawgiver loosened the mouth of the little bag to peer inside. The amount appeared to be satisfactory.

'I'll let him go this time,' he said severely to Shree, 'but next time I may not be able to save him – the things he was saying! Canzitar indeed! What kind of a father are you, to let your poor feeble-minded son go wandering about on his own?' Then he turned to me and laid a heavy hand on my shoulder. 'And you – don't you know you should take better care of your poor mad brother?'

'Yes, master,' I said.

'I've got eleven younger brothers myself, and there's nothing I wouldn't do for them. And since yours is, you know,' he tapped lightly between his eyebrows, 'you should take even better care of him.'

'Yes, master,' I said.

'Now get him out of the marketplace before he causes any more trouble, and don't ever let me see him here again.'

'Yes, master,' I said.

'A thousand thanks, master,' said Shree. We turned to go, the three of us, one of us perforce, and made our way through the heaps of strange roots, herbs and vegetables, the mats laid out with Ansatz icons and cheap clay pots, the beggars waiting patiently to pillage the leavings when the market closed at curfew. Shree did not set him loose until we were well out of the square and halfway down a dark, windowless lane.

'Tig,' he said wearily, 'you've got to stop doing that.'

'He's right, Father,' I said. 'Mother was very worried.'

It was bad enough being in this squalid Tatakil outpost without my father doing his best to enrage the natives, though it could have been more serious. At least it was civilized enough here for bribery to be an option. It was not even the worst place he had ever chosen to be awkward in – that distinction, in my opinion, was reserved for a vicepit called Uagolo on the west coast of Storica, where owning a money purse was equivalent to inviting a death warrant, and the biggest thief of all was the one sitting on the law-chieftain's stool.

Shree's opinion leant towards an icebound clutch of hovels near the ruins of Myr, on the grounds that one ran the risk there of being eaten as well as robbed and murdered; whereas Chasco held out for a small island in the middle of the South Ronchar Sea where, according to local repute, the inhabitants would eat their visitors without bothering to murder them first. Luckily for them, they didn't try it with us, but Chasco stubbornly stuck to his choice.

My sister Katlefiya's opinion did not count – she had an equal dislike for all the ports where we had ever landed, except perhaps Gafrin-Gammanthan. My father's opinion did not count either, since he had forgotten about eight years before that such a state as danger existed except in rather interesting hypothetical terms. His habit of testing hypotheses explained why we spent so much energy trying to keep him out of trouble.

Calla, my mother, took what was probably the most sensible view of all: that wherever we were at the moment should be considered the most perilous place we had ever been.

Chasco was waiting for us on the quayside, guarding the empty smallboat. While we'd been searching for my father, he had finished taking the supplies aboard the *Fifth*, and the front of his dark cloak was powdered with flour from the ill-sewn Tatakil sacks. He whistled on a falling tone as we helped Tigrallef into the bottom of the boat, and was answered almost at once from some distance across the water. The answer was similar but not identical, a shrill and vehement whistle blast that took the same sliding note and turned it into a clear statement of fury.

'Tig,' Chasco said with a grin as he unshipped the oars, 'I think you're in trouble.'

My father, hunched between the thwarts, looked up at him innocently. 'Physical, metaphysical or domestic?' he asked.

'Domestic. Kat isn't pleased with you. She said, if you were going to go off and start a riot in the town, you could at least have taken her with you.'

'Riot? I didn't start a riot,' my father said. 'I wanted a look at the shrine, and got talking to some of the local people, that's all.'

'He was telling them a few interesting things about the Shining Ansatz cult,' I put in.

Chasco shuddered.

'Fortunately,' I added, 'we got there in time to prevent anything terrible happening.'

'I wouldn't have hurt them,' my father protested.

'We won't go into that,' said Shree.

We traded glances over my father's bent head, Shree and Chasco and I – I had a good idea what they were thinking about, because it was haunting me too. The last time we were late in rounding him up, the death toll was somewhere between ten and fifteen. He never meant to hurt anybody, of course. He never even meant to wander off. When I looked back at him, he was humming softly and experimenting with the wake his fingers made in the water beside the boat; but a few moments later the humming stopped, his hands curled into fists, his neck and shoulders began to stiffen. Chasco saw that too, and quickened his stroke. The Pain was striking again.

*

12

It called itself the Harashil. *We* called it the Pain. My father often referred to it as 'the old sow'.

It had many other names. The Great-of-Fangs was what they called it in Nkalvi, almost five thousand years ago. The Burning Child of Baul, the White Dragon of Khamanthana, Itsant's Master of Hands, the Myrwolf, the Sun Serpent of Vizzath, the Flaming Skull of Fathan, the Lady in Gil – but of all its names, the Pain was probably the most frank and descriptive.

It was my father's private demon but potentially a very public one, a doom tapping its foot with impatience while it waited to bring down the world. It was a burden my father had carried inside his own skin for the last twenty years; and while it held off the effects of age upon his body for all that time, it waged an unending war of attrition upon his spirit. Nor did it leave the rest of us entirely unscathed, since we were the poor sods who had to live with him.

Kat and Calla were leaning over the rail as the smallboat nosed past the anchor chain and bumped against the ladder. My mother sheathed her sword as she identified us; Kat's chain glittered as she poured it back into the compartment in her belt. I helped my father up the ladder – I could see from the brightness of his eyes and his set smile that the Pain had taken a firm grip during the short ride in the smallboat, and he was already too busy battling it to watch where he put his hands and feet. Kat saw it too, and turned away with a sour face. It was no use berating him now, because he simply wouldn't notice. Calla bent over the rail to take his arm and guide him up the last few steps.

'How long since the Pain began, Vero?' she asked over her shoulder as she helped him towards the cabin.

'Only a few minutes.'

'Any problems in the town?'

'Nothing much – Chasco was right about the local susceptibility to bribes.'

'Thank the lords for that. Careful, my darling, the doorstep . . . I'll have words with you three later, letting him wander

13

off like that,' she added ominously. The cabin door banged shut behind her.

Shree had reached the deck by then, and Chasco was already securing the painter of the smallboat in preparation for departure. Tig's venture into town had cost us the best of the tide, but we were still determined to leave that night. It was not just the general nastiness of the Tatakil port that impelled us. For twenty years we had followed the meandering trail of the Pain's history, and in Nkalvi we had struck a dead end; for want of anything better to do, we were now setting a course for Gil, and our elders had suddenly found themselves in a tearing hurry to get there.

Pearl of the World, my father kept calling the place, with a dreamy look in his eyes; *more like the Arse of the World*, my mother would reply, and Shree would add, *yes, once your tupping Flamens finished what we Sherank began*, but they seemed to be no less eager to get there than my father did. Katlefiya and I, who had seen many shores but never the one that belonged to Gil, who had lived much of our lives on salty deckboards in the great unknown world, felt no particular affinity for this homeland of our forefathers. I was curious at most, though I welcomed making a landfall that was unconnected with my father's antiquarian researches. Kat was already preparing to be unimpressed.

She was sitting on the deck by the foremast, shadowed from the lamplight, waiting for Chasco's signal to help with the sails. It looked as if she had just cut her hair again, cropping it close at the neck in the shape of a pudding basin. Like my father, she had often been mistaken for my younger brother, a misapprehension which I reckoned would not be possible for much longer, no matter how loosely she wore her tunics. Though she had said nothing as we brought Tigrallef aboard that night in Tata, I knew her well enough to feel the heat of her resentment at several paces.

'Katla?' Taking my place beside her, I reached out and touched her arm.

'Leave me alone.'

'The town was a pisspit, little Kat. You wouldn't have liked it.'

'I don't care about that,' she snapped back. She jerked her arm away.

'What's wrong, then? Surely not that handsome lad you saw on the quayside. I saw him up close. *Not* freckles. Pimples.'

'I wouldn't care if they were boils. Just leave me alone, Vero.' She shifted until all I had was a three-quarters view of her back. We sat for a few moments without speaking; a dog howled ashore, a promising breeze pressed against the still-rolled sails, Chasco and Shree conversed in low tones in the stern.

In the cabin, our father cried out. Kat sat up rigidly and slumped back again.

I pulled her around so that I could see her face. In the meagre light, she looked like a younger version of a mask we'd seen in the fetish temple in Uagolo, the face of the Bitter Goddess, eternally furious since the Makers used her children's bones and blood as raw material in the construction of the world. When Tigrallef cried out a second time, the resemblance became truly noteworthy. Of course I had known all along what was bothering her.

'He can't help it, you know,' I said.

She turned away again. 'He's getting worse. It's the third time since this morning.'

'It's not his fault.'

'I'm not saying he does it on purpose,' she snapped. 'But what does he actually think he's doing? Why does he keep dragging us around these terrible places? I don't think he knows what he's looking for.'

'Of course he knows. He's looking for a true version of the Will that will banish the P . . . the Harashil.'

She swung her head around on her slender neck until I was looking full into her eyes. 'That's what he thinks he's doing,' she said, 'but I sometimes wonder. Never mind. Leave me alone, will you?'

I shut my mouth. I always thought it was hardest for her.

15

Calla, Chasco, Shree had all known my father before the Pain became a part of him; even I could remember a time when he was no more than a little strange. But Katlefiya was fifteen, ten years younger than I, and our father had been extremely peculiar all her life. Her first specific memory of him was on the night of blood and fire when we left the Mamelons of Itsant behind us, with a death count that probably topped three hundred. My first memory of him was on a different night of blood and fire, but it had made less of an impression on me; and of course I had better memories of him to balance it.

I can hardly recall how it felt to be a Vassashin child-messiah. For the first five years of my life, my world was divided between those who fell to their knees at the sight of me, whom I ignored, and those who actually mattered − my mother, my tutor, the Divinatrix Valsoria, and a few high-ranking Daughters of Fire, none of whom took any nonsense from me. It never occurred to me that other children might live any differently. Nor did it occur to me to wonder who my father was until he actually appeared.

Manners, archery, prayers, training in ritual and ciphering and dancing and the significant Vassashin art of oratory − one day I was learning etiquette from my Vassashin tutor, and the next, Chasco was teaching me how to tack into the wind. The intervening night of blood and fire exists in my memory as a few scattered pictures, nothing more; my first detailed recollection is of the day we crossed the outer boundary of the known world.

According to Chasco's log, this was about four days after Vassashinay dropped under the horizon behind us, an early afternoon that burned under a molten sky, with a hot steady westerly filling the sails of the lorsk and drying the sweat on our faces. My mother was down in the cabin finding her sea-belly, which she wanted to do in privacy, so the rest of us were under orders to amuse ourselves quietly on deck. Chasco was on the little foredeck with me, showing me how to tie sailors' knots. Shree was in the stern minding the tiller

16

and keeping a watchful eye on my father across the roof of the squat deckhouse. My father, propped against the bowrail a few feet from our lesson in knots, was alternately watching us and scribbling in his notebook.

It was already hard for me to remember a different life. After the routines and restrictions of the Sacellum, the boredom of being worshipped, the constant cloying attention of scores of Daughters, it was a strange kind of freedom that I was finding on the tiny lorsk. I was not told that our position was perilous and our future uncertain.

'Chasco,' my father said abruptly, 'we'll be passing the south point of Zaine in an hour or so.'

Chasco put down the death's-head knot he was tying for me and got to his feet to look around. 'Will we indeed?' he said. 'If you're right, then we need to decide now, Lord Tigrallef. Once we're past Zaine, we don't know what we'll find.'

My father stoppered his ink, closed the notebook and put both items carefully down on the deckboards. There was something odd and deliberate about all his movements in those early days, before he taught himself to block out the confusion of the Pain's multiple layers of vision. He tugged me to my feet, closer to the bowrail; I could just see over the weatherbeaten edge of it to the sea that glared around us. 'Look, Vero,' he said, 'and tell me what you see.'

'No.' I wanted to return to Chasco's enchanting knots. Also, I was still trying to decide whether my father fitted into the category of people I had to listen to. He did not fall to his knees at the sight of me, which pointed in one direction, but at least twice in those four days I had seen him fall to his knees anyway, with his hands shaking and great balls of sweat rolling down his face. His lips had moved as if he were praying, and experience had taught me that people who prayed could mostly be discounted. Shree and Chasco, however, whom I had easily classified as to-be-noticed, talked to him as I'd seen the Daughters of Fire talk to my erstwhile godmother, the Divinatrix, which seemed to indicate that Tigrallef was to-be-noticed as well. He smiled at my refusal,

17

with such good humour that I contrarily decided to oblige him and peered over the rail.

'Do you see any land?' he asked.

'No.'

'Chasco?'

'No, Lord Tigrallef.'

'The odd thing is,' my father said reflectively, 'that my eyes used to be much worse than yours, and yet I can see Zaine very well.'

'Zaine? Where?' Shree was edging towards us along the narrow walkway that ran along the side of the deckhouse. He joined us at the rail and looked keenly to the north. I remember how close and heavy the air felt, pressed down by the copper sky and not at all cooled by the sultry breeze. 'I don't see any land,' Shree said.

My father pointed to the north-northeast. 'There it is, that darkness along the waterline. Those are the clouds of Zaine, Vero.'

Chasco said, 'All right, my lord, we'll take your word for it. Are you sure you want to bypass the islands? We could still reach the cape on this wind if we started tacking now.'

'We don't want to go there,' my father said. 'They've got no food to spare, believe me, and the water isn't worth having. Too many bodies rotting in the sinkholes. The plague's raging there, and not just the Vassashin chorea: plagues are very sociable, they keep each other company. Anyone who doesn't dance himself to death could end up perishing of the squits, or maybe the sweats or the Storican pox. They're digging a mass grave on the edge of that little beach, do you see it?'

'What little beach?' said Shree.

My father sighed. 'I keep forgetting. Never mind. But I think we'll bypass Zaine, and you'd better pile on some more sail, Chasco, or whatever you can do to make this tub go faster, otherwise that rather large Zainoi wind-galley is going to cut us off.'

'What Zainoi wind-galley?' said Chasco.

My father sighed again.

There were two lessons for me in this. Shree and Chasco, both of whom were larger, handsomer, stronger and overtly more significant than my father, nevertheless raised the aft highsail simply because he told them to. Lesson one, therefore, was that my father was in charge. Second, there actually was a Zainoi wind-galley, though it was another half-hour or so before the rest of us spotted it. It saw us at about the same time; a distant flashing at its sides showed that the oars were being unshipped, and it changed course in our direction almost at once. Thus, lesson two was that my father really could see the things he claimed to, even when no one else could.

My mother wandered palely on to the deck just after Shree first sighted the Zainoi ship, and came to stand by my father and me in the bow. 'What do they want, Tig?' she asked. 'Are we in danger?'

He put his arm around her. 'The future,' he answered, 'is still something I can't see, by grace of the Old Ones. I can see they're quite a rabble, though. Refugees from the dancing plague, I guess, all of them men – the least they'll want is our stores to help them on their way. They'll probably want to take you too.'

'Not alive, they won't.'

My father smiled and clasped her hand. Watching jealously, I saw her turn to him to say something else, but she caught her breath instead. All of us were sweating in the cauldron heat of that afternoon, but my father was drenched, as if he had just climbed back on board after a dip in the sea. Still smiling at my mother, he bit his lip hard enough to start a thin dribble of blood running down to his chin.

'Oh gods,' said my mother, 'it's happening again. Shree, come quickly!'

Tigrallef thudded down on to the deck, cupping his head. Shree, arriving from below with our pitiful stock of weapons, dumped them in a heap and leapt to my father's side. I sat down close by, where I wouldn't miss anything.

Glancing over her shoulder at the approaching wind-galley, my mother knelt on the deck. 'Keep hold, Tig,' she said.

With Shree's help, she dragged him away from the rail and propped him against the side of the deckhouse. 'Keep hold,' she said again. I had no idea what she meant.

The Zainoi galley was gaining on us, its oar banks glittering as they shuttled in and out of the water. Chasco came around from the stern, shaking his head when he saw the state my father was in, frowning as he picked through the small heap of weapons and selected a dagger long enough to be called a short sword. The galley was close enough now so that I could distinguish long forked beards on the faces of most of its crew. Their shouts came clearly across the glassy water.

'Don't worry, Tig,' my mother was saying. She was still half-supporting my father, but I could see her eyes working critically through the pile of knives. My father looked even worse: hunched and trembling, wild-eyed, sodden with sweat, bearded with blood.

'Calla,' I asked, 'why is he being like that? Is he afraid?'

'No, Vero,' she said, 'he's not afraid. Keep hold, Tig.'

I wriggled closer. 'Why do you keep saying that? What's he supposed to keep hold of?'

'I'll explain later.'

'He shouldn't bite his lip like that.'

'Later, Vero.'

'But why is he—'

'*Later*, Vero! Come sit over here.' She pushed me against the deckhouse wall beside my father, propped him against me, then scrambled to the weaponry and snatched up a handful of knives. Leaning around my father's shaking body, I could see the wind-galley was only seven or eight lengths away, bearing down on us on a nearly perpendicular course as if to ram us with its blunt prow. Several men with clubs and swords in their hands were grinning in the bow.

My mother, Shree and Chasco were piling the throwing disks in the scuppers; a powerful voice bellowed in the wind-galley, and Shree bellowed back. Another sweep of the oars – the galley leapt a length closer. 'Vero, go below,' my mother cried to me. She had a knife in each hand, and three more quivered on their points in the rail beside her.

Another length closer, almost within throwing distance. Beside me, my father stirred.

'Help me up, Vero,' he said hoarsely, '*she*'s doing her best to stop me.' Somehow I understood he was not talking about my mother. I watched him tip drunkenly towards the deck on to his hands and knees and begin to work his way up from that position. Fascinated, I put my shoulder under his groping hand. With that support he managed to rise to a crouch, then painfully straightened his body. He shuffled forwards a few steps and, spreading his arms for balance, twirled clumsily on one foot. The effect was so comical that I laughed out loud.

'Vero,' he grated, 'dance with me.' He twirled again and made a series of little hops, swaying his upper body. I laughed at him again, then looked guiltily at my mother. She had her back to us, facing the wind-galley, which surged so close while I watched that I could actually smell the fork-bearded assassins in the bow. The largest and fiercest of them was petrified in the act of raising a grappling hook over his head; his eyes were fixed on my father. His gaze swivelled to me, so I did the first few steps of a Vassashin courting dance for his benefit, and he gasped and dropped the grappling hook into the sea. A chorus of many voices rolled out from the galley, counterpointed by frantic splashes and the clattering of wood. For some reason the wind-galley was falling over itself to get clear of us, oars tangling as the rowers fought to back water.

Of our armed defenders, Shree recovered first. He turned his back on the wind-galley while it was still sorting itself out, tossed his knives down and propped himself by his elbows against the bowrail. 'Tig,' he said, 'that's the worst Crane Dance I've ever seen – assuming it's intended to be the Crane Dance. How's the boy going to learn? Watch me, Vero, this is how it's done.'

He stepped away from the rail and began a series of movements that had a generic resemblance to my father's but were much more graceful and controlled. This led to a renewed outbreak of howling on the Zainoi wind-galley, which I imagined was applause. Watching Shree's feet closely, I did my best to follow his steps. I did not look at my mother in case she tried to order me below deck again.

But she didn't. She said, 'Let's show them the other courting dance, Vero, the one Silvir was teaching you.' She had left her post as well, though her knives were still lined up in a point-down row in the railing. She put her arms around my father and guided him through the dance – he sagged against her and kept stepping on her toes. After a while she steered him back to the shade of the deckhouse, helped him collapse on to the boards and slid down beside him to cradle his head in her lap. 'That was clever, Tig,' I heard her murmur, 'unless you really do have the plague.'

He did not answer. His eyes were closed, his breathing ragged.

Shree carried on at my insistence, with a sombre look in the direction of my father, though he cheered up at last and even showed me some Sherkin dances that were far too energetic for the southern climate and tired us both out nicely. Chasco declined to join in on the excuse of minding the tiller. He said he couldn't dance to save his life, that it was a good thing we'd done it for him. When I remembered to look for the wind-galley, it was a toy shrinking rapidly to the northwest.

And so it was, late that afternoon, that I danced my way across the invisible line that divided the known world from the unknown, while my father twitched in his sleep in my mother's arms. It was to be nearly twenty years before we crossed back again, and by then my dancing days would be over.

2

We bade goodbye and good riddance to Tata on the same night that Tigrallef blasphemed the Shining Ansatz, and set our course eastwards for the Island of Gil. After groping without guides through the unknown world, travelling through a geography familiar to our elders felt like a stroll in a pleasant garden.

The late spring weather which had caught up with us in Tata continued to be brilliant. The shallow seas supplied us so abundantly that we hardly needed to touch the leathers of dried meat in the hold until we grew thoroughly sick of fish. Only twice did we sight pirates and both times the sleek *Fifth* outran them without much effort. The prevailing winds, which were fair and strong, enabled us to work our way east by easy stages, watering mostly on islands that were empty or only sparsely inhabited, bypassing Plav and Zelf altogether. With hindsight, this was a mistake.

As we neared the Archipelago, my father was in two minds. He had a sentimental desire to see Exile, where he grew up, if only to make sure it had recovered from the effects of seventy years of Flamens; but Gil was so close now, and the Pain was intermittently so crushing, that he decided the diversion would not be worthwhile. Calla and Chasco, on the other hand, thought it might be wise to put in at Sathelforn itself to get some idea of what was happening in Gil, and we duly set a course in that direction.

What put us off at the north end of the Archipelago was the sight of three large black windcatchers, obviously naval but not flying Satheli colours, heading up the Forn Channel behind us. We pulled into a cove to hide while they sailed past, and decided, after viewing the arrays of spearchuckers and bouldershots on their various fighting decks, that it might be more prudent to find out in Gil what was happening in Sathelforn. In the end we avoided both Sathelforn and Exile, which also proved to be a mistake, a grave one, and made our last watering stop on a deserted islet at the southern tip of the chain. Three days later, on a limpid summer morning some five weeks after leaving Tata, we at last approached the Island of Gil.

Only Chasco and my father were in calm spirits as we waited to catch the first glimpse of the Gilgard across the sea. Chasco was sitting at the wheel, though the breeze was of the cooperative sort that left nothing much for him to do. Tigrallef was sitting not far from him in his special chair on the afterdeck, chatting about the tablets from Nkalvi between skirmishes with the Pain.

It was bolted to the deck, that chair, and fitted with restraints made of padded leather – when my father designed it, he aimed as much for comfort as for strength. Of course, the bindings would have been as effective as so much cornsilk if he really lost hold; anyhow, he'd invented a cunning little device that enabled him to manage the bindings without help from a second pair of hands. No, the chair was only meant to slow him down, to keep him from blundering about the deck in a blind daze if the Pain addled him without warning, to save the rest of us the trouble of nursemaiding him or the inconvenience of fishing him out of the sea.

That day, only he and Chasco could work up any interest in the Nkalvi texts. Shree was pacing the decks from bow to stern and back again; Calla was mostly haunting the bow, peering impatiently through the slight morning sea mist ahead of us. Kat and I were high up on the crosstrees, supposedly on lookout for the Gilgard, but also monitoring the activities of a fishing fleet not far to the south and marking off the succession of minor navigation points as we sailed past them. Primarily, though, we were keeping out of Calla's way.

This was because our mother was working through a series of difficult and contradictory frames of mind as we drew near to her birthplace. One minute she was anxious to have the *Fifth* shine from a swabbing the like of which it had never seen since it left the shipyard in Amballa, in order to impress any friends who may have survived the Sherkin oppression, the liberation, the Flamens, the plagues and the subsequent two decades of Gil's history, a period we knew woefully little about. The next moment, she was sure we should sail into Gil incognito, avoid all old acquaintances, skulk about the city in disguise. The moment after, she'd wonder if we shouldn't omit Gil from the itinerary altogether, especially as Tigrallef seemed to have no very clear notion of what to do when we got there. She accosted Shree at the foot of the mast, just below us.

'No,' Shree said. 'Whatever it is, the answer is no.'

'I just think we need to be better prepared,' she said.

'How? In what way? You've been through it a hundred times with me, and a thousand times with Tig. We're as well prepared as we ever are for a landfall.'

'But it's *Gil* we're going to, you Myrene ice-trog, not some scummy midden on the edge of nowhere.'

'So?'

'We should be better prepared than usual,' she repeated. Her voice was at its flintiest.

Up on the crosstrees, Kat and I exchanged weary looks. The *Fifth* had no captain. Tig's will might be the wind that blew us in a particular direction, but Shree and Calla shared the practical planning that got us there and the strategic planning that kept us breathing when we arrived. Chasco effectively ruled when it came to matters of seamanship and of commerce, where he had considerable quiet talent, ensuring we never left one port without a cargo that would be profitable in the next. I had a voice in all councils, when I cared to use it. This was a non-system that worked well most of the time, but the rare occasions when Shree and Calla did not agree could be tense for everybody except perhaps my father, who never paid attention. This was turning into one of those occasions.

'You're right,' Shree went on, 'about one thing. Sailing

into Gil will be different from any landfall we've ever made – for a change, we'll know something about the place beforehand. For a change, we'll be among friends.'

Even from above, the tilt of my mother's head looked sceptical. 'Or enemies.'

'What enemies, Calla? The only real enemy Tig had was the Primate, and he'll be long dead. Whereas if Tig's mother is alive or if his brother Arko is still on the throne, we'll be made welcome. Arko was always fond of Tig. He was even quite fond of me when he could remember who I was. He mostly mistook me for one of the butlers.'

'If they're alive,' my mother said tightly, 'we'll have an interesting time explaining why Tig hasn't aged in twenty years. And what if the Lady Dazeene is dead? What if Arko isn't on the throne? You've always said the people weren't happy living under the Flamens. What if they revolted after the Last Dance? What if Oballef's line was overturned? It could be dangerous to be a Scion in Gil now.'

He sighed. 'We've been through that already, too. We won't announce ourselves until we're sure of how we stand.'

'We'll be recognized.'

'No, we will not,' Shree said, quite sharply. 'Think hard: you've been away from Gil for twenty-five years, the rest of us for twenty years, and Kat and Vero were never there in the first place. We've *changed*. Be honest, cousin, how long ago did you give up pulling the grey hairs out of your head?'

'About when you gave up pulling them out of your beard,' my mother retorted.

'About seven years,' Kat murmured. I nudged her to be quiet.

'But no matter how much you and Chasco and I may have changed,' Calla went on, 'Tig has not. He looks just the same now as on the day he first arrived in Gil, and on the day he left.'

'That's his protection, if he needs it. Who will think he's the same man, if we don't tell them? Furthermore, Tig doesn't have the sort of face people remember.'

'Then what about Vero? You've always said he's the image of his uncle Arkolef.'

'We don't need to borrow trouble, Calla.'

'Oh gods, that's true enough. But I'd feel better about it all,' my mother said with a deep sigh, giving up for the moment, 'if I knew what Tig's plans were in Gil.'

'He doesn't know himself yet. Ho!' Shree jabbed a finger to the southeast. 'I think that's it – do you see it, Vero? Kat, do you see it?'

We had been paying attention to the deck instead of the sea; also, the waters to the east had taken fire from the sun as it rose higher, burning off the mist, and for the last while the horizon had been vanishing behind great blots of green dazzle whenever we tried to watch too conscientiously. Now the glare was cut as the sun passed behind a cloud and I saw, far off, the blunt grey snout of an island just poking above the horizon. There was only one thing it could be, I thought, the fabled mountain itself, the Gilgard, the centrepiece of so much history, of Tig's stories, of Chasco and Calla's grim reminiscences about the Web and Shree's matter-of-fact accounts of his Sherkin years. Kat went rigid beside me. 'I don't like the look of it,' she whispered.

Kat could be very hard to please. I didn't bother to answer. 'Landsight,' I called down to Chasco, who waved back with unusual animation and began to lash the wheel so he could go forward for our planned celebration. Beside him, Tig loosened his leather bindings, stretched, and strolled over to join Shree and Calla at the bowrail. He appeared to be in good control of himself, moving easily and walking a straight line. His smile looked genuine, very different from the manic curve the Pain often clamped to his lips. As he reached the others in the bow, the sun reappeared and bathed the three of them in a golden light, as if obliging us with a happy omen. High up in the rigging, I felt my spirits rise.

'So, Gil at last,' I said. 'Just think of it, Katla – where Oballef worked all those miracles and founded a dynasty; where our ancestors ruled as priest-kings for nearly a thousand years; where our father stood when he willed the sinking of Iklankish; where—'

'Shut up, Vero. I tell you, I don't like this.'

She was watching the slow rising of the Gilgard above the horizon, pointedly without the good cheer that was permeating the rest of us. When Tigrallef's laughter floated up to us from the bow, Kat looked down at him with narrowed eyes. I reached across the lines to tug gently at her cropped brown hair.

'What's the matter, little Kat? Come on, tell big brother.'

She glanced at me coldly. 'That was a reasonable approach, Verolef, when I was a small child with a grazed knee. Shut up and watch Father.'

'Tig's just fine,' I said, 'in fact I haven't seen him in a better way in a long time.'

'No, Vero, *look* at him. Watch the way he moves. Wait for another cloud.' I frowned at her, then at the three figures in the bow. Our mother was laughing as well, her fears apparently forgotten. Shree was looking pleased and clapping Tigrallef on the back. Below us, Chasco was just striding past the foot of the foremast carrying flagons of wine and water and six beakers on a tray. He looked up at Kat and me and motioned with his head for us to join them. *Homecoming*. I grinned back and started to pull my feet up on to the crosstrees.

'Watch him now, Vero!'

Another ragged cloud bank was just drifting between us and the sun, dimming the light to grey, dousing the fires on the water. For a broken second I saw what Kat had seen; a few heartbeats later I had shinnied down the mast and crossed the foredeck in a bound. Already the sun was clear of the clouds again.

They looked a little surprised at my precipitate arrival. 'Wine, Vero?' asked Chasco.

'He's glowing,' I panted.

'*What*? Are you sure?'

'He's glowing. You can't see it when the sun's out, but he is.'

28

We stood uncertainly around my father wondering what to do for him, which would be a fair and accurate summary of how we had spent the preceding twenty years. Light glowing through his skin was something we had seen before, several times, and recognized as a measure of the Pain's most powerful assault – and most of those times it had been like the groaning of rocks before an avalanche or the heavy air before a storm, a signal of danger that was grave enough to tempt Tigrallef to lose hold of his will.

This occasion did not seem to fit the pattern. It was a celebration, and there were no enemies in sight. It was a homecoming – after twenty years, the Gilgard was no more than a few hours' sail away. No wonder Shree looked incredulous at first. He said, 'Vero, are you sure about what you saw?'

'Absolutely.'

He stared at me, shaking his head. 'No, I don't believe it. Just look at him, he seems all right.'

Tigrallef, who was used to being talked about as if he wasn't there, beamed at us across his beaker like a man at a wine-tasting in a rather superior vineyard. 'I should imagine Vero's right, though,' he said.

The rest of us were silent as he took another sip from the beaker. My mother reached out to him, and he turned a smile of terrible brilliance on her. She said, 'What is it, Tig? Is it Gil? Should we bypass Gil after all?'

'Turn aside?' he said. 'Certainly not.'

'But—' She swallowed, started again. 'Tig, dearheart, if it's going to be like Itsant . . . Amballa . . .'

As he laughed, I could swear the brightness intensified inside him, until even the naked sun could not overshine it entirely. 'Not like Itsant, Calla. Not like Amballa or Nkalvi. Like Myr! A different matter altogether.'

'But—'

A trace of impatience came into his voice. 'Don't you see that *she*'s in terror at the thought of returning to Gil? She's trying to turn me aside.'

'But the danger—'

'Is to her, it may be,' he broke in. 'Remember how she tried to keep me from Myr, way back at the beginning of things?'

Other signs were appearing now, confirming that the glow I'd seen had not been a trick of the variable sunlight. His eyes were dilated until only the thinnest of blue rings divided the black pits of his pupils from the surrounding whites. His fingers paled around the beaker – Chasco saw that too, and reached to take it from him a broken second too late, just as it fragmented into shards. My father looked down at the pool of red wine at his feet, blood-coloured on the polished boards. 'Oh, damn,' he said. Very slowly, he began to drop.

Shree swung him up into his arms and ran for the deckhouse, my mother racing ahead of him to throw open the door. I knew they would not be back for some time.

'Will you have that wine now, Vero?' Chasco asked.

'Just a drop,' I said.

'Isn't Kat joining us?'

'Doesn't appear to be.' She was still sitting up on the crosstrees with her shoulder pressed against the foremast. I waved at her. She shook her head and looked away. 'No, she's not joining us.'

'Poor child,' said Chasco. He held my beaker out to me and took a measured sip from his own.

'Do you think I should go back up and talk to her?'

'No, Vero. I think you should leave her alone.'

I peered back up at the slight figure in the rigging. Her posture was not welcoming. 'You're probably right.'

Chasco usually was right, and of course he knew my sister as well as anyone could. He had taken on much of the burden of Kat and me when each of us was little: amused us, fed us, bathed us, taught us our lessons, even soothed our nightmares when Shree and Calla were too busy watching over Tigrallef's. It was he, not my mother, who used to brush and braid Kat's hair before she decided to cut it short. It was he, not my father, who took me to my first tavern and later my first brothel. It occurred to me now, looking at him, that outwardly he had aged hardly more than my father had – a slim straight man in his mid-forties who could have passed for thirty, with just a frosting of grey at the temples of his dark hair. Handsome, too; in his quiet self-effacing way he had broken hearts all over the unknown world, and a certain rich widow in Amballa had tried very hard to keep him. Sometimes I wondered why he stayed with us. Other times I knew he would never leave.

'Do you think Kat's right?' I asked. 'Is the Pain coming more frequently?'

He shook his head. 'The Pain is always there. Always. Your question these days should be, how much closer to the edge is it pushing your father?'

I stooped and started picking up the shards of Tig's beaker. 'The glow is a bad sign.'

Another slow shake of the head. 'Maybe, maybe not. It's hard on Tig, but it could mean we've picked up the trail we lost in Nkalvi. It meant something of the sort once before. Surely you remember the approach to Myr?'

I tossed the shards overboard. Remember Myr? Didn't I just.

Our first landsight in the unknown world, according to logs kept by Chasco and my father, was made just over nine weeks after our flight from Vassashinay. Such an empty sea would have been unusual west of Zaine, where landsights were commonly no more than half an hour apart and formed a solid basis for navigation in the Great Known Sea; but east of Zaine there were no markers. The sea stretched ahead of us featureless and unbroken, and even the patterns of the stars changed as we fared, first eastwards, then southwards. Chasco's log entries grew gloomier as the weeks went on and the water level fell in barrel after barrel.

My father's spirits, however, rose steadily at first. His movements became easier, he stumbled less, he stopped handling objects as if their size, weight and distance kept shifting on him. He slept badly, though, twisting and muttering on the pallet he shared with my mother in a curtained end of the cabin, often crying out in his sleep in words that no one could understand. After a week or so of this, Shree and Chasco took to moving their pallets to the foredeck at night with mine between them, so we could sleep undisturbed. My mother claimed she didn't need much sleep.

Five weeks into our journey, at about the time my father decided we should turn our course southwards, he fell sick for several days. That, anyway, was what they told me; but in fact the Pain was making its most vicious assault so far, long and brutal enough for me to remember it, many solid hours of my father curled up on his pallet, sweating, twitching, arguing with the invisible, reading horrors on the blank page of the cabin wall. When at last he seemed to be over it and could come on deck again, I heard him explain to Calla that *she* was trying her best to turn him north.

A few nights later I was lying on my pallet on the foredeck under the stars, supposedly unconscious, while the grownups talked softly around the last wine keg a few feet away. I was pretending to be asleep because I had noticed my elders' tendency to talk about the most interesting things when they thought I wasn't listening. That night, though, the talk was boring and incomprehensible, mostly about the dwindling water supplies, the lack of the small islands that had been so common in the known world, the urgent need to make landfall in the next week or so. With all the curiosity in the world, it was difficult for me to stay awake.

'But we've already crossed the deeps,' I remember my father saying. 'For two days now I've been watching the seabed rise towards us, just as I watched it fall away after we passed the cape of Zaine. I should say we're due to make landsight in the next week or so. By the way, I suppose you're all wondering why we're heading due south . . .'

I was dropping helplessly towards sleep by then and did not catch what he said next, but I dreamt that the voices suddenly got much louder, and Shree's voice, raised and angry, said things like 'madness' and 'get us all killed' and 'tupping Harashil', all of which sounded quite interesting; but the next thing I knew, I was waking up under a clear dawn sky with only Chasco asleep on the pallet beside me.

Somebody had furled the sails during the night, but I could tell the lorsk was still moving along rapidly. I got up and looked around.

Shree was in the stern doing his watch at the tiller. He was also tearing chunks off a piece of bread with his teeth, and looking grim. He held the loaf out to me as I hopped across the roof of the deckhouse.

'Where are we?' I asked between bites.

'Nowhere in particular,' he said.

'Why are we moving so fast?'

'We're in a very strong current.'

'Are we going to make landsight soon?'

'I could not say.'

I thought about the words he had shouted at my father in my semi-dream. *Madness. Get us all killed. Tupping Harashil.* 'Are you angry with Tig?' I asked.

'No.'

'Is Tig crazy?'

Shree drew in a long breath. He would not meet my eyes, but after a few moments he sighed and put his arm around my shoulders. 'No, your father's not crazy. Don't worry, Vero.'

'Is he going to get us all killed?'

'No, no. Of course not.' He grinned at me with a cheerfulness that would not, and did not, fool a five-yearling. I gave him what must have been a hard, penetrating look.

'What does "tupping" mean?'

'Raksh! Were you listening to all that?'

'I had a dream,' I said with partial truth. 'What does tupping mean?'

'Ask your mother,' he said; this time his grin was real. 'No, not your mam, she may wash your mouth out with gallroot. Ask your da, he'll tell you more than you want to know. Come on now, little Vero, there's work to do. Let's wake up that lazybones Chasco.'

I wanted to ask him about the other word, but I couldn't bring it to mind just then, the long word with an alien but not unattractive sound. Later it came back to me: Harashil.

In due course I did ask my father about tupping, and learnt a great deal about its etymology and not much about what it meant, but I put off asking about Harashil. It became obvious without asking that it had something to do with the Pain.

In fact, my father had decided to commit the lorsk to the Great Southern Current and follow wherever it led, which is why Shree had been so angry with him. Nobody knew for sure where the Great Southern Current fetched up; all they knew was that any vessels caught too firmly in its watery grip were swept into oblivion, never to return. In the known world we had come from, all sorts of terrible fates were envisioned for those vanished ships and their crews: pits of fire, sea-beasts big as mountains and hungry as babies, pirate demons, demon pirates, boiling water whorls, an edge of the world decisive enough to fall off of. None of the myths were more bizarre than the reality we found, though the reality had the agreeable characteristic of being survivable, with luck. We had located the current by the simple expedient of sailing due south until, in the middle of the night already described, we suddenly found ourselves careering east-south-east.

The next events I remember happened a few days later. The air had been growing steadily colder since the current captured us, until we were forced to don all our clothing in layers and wear our blankets as cloaks, even at midday. The spray hardened on the lorsk's yards and shrouds, the tattered web of her halliards glittered with a strange new substance which my elders called *ice*. Strangest of all, the days grew much longer, the sun dipping below the horizon for no more than three or four hours of each night. By day, its light was wan and watery.

My father sat in the bow for many hours each day watching the sea, looking perfectly well, if a little pale. In the evening of our sixth day in the current, I was sitting with him in his usual spot when he stopped in the middle of a story and pointed to the southeast, where a white line glinted far away on the horizon. It was only just distinguishable from the sky, which was also white, but with a luminous pallor the colour of pearls.

'Could you give my respects to Chasco,' he said to me, 'and tell him it would be a good time to raise the sails.' Then he sat up straighter and narrowed his eyes; I followed his gaze and saw that the white line had leapt up from the sea quite suddenly, becoming a thin strip coloured the blue-white of skimmed milk, cleaving the tarnished silver ocean from the sky. The strip began to thicken. 'Could you also tell Chasco,' Tig said, 'that he had better hurry. The pocketing old sow is up to her games again.'

I trotted to the stern, where the others were playing fingersticks, and delivered the message. They gazed open-mouthed at the horizon for a few seconds, then leapt to tear at the sheathing of ice that glued the furled sails to the yards, to twitch at the stays until their icy patina shivered into tinkling fragments on the deckboards. My father stayed where he was. I crept back to his side and craned to look over the bowrail, trying to work out what had so disturbed the others.

It was astonishing how rapidly the view had changed. A few minutes before there'd been an empty sea with a blue-white streak along the waterline; now there was a line of cliffs, not continuous, but tall and shining, heightening as we watched – the milky blankness resolving into stripes and mottles of detail, violet and pale blue, silver and dazzling white. Quite pretty, I thought, also interesting and worthy of further investigation, but not yet at the top of my list of questions. My father, paying no attention to my return, was staring at the cliffs with eyes that were no more than black tunnels drilled through the bloodshot whites, like the eyes of cats or certain lizards. I gathered my courage and pulled at his sleeve.

'Who's a pocketing old sow, Tig?'

He gazed down at me without focusing. His eyes drifted back to the swelling cliffs, so I tugged harder.

'Who's a pocketing old sow?' I repeated. 'Is it Calla who's

a pocketing old sow, Tig? Because *I* don't think she's a pocketing old—'

'Hush, Vero.' He blinked rapidly until his eyes shifted into focus. 'No, of course your mother is not a pock— not a sow of any description. Your mother is lovely. I – I'll explain later. Come on, let's help them get the sails ready.' He glanced at the cliffs again. 'There's not much time.'

The four of them worked like demons, too preoccupied to maintain the fiction that I was a useful member of the crew. Philosophically, I gave up trying to direct them after a while and returned to the bow to watch how fast the cliffs were growing.

Fast enough; by the time the sails were raised, the cliffs were a palisade from one end of the horizon to the other, mighty as mountains. They even had foothills, jagged hillocks that looked like a picket fence guarding a towering rampart – it was only when we were swept in among them that I realized they were islands, and that some of them were respectable mountains in their own right, all shades of white and grey and purple. One of the smallest, an angular tump not much larger than the lorsk, was directly in our path until Chasco calmly pulled at the tiller and swung us on a tight curve around it. We were safe for the moment, but a thousand others loomed beyond it, and the light was beginning to fail.

Now a chaotic battle commenced, a controlled frenzy of hauling on the tiller and angling the sails, of steering a drunkard's course through the maze of those floating foothills. The current became unpredictable and strewn with hazards – stretches of turbulence, savage cross-eddies, broad dimpled whorls that sucked at us as we skirted their edges – the wind was almost no help, being the erratic wheezing of a crazed giant. Chasco sang out terse orders, even in this crisis managing to sound courteous and precise; the others, including my father, scrambled to obey. There were many near misses. At that age I found it all very thrilling; in retrospect, terrifying.

Sometime during this wild ride I made the connection

between those huge haggard islands and the substance that had congealed so prettily on the lorsk's rigging. The islands were simply great chunks of ice, and they were indeed floating; some were even moving with the currents, though sluggishly and far more slowly than the lorsk. I raised my eyes to the great fissured cliffs beyond and saw with wonder they were crowned with greenery but caped with ice.

As we drew nearer the cliffs, the floating tors began to crowd more thickly, until I could imagine they were jostling each other for the privilege of getting in our way. Chasco worked marvels of steersmanship, dancing around one, swerving to avoid another, shaving past a third with a few spans to spare, finally slamming the lorsk to starboard as a great purplish mammoth reared up in our path. At first it seemed impossible that we would clear this one's bulging sides, and then it seemed we had miraculously done so; but the next moment the lorsk heeled almost on her beam ends as her keel scraped across a jutting shoulder of the ice-mountain just under the surface. Very sluggishly, the lorsk righted herself – but even I could tell, from the strange feel of the deck under my feet, that the sea was pouring in below.

The irony was that, through a narrowing gap between two enormous bergs ahead of us, I glimpsed an expanse of uncluttered water and a wedge of flat grey beach. Chasco must have seen it too, for he cried out and angled towards the gap with all the lorsk's remaining wayspeed.

That was when my father rejoined me at the bowrail, putting his arm around my shoulders and pulling me close to his side. When he looked down at me, I thought at first that the brightest and coldest of winter moons was being reflected in his face, but there was no moon that night.

'Tig?' I said. 'Father?'

He did not answer, but the light grew under his skin until it hurt my eyes to look at him. I pulled my gaze away and looked ahead to the gap, where the flanks of the two great ice-islands were closing together like the leaves of a double door, only a length from the point of our prow – and then the dark walls were sliding past us on either hand, cutting off the sky, sheer and louring as the sides of a steep ravine. From midship, I heard a terrible sound like a cloth being ripped across, probably indicating an unwelcome second hole in the hull. Seconds later we burst through the gap into clear water, while the two bergs ground thunderously together behind us.

My father's face, shining with that clear frigid light, was blinding in the dimness of dusk. He said, 'The answer is still no. Oh, we'll make it, all right, but *without* your help, so you might as well bugger off back to your pit.' He seemed to be talking to himself.

A drastic and worsening list suggested that the lorsk had no more than a few minutes left to live, but she limped on in the slack remnants of the current. We were in a race – the shore was close, but perhaps not close enough. Across a maddeningly short stretch of water the great ice-covered massifs towered halfway to the sky, and at their feet a low city tumbled along the waterline as far as my eyes could follow. That is, it looked like a city at first glance; at second glance, a city of ruins; at third glance, not a city at all. In the next instant the bottom finished falling off the lorsk, but before she had a decent chance to sink, the current flipped what was left of her up on to the shore.

Within minutes of extricating ourselves from the wreckage and tottering above the sideline, two things happened. First, the light faded inside my father's body, leaving him weak but cheerful; the pocketing old sow had conceded for the moment. Second, we solved the mystery of what the Great Southern Current did to the vessels it captured. There were no sea-beasts, no fiery fingers reaching from the deep, no sharp edge of the world – just miles of beach mounded with the rubble and carrion of whole fleets of wooden ships, hulls, prows, splintered masts, rat-kings of rope, crates, keels like the ribcages of dragons, some smashed and weatherbeaten, some as fresh as if the wood had been planed within the preceding year.

The youngest wreckage we identified was from a Satheli windcatcher, possibly a whaler; the oldest was a carved rostrum that made my father whistle with astonishment, because its like had last been built about fifteen hundred years ago at the imperial shipyards in Fathan. Given that it overlay an accumulation of earlier wreckage, my father estimated that this graveyard of unburied ships could be upwards of two thousand years old.

Bones of many men and women were mixed with the bones of the ships, but we were not the first crew to survive that landfall. As a direct consequence of this fact, the five of us were full of hot broth and snug under warm blankets by daybreak, in a ship on a mountaintop with a stunning view of the sea.

It seemed that, over the centuries, castaways of many nations had crawled up on the same beach; their descendants lived on in strange polyglot villages built of salvaged wood, scattered about the relatively temperate highland that crowned the cliffs. They had become a curiously hospitable people over the years, with a tradition of adopting all newcomers delivered to them by the Great Southern Current – the theory was that anyone who survived the long waterless drift and the final gauntlet of ice had been chosen by the gods themselves, and who were they to argue with the gods? Bad winters aside, it may have been the most benign landfall we ever made; and the smattering of languages we picked up in the plateau townships proved to be very useful in the long term.

My father, however, was not content to settle down in a cabin made from parts of an old windcatcher, to grow salt-resistant corn and raise sheep. My father had a mission.

Not long after our arrival, he announced his intention of taking a stroll into the interior of this small continent, a prospect that horrified our hosts. The continent, they said, was like an enormous saucer, sloping inwards from the coastal cliffs to a sinister hub where winter's hold was never broken, and the sombre white wastes were prowled by wraiths and cacodaemons; where disembodied siren voices lured trespassers into the bottomless crevasses that scarred

39

the continent's icy heart; and, more to the point, where the corporeal but possibly not human tribes of the Eyesuckers retreated after their occasional raids on the plateaux, to their filthy habitations built from the longbones of their victims – after dinner, of course. My father said it all sounded terribly interesting, and could they spare him some paper?

In the end, he borrowed furs and food as well, for himself and Shree and Calla. I stayed on the coast in Chasco's care, more because my short legs would slow the party than because of the insane riskiness of the venture, or so my mother told me. *Why* Tigrallef insisted on going was not told to me, though I gathered it was largely because the Pain was pressing him not to. At any rate they were gone for just over three weeks, and all I know of their adventure was picked up by pretending to be asleep when Shree and Calla described it to Chasco.

This is what I pieced together: that it took two full days to reach the edge of the ice-field and seven more to reach Tigrallef's unknown goal, walking downhill all the way into deepening cold and a furious snow-laden wind. The crevasses were no myth, though the wind probably accounted for the siren voices. The Eyesuckers were no myth, either – furtive, quick-footed skulkers with a gift for staying just on the edge of sight – and they in turn probably accounted for the reports of wraiths and cacodaemons. Shree and my mother knew almost from the beginning they were being followed, spied upon, sized up, but not until mid-morning of the ninth day did they get a good look at the lurkers.

Shree and Calla had been trudging, head down, all morning through a blinding snowstorm, with Tig striding confidently in the lead. At no time did he seem to be in doubt about where he wanted to go, and he was infuriatingly blithe about the weather. At last he called a halt on the edge of a much steeper slope, slanting down at a vertiginous angle into the obscurity of the swirling snowclouds.

'This is the place,' said my father, 'but I'm afraid you shouldn't come with me. Better if you wait for me here.'

'I hope you're joking,' Shree said.

40

My father took no notice. He swung his load off his back and took out of it a smaller knapsack containing paper and drawing sticks. 'This is all I need – I shouldn't be more than three or four hours, five at the most. Incidentally,' he added, 'don't worry about *them*.' He pointed at something behind the others' backs.

They whirled around at the same moment as the wind dropped and the snowclouds thinned and fell away. For the first time that day it was possible to see farther than a few feet, and it became immediately apparent that the story about houses built of longbones was also rooted in truth. In fact, my father's walking party had just unwittingly trailed through a sizeable encampment of the dreaded Eyesuckers.

Thirty or forty grisly hovels were huddled together within the throw of a heavyweight spear, coming nearly to the edge of the steep slope; uncountable fur-packaged ogres with gleaming silver eyes and long pointed buckteeth drifted in clusters among them, looking fully capable of sucking eyeballs for appetizers. Tigrallef moved forwards as if to greet them, and Shree and Calla instinctively caught at him to drag him back. He shook their hands off and stood with his arms folded for a moment, staring around the advancing semicircle of Eyesuckers with an air of polite interest. Then he threw back the hood of his fur cape.

He was glowing.

The ogre-people stared at him without changing expression – their faces wore a look of imbecilic sullenness throughout the encounter, according to my mother – and then slowly turned and plodded back into the grey boneheaps of their houses and closed the doors, and that was the last my elders saw of the Eyesuckers. Oddly, my mother had no feeling that it was fear that drove them indoors; rather, that the glimmer under Tigrallef's skin was something they recognized and respected, and most of all wanted no part of. By the time my mother turned around to remark on this, my father was already over the edge and starting down the precipitous slope with nothing but his little knapsack in his hands.

'I won't be long,' he called again. 'Just wait there and have a nice rest.' He was still glowing. Calla cried out in fury and started after him, but Shree caught her by the scruff of her cloak.

'He knows more about what's going on than we do. Let's do as he says.'

And that is what Calla and Shree did for the next five hours, barring the instruction to have a nice rest, which was not practical in such close proximity to the Eyesuckers. Mostly they sat back to back with as many weapons as they could manage spread out ready around them, taking turns watching the bonehouses on one side and the slope where Tig had vanished on the other. Every so often they had to get up and stomp around to keep themselves from freezing to death. They were nervous, hungry, cold and bored. Only once did the wind drop and the whirling clouds of snow settle out, and for a few moments they had a clear view across the valley.

They were perched on the lip of a giant bowl, an ice-encrusted amphitheatre perhaps half a mile across, too round and regular to be a natural formation. There was nothing natural, either, about the thousands of round black windows that stared at them from the sweeping walls of the bowl . . . and then the wind began to howl again and a heavy white curtain rose up between them and the view.

This was Myr, once a great city, where the ice lay spans-thick over the scars of an ancient fiery destruction. It was more of the discarded handiwork of our Naar ancestors, where the Harashil ruled for two centuries under the name *Myrwolf* in the cycle before the omphaloi of Vizzath were raised; these facts were worked out from the inscriptions my father copied among the ruins. More vitally, the inscriptions also hinted at where we should go next. *Before Vizzath, Myr; before Myr, Itsant; before Itsant, Khamanthansa . . .* By the time my father pulled himself back on to the lip of the dead city, he knew where to start looking for Itsant.

*

But first we needed to build a boat, a corporate task that took us more than two years. Naturally the Myrene villagers thought my elders were insane, and pitied me for how soon the stalk of my brief life would be snipped off close to the root, but they put no obstacles in our way. The *Second* was a patchwork vessel, the keel and ribs from a small Plaviset fishing boat, the strakes and deckboards carefully scavenged across miles of beach, the deckhouse frame and many of the fittings salvaged from the lorsk, even part of the ornate Fathiidic rostrum incorporated into the bowsprit as a decorative folly. Nautically speaking she was a mess and a mongrel, but she was a snug little ship, and I loved her better than any of those we sailed in after she was wrecked in the stormbowls of the Kerossac Sea.

My father, who became a danger to himself and others when he picked up any given tool, was gently discouraged from helping with the boat. Instead he spent those years asking questions and gathering information, and what he was able to piece together was startling: that the world was indeed a globe, as the Zelfic mathematicians had surmised; that there were four great clusters of continents and islands spread around this globe, divided from each other by deeps of such daunting breadth that only an idiot would set out to cross them intentionally; and that each of these clusters, not surprisingly, had come to think of itself as the entire world. The map my father compiled was probably the first of its kind.

That was not the limit of his activities. He salvaged his books and papers from the wreckage of the lorsk; he brought his memoirs up to date; he collected languages of the three unknown worlds; he charted the pattern of the great currents along Myr's complicated coastline, data which eventually enabled us to launch the *Second* safely. He also gathered fresh information from the castaways tossed up on the beach after us, which included a few each from Canzitar, Glishor, Sathelforn and Zaine; from them we received the last snippets of news for many years about our own part of the world, and also learned about the origins and spread of the plague they called the Last Dance.

My own feeling is that it was no accident that took us to Myr, nor was it an idle desire on Tigrallef's part to investigate the Great Southern Current. Myr was the best place, perhaps the only place in the world, where we could prepare ourselves for the long journey to come. Where else could my father have sat in one spot and let the information come to him with such obliging regularity? The Great Southern Current spread a very wide net. That, I am certain, was the prime reason for the Pain's savagery as we approached Myr's bleak shores, in a struggle so intense that the fire of it was visible in my father's face.

And now, nearly two decades later and half a world away at the approach to the harbour of Gil, we were again seeing that light inside his skin. I tried hard to see it as a good sign, as Chasco suggested. I tried not to think about what happened at Amballa, Nkalvi and especially at Itsant.

3

From the sea, Gil City looked nothing like the cesspit of danger, vice and oppression my mother had described, but it was no Pearl of the World either. To Kat and me, resting our elbows on the *Fifth*'s bowrail as Chasco manoeuvred towards the gap in the breakwater, it looked like a prettyish little port city with a scenic castle, a promising number of masts inside the harbour and a few more treetops than most visible along the waterfront. If anything jarred, it was the castle itself, which was almost outrageously scenic, looming over the modest town like a marble telamon in a kitchen garden.

'What's happened here?' Our mother joined us at the rail. 'Except for the Gilgard, I'd hardly believe it was the same place.'

'Better than you expected?' Kat asked.

Calla nodded slowly. 'Much cleaner, that's for sure. The walls the Sherank built are gone, but that happened before your father left. And I don't remember the breakwater coming out this far, or being so high and strong, and I certainly don't remember those watchtowers, though of course I never saw the harbour from the outside before – oh gods . . .'

Chasco was now threading the gap. We were passing between the watchtowers, squat blackstone structures hulking over the mouth of the breakwater, aware that we were being studied intently from both flanks. In another moment we knew the real reason why everything looked new and strange to Calla – another breakwater, which must have been the one she remembered, was still several hundred yards ahead of us, marking the line of an inner harbour. My mother's startled reaction was to a double row of enormous black windcatchers just coming into view behind the towers, moored four or five to a side in the outer harbour basin.

'Those ships look familiar,' said Kat.

I agreed. 'You're thinking of the naval windcatchers we saw in the Forn Channel.'

'The ones,' my mother said drily, 'that persuaded us it was unwise to go to Sathelforn.'

We were already among them, watching their imposing prows slide past us as we moved down the narrow channel of open water leading to the mouth of the inner harbour. Somebody somewhere was making a fortune in spearchuckers and bouldershots. Somebody else was making a fortune in banners. The latter were black or a deep blue-black in the bright sunshine, almost square, with some indecipherable logo worked on them in pale green and gold. Green and gold on their own would have been the royal Gillish colours; on a dark field they meant nothing to me, though I had been taught all the colours of the known world. On instinct, I disliked and mistrusted that flag.

Emerging from between the last two warships on the left, a little galley cut towards us with seven or eight men visible in the prow, all dressed in uniforms of dun-coloured tunics and britches. The craft looked tiny beside the great wind-catchers, but as it came closer we saw it was not much smaller than the *Fifth*, though lower built and only single-masted, with half a dozen oars on each side. A figure in the bow was hailing us. He waved us, not towards the jetties and anchorages of the inner harbour, but towards a blackstone moorage platform built into the inner edge of the new breakwater about three hundred yards to starboard. His request was more of an order, given the number of spears, swords and bows we could see among his companions.

'The Sherank used to inspect all ships that came into the harbour,' said my mother. Something in the flatness of her voice made me uneasy.

Shree came out of the cabin to help with the sails as we furled all but one and changed course under the vigilant eyes on the little galley. As we worked, he told us the disturbing news that Tigrallef was awake and in a 'strange mood' – a euphemistic understatement that we understood very well. It was with increased foreboding that we watched the moorage platform approach. Not for the first time, I reflected how much easier life would be if Tigrallef could be sedated or knocked gently on the head or reliably locked in a closet when the occasion demanded it. I glanced at Katlefiya and saw she was very pale.

There were more spearchuckers set up on the moorage platform, together with the crews to work them. Another little black galley nosed out of its nest of warships to glide along beside us, as the first trailed us watchfully at a distance of a few lengths. Three men in green tunics were waiting by the bollards on the moorage platform, armed only with pens and writing boards instead of weapons with sharp glittering points, which made them the friendliest sight around. I felt a little better when I saw them – the writing kits made it seem less like we were being taken prisoner, more like we had a lengthy but not physically threatening bureaucratic procedure in store for us.

Still, I did not like it. We had been expecting some kind of formality when we entered the harbour – most ports had a harbour master, quite a few had customs officials as well, and we were used to dealing with them – but we had not anticipated anything like this. In the Tatakil port, the formalities consisted of two old men ambling along the grimy wharf to meet the smallboat when Chasco and Shree first put in, to accept a reasonable bribe and ask a few gossipy questions. Other ports, Amballa for example, had been a little more businesslike; in a few the bribes or landing taxes demanded had been exorbitant, and in a few others an outrageous duty had been levied on our visible cargo, which was one reason why the *Fourth* and *Fifth* had been built with false bottoms and several hidden holds. The austere efficiency in the harbour of Gil City, however, the unsmiling and largely wordless show of force, were of a scale and quality we had never encountered before.

Between this and the surging attack of Tigrallef's Pain, our sense of homecoming was not what it had been in the early morning. With serious misgivings, we threw the lines to the moorage crew and suffered ourselves to be warped in. The tension increased when we saw that a guard of six armed troopers was waiting to accompany the three scribes on board.

'Use Storyline Two,' my mother whispered to Shree.

Shree nodded. Storyline One was the carefully edited truth. Under other circumstances we might have been tempted to use it, but these circumstances warranted something more convincing than the truth.

Storyline Two was a poignant saga about two Gillish brothers, Selki (Shree) and Masli (Chasco), torn from their starving elderly parents in one of the infamous Sherkin labour levies and shipped off to be worked to death in the copper mines of Calloon about half a year before the liberation. It was plausible. Shree said such things had happened frequently, though most levy-loads were taken directly to Iklankish. When freed by the wrack of Sher, the two brothers had gone into the copper business in Calloon and built up a good trade and a modest fortune. Selki married Shanna

(Calla), a Gillish girl liberated from the shintashkr of a garrison in Tata, and together they produced several fine children who had never known want, hunger or the heel of oppression.

Now the three Gilborns were fulfilling a vow to themselves, to return to their beloved homeland with their exile-born Gillish children, to walk once more the streets sanctified by the blood of their forefathers, the streets of the Pearl of the World. And, incidentally, to seek a good Gillish price for the Calloonic copper vessels and traditional Tatakil ornaments they had brought with them in the cargo holds. That homely commercial detail was intended to add a gloss of authenticity to Storyline Two.

The moment the officials came on board, it seemed that our fears had been unnecessary. The demeanour of both scribes and troopers was courteous, professional, impersonal; Shree, whom they instinctively but not quite accurately identified as the *Fifth*'s master, was greeted with a welcoming sweep of the hand that was straight out of the old gestural system. Another curious revival occurred when I took my first close look at the device on the scribes' green tunics, identical to that on the flags – two golden glyphs entwined on a grass-green circle, bordered with a thin black band. With an unpleasant lurch of the heart, I recognized one glyph as the name of the Lady in Gil in hieratic Old High Gillish, which had not been used for over five hundred years except in the most secret and sacred of the Flamens' records. The other glyph was unfamiliar. I saw Shree frown at the logo several times as if it reminded him of something he could not quite remember.

We were soon too busy to think about it. One of the officials, in a respectful but no-nonsense fashion, began by interviewing Shree/Selki about our past, our plans, our cargo, our intentions in Gil, and a large number of other pertinent or impertinent questions. A second inspected the cargo of copper and wooden ornaments in the holds, guided by Chasco/Masli and myself. The third, who was obviously in charge, a gaunt man with thin-pressed lips and cold eyes, stood by the foremast and watched and listened to everything.

Kat sat quietly on a bench in front of the forecabin door; Calla joined her after slipping into the forecabin and out of it again, signalling that all was well and Tigrallef was sleeping again. This was a relief – with luck he would stay asleep until the danger was over, and the inspection would both begin and end with the contents of the hold.

So it turned out for the first while. My poor father slept on. The customs scribe, who was not unfriendly, asked routine questions and scribbled many notes, doing an expert job of surveying the visible cargo but showing no great interest in sounding for secret holds. He loosened up far enough to exchange small talk with Chasco about the weather as we climbed back up the aft companionway, and even recommended a merchant in Coppermonger Yard – no doubt one of his relatives – for our load of copper. It was obvious this inspection was nothing special in his eyes. Chasco and I began to relax.

On deck, we found the same workaday air among the rest of the boarding party. Shree was getting hoarse from answering questions. Chasco was immediately drawn aside to fill out a sheaf of documents under the customs scribe's direction, and to pay a fee which was significantly smaller than many bribes we had cheerfully paid in other ports. I lounged unimpeded by the rail and watched two other small wind-catchers being escorted from the channel towards the moorage platform, which further reassured me. We had not been singled out, as I feared at first – it looked like all non-Gillish ships coming through the breakwater were inspected in this way.

More than an hour had passed since we were boarded, and the afternoon was becoming hotter and we were becoming drowsy. All vestiges of threat had faded; what was left was boredom, lassitude, and some slight irritation at the ponderousness of the Gillish bureaucracy. A seaward breeze wafted past, laden with the smell of a good marketplace – incense, spices, stall-cooked food, woodsmoke – and still the damned pen-pushers carried on, though there were signs they were running out of procedures. The customs scribe was writing out the fourth of four copies of Chasco's receipt; the scribe interviewing Shree, having asked at least fifty questions, had only a few sheets left to go. I stifled a yawn.

'You declared a complement of six,' the scribe said to Shree, his pen poised over the writing board, 'your wife and brother and three more. You will identify the others for me.'

Shree nodded. 'They are all my offspring, my sons Vero and Tilgo and my daughter Katla,' he said promptly, remembering to omit the Scions' tags. 'Vero, my elder son, is the one by the rail; my daughter Katla is over there on the bench; and my second son, Tilgo, is in the forecabin.'

The scribe peered serially across the writing board at me, at Katla, and finally at Shree. 'I need to inspect them all. You must show me your second son,' he consulted his writing board, 'the one called Tilgo.'

'If you must see him, you must,' said Shree, 'though I'd rather not waken him.'

'He's sleeping? At this time of day?'

Shree also suppressed a yawn. 'Can you blame him? I'd forgotten how hot these Gillish summers can be. But the truth is, he's not feeling well.'

This was a mistake on Shree's part, a transgression of one of the first rules he ever taught me: *never volunteer information*. It was also the first turning point. Every man in the boarding party stiffened. The scribe's chin snapped up; he stared hard-eyed at Shree for a few seconds and twisted in his tracks to look at his chief. Ominously, the chief scribe cleared his throat.

'Did you say he's not well?'

'It's nothing,' Shree answered firmly.

The chief scribe. moving a couple of paces forwards, came very close to standing on Shree's feet. 'Nothing?' he repeated. 'Nothing? What does *nothing* mean? Is your son ill or not?'

50

His voice retained a veneer of courtesy that I found more worrying than bluster.

Shree was quick to pick up this sudden shift in the wind. With a casual air, he stepped back from the chief scribe and reached down to adjust his broad belt – inside it was a fighting chain forged in Gafrin-Gammanthan, like the one in my own belt and Katla's, with flat razor-edged links on the business end and a flat leather handgrip on the other.

'He's been seasick, poor lad,' he said. 'He's not used to travelling by ship.' This of a man who had spent the last twenty years aboard ship, had circumnavigated the known and unknown worlds, and had never once in my memory thrown up, courtesy of the Pain; but it was a good lie, because seasickness was not a disease that could be passed from person to person. I was beginning to understand that the boarding party's concern was most likely a legacy of the Last Dance.

'We'll need to see him before I can issue an Affidavit of Clearance,' the chief scribe said in the same deadly tone. 'You must know of the Most Revered One's fiat, that no sickness shall be allowed to invade Gil City from the sea. I warn you, I am empowered to take stern measures to prevent the entry of any kind of contagion.'

'I understand,' Shree said quickly, 'but it's nothing like that – he's been seasick, also he took the late watch last night and he sleeps through to suppertime when he's taken the late watch . . .'

Tigrallef, fairly typically, chose this moment to throw open the cabin door. Blinking and smiling, he emerged on to the deck and was past Kat and Calla's bench before they could move to intercept him. He was not visibly glowing, fortunately, but his cheeks were flushed and his eyes were glittering with a sort of mad amiability. His appearance on deck brought about the second and more dramatic turning point.

Before he'd gone three steps from the door, one of the underscribes and two of the troopers gasped and fell to their knees; the other underscribe followed a moment later, and the remainder looked as though they were thinking about it

– all but the chief scribe, and even he looked shaken at first. Then he stepped back a pace and stared searchingly at my father. Ignoring them all, Tigrallef drifted across the deck taking deep lungfuls of the humid Gillish air.

By this point, three broad belts had already been discreetly loosened; Chasco owned a Gafrin-Gammanthan fighting chain but found the throwing disks more effective, and my mother preferred the little knives in the calf-sheaths of her britches. Then there was the razor-edged shark tooth on a thong around my neck – relic of a Bloody Spirit of the Sea who made the mistake of trying to eat my father – with which I once removed most of some pirate's throat when we were attacked near Amballa. I toyed with it idly, ready to snap the thong.

The chief scribe, not a happy man, looked away from Tigrallef long enough to scowl at his subordinates and the troopers, one of whom was now grovelling on the deck. 'Get up, thickheads,' he said, 'any more of that and you'll find yourselves on the Mosslines. And not as guards, either.' As Tigrallef floated past him, the scribe closed his fingers around my father's arm. My father stopped and surveyed him with a pleasant smile. The scribe did not smile back. 'You, lad,' he said, moving his hand up until he could dig his fingers into my father's shoulder, 'you're this Tilgo who's been seasick, is that correct?'

We all stopped breathing, but after my father had spent a rapt moment examining the chief scribe's hand on his shoulder, he said, 'Tilgo? Yes, I suppose I must be.' His eyes dropped to the device on the scribe's tunic, and his smile became broader and more delighted.

By this time the rest of the boarding party had struggled back to their feet – presumably out of fear of fetching up on the Mosslines, whatever they were. None of them had reached for his weapons, and they all looked more thunderstruck than hostile, but trouble still seemed much too possible. Kat and my mother were poised to throw open the lid of the bench they had been sitting on, which is where we kept an emergency cache of swords and knives. Chasco was hovering beside the slot in the midmast that held another supply of throwing disks. On the underside of the rail not far from where I stood was the switch that would release the anti-boarding nets and buy us a bit of time, though I doubted it could buy us enough. We were seriously trapped: the spear-chuckers and their crews were primed on the moorage platform and four little armed galleys were now in sight, not to mention the black fleet and the watchtowers standing between us and escape. I saw a vein swelling in Shree's neck, a reliable indicator that he was preparing to give a familiar signal. It was my father, though, and not the chief scribe, whom Shree was watching with such grim and fearful intensity.

But wait, I said to myself. Perhaps we were still seeing a threat where none existed. The worst those tinpot Gillish officials had done to us to that point was wave us over and document us half to death. On that basis, it seemed the most likely procedure for a suspected health hazard would involve a thick sheaf of forms filled out in quadruplicate. But why, then, the armed guardparty? Why the primed spearchuckers? Why the wolf pack of little galleys and the mention of 'stern measures'?

Tigrallef was gazing at the gold-stitched glyph of the Lady on the chief scribe's tunic, cheerfully blind to the man's searing close-range scrutiny. The others of the boarding party were standing still as wooden posts, barring a few nervous tics when Tigrallef happened to glance around at them. As the silence lengthened, I shifted along the rail and positioned my hand near the switch. Another armed galley hove into view.

'Well, he looks healthy enough to me,' the chief scribe said abruptly, releasing my father's shoulder. I almost pulled the switch anyway, out of plain shock. One of the underscribes dropped his writing board. My father beamed. Oddly, there was no lessening of tension on the deck of the *Fifth*, the troopers were still pop-eyed, we were twitching with the need to keep Tigrallef calm in case the dangerous glaze on his face turned into something else, and we heartily wished our guests would leave. I felt like the host on the final day of one of those two-month sacramental picnics the Plaviset love so much.

'Ship's master,' the scribe continued to Shree, becoming much brisker, 'I'll be able to issue you with the Affidavit of Clearance after all, but there will be a delay. It should not take long.'

Smoothly, Shree hooked a finger in my father's belt and tugged him away from the scribe. 'How long?'

'Not,' the scribe repeated, 'very long. Your ship will remain here until the documents are ready. If the delay drags on, I shall have fresh water sent to you. Welcome to Gil.'

Later, we all agreed that last remark was a nasty joke. We did not feel welcome, or anything resembling it. A cloud of uneasiness hung over the *Fifth* long after the scribes had moved on to their next victims, much of it because of the way the entire boarding party watched Tigrallef from the corners of their eyes for as long as they physically could. I got one or two curious looks as well, but characterized more by puzzlement than awe, as if they'd seen me somewhere before and were trying very hard to think of my name. The last trooper to leave our deck began to whisper something in my father's ear, until a peremptory shout from the chief scribe sent him hurrying over the side. Tigrallef stared dreamily after him.

'What did he say to you?' Calla asked.

Tigrallef focused his disconcerting smile on a point behind her shoulder. 'He called me *lord*. Laughable, really.' He commenced laughing, in a way that was wild and innocent, like a simple shepherd in a field of daisies, and also wild and fiendish, like an axe-wielding berserker in a field of simple shepherds.

Kat turned on her heel and climbed to her usual refuge on the foremast.

Even without the garniture of later events, this 'lord' business was dismaying. Tigrallef had been taken for a madman many times before, not without good reason, but he had never been taken for a lord. Greatly disturbed, Calla steered him back to the forecabin, leaving the rest of us to keep an anxious watch over the moorage platform.

The second distressing factor was the treatment we saw being meted out to the other four ships that were escorted to the customs moorage that afternoon. In essence, nothing happened to them, nothing at all. Not one of them was held for more than an hour, not one had to wait for clearance documents. The last of the four, a medium-sized trawler, was off and headed for the inner harbour less than forty minutes after it first moored. That made us feel unpleasantly distinguished.

The third distressing occurrence happened well after dark, when Shree had retired to record the day's events, Chasco and I were dividing up the night's watch, and Kat finally climbed down from the foremast. I had saved some supper for her, which she accepted with a mumble of thanks. She stood beside Chasco at the rail as she ate, overlooking the moorage platform, and after a few bites she said, 'He's back.'

I looked down. No scribes were visible, just troopers of various ranks standing in alert formation around their spear-chuckers. They appeared ready to repel a full-scale assault, though nothing was moving in the mirror-calm outer harbour except three of the little wolf-boats, and the *Fifth* was the only ship at the moorage. 'Who's back?' I asked.

Kat took another bite and motioned with her head towards the corner of the blackstone customs shed that ran along the rear edge of the moorage, where it connected with the breakwater. A youth in a plain dark tunic was standing there, barely visible until he moved a little and was sidelighted by a lamp on a nearby pole, apparently talking to someone out of sight around the side of the building. As we watched, the youth held out his hand and received something that might have been a bundle or might have been a message packet, then turned and ran shorewards along the walkway built just below the crest of the breakwater. We lost sight of him in moments, but I glimpsed a tall thin figure poking cautiously around the corner of the customs shed and drawing back as soon as my face turned towards it. Brief as the glimpse was, I recognized him as the chief scribe from the afternoon boarding party.

Kat swallowed. Before she could fill her mouth again, I intercepted the hand holding the bread and cheese. 'Who's back?' I repeated.

She glanced at the customs shed. 'Never mind, he's gone again.'

'Who? Who?'

'I told you, fishbrained brother. The messenger who just left. That scribe sent him off with a message packet hours ago, about ten minutes after I went aloft, and he only got back a few minutes ago, and now he's gone again. Let me eat.'

'Did it never occur to you—' I began, but Chasco nudged my side pointedly and quite painfully and shook his head, so I broke off and left the child to her bread and cheese. A few minutes later she bade us both good night and wandered aft towards the tiny cubbyhole we called her cabin. Chasco waited until she was out of earshot, then said in a low voice, 'Don't trouble her. There's no good reason to think those messages had anything to do with us.'

'She should still have told us earlier. And what else could they have been about?'

'Any number of things,' Chasco murmured tranquilly. 'Scores of ships pass through the customs post every week, and wainloads of provender have to be arranged for the troopers quartered in the outer harbour, and there would be orders and reports to exchange with the harbour master, and—'

'But what if the message did concern us?' I broke in. 'Suppose these damned Gillish bureaucrats are the first to see my father for what he is?'

He pondered my question while we watched the troopers just below us. A maintenance crew had arrived and was lovingly dripping grease into the mechanism of the spear-chucker. At last Chasco said, 'They were seeing *something* in him, but I don't think it was the Pain. Cheer up, Vero. My feeling is that Tig was right to bring us here.'

'But why?'

'I couldn't say why. Who knows? I'm going to sleep now. Don't forget to wake me for the second watch.'

Alone, I hung over the bowrail and traded occasional cold glances with the spearchucker crews, but mostly I watched the lamps of Gil City wink out in ones and twos, until the illuminated tracery of windows that marked the castle seemed suspended over darkness, a lighted ship sailing on a calm unreflective sea. Even by night, Gil City was too picturesque to be taken seriously.

But what struck me as odd was this: at no port larger than a small village had I ever encountered a waterfront as dead as this one. Not a single shout reached my ears from across the harbour, no screams, no tavern ruckus, not one burst of music through a brothel door as some hapless drunken patron was thrown out on his ear; just a bell that tolled out the watches of the night, and the gentle sucking of the wavelets around the *Fifth*'s hull when the light breeze blew across the water. It was so disquietingly quiet that I could not face going to my pallet in the aftercabin when I woke Chasco for his watch. I just hung the heavy Gafrin-Gamman-than belt over the wheel and rolled up in a blanket by the foot of my father's special deckchair, and slid into an uncomfortable sleep.

I was wakened at dawn by the arrival of another trawler at the moorage platform. Rolling over, stiff and sore, I saw Chasco standing near the bow where I had stood the night before, taking his turn at enjoying the spectacle of the Gilgard. Surprisingly, Tigrallef was beside him. Together they were watching the early sun flame on the upper pinnacles of the mountain, which was floating on the white pillow of mist that still lay over the city and the inner harbour. In the attenuating light, the great plug of solid rock looked as frail as a blown-glass bubble. The three palaces terraced up to its

57

heights were more unearthly than ever, palaces poised on a cloud, far too fine to be the work of human hands.

My father beckoned me over with an enchanting smile. He was fully himself for the moment. 'Look at that, Vero! What did I tell you? Beautiful!'

'Beautiful,' I agreed, not very happily. Not only was I still half asleep, but I could not forget the *Fifth* was under detention in a strange and unwelcoming port. I caught myself counting and recounting the spearchucker crews, coming to the conclusion that the moorage was almost twice as well manned as it had been the day before.

'And to think,' Tigrallef went on, 'that in all the world, Gilgard Castle is the only monument to the Harashil that hasn't been burned or drowned into a sad state of ruin. There must be some significance to that, if only . . .'

'What does a trawler need with that many crew?' Chasco interrupted, speaking to himself, but out loud. 'I sailed on one like it before the liberation – it needed no more than seven or eight of us.'

The newly arrived trawler's stern was only a few spans from our bow, with its high afterdeck not far below our feet. It did seem to be over-supplied with crew, many more than ten or even twenty, not counting those who may have been on the main deck but occluded by the stern. Chasco nudged my arm. Three of the little black galleys were hovering just off our port side, effectively blocking us in. A fourth was just being warped in at the far end of the moorage platform, well beyond the trawler. I began to get a very bad feeling.

'Chasco, Vero, you mustn't resist.'

I could not make sense of that for a moment; then I turned angrily on my father. 'They're about to spring a trap, aren't they?'

He was back to admiring the Gilgard. 'Oh, it was sprung some time ago. But when they come aboard, which will be any minute now, you mustn't resist. Chasco, no, don't sound the alarm. Let the others sleep in comfort while they have the chance. It'll make no difference in the end.'

Chasco stopped with his hand already on the rope of the

alarm, looked steadily at Tigrallef for only a few seconds, dropped his hand without ringing the bell, and stepped away towards the rail. His face was pale but without expression. I could not credit his ready compliance, especially as I could see a large party of troopers in dun-coloured tunics moving along the moorage platform towards the *Fifth*.

'Raksh take you both,' I hissed, pushing past Chasco towards the wheel, where my belt was hanging. He leapt after me and grabbed my arms from behind.

'Your father has told us not to resist,' he said firmly. 'We must do as he says.'

I easily wrenched free. 'Chasco, he's affected by the Pain. He doesn't know what he's saying.'

'No I'm not,' said Tigrallef behind me, 'and yes I do.'

I turned on him again. 'We may be in a trap, Father, but why should we surrender without even a token struggle? Unless,' I added cruelly, 'you're planning on handling this in your own way, like you did in Itsant.'

Chasco glared a warning and reproof at me, but Tigrallef smiled sunnily. 'Action for action's sake – you take after your mother, Vero, fortunately. But sometimes the best action is no action at all.'

I hesitated. It was depressingly clear that resistance could get us killed, and could not possibly get us free. Perhaps my father was just being sensible. He did that sometimes. Already we could hear the scratch of a gangplank against the starboard side, a voice giving terse orders in tones low enough to hide the words. A breath later, two helmets poked above the scuppers side by side.

'Verolef, remember what I said. I think this is going to be very interesting.'

Interesting. He could not have chosen a more inflammatory word. Tigrallef defined *interesting* in the way the rest of us defined *hideously dangerous* or *impossibly bizarre*. My hesitation ended. I lunged for the weapons cache in the midmast, but found my father blocking me with his hand raised in a calm-down gesture and a new and strange kind of brightness, scintillant rather than glowing, in the pupils of his eyes. It called to my mind the flickering of the fires of Itsant, the rain of bright brands arcing down to meet their reflections in warm black water as the tops of the ancient towers exploded. Uncertainly, I backed away. Then a more familiar cast overtook his features, and I knew his respite from the Pain was over.

'Don't resist them,' he repeated thickly. 'Let them take us.' He swayed on his feet.

Chasco and I grabbed an arm each and hauled him a safe distance away from the rail. Movement caught the corner of my eye: the chief scribe was on deck and moving towards us with six troopers in a neat double rank behind him. They were not the guards who had come on board the day before – their tunics were black instead of dun, and showed no insignum except a narrow green band high on each forearm. Tigrallef was the lodestone of all their eyes.

'The harbour master's compliments and regrets,' the scribe said smoothly, 'but we need to clarify a few minor matters before your ship can be allowed to proceed.'

He was only a few steps away. I neither heard nor saw him give a signal, but suddenly the troopers had bows in their hands, and arrows the size of small harpoons were aimed at Chasco and me. Nothing was aimed at Tigrallef.

'Get away, Tig,' Chasco said in the language of Gafrin-Gammanthan. 'Go over the side if you must, but get out of here.'

'Go, Father,' I urged him in the same language. I called him 'Father' only when I was annoyed with him, or when I was trying to impress on him the importance of something, usually his own safety.

He gave us a reproachful look, marred by the peculiar flying sparks deep in his pupils. 'Don't be rude to our hosts,' he said. 'You must speak to me in Gillish, or they'll think you're telling me to run away.'

'No need for that,' said the scribe soothingly, 'you're in no danger, any of you, if you do as you're told.' He nodded to one of the troopers, who stepped past him and headed straight for Tigrallef. In his hand was a small scarlet sack of some fine material. While Chasco and I stood paralysed by the arrows at our throats, the trooper pulled this sack over my father's head, in a manner I can only describe as reverent, and secured it by means of a drawstring at the neck.

I bellowed at the indignity – and also at the chilling reminder of Itsant, where such masks, eyeless and scarlet, along with heavy stone fetters for the hands and feet, constituted the entire ritual attire of human offerings to the Bloody Spirits of the Sea. I half expected the troopers to pick my father up and throw him overboard. The arrows suddenly didn't matter.

'Leave him alone!' I pulled the dagger from my belt and leapt for the scribe's throat; a half-moment later I was flat on the deckboards, and it was Chasco who had put me there. He kept his knee on my chest for a few seconds – 'Sorry, Vero, but Tig told us not to resist' – before climbing off and helping me to my feet.

I shot him a look of pure disgust. He shook his head sadly in something like apology as rough hands yanked my arms behind me and wrapped enough rope around my crossed wrists to have raised a highsail on a tall ship. Tigrallef, however, having obligingly turned around and clasped his hands behind his back, was left unsecured.

'Just these two,' the scribe said. 'Hurry, they're waiting for us ashore. Mollo knows what to do with the others.'

As our small party swept towards the gangplank, a more powerful reverse current began to sweep up it, a spring tide of troopers in dun-coloured uniforms, armed and businesslike. Turning my head, I could see another such tide leaping the short distance from the moored trawler to the bow of the *Fifth*. There was no shouting. The only sound was the thudding of their boots. A last glance, snatched as I was shoved on to the gangplank, showed a silent press of troopers around the spot where Chasco had been standing, and others moving purposefully towards the cabins where the rest were asleep. When I tried to cry out a last-minute alarm, somebody's mailed hand shoved a leather mouth-stopper between my teeth.

The fact that I was furious can be taken for granted; and it was a comprehensive fury, encompassing not only our captors, the gods, the Pain and the entire population of that damnable island, but also Chasco and especially Tigrallef. Mixed in with the anger was a strong element of mystification: as I stumbled along the smooth stone pavement surrounded by guards, I became wildly obsessed with how little sense this trap made. Why? Why? Why bring up fifty or sixty men to capture six persons, three of them sleeping, one of them a girl hardly out of childhood – at that reminder of Kat, fear hit me for the first time. I was still enraged with Chasco, but now there was fear for him as well, and for my mother and for Shree; but the fear I felt for my sister was like a sharp knife in the heart. In the peculiar silence that now hung over the moorage, I found myself listening for her screams. The fact that none came was no great comfort, giving rise to visions of the poor child lying in her bed with a cut throat, or – or worse. The thought of 'worse' made me frantic, to the point where my guardparty saw the wisdom of stopping to tie my feet together as well as my hands, because they preferred carrying me to being kicked by me. One of them noticed the lethal nature of the shark tooth hanging at my throat, and snapped the thong.

Ahead, I could see Tigrallef being handed gently into the little black galley moored at the end of the platform. When my turn came, they simply threw me into the bow. Stunned and breathless, it took me some time to regain any interest in events; and when at last I was able to sit up and look over the side, we were passing through the second breakwater and into the heavy mist that still shrouded the inner harbour. Visibility was no more than twenty or thirty feet; dim ghosts of ships rocked at their moorings all around us.

Still hooded, Tigrallef was sitting quietly in the stern on a pile of large cushions. Someone had even put a sheepskin around his shoulders, while I sprawled on the bare deck chilled by the mist and collecting splinters through the thin cloth of my britches. I raised my head again as the prow of the little galley nosed up against the end of a quay. Tigrallef was helped tenderly to his feet by the scribe himself; I was hauled bodily out of the boat between two black-clad troopers.

The shore was still hidden, but my eyes were caught by a massive grey form hovering behind the mist at the far end of the quay, a great vague circle shadowed with random darker patches, like the moon. I watched it as we proceeded down the narrow walkway. The circle grew; the dark patches resolved into a pattern, an eerie impression of eyes and mouth in a face that reminded me of a child's sketch of a demon, malignant and grinning; but gradually, as we came even closer and the mists thinned before it, the malignancy softened, the demonic features clarified and became human, though impossibly huge – stone features on a stone face the size of a cottage, set on shoulders thirty feet broad. Dimly behind it rose the serried ranks of the buildings along the corniche.

Astonished, I stared up at the stone face from the foot of the jetty. The giant lips were half-smiling, the chin raised, the brows drawn together into the beginnings of a frown. A noble young guardian god, that face suggested, keeping a kindly but stern and inescapable watch over the harbour with his great stone eyes, equally ready to bless the good and scuttle the bad. A most impressive piece of statuary. It was odd that it managed to look so handsome while being a very decent portrait of my father.

4

That was the extent of my sightseeing in the Pearl of the World for some time. While the black-clad troopers were loading me into a litter at the waterfront, I seized an irresistible opportunity to kick the customs scribe in the belly with my bound feet. The troopers reacted to this by knocking me into a grey daze; worse, the scribe reacted by vomiting on my legs. Consequently, I have only vague impressions of the litter jogging along with more jolts than seemed strictly necessary, each jolt sending livid streaks through the fog in my head, voices skimming across the waterfall in my ears, a disgusting bilious stink in my nostrils. At some point, out of sheer nausea, I fell asleep.

The next thing I remember is waking up on a soft clean-smelling pallet, without my britches and bonds and the mouth-stopper. Only a dull ache remained of the pain in my head, but it was worse when I moved. I worked my eyes open and found myself in a large room, dim and comfortably cool, with a few heavily latticed windows in the wall opposite my pallet and furnishings that were good and solid and reasonably ostentatious, the sort one would expect in the receiving room of a prosperous merchant's residence.

Tigrallef was sitting cross-legged on the bottom end of my pallet humming softly to himself, as he often did when the Pain was not giving him much trouble. He took no notice of me until I managed the daunting feat of sitting up, when he leaned over and put his cool hand on my forehead. At once I felt better. Disturbingly better.

'Careful, Tig.'

He pulled his hand away and examined it suspiciously.

'No, don't worry about it,' I said, 'just tell me what's happening.'

His eyes brightened. 'Well, they've done some marvellous restoration work on the Gilgard.'

'That's nice.'

'Tallislef Second's postern and the gardens outside it – Tallislef himself wouldn't know the difference.'

'Oh, really?'

He leaned closer, dropping to a conspiratorial whisper. 'Mind you, I suspect they've committed a few infelicities in the Scion's Ride.'

'Surely not.'

'Alas, yes.' He shook his head sadly. 'For example, though

I couldn't see very well through the mask, I suspect the figures on the keystones—'

'Tig.'

'—are only in low relief, or even,' he added with creeping horror and contempt, '*or even just incised into the stone-work*—'

'Listen to me, Tig.'

'—whereas, unless I'm almost impossibly mistaken, the originals were in very high relief, virtually in the round—'

'Father, shut up and listen.'

He gazed at me with suddenly clear eyes; his fingers moved. *You should not call me Father. Not here. Not yet.* The eyes held mine for a few seconds before shifting back into shining madness. 'I think they've retained some portions of the old Sherkin bastion—' he began. I seized both his shoulders and shook him just hard enough to get his attention.

'I don't want to discuss Gillish architecture.'

He looked shocked.

'Listen carefully. We're in trouble. We don't even know if the others are alive or dead. Right now, I don't give a fart about the old Sherkin bastion.'

He looked hurt.

'Try to listen,' I said. 'There's something important to tell you, something that might help explain what's going on. No, Tig, look at me, *listen*. I saw a monumental stone icon at the waterfront, a huge head-and-shoulders, half as big as the *Fifth*, placed where every ship in the inner harbour could see it.'

He frowned. 'I missed that. What a pity. It must be new – I don't remember it being mentioned in any history of the corniche. Was the face mine?'

Astonishment gagged me as effectively as any mouth-stopper. I nodded.

'Well,' he said, 'is it a good likeness?'

I nodded again. 'Very good – a bit flattering, even.' Choking a little, I added, 'How did you know?'

'The glyphs on the banners.'

65

'What about them?'

'One of them's my name. But I was only guessing about the statue, really. They'll be here in a minute.'

From long experience, I was adept at following the dog-leg turns in my father's conversations. I straightened up and swung my feet on to the floor. 'How many?'

He cocked his head as he listened. 'Two Flamens in the lead. I'm sure about that – it's the sweeping noise their robes make. A young one and an old one,' he added helpfully.

'How many guards?'

'Twenty.'

'Damn. That's too many. Any ideas?'

'A few. First of all, they should demolish the rest of the Sherkin bastion . . .'

About an hour later, twenty troopers and two Flamens (one young, one old, as promised) were marching us along a broad, deserted corridor in what Tig whispered to me was the Temple Palace. The troopers, who were of the black-tunicked variety, treated us with courteous efficiency, neither gawking at Tigrallef nor using me for boxing practice. The elder priest, a kindly looking greyhead in his early seventies, introduced himself as the First Flamen; the other, whom I judged to be no more than thirty, turned out to be the Second Flamen. One glance at his well-cut but icy face, the stone hardness of his glossy eyes, and I had a good idea how such a relatively young man might have risen so high in the ranks of the priesthood.

It seemed we were still prisoners, but we were honoured ones. The Flamens issued what amounted to a gracious invitation to accompany them to the audience room. They were apologetic about my bruised face and burgeoning black eye and the lumps on the back of my head. The tonic they gave me to drink chased away the last of the pain. The clean britches they brought me were of the best quality, and fitted as though they had been tailored just for me. Despite all this, I remained on my guard and had to keep squashing impulses to kick people.

There was one sticky moment as they conducted us through the Temple Palace, but it was Tigrallef's turn to be difficult. Doorways were set at intervals along the corridor, some fitted with wooden doors, others opening directly on to narrow passages that faded into shadow within a few feet. Tigrallef and I were marching pretty smartly along in the middle of the column, the Flamens and ten troopers ahead of us, ten troopers behind, when Tigrallef smoothly wheeled into one of these side passages without breaking stride and vanished into the darkness. He did not get far – two troopers from the rearguard pounded down the passage and retrieved him within seconds – but their captain was furious and the First Flamen was visibly shaken. Tig was unruffled by his recapture.

The captain, with a glare at the rearguard that said volumes about their competence, parentage and future prospects, ordered the column to continue. As we went, I muttered sidewise into Tigrallef's ear, 'By the Rages of Raksh, what was the point of that? Surely you weren't trying to escape?'

'Of course not,' he answered, in a voice so loud and clear that the captain turned his head and scowled back at us.

'After all,' I whispered, 'you're the one who told me not to resist.'

'But I wasn't resisting, Vero. I was following my feet.'

'Well, don't do it again,' I said crossly. 'Follow my feet, not yours. This is not the time or place to try escaping. Really, Father.'

'I was not trying to escape,' he insisted. 'It was habit. That was the way to the archives.'

While I was thinking this over, we came to a point where the corridor turned at right angles and then dead-ended at a pair of tall wooden doors, broad, plain and solid, flanked by troopers in the same black livery with green armbands. Tig slowed as we turned the corner, then stopped altogether; and finally responded to a gentle prod from the trooper behind him by bolting ahead a few paces, all in astonished silence. I caught his arm and pulled him into step with me, whispering fiercely, 'What is it now?'

Nothing trivial, to judge by the death-hold he took on my arm. 'There's a familiar voice behind those doors, Vero, an old, old friend.' I stared down at him with dismay. He was wearing the kind of expression that made me want to throw a cloth over his head, as if he were a raucous bird in a cage. I didn't dare to ask whose voice he meant, or which old friend, only whispered the phrase that had become a reflex response over the years: 'Keep hold, Tig, keep hold.' The doors swung open before us.

A vast chamber lay beyond, a curious mixture of opulence and emptiness. The floor was an expanse of grass-green carpet, apparently seamless, smooth as a lawn trimmed blade by blade. I could not begin to imagine what it must have cost. The walls were masked by a sweep of figured tapestries of equally unguessable worth. The crystalline panes in the high-arched windows to our left could only be of Crosthic manufacture, and were larger and more transparent than I thought was technically possible.

But despite all this magnificence of setting, the chamber was nearly bare – nothing but a cluster of settees, chairs and low tables around a great stone hearth at the far end. I could see one personage sunk into a large armchair near the empty fireplace, with a blanket tucked around him although the room was warm. Beside him, three figures in green tunics were sitting in a prim row on the edge of a settee, each stiffly holding a beaker of wine in one hand. They turned their heads to watch as we approached.

I recognized them at once: the three scribes who had boarded the *Fifth* the day before and presumably brought the full force of Gillish authority down upon our heads. In the middle was the one whose scrawny white underbelly I had kicked and would dearly love to kick again. Tig nudged me. 'Keep hold, Vero, keep hold.' I gritted my teeth and walked on.

Busy controlling myself, I did not even glance at the man in the armchair until the Flamens led us in front of him. Besides, it was a deep chair and he was sunk almost invisibly into it, shadowed by its winged sides. I saw only that he must be terribly thin or wasted, that the chair could almost have been empty under the heavy green blanket.

Then he leaned forward, and I recognized him at once from Tigrallef's highly coloured descriptions; told myself not to be so bloody stupid; did the arithmetic in my head and realized it was just possible; looked at him again and knew that it was true. He'd be late in his nineties now, but my father always said the old goatfish was too cussed to let himself die. He still had his teeth, too.

The Primate Mycri.

An old face. Older than time, harder than stone, colder than the ice-mountains of Myr. A mask of mottled yellow marble, I thought, carved by a sculptor who was paid by the wrinkle; only the eyes were young and strong, twin dark glimmers under a shelf of white eyebrow. Tigrallef was vibrating with excitement. I found his hand without looking down, spelt into the palm: *Keep hold.* Tigrallef laughed out loud.

'You seem happy to be here, boy.' The Primate's voice, deep and harsh, was still powerful. 'Sit down over there, close to me. Let me have a look at you. By the Lady, it's like seeing a ghost.'

The two Flamens waved us to the settee opposite the old man's chair, divided from it by a low table set out with wine and biscuits. Long moments passed while the Primate studied first my father's face, then mine. At last he said to the Flamens, 'The little one's resemblance is more than remarkable, it is exact. The other one is less like, but it's been years since anyone saw the Priest-King; it may be that we can find a use for him too.' He turned to the scribes. 'You did very well to bring these young men to our attention.'

The scribes' settee was at an angle to ours, so I had a good view of their faces. Stark terror was politely disguised in the two underlings, but their chief wore a look of such soon-to-be-richly rewarded smugness that my fists hurt from clenching. It was a minor satisfaction to see him flinch when our eyes met – the unconscious move to protect his belly was especially heart-warming. After that he looked a little less smug.

'Tell me, Scribe,' the Primate went on, 'did anyone else see this young man up close?' He indicated Tigrallef.

The scribe answered eagerly. 'Oh no, Most Revered One. Only we three and the guardparty who went on board with us yesterday. I was most careful in carrying out your instructions.'

'And this morning?' The old man looked to the captain of the black-uniformed troopers.

'Only the Flamens' Corps, Most Revered One. The regular troops did not go on board until the – the young man's face was covered.'

'Very good. Report?' He extended a hand like the claw of dead lizard, to take a neat sheaf of papers from the captain. The Most Revered One read with amazing quickness, nodding to himself, obviously approving in a grim sort of way, until he reached the top of the final page. There he paused, hissed between his teeth, and scowled. The captain shifted nervously on his feet.

'We're already searching, Most Revered One. I've got fifty men out, and the cordons went up an hour ago.'

'Then let us hope fifty men are enough, and an hour ago was not too late.' The Most Revered One glared at the captain for only a few seconds longer, but they were sizzling seconds, and I saw beads of sweat begin to pop out on the captain's neck above the black tunic; then the Most Revered One startlingly rearranged his face into something like a benevolent smile, and turned to the trio on the other settee.

'You did well, scribe, and I am grateful. You may go now. Second Flamen, go with them and make sure they find their way out.'

'Most Revered One?' the scribe began.

'Don't worry, you'll get your reward. Now go.'

With a last filthy look in my direction, the scribe put his beaker down on the table and departed with his colleagues. I wondered why there was such pity in Tigrallef's face as he

70

watched the doors close behind them, a pity that I saw mirrored in the old First Flamen's expression.

Hesitantly making a formal gesture that I did not recognize, the First Flamen said, 'Most Revered One, I ask once more, is it really necessary to – could we not—'

'Be quiet, Kesi,' the Primate broke in, 'we went through this already.'

'But Most Revered One—'

'I told you, the Mosslines are fine for illiterate soldiers, but these ones are scribes – the tongues alone would make no difference, not while they had hands to write with. And what use would they be in the Mosslines without hands? I agree, it is most unfortunate. Now be quiet.'

The First Flamen subsided unhappily and slumped on to the settee vacated by the doomed scribes. As for me, I may be slower than my father, but I understood. I felt a moment's regret for having wasted a perfectly good kick on the belly of a dead man, even if he was still breathing at the time; it was just a pity about the other two.

And now it was our turn. The Primate had featured as a ruthless tyrant and schemer in my father's stories, and I was getting the impression that extreme age had not mellowed him. At least three men were dying, apparently for the misfortune of having met us – what, then, was going to happen to Shree and Chasco, to my mother and sister? What were the Primate's plans for them? How easy it would be, I thought suddenly, to leap across the low table that separated us, to take his furrowed neck in my hands and snap it like a chicken bone before the troopers struck me down . . .

Tig's fingers clamped painfully around my wrist.

'A hundred pardons, Most Revered One,' he said, 'but what have you done with our family?'

The Primate stared at him, shaking his head. 'Even the voice, Kesi. Astonishing. If I didn't know better, I'd think it was Tigrallef in the flesh. What a dreadful thought. As for you, boy, you do not yet have permission to speak. You have permission to listen.'

'Most Revered One?' said the First Flamen hesitantly. 'It

71

would do no harm to assure them their family is safe and well.'

The Primate's claws tightened in anger on the armrests of his chair; but I filed Kesi's small act of kindness away in my mind. Someday I would thank him for it. Tigrallef's tension, however, was as powerful as before. The Primate, after a short statutory glower at the First Flamen, picked up the sheaf of the captain's report again and leafed through it.

'Correct me if any of this is wrong,' he said to us. 'You are Vero and Tilgo, sons of Selki, a Gillish copper merchant who resides in Calloon. Yes? Good. Born in Calloon, both of you? And you arrived in Gil yesterday: small windcatcher, cargo of copper and wood, well nourished, good health, visible means of support, no security risk, Affidavit of Entry recommended – that's how the report would have read, young Tilgo, if you hadn't poked your head out the cabin door. Do you know what made the difference? Do you have any idea why you're here?'

Tigrallef frowned and put his chin on his hand in an exaggerated posture of deep thought. *Don't overdo it*, I prayed silently. 'I look like somebody famous?' he suggested at last.

'By the Lady, it could have been the Scion himself speaking. Even,' and the Primate's voice hardened, 'to the implied insolence. I warn you, young man, the Scion Tigrallef learned to fear and respect me, and it's a lesson you should learn right now.'

Tigrallef managed to look truly repentant, while I wondered what other rearrangements of history the Primate would be serving up. I was about to find out.

'I will assume,' the Primate began, 'that your Gillish parents have told you something of Gil's glorious history – the Scions of Oballef, the Lady in Gil, the Bright Ages—'

'The Pearl of the World,' Tigrallef interjected.

'Yes, quite. Don't interrupt, boy. I'm sure you have also heard of the atrocious brigandage of the Sherank, the invasion, the concealment of the Lady in a secret place in the

72

Gilgard, the many years of suffering under a heavy Sherkin yoke—'

'Our da was taken in the levy.'

'Yes, all right, so you do know something about it. Can I assume you also know the history of the rise of the Second Empire of Gil?'

Tig and I exchanged startled glances. *Which* Empire? The Second *What*? I cursed myself and my elders for sailing so blithely into the middle of a surprise like this; perhaps returning to the known world had made us careless. We should have asked more questions in Calloon. We should have bought new maps in Tata. We should have stopped in Glishor, Zelf, Plav, Sathelforn, for the latest news. In short, we should have examined the turbid waters of the known world very carefully before jumping into them headfirst after all those years away. I gritted my teeth. Tigrallef said, quite winningly, 'We weren't taught much about it in Calloon. The Calmen have their own views, of course, but I'd really like to hear the Gillish account.'

'Then listen carefully – it begins with the end of the Sherkin Empire. Now, many stories were told about the wrack of Sher, but the truth of it happened here, right here in the Gilgard, and it was a Scion of Oballef who accomplished it: a fool, and no hero, and no friend of mine, but the truth is that he alone destroyed the appalling Sherank using the great power of the Lady in Gil. I'll give him that much credit.'

He paused, scowling over his thoughts, and quite suddenly turned a bright angry red; from calm to enraged in three seconds flat, by my estimate. 'And then,' he continued through clenched teeth, 'the traitorous young clodwit *destroyed* the Lady.'

'I'd heard that, actually,' my father said.

'Don't interrupt! All the power in the world, enough to restore Gil, to make us the greatest nation – yes, the greatest empire – ever to arise in these oceans, and that tupping young fool smashed her to pieces and tossed her away! I could have killed him then, you know, and perhaps I should have . . .'

He collapsed backwards into the recesses of the chair, just wheezing at first, but the wheezing hardened into a threatening rattle within a few breaths; the First Flamen gasped and tumbled on to his knees beside him – 'Mycri!' – but a dry yellow corpse-hand emerged from the depths of the chair to shove him away. A moment later, breathing more easily, the Primate sat up again.

'Kesi, you cretin. If my own anger could kill me, I'd be twenty-five years dead. Where was I? Oh yes – that double-dyed traitor and clodwit Tigrallef had just broken the blessed Lady. And so, there I was after the liberation of Gil, with a hungry, rebellious people to govern and a shattered nation to rebuild—'

'Wasn't there a Priest-King?' my father asked in a wide-eyed sort of voice.

The Primate regarded him thoughtfully; I was expecting another explosion of wrath and perhaps wheezing, but he simply folded his hands on his lap and nodded. 'A good question – very good. Yes, there was the Priest-King Arkolef, but he was quite incapable of ruling, just as useless as his unusable brother. Tigrallef was a fool, but Arkolef was actually stupid. I have no regrets about taking the reins – somebody had to. And without the Lady's powers, it was not easy to lead the people in the direction that was best for them.'

'What happened to the Scion?' I asked. This was partly to forestall any dangerous political commentary from my father – for example, about why the Primate was so damned sure he knew what was best for the people.

'You mean the Scion Tigrallef? May his bones bring forth flowers,' said the Primate without a trace of grief, 'he was killed far away from Gil. Before you ask, I had nothing to do with his death – it was a natural disaster at the eastern edge of the known world, some no-name island with a volcano. I'd arranged a marriage for him, an excellent alliance with Miishel, which was still a power in those days – the damned

74

woman was quite fetching then, if I remember correctly –
and all he had to do for the nation was eat and drink and
tup himself silly in comfort for the rest of his natural life. He
even managed to make a mess of that. He was useless.
Useless.'

'To be fair,' the First Flamen said timidly, 'it was the Last
Dance that broke the alliance, not the loss of Tigrallef.'

The Primate sighed. 'If you irritate me once more today,
Kesi, I'll appoint you to be resident governor of the
Mosslines.'

Poor old Kesi, whom I was beginning to like, sat back with
a pale face.

'Kesi fancies he's a memorian,' the Primate went on, 'like
the lost Scion himself. The Last Dance – yes, that came next.
The great plague, the dancing death. You two are probably
too young to remember it, but it was a bad time, perhaps the
worst the known world ever saw – thousands died. Hundreds
of thousands. Gil was hit less terribly than most, but even
here it was a catastrophe.'

'Were the Scions wiped out?' Tigrallef asked in a carefully
neutral tone. Subtext: *Is my brother dead?*

'Most of them died, yes.' Shifting his body to the edge of
the deep chair, the Primate signalled for the First Flamen to
pour out a beaker of wine for each of us. Tigrallef accepted
the beaker with subtly unsteady hands – I realized the
question was about more than his brother Arkolef. We had
learned of the deaths of his father Cirallef and his uncle the
High Prince of Sathelforn from survivors in Myr, but there
had also been cousins, nephews, nieces, a mother; friends as
well as family. Grief that was properly twenty years old was a
spectre creeping up behind him at last, raising a cold hand
to lay on his shoulder. Grief was also a powerful friend and
ally to the Pain. I prepared myself to grieve with my father
for these relations I had never met, but I also reviewed our
emergency procedures for helping him keep hold.

'They all died but the Priest-King,' the Primate continued
when the wine arrangements were to his satisfaction, 'and if
poor Scion Arkolef was stupid before the plague, he was

worse than stupid after it. Mad, you see, quite broken, nothing left of him. If his cousin Lady Callefiya had survived instead of him, or any one of the children, my task would have been much easier.' His tone was aggrieved; destiny should have consulted with him before having the effrontery to spare my uncle Arkolef.

'How very sad,' Tigrallef said softly. I glanced at him, amazed at how normal he appeared. Where was the grief? Where was the Pain? 'Where is the Priest-King now?' my father added.

'Well cared for and still on the throne of Gil, my boy, and that's all the nation needs to know. No one will ever accuse me of killing him by neglect. Of course, it is not generally known that he has the sanity and intelligence of a spud-root.'

'Why are you telling us, Most Revered One?'

'I'm coming to that. You'll understand your position better, I'm sure, when I've taught you a little history. You must have been a very small child at the time of the Last Dance; you may remember a little hunger, you may have heard a few stories from your parents, but you're not old enough to know in your heart how desperate the world was in the aftermath of the plague – not from the dancing deaths alone, but from the untended fields, the starvation, the civil strife, the fires burning unchecked, the fleets rotting in the harbours for want of crews to man them . . .'

'It always sounded to me,' said Tigrallef with a straight face, 'like a time of immense opportunity.'

I nudged him desperately with my elbow; but the Primate raised a wattled chin to peer at him with surprise.

'How perceptive for such a young man,' he said, recovering. 'Yes, as you say, it was a time of opportunity, for a strong leader that is, and nobody saw it more clearly than I. Gil was not the only nation to have lost its royalty – the Last Dance had a taste for kings and powers. Four High Princes in turn succeeded to the throne of Sathelforn during the first fortnight of the plague, and after the fourth one died it stayed empty – those of the rank to refill it were also dead. Miishel and Grisot, both kingless, went to battle with each other

76

while their own civil wars were still raging, and thus they devastated the eastern edge of the known world; Storica set itself on fire and spilled a great deal of its own blood. Calloon and Tata you know about. The little mid-kingdoms, Plav, Luc, Glishor and the rest, sat around starving, weeping at the loss of their princes and the impotence of their gods.' The Primate paused. 'For the right kind of leader, it was indeed a world of opportunity.'

His voice, so powerful until now, cracked on the last words, reduced to an old man's quaver. The First Flamen reached out to him with what I could see was genuine solicitude, and again he was rebuffed. In fact, it looked increasingly like the First Flamen and I could take the captain of the guard off for a quick one in the nearest tavern without the Primate noticing, because he seemed hardly aware we were there. Only Tigrallef existed for him, sitting quietly and attentively beside me with his hands resting flat on his knees.

There was still no sign of the Pain.

The Primate sipped his wine and coughed to clear his throat. 'So there I was, boy, empty-handed in Gil: the Lady gone, smashed by the Scion Tigrallef; the proud bloodline of the Scions shrunk to one weeping lunatic without living issue; both my claims to authority gone; the nation in ruins; the people in shock, without gods, without kings, without hope – what was I to do?'

'It's obvious,' Tig said calmly. 'You gave them a new myth.'

'Myth' was probably a tactless word to choose – it looked to me like Tig had gone about half a step too far. I could see it in the First Flamen's eyes and hear it in the shuffle of the captain's feet behind our settee. The Primate, nursing his beaker, appraised Tig silently from under the louring eyebrows – Tig smiled back. *Still* no sign of the Pain.

'That's right,' the Primate said, so softly I had to strain to hear him. 'I gave them a new myth. The myth gave them new hope. Their hope gave me the power I needed to weave them into a new nation and bring them out of the shadow of the plague – almost alone among the nations, Gil did not descend into general famine and civil war. And that was only the beginning.'

He was enjoying telling this story. His voice hardly rose in volume, but every word was an arrow twanging from a tight bow.

'We were not very strong at first, but we did not need to be when the others were so weak. We organized Sathelforn first – it was a pitiful chaos when our army arrived, with the High Peerage dead and all the islands of the Archipelago armed against each other and warring for food; but I had the Scion Arkolef's claim to Sathelforn through the Lady Dazeene, and I had the Lady Dazeene herself – she wanted no power, but as long as I allowed her to tend to her surviving son—'

'She's alive?'

'Yes, boy, and you're interrupting again.' Such quiet force; behind the yellow-domed corrugated old man, I saw the imposing shadow of what he must have been before age sucked him dry. I also saw why he and my father had loathed each other from the time my father was a child. 'So we organized Sathelforn; and over the next few years we organized the mid-kingdoms, one by one; and then we took in Koroska, who begged to come under our dominion. Now we have treaties with the far western kingdoms, bits of paper which I have so far had no reason to tear up; and the eastern kingdoms pay us a very heavy tribute, so heavy that they may as well be counted as part of the empire, and they ceded us the Mosslines as well. The known world is at peace, and Gil is once again its heart. Any questions?'

'Two,' said Tigrallef without pausing for thought. I tensed – there was a timbre in his voice which we who knew him dreaded. *Not the Sherkin bastion*, I prayed; but he asked with reasonably normal inflections, 'What have you done with our family?'

'As the First Flamen told you,' the Primate said with a black glance at the other old man, 'your family is safe and well. I imagine they're even comfortable – is that right, Kesi?'

Kesi looked straight into Tig's eyes, then into mine. 'I have seen to their comfort myself.' I believed him.

'You see, Vero, young Tilgo, there's nothing to worry about. Your family will be treated like the Scions themselves, if you do as I tell you.'

Personally, that did not reassure me. My father had told me how Flamens tended to treat Scions, from the time of the Sherkin invasion onwards; no wonder Arkolef was the only acknowledged survivor of the line. Even less reassuring was the way my father was beaming at the Primate. A little uncertainly, the Primate smiled back. I wiped my sweating palms on my nice new britches, because I could see my father was on the verge of what he'd call *interesting* behaviour.

'So our family is the surety for our good conduct,' Tig said. 'That's natural, Most Revered One, but I think it's only the half of it.'

He casually picked up the wine flask and refilled the Primate's beaker. The First Flamen gasped at this, the captain began to jerk his dagger from the sheath on his arm – the Primate stopped him cold with a very small gesture. 'Go on, young man,' he said to my father.

'It's also secrecy, isn't it? Our poor family may have to be hidden away for ever. If you decide to use Vero and me to your advantage, we can't be known as the sons of a copper-monger from Calloon and a woman who whored for the Sherank. Isn't that right?'

The Primate, after the briefest of hesitations, picked up his beaker and raised it to Tigrallef in a kind of salute. 'Keep talking.'

'It's why the scribes had to die, and why yesterday's guardparty is going to the Mosslines with their tongues torn out.'

'Obviously. Is there a question in this? You said you had two.'

Softly: 'Tell me a story, Most Revered One. Tell me the myth you told the people of Gil.'

'No – you tell me.' The Primate's tone was amiable, the undertone challenging.

'All right.' Tig took a deep breath and raised his right hand in the manner of a Tatakil storymonger declaiming his wares. Sonorously, he began: 'The power of the Lady is not lost to Gil. The Scion Tigrallef is not dead. The power became invested in Tigrallef when he broke the old vessel, and even now it is growing in him, perfecting and purifying him; and someday he will return to the Gilgard, glorious and powerful, to rule the righteous and destroy the wicked.' He dropped his declamatory hand. 'Have I got it right?'

'Of course you've got it right. Every toddling child in the empire knows the story. There are shrines dedicated to the Scion Tigrallef, the Ark and Sceptre of the Lady in Gil, in every hamlet from here to Zelf.'

My father grinned cheekily. 'Shrines dedicated to me?'

'Not necessarily.' The Primate grinned back; no hesitation this time. 'You must give me a chance to think, my boy, you only landed in my lap this morning.'

'You had to get me off the streets, though. I can understand that.'

'Quite so. I couldn't let someone with your face wander about freely. The results could be—'

'Awkward,' suggested my father.

'Confusing,' said the Primate. They grinned at each other again. The Primate reached out with a creaking of old shoulders and slopped more wine into my father's beaker. They raised the beakers and clinked them across the low table. Kesi and I, both excluded from this developing love-feast, caught each other's eyes uneasily.

'But what is there to plan?' my father asked. 'It seems simple enough to me. You told the people Tigrallef would return – here I am.'

'It's not at all simple. If I decide to use you instead of having your throat cut, timing will be everything. Yes, I told the people Tigrallef would return someday, but I had the indefinite future in mind. A few centuries. A few millennia. Effectively never.'

'Well, when would suit you? I could come back later.'

The Primate laughed out loud, a peculiar laugh that was

something between the sound of strangling and the cry of an exceptionally obnoxious species of waterfowl that used to keep us awake in Gafrin-Gammanthan. 'Don't worry,' he said, 'if and when Tigrallef returns in glory, we'll have no trouble making the prophecies fit the occasion. By the Lady, if only the real Tigrallef had been like you!'

'What if I were the real Tigrallef?' asked my father roguishly. 'What would you do?'

This managed to wring an actual, if solitary, tear of laughter from the corner of the Primate's eye. 'I suppose I'd have your throat cut straight away. It's what I really should do anyway. But you're very good, you know. You shouldn't waste it on Kesi and me, you should save it for the faithful.'

'But are you *sure* I'm not the Scion? Maybe the story is true.'

'Dear boy,' the Primate said as he wiped the tear away, 'you mustn't carry the joke too far. Tigrallef died twenty years ago. As for the story, remember I'm the one who made the whole nonsense up.'

They laughed together, at entirely different jokes.

At the far end of the room, the double doors swished open. The young Second Flamen entered and hurried across the sward of carpet with a scrolled paper in his hands, greeting the Primate with a quick full-arm gesture and a meaningful look. The Primate immediately sobered.

'Go now. You will continue to be our honoured guests for the time being. The First Flamen has arranged suitable quarters for you – I've often thought he'd be happier running an inn than an empire. Isn't that true, Kesi?'

The First Flamen blushed but made no comment, just beckoned to us and led us towards the doors accompanied by the same twenty troopers. Even before we were out of the room the Second Flamen was sitting in the place Tigrallef had just left, almost doubled over the table and talking to the Primate in a low, vehement voice. The First Flamen glanced back at them just before the door closed behind us. His face was anxious and even fearful, and he avoided catching my eye again. I wondered what his idea of suitable quarters would entail.

5

I picked half-heartedly at a plate of incomparable tripe pastries, wishing I'd gone a little easier on the merely memorable fig-mutton. In the other hand was a crystal wine beaker worth about the same as the wine inside it – the two together could probably have been traded for a small house. The carven and cushioned settee I was lounging on, with my boots off and my feet up, could probably have been traded for a farm. After some heated discussion we'd sent the Tatakil girls away, all four of them.

My father had taken nothing but a little water and a small bowl of lentil hotty, and he was wandering barefoot and thoughtful among the expensive marvels of our new quarters, hardly seeming to notice either them or me. From time to time he gave the ceiling an abstracted smile. Finally he bumped into the settee I was occupying, focused on me, and frowned. 'Haven't you stopped eating yet, Vero?'

I was still annoyed about the Tatakil girls. 'I was hungry,' I said sharply. 'I missed breakfast and was unconscious through midday, if you can think back that far. Starving ourselves wouldn't help the others; anyway, they're probably being fed from the same kitchen. I think the First Flamen is being truthful when he says they're safe.'

'Oh, they're safe for the moment. Just like us.' His eyes wandered back to the ceiling.

'Well, then. Since we're all safe, and there's no action we can take for the time being that would make a blind bit of difference, the sensible course is to rest and eat and build up our strength – and by the bye, that's the best tripe I ever tasted.'

'Don't get too comfortable. We're not staying long.' There was a crystalline overlay to his eyes, which were a little too bright for my liking. Putting my feet back on the floor, I pulled him on to the settee beside me.

'Do we have a choice?' It was a serious question.

'No, we don't. It's an entertaining situation, but I really can't spare the time.'

'I meant, do you think we can just choose to leave?'

'Well, yes, in an informal fashion . . .' Tig's voice faded as he resumed his scrutiny of the ceiling.

I sighed and gently pushed on the top of his head until he was looking down at the plate of pastries. 'Eat something first. That spoonful or two of hotty won't get you very far. Have some of the tripe. And while you're doing it, you can tell me what you're talking about. I assume it's because you think the Primate will decide to have us killed after all, though he seems to like you so much.'

'That goes without saying,' Tig answered, taking a pastry from the plate and examining it earnestly. 'You heard him, Vero, he won't want us upsetting his nice tidy mythology. But that's not why we have to go.'

He leaned back into the cushions of the priceless settee and put his feet up on the equally priceless table as he ate. I did the same, licking gravied flakes of pastry from my fingers. 'One thing at a time,' I said. 'Do you think he'll want to kill us fairly soon?'

'Maybe as early as tonight; maybe tomorrow, maybe in a year or two. We're an extraordinary find from his standpoint, two brothers who look so much like the brother Scions. He must be tempted to think up a scenario that would let him use us, otherwise it would seem like such a waste of a good coincidence. But I'm sure he'll be sensible in the end.'

'And the sensible thing is to kill us.'

'Yes, of course. Wouldn't you, in his place?'

'No, but I can see his point. He wouldn't hand power over to a nobody he thinks is a fake Scion.'

My father looked at me with surprise and disapproval. 'Hand over his power! What a foolish idea. Really, Vero.'

'Then what?'

The last crumbs of the first little pastry vanished; Tig surveyed the rest of the platter with the eye of a horse trader in an auction barn before taking another. 'Look at it this way: for centuries, as long as the blessed Lady in Gil was around and the Scions were the only ones who could conjure her, the Flamens had to put up with us – but as far as they know the Lady is gone forever, and when poor Arko dies the Scions' line dies with him. It puts the Flamens in an absolutely secure position. Their stewardship is validated by the memory of past Scions, buttressed by the promise of future Scions, and without the awkward complications of present Scions – which means the Flamens can get on with the business of being in complete control. Now that he's got over the Lady's loss, the Primate must be rather pleased with the way things have turned out.'

'I don't see that their position is so secure,' I objected. 'What will happen when the prophesied Scion – the Ark and Sceptre, was it? – doesn't return within a reasonable span of time? Won't the people lose faith?'

'Vero, Vero, nobody notices when prophecies *aren't* fulfilled. In fact it's often a damned inconvenience when they are.'

'Oh, right.'

'Anyway, by the time the Primate's dynasty has carried on a few generations, the myth will be so well entrenched that nobody will even think of questioning—'

'Dynasty?' I broke in.

'Don't interrupt me, boy,' Tig said in a precise and merciless imitation of the Primate. 'This priesthood is a dynasty in the making. For example, Kesi, the First Flamen, is the youngest of Mycri's eight brothers – a good man, he was always kind to me when I was a child in Exile; but I suppose old Mycri's other brothers must all have died, because Kesi was never the type to seek high office. I doubt he could stomach becoming Primate.'

'What about the Second Flamen?'

Tigrallef roused himself sharply. 'A different matter. I

recognized him too – I taught him to read. He's the Primate's great-grandson Lestri, whom I remember as a devious and unlikeable little lout of eight years old. He came to me as a pupil in the archives, but I suspect the Primate was only sending him to spy on me. He's grown up true to form. I should think he's the one Mycri's grooming to be his successor.'

'The second in a dynasty of Flamens,' I said, watching him closely, having noticed his hands were twisted together as if to discourage each other from trembling. This was something we'd learned to look out for. 'How do you feel about that?'

'I feel nothing. Why should I? The Scions are gone, the Flamens may as well be the ones to pick up the pieces. Look how long the Divinatrixes lasted in Vassashinay.'

'We're Scions,' I reminded him mildly.

'Not any more, Verolef – we're the heritors of Naar. The Scions are becoming a memory, like the kings of Fathan, Itsant, Nkalvi and the rest. There's nothing for us now in Gil. Isn't that right? *Isn't that right?*'

I opened my mouth to answer, but shut it again when I saw the question was not addressed to me. The eyes he turned to mine were fixed and glistening, his neck was corded. Sighing, I loosened the drawstring at the throat of his tunic. The table was just starting to vibrate in synchrony with his hands; I moved the crystal decanter and beakers to safety on the floor below it. Tigrallef started to rise in strange jerks as if each muscle had to be individually sought out and instructed, a process that was obviously agonizing, so I took him by the wrists and pushed him back on to the cushions of the settee.

A normal first-line procedure involved the Zelfic Mathematical Protocols: orderly, invariable, symmetrical, a formal perfection that owed nothing to magic. Eye contact was necessary, even on those occasions when my father was blind at the onset of the attack. The rhythm of the words was important, also the tone of voice. Too loud, and the Pain would rise to smother it and my father's torment would increase and be prolonged. Too low, and it would be lost in the multiple voices that filled his ears, all the snarls, yips, howls and oily suggestive whispers of the Pain's extensive repertoire. The best voice to use was firm, clear and insistent, delivering the elegant Zelfic equations in a steady pulse that would thread through the chaos like a slender steel lifeline.

This was fortunately not a very bad attack, hardly more than a lash of the Pain's tail. By the Sixth Protocol my father's dilated pupils were contracting, by the Eighth he was managing to repeat the equations along with me. I faded out by the Eleventh and let him carry on by himself in a voice that gradually took on strength and colour. Relieved that we would not need to go on to the insanely numbing qualities of the Lucian proverb lists, I left him to it and toured the room to see if anything was broken. When he drifted off to sleep in the middle of the Seventeenth Protocol, I lifted his bare feet on to the settee and covered him with a brocade throw. Then I retrieved the crystal beakers from under the table and drained the one that had more wine left in it.

We should never have come to Gil, I thought. Tigrallef was right; there was nothing for us here. For twenty years we had followed the Harashil's trail backwards through time, each footprint a blasted or waterlogged ruin with the Harashil's hallmark on it, and at Nkalvi the trail had ended; but Gil was not the place to pick it up again. Gil was at the wrong end of history, the last of the Harashil's empires. We would find no clue here to the Great Nameless First. The spell of banishment was not in any Gillish archive. We were here only because we could think of nowhere else to go, and we'd made a bad mistake in coming.

Pearl of the World, I thought bitterly. I drank what was left in the other beaker.

My father was twitching and murmuring in his sleep – all normal. It was twenty years since he had taken an easy night's rest, I thought as I watched him, and I could not imagine the next twenty years were going to be any different. I reached under the table for the decanter and poured some more wine into my beaker. In a few years I would have to start passing as his uncle or his father, someday his grandfather. Someday, if I ever had the chance to beget any, my children would still

86

be chanting the Zelfic Mathematical Protocols into his ears to help him keep hold; unless, of course, the Pain defeated him first.

Surely it was the wine that was depressing me; I wondered if more of it would reverse the effect. I filled my beaker again. And again.

And again.

'Wake up, Vero.'

I was obviously on the *Fifth*, and the weather was against us. The deck was rocking gently under me, while the ship was simultaneously rotating in a smooth, leisured sweep, as if we had happened on the centre of a shallow water whorl. Somebody had kindly placed a thick-napped carpet under my body, but had forgotten to do anything about the stench of sweat and stale wine. My head and eyes could also have done with some maintenance, and the inside of my mouth was like the nest of a fieldmouse, furred and fouled. Groaning, I raised myself on to my elbows and blinked my eyes open, immediately regretting it. My head was an anvil under the hammer of an apprentice blacksmith; the single lamp burning on the table was a flame-sling aimed with deadly accuracy at my eyeballs. I let my head fall back.

'What time is it?'

'It's about two hours after midnight – I heard the bells in the city a few minutes ago. Is something wrong, Vero? Are you unwell?'

'No.' I was dying. I *wanted* to die.

'Come on, then, get your boots on. It's time to go.'

I contrived to get about halfway to a sitting position before falling back. By hooking an elbow over the seat of the settee and hoisting myself up, I slowly became more or less vertical from the waist up. 'Does it have to be tonight?'

'The others are being moved out of the Gilgard very soon. Fetching them now will save us a lot of trouble later.'

'Oh.' Struggling with the boots, I mumbled some vile phrases I'd learned from a tavern-creeper in Tata; but then, through the sick irregular rhythm of the headache, it occurred to me to wonder and doubt. 'How do you know they're being moved? Did the troopers tell you?'

'The First Flamen, among others, was here while you slept. Come on, Vero, you're wasting time.'

He pulled at my arm – he was stronger than he looked – hauled me to my feet and guided me, not towards the impressive doorway framed by tapestries but to the narrow arched casement that faced it across the room. It was a dead end, as far as I knew. I had already rejected it. We were high up on the northwestern face of the Temple Palace, a segment where each storey projected as a cunning stone cantilever about six or seven feet beyond the storey below, a miracle of engineering that impressed even me when I saw it from the *Fifth*. At that long distance, in profile, it had the effect of a great slanting wing flaring outward and upward from the white eagle-breast of the mountain.

My current perspective, propped uneasily against the window frame, was very different. Downwards, a few hundred feet of empty space ended abruptly in the rock-strewn tidal flats north of the harbour, at this moment visible only as a glimmering of wet sand in the dark night; upwards, the smooth soffit of the next storey up overhung us like the underside of a half-open drawer. No handholds, nothing to cling to, nothing much to secure a rope to – assuming we had several hundred feet of rope. Short of growing wings like birds or sticky feet like lizards, we could not possibly escape by this route.

My father climbed up on the broad marble window sill and threw himself into the abyss of the night.

I closed my eyes and slumped back against the window frame, feeling too ill to be more than mildly cross. Fine for him, I thought, but if he was expecting me to leap out after him, he was in for a very long wait at the bottom. I knew I should watch what was happening, if only to determine for future reference exactly how the Pain dealt with the mechanics of such a long drop. Was she halting him in mid-air? Floating him gently down the air currents? Arranging for him to land catlike on his feet without driving his shin bones up to his shoulders? Or simply letting him smash himself to pulp on the sand, and then knitting him back together again? The last seemed most likely. No, I couldn't watch.

'Vero?'

His voice was not far from the window and on a level with it. I opened my eyes cautiously. There was no moon, and the sky was spattered thickly with stars, merging far away with the reflections on the black burnished surface of the sea. Tig was visible mostly as a dead-black silhouette defined by the stars, swinging gently to and fro like a man on the end of an invisible rope. His hands were raised level with his shoulders and curled around something I couldn't make out. I tottered to the table to get the lamp, tottered back again, held the light high in the arch of the casement. This time I could see a ladder, a spindly looking article of rope dangling down past the edge of the soffit, with Tig clinging to it as casually as I might sit on a chair.

'Vero,' he said, 'it occurs to me that I forgot to mention what the plan is.'

'I did wonder,' I said.

'Well, we're going to climb up there,' he took one hand away from the ladder to wave vaguely towards the heavens, 'and then we're going to go for your mother and the rest.'

'That's clear enough,' I said.

'But I've been thinking . . .'

I looked down, far down, at the expanse of beach and black sea below, then back at my father. 'Just climb,' I said.

'Yes, of course, but I was wondering – it seems to me that you're not looking very well, and you may not feel much like jumping for the ladder. The gap's only about seven feet, but it's rather a long drop if you miss.'

Another glance downwards. Another glance at the rope ladder, which now seemed worse than spindly. An impossible target, especially in the light of my recent experiment with the wine decanter. 'That's true,' I said.

'Then this is what we'll do. When I'm at the top, we'll start swinging the ladder back and forth until you can reach the end of it from the casement. Sing out when you've got it, and we'll start pulling you up. Will that suit you better?'

'Very much.'

With a cheerful nod he resumed his climb up the ladder, hand over hand. The double filament of it danced below him after he climbed out of my sight, and then was still, by which I reckoned he had reached the top safely. Wherever the top was, and whoever he meant by 'we', it was now too late to ask.

I kept my eyes fixed on the end of the ladder, which began to twitch again after a few moments of stillness. Back and forth, back and forth, a few inches at first, then a few feet, further each time, out into the shadowy vaults of the night sky, back into the orb of light surrounding my lantern; looming, receding, looming, receding. After a while it was impossible not to watch it. Some part of me, however, perceived that this was unwise.

Back and forth, back and forth. Nearer every time.

Odd things began to happen. The night sky lost its depth, was pushed much closer, became a flat black wall pinholed with light only a few feet away. Back and forth, back and forth. The distant tidal flats were uplifted until they were no more than a step or two below the sill; how amazing it seemed that I had ever been afraid of falling. The chamber at my back seemed to be shrinking to the size of a coffin just large enough to hold me, though I could not confirm this without turning around.

At some point the ladder stopped moving altogether, whereas the rest of the world began to swing back and forth. This did not strike me as strange at the time. Passengers on a vast pendulum, the window frame and I swooped towards the ladder and away again, up in a mighty arc, down in a mighty arc, each time a little nearer. The ladder even spoke to me – it told me to jump. It said, quite persuasively, that nothing bad could happen.

I believed it. Dreamily, I climbed up on the sill and poised myself – how easy it was, really – and the next time the window swung downwards on its nearest approach to the ladder, I leapt forth with a glad cry. Naturally, that was the moment I woke up.

I could hear them talking as they pried my hands loose from the ladder, finger by finger. 'Quite unaccountable,' my father was saying. 'I had no idea he was afraid of heights.'

I was too offended to remain in shock. Half my life had been spent aloft in some rigging or other, not infrequently in a vicious gale and/or mountainous seas; I was the one who had scaled a near-sheer rockface in Nkalvi, carrying the rope that would enable the others to follow in ease and safety; I was the poor sod who was always sent creeping up the treacherous sides of the Khamanthana pyramids outside Gafrin-Gammanthan to scramble down the crumbling central shafts and open the portals from the inside.

'I'm not afraid of heights,' I said, snapping my eyes open to glare at my father. That was the intention. Instead, I fell in love.

Lust, anyway.

It would have been too much to expect Tigrallef to introduce us. All he said was, 'Good, Vero, you're awake. See to the door, Mallinna.'

As he spoke, the unknown beauty was rolling the ladder into a tight coil. By the time I managed to sit up, she had vanished so silently into the encompassing shadows that I began to doubt I had even seen her. All I had to go on was the impression of dark eyes, deep brown if not black, buried in lashes; a firm chin and sculpted cheeks; black hair plaited rather untidily in a thick tail hanging over one shoulder; and yet I was sure I'd know her face again even if the next time I saw her was a hundred or a thousand years from then.

'Who is she?' I whispered.

'Mallinna? Like Lestri, she's somebody I taught to read. She knows who we are, by the way. Are you feeling better now?'

'Much.' My legs were wobbling, but the terror on the ladder had effectively disposed of the headache, and any residual pains and fears were swallowed up by an urgent curiosity to see this Mallinna woman in a stronger light. Whatever chamber we had landed in this time was as dark as a cave except for the archway of stars framed by the window and a purely localized glow from the tiny oil lamp, extending no more than a span or two from the wick. By the expansive timbre of our whispers, I knew the room was large and probably empty, and a faint mustiness in the air suggested it was not in frequent use.

Then I became aware we were not alone. Somebody was watching us from just outside the feeble corona of the lamp, somebody whose breathing was soft and ratchety, whose eyes were little twin sparks of reflected lamplight against the black gloom. This person also accounted for the hand I noticed in the next few seconds, an emaciated, liver-spotted and amazingly wrinkled old hand, truncated at the wrist where it passed into the darkness, its fingers knotted in the edge of Tigrallef's tunic. When Tig rose to his feet with the lamp, the stranger maintained that death clutch and rose as well. Tig made no comment.

I sighed and climbed to my feet. 'Do you realize someone is holding you by the tunic?'

Tigrallef raised the lamp higher. 'Of course. Come along, Angel, show yourself.'

Angel. Surely this could not be *the* Angel; not the lonely orphan of the between-ways, raised in the shadows, named by the harlots, the shaggy rescuer in one of my father's favourite stories, left behind in Gil as First Memorian when my father inadvertently set off to circumnavigate the globe. He blinked in the light. I saw he was old enough, all right; a floss of thin white hair fell in tangles to his shoulders, in wild contrast with the trim of his neat white beard, and his face was not so much wrinkled as etched with permanent lines of bewilderment. His bleached blue eyes flicked over me, and he made a polite gesture of greeting with his free hand. Then he returned to his rather touching fixation on my father. He put me in mind of a very ancient puppy.

Tigrallef forestalled any questions at that point by dousing

92

the lamp, taking me by the elbow and setting off with immense sureness into the gloom, with the old man pattering trustfully behind us. Only by glancing backwards and orienting myself by the diminishing patch of stars could I reckon that we were heading on a direct line across the chamber. The floor was bare, hard and empty, and seemed to go on for a very long way. At last there was the indefinable change in the air that meant we were approaching a wall, also a scent that I eagerly recognized from my brief exposure moments ago, a mixture of clean hair, soap and – oddly – fresh ink.

'Mallinna, there's no sound at all out there,' my father whispered. 'It's safe to open the door.'

She did not answer in words, but the darkness split as she pulled the door open a few inches and peered through the crack. Her silhouetted profile, I noted, was flawless. I had never known that ink could smell so enticing.

Moments later our oddly assorted party was walking softly but briskly along a corridor where the darkness was punctuated at intervals by peculiar oil lamps in crystal hoods, a type I had not seen before, casting a light that was steadier than a torch and not so smoky. Mallinna prowled along about half a dozen paces in the lead, a long body moving lithely inside a rather shapeless brown robe – a very long body, I realized, an inch or more longer than my own. Then came the strange composite figure of my father and the old man, apparently joined at the hip; and then me, a few paces behind, on legs that still felt as if they were stuffed with aspic.

I did my best to stop watching how Mallinna moved. Indeed, I had never had much time for watching women, and this was not a good moment to form the habit. Not ten minutes before, I had nearly turned myself into a thin puddle of red paste by jumping out of a window so high I didn't want to think about it; my beloved family was in dire danger at the hands of my father's oldest enemy; my father and I were still in danger, same source as above; a hero of my childhood and the woman I was trying to avoid looking at had probably imperilled themselves just by helping us. And then of course there was my duty to my father – how many pretty women had I turned away from for the sake of the Pain?

Mallinna, halting near one of the lamps at the top of a stairwell, glanced around just as that thought was running through my mind. She caught my eye and smiled with her underlip between her teeth. A heavier portion of pure lust was added to my burden. Fortunately, I was distracted at that moment by the outbreak of a great uproar funnelling up to us via the stairwell, a bull-cry of rage or distress, shouts, orders, marching feet, running feet – I reached for the shark tooth at my throat, remembered it had been confiscated; reached for the fighting chain in my belt, remembered it was back on the *Fifth*; cursed softly.

'The old goatfish,' Tigrallef breathed beside me. His chin was up and his eyes were distant as he listened to the tumult below. Angel was clutching his arm fearfully with both hands. 'The old goatfish,' Tigrallef repeated, 'was very quick in deciding to keep things as they are. A lamentable lack of imagination on his part, I think. There must be many options he didn't even consider.'

'Were the troopers coming to murder us?'

'Yes, Vero.' His grin was just a shade too manic.

'Who are you listening to?'

'The captain from the Flamens' Corps is one.' He closed his eyes, held his breath, moved deeper into the shadows as if that would help his ears sort out the threads of the voices. Angel moved with him. After almost a minute Tigrallef said, 'The other is Lestri, the Second Flamen. They know we used the window.'

'That's bad.'

'They've sent a search party down to the beach to look for our bodies.'

'That's good.'

'The Second Flamen is unhappy.'

'That breaks my heart. Anything else?'

Another long silence. I peered at him anxiously. Even in the shadows I found I could see him quite well – too well.

He was phosphorescent as a moonfish and getting brighter by the moment. My headache returned.

'Mallinna,' I said, addressing my beloved for the first time, 'let's *move!*'

She glided back to us, smiled at me again, and peered with great interest at Tigrallef's luminous face and glazed eyes. 'That's a curious phenomenon,' she said in a voice that was both sweet and husky. 'Is it something he ate?'

'In a sense.'

He was sagging; Angel's mouth was opening and closing in distress, though he made no sound. I gently disengaged the old man's grip and handed him over to Mallinna, then bent and slung Tigrallef across my shoulder, grimacing at the contact with the white-burning heat of his skin. He felt heavier than usual, possibly because I felt worse than usual.

The clamour below us was getting even louder, moving closer to the foot of the stairwell. If they decided to search the floors above and below our ex-prison, we'd be easy game.

'Wherever it is we're going,' I said bluntly, 'let's go there now.'

Mallinna shook herself out of her fascinated observation of my father. 'Oh yes, of course.' She turned immediately, took Angel by the hand and set off down the corridor in an undulant walk that looked unhurried but was not easy to match with my father on my back. The old man allowed himself to be towed along, but his eyes kept turning back to Tigrallef as if he feared we would vanish if not carefully monitored. Several turns, another down-spiralling stairwell – the guardtroops' discord swelled briefly and faded again as we descended to and past their level – another corridor, more turns, a change from plastered to solid stone walls, and at last we were in a dusty little passage about thirty feet long, narrow and made narrower by the scroll racks and book-shelves that lined it from one end to the other. All of them were full and neatly ordered. At the end of the passage was a small unmarked door which Mallinna pushed open without hesitation, propelling the old man tenderly ahead of her. I followed her through and stood panting under Tig's weight while she lit the first of several lamps.

'There's a pallet over there you can put him on.'

I located the pallet and staggered towards it, dimly seeing that I was moving through a landscape composed almost entirely of more bookshelves and scroll racks, also dimly aware that Angel had latched on to Tig's tunic again and was shuffling along beside me. Thankfully I eased Tigrallef's dead weight off my shoulders and on to the rumpled pallet. Mallinna had lit four or five lamps by then and it was hard to tell whether Tigrallef was still glowing, but one of his eyes was blinking madly while the other was staring straight up at the dust swirls on the ceiling. I had once seen someone else who could do that, a buffoon in a travelling comedy show in Gafrin-Gammanthan. When my father did it, it was not funny. I dropped to my knees beside the pallet and launched wildly into the First Protocol. Against all experience, his eyes cleared almost at once, and he stared up at me with a blank expression on his face. My words faltered.

'Too late,' he breathed, and added something almost inaudible about the breakwater. That was all. His head drooped sideways as he fell into a shivering sleep. I found a blanket crumpled at the foot of the pallet and pulled it up around his shoulders.

Angel was on his knees on one side of me, looking stricken and more bewildered than ever. Mallinna was kneeling on my other side. Thoughtfully she touched Tig's cheek. 'His skin's cold. First fever, now chills. But it isn't swamp sickness, is it? Because that wouldn't explain the luminosity.'

'No,' I said sadly, 'it isn't swamp sickness. Swamp sickness would be easier to deal with.'

She frowned as she studied him; I took the opportunity to study her in turn, in the stronger light I had wished for. I noted that her skin was darker than her light brown robe; that her hands were longer and much slimmer than mine; that her black eyes were bright with intelligence; that she did not bother with how she looked and was beautiful enough to get away with it; that her long slim body under the plain robe was an attenuated version of perfection; that her mouth . . .

I stopped there and looked away quickly from her mouth, as it brought the lust rushing back, and I knew perfectly well that lust and duty didn't mix. It was time to address the necessary task of falling back out of love with her – bitterly, because it was not the first time the Pain had sabotaged my love life but it was the first time I had minded very much. Mallinna, ignorant of the quick birth, short life and imminent demise of our love affair, made the process harder by putting her hand on my shoulder and gazing earnestly into my eyes.

'The luminosity – does it indicate an exotic disease of some kind?'

'Uh – not really.'

'An exotic parasite, perhaps?'

'Well . . .'

'Or is it related to the Lady in Gil?'

Too far, too fast. 'What do you know about the Lady?' I countered sharply.

Angel tapped my shoulder. 'The Harashil,' he said in a matter-of-fact voice. They were the first words I had heard him speak, but it was the shock of hearing that hated name, which I had thought was known only to the company on the *Fifth*, that nearly knocked me off my knees.

'The what?' I asked, still nurturing the hope I had misheard him.

'He's referring,' Mallinna clarified, 'to one of our working hypotheses. We have reasonable evidence the Lady was an aspect of something more properly called the Harashil.'

'Mmmm,' I said non-committally.

'The Vassashin texts,' Angel prompted, nodding at her.

'He's referring to a study we did of archival material from a place called Vassashinay, fragments of a very intriguing story. Unfortunately the texts were too badly preserved to give us the rest.' She waved her hand vaguely at the mountain range of written matter around us. 'We have some parallel texts that we think originated in Fathan, but they were badly damaged in the sackings of Cansh Miishel. Perhaps Lord

Tigrallef can help us interpret them. And we were also wondering why he hasn't aged since the last—'

'What excellent questions,' I said, closing my eyes wearily, 'but I have other things on my mind right now, and I'm sure Tig will as well when he wakes up. Our family, for example.'

'The Harashil?' Angel repeated, this time as a question.

'He's referring—'

'I know what he's referring to,' I said, opening my eyes just as wearily. 'We call it the Pain, and it's probably the answer to any working hypothesis the two of you would want to think up. But I can't take the time to tell you about it this moment, and Tig could be asleep for hours. If you know what his plan was for freeing the rest of our family, please tell me now.'

Angel and Mallinna craned around me to see each other's faces.

'Contingent,' said Angel unhappily.

'He means,' Mallinna said, 'that he doesn't believe Lord Tigrallef had a plan yet, exactly.'

'I see. He was going to make it up as he went along. That's a great help.' I took a moment to glare at my father, moaning and sweating on the pallet. 'Do you know where they're being kept?'

Mallinna looked pensive. 'I know where they were earlier, a comfortable suite of rooms in the Middle Palace. But I would wager they've been moved.'

'What do you mean?'

'Hostages,' said Angel sagely.

'He means, they were being kept in that comfortable room only as long as you were being kept in yours. But since the First Flamen said they were being moved, and Lord Tigrallef said the Most Revered Primate had decided to kill you instead of using you—'

It hit me with the force of a collapsing ceiling. I shot to my feet, pulling Mallinna up with me. 'Quickly! Can you see the outer harbour from here? Can you see the breakwaters?'

She caught my urgency. 'Yes, Lord Verolef, you can see the whole harbour from the main workroom. Come with me.'

I had a blurred impression of more books and scrolls, more and more and again more, ranged with exquisite tidiness on the piers that flashed past us; then a door and another dark room. Mallinna guided me across it without bothering to light a lamp and slid to a stop in front of a large double square of starry sky.

Gil really was relentlessly scenic, even on a pitch-dark moonless morning an hour or two before dawn. There was no mist bank this time, and the harbour was visible in full from where we stood. Each of the breakwaters was outlined like a crystal necklace by a bright string of lanterns; festive-looking clusters of white and coloured guide lamps stood on the summits of the guardtowers at the outer breach; fire buoys flamed here and there among the dark ships moored inside the harbour; and well beyond the double arc of the breakwaters, other lights moved on the open sea, the mast lamps of a large vessel.

Mallinna caught her breath. I lost mine.

The great ship, a three-masted wind-galley, was stern-on to the shore at that point; but she heeled and swung slowly northwards as we watched her, and then a few points to the east, as if to round the base of the Gilgard on as tight a course as possible.

'They're on that ship,' I said flatly. 'That's what Tig meant about the breakwaters.'

'That is not good news,' said Mallinna after a moment. 'In fact it's very bad news.'

'Why? What ship is it?'

She shook her head without looking at me. 'I only know its destination. There are four wind-galleys of that grade plying the route, as well as two Warrior-grade windcatchers and two non-specific rammers. That's probably the *Dowager Dazeene*.' She glanced at me. 'She's named after your grand-mother – Dazeene used to come to the archives daily until the Primate sent her away from Gil—'

'Why are you changing the subject? Where's the ship bound?'

She went back to avoiding my eyes. 'Only the Mosslines.'

'Nowhere else?'

'Nowhere else. Straight to the Mosslines, straight back.'

'Cargo?'

'Outward bound,' she said steadily, 'those ships carry labourers for the Mosslines and the troops to keep them in order. On the return journey, the only cargo is the moss itself. The refinery is in Gil, you see.'

The Mosslines again. Every mention of them in my hearing had been hung about with nasty connotations like the smell of rotten meat. 'Tell me about the Mosslines. Where are they? What moss? Why? *Who gets sent there?*'

She looked out across the dark ocean, frowning. 'The Mosslines are far over the sea in the wasteland that used to be called Fathan, the only place in the known world where the moss is found. It's strange stuff, can't be cultivated, but it grows very fast in natural rifts in the slag-cover – it has potent healing properties as well as the power to give dreams, and the Flamens guard their monopoly very carefully. As for who gets sent there – mostly convicts. Thieves, murderers, milchers, smugglers, blasphemers. That's officially, and it's also nearly true.' Her voice dropped. 'Unofficially: a few citizens who don't like the rule of the Flamens; a few citizens the Flamens don't like; a few citizens who have said unwise words or seen sights they weren't meant to see. They're called treasoners, and they don't last long on the Mosslines.'

Shree, Chasco, Calla, Kat. Four inadvertent treasoners who had seen something they were not meant to see, Tigrallef's face and mine. Watching the ship's mast lamps recede around the curved flank of the Gilgard, I knew that we had already lost this battle. I could hardly swim after them. Until we could somehow get hold of a sea-going vessel, there was nothing in the world we could do for them.

'You don't happen to have a ship we could borrow, do you?' I asked Mallinna bitterly.

She took it as a serious question. 'Not at this moment. However we put in a requisition for one several months ago.'

I almost laughed.

'When we do get a ship,' she went on, 'we'll be happy to take you anywhere you want to go, even to the Mosslines.'

'Thanks, but they'll be dead by then,' I said, not very graciously. I had previous experience in how the Gillish bureaucracy worked.

Angel, keeping vigil over the pallet when we returned, was clumsily but tenderly wiping the sweat off my father's forehead with the sleeve of his brown robe. There were no questions in his eyes as he looked up at us, and he came out with the longest string of words I'd heard from him so far. 'He says they've been taken away on a ship,' he sighed, shaking his aureole of white hair. Tigrallef muttered and ground his teeth in his sleep.

6

Breakfast time in the archives: a far cry from the kind of archival slop Tigrallef and Shree had described to us, the stale bread dipped in mutton lard, the leftovers from whatever culinary atrocity had been served up the night before, the lumpy sand-leavened porridge that tasted of dust. The others, Tigrallef included, were eating steadily through a platter of boiled eggs, salted fishpaste, fine fresh bread, and fruits gathered from half a dozen climates, washing it all down with a hot infusion of herbs sweetened with honey. I managed some of the liquid, but between the despair and the hangover, I had no appetite for solid food. I was surprised and faintly resentful that Tig could eat at all.

Catering was not the only aspect of the archives to have changed over the years. The shelves and racks that surrounded us were not cobbled together out of scavenged and mismatched boards, but were inbuilt of hardwood, carved and polished. The work tables were steady on their legs and veneered on top with smooth granite sheets. The stacks had grown to a labyrinth twenty times the size that Tigrallef remembered, room after room of works in all scripts and languages of the known world. The walls were well plastered and recently painted; the floors throughout were covered with plain Flamen-green carpeting that was comfortable on the feet, durable and conveniently easy to clean, as we discovered when Tig dropped his bread on it with the fishpaste-side down. In the spotless and tidy main workroom, the one with the view of the harbour, ten or eleven apprentices or assistant memorians of assorted ages were already hard at their scholarly tasks.

But we were breakfasting in Angel and Mallinna's private workroom behind the stacks, which was a very different prospect. However plush the carpet, and however neatly the books stood on the shelves, it was clear nobody had dusted or tidied in that room for a very long time. Great piles of books, scrolls, tablets and loose papers, some of them rare and ancient, lay in drifts across four broad work tables. They had the look of papers in precisely ordered chaos, like those on the table of the hidden study on the *Fifth*. At a glance, many of those I could decipher described the landmass shared by Miishel, Grisot and what used to be Fathan.

Tig had wakened about an hour after dawn, ravenous and bizarrely cheerful, and insisted on waking me up too, though I'd managed less than two hours of exhausted sleep. It was, of course, no news to him that the others were on their way to the Mosslines. He embraced Angel heartily, and then Mallinna. When it came to my turn, he looked past my shoulder as if not quite willing to face me, which I did not understand at that point. Then he demanded food. He refused to discuss the others. He wanted to hear all about what Angel and Mallinna had been doing for the last twenty years.

Even weighed down by misery, I found myself watching

Mallinna. What was she to Angel besides disciple and, apparently, interpreter? Was she his granddaughter? His mistress? Was she spoken for? How did my father know her? And how, by the Eight Rages, did she and Angel just happen to drop a rope ladder from a particular window at a time when my father and I just happened to need one? I lay prone on the pallet, not saying much, letting the answers slowly come together.

First, I found out who she was. Mallinna's mother was an old friend of the family, a whore named Lissula who had progressed from the Gilgard shintashkr into running a highly successful bawdy house of her own after the liberation, a liberation in which she played no small part. The father was a nameless client, evidently a Storican, from whom Mallinna inherited her dark brown skin and long slender frame. At the age of four, when my father was still the First Memorian in Gil, she became one of his day pupils in the archives; at the age of five she became an orphan and a scholar. It happened in the time of the Last Dance.

Angel told this part of the story in his halting fashion: how for a number of days he had been sequestered in the archives, mourning the departure of Shree and my father for Miishel, mechanically continuing the tasks of reading and annotating and cataloguing. One day it occurred to him that no pupils had climbed the stairs to the archives for some time, that the water barrel was empty, the makeshift pantry critically depleted, the slop pails full, the laundry neither collected dirty nor delivered clean. He waited another day, puzzled, and then ventured out through the silent halls of the Temple Palace, down the echoing stairs, meeting nobody, until he passed through the unmanned gates of Gilgard Castle into the hot reeking streets of the city. Gradually it began to dawn on him that something strange was going on.

Except for my grandmother the Lady Dazeene, the only person Angel knew outside the archives was Lissula. He had never been to her brothel – he had only once or twice left the Gilgard since the day he was born – but he had seen it daily from the window of the workroom, and carried an aerial view of that quarter like a map inside his head. He set off down the broad avenue that led to the waterfront, observing with wonder the abandoned wains and empty byways, the shuttered houses and barred taverns, the deserted scaffolding of a building under construction, the dog-eared remnants of the banners raised for my father's wedding recessional. He began to think it was a holiday nobody had told him about. Until, that is, he turned a corner and came to a cordwood of corpses in a small market square.

There were a few living persons around as well, but Angel was too shy to ask for explanations. Some were desultorily stacking the corpses, a few skulked out of sight at his approach, a few simply stood around with dazed eyes and dangling hands and took no notice of him. As Angel passed, one of these began to shuffle her feet in a little dance, pirouetted straight into the edge of the neat heap of the dead, and fell over to join the others. Angel kept walking.

The other wonder he saw on the way to the brothel was in the mouth of a narrow lane off a street of provisions warehouses, where half-glimpsed movement caught the corners of his eyes as he passed. He thought about it for a few steps and then went back to look. It was a concourse of shulls, leaping, twisting, jerking, falling over, and lying where they had fallen. Angel kept walking, only faster.

Lissula's brothel was a grand one with a guard's kiosk at the door and a fine entrance court equipped with flower beds and a fountain, but the kiosk was empty and a corpse was digging its fingers into the cracked earth around the natch-blossoms. Inside, intimidated by the silken cushions and lattice-work partitions, the job-lot but rather good tapestries on the walls and the overhanging silence, Angel crept from compartment to compartment of the brothel and found plenty that stank but nothing that breathed. Last of all he penetrated the good solid door that led to Lissula's own living quarters, and found Lissula, dead, and Mallinna, alive but hungry and beginning to be annoyed. Her mam, she explained to her teacher, was so tired from dancing that she wouldn't get up and make supper. Angel took his little pupil back to the archives. Twenty years later she was still there.

As for Angel's empire-within-an-empire, the archives had shared richly in the general fortunes of Gil. I learned a startling fact at this point: that the Primate Mycri was in a strange way a man of his word. Promises he made were always kept to the letter – though the spirit was often twisted into shapes the other party had neither intended nor foreseen. Any treaty he signed was honoured with exquisite legalistic nicety – until the other side gave him some excuse, however slight, to piss on it. A satirical catchphrase – 'Primate's honour' – had entered the Gillish idiom, though to be heard using it could mean a quick one-way trip to the Mosslines.

Twenty years ago, this honourable Primate had made a bargain with my father regarding Angel and the archives. It was a bargain which the Primate may have been prepared to invalidate when Tigrallef had the apparent inconsideration to die; but my grandmother, the Lady Dazeene, had made a promise to Tig as well. When she struck her own bargain with the Primate after the Last Dance, Angel and the archives came under her patronage and protection, and so they remained.

In due course the canny Primate began to understand the advantages of owning a well-managed national library with a non-political work fiend like Angel in charge – the prestige, partly, the visible guarantee of Gillish superiority in scholarly matters, but also the access to odd bits of lore that could shore up the Flamens' claims and arguments, to dazzle those who supported them and confound those who did not. Angel, it must be said, had always given some form of satisfaction.

Gradually at first, then rapidly, the archives had begun to grow. Client nations were honoured, in theory anyway, to contribute their holdings to the centre of empire. Treaty nations, like Miishel and Grisot and Zaine, were relieved to pay a portion of their tribute in ancient manuscripts rather than gold palots and grain. As for those nations misguided enough to require being 'organized' by the Primate's armies, they had only themselves to blame when their national treasures, written and otherwise, were carted off to a new home in the Gilgard. And thus the archives overspilled the few miserable rooms Tigrallef had first co-opted, and expanded to fill an entire floor of the Temple Palace; one whole aisle was devoted to inscribed Plaviset tortoise plastrons. Angel (through Mallinna) estimated his holdings at more than two hundred thousand documents in a dozen different forms, thirty-two languages or dialects, and nineteen different scripts.

All of this shocked me in a strange and not very reasonable way. The Primate was a major ogre of my childhood, devious, power-thirsty and ruthless. He was the kind of remorseless plotter who would serve wine to three innocent men in one moment, and send them off to be murdered in the next; who was prepared to wipe out an entire family – mine – because he thought one of them bore a chance resemblance to a fraudulently prophesied demigod – his wrongness about us on every conceivable account was irrelevant. We had no way of knowing what other cruelties he had found to be expedient in the last twenty years, but I suspected there was an ocean or two of blood on his gnarled hands. How could Angel, my father's friend, and Mallinna, daughter of the intrepid Lissula, submit to being a part of it?

And anyway, I asked myself bitterly, when were we going to discuss the fates of Kat and Calla, Shree and Chasco? At the thought of them tossing about in the dark hold of a slave ship, I felt my belly and all its contents churn with impatience. Tigrallef's blitheness was infuriating. Mallinna's loveliness was an affront. Angel, frankly, was not measuring up to the heroic image I'd formed of him, and not just because of his age. The three of them were having a pleasant time chatting about the archives and matters of scholarship while our loved ones were being carried farther away from us every moment, probably suffering, perhaps even now beyond our help, and my father did not appear to care. He was being brilliantly snide about a scroll submitted by the Lucian Clerisy, actually chuckling over it with Mallinna, when my self-control snapped.

I flung myself off the pallet and turned on Angel and Mallinna, the easier targets. 'I can't listen to any more of this hypocrisy. You can't deny you've profited by the Primate's crimes, can you? You're just as much his lackeys as those bastards in black, or the Flamens, or the drones in dun tunics down by the harbour. You accept his pilfered booty like any picklock thief's receiver – you feed him the lore that helps him lie to the people – you do nothing to protest his tyranny, you . . .'

And so I ranted on in a way that makes me cringe to remember, even then knowing but not caring that I was being unjust. Fortunately it was wasted. Tig carried on skim-reading the Lucian scroll; Angel and Mallinna listened to me with great interest and attention, as if I were stating a position in a scholarly debate. When my words ran down without effect, I glared at the two of them in frustration and turned furiously to my father.

Looking up from the scroll with his eyebrows raised, he quietly ambushed me. 'Have you forgotten, Vero, who helped us escape?'

I felt as if someone had kicked me in the gut. 'No, I haven't forgotten, but—'

'And who it is that's hiding us in the very heart of the Gilgard, at great peril and inconvenience to themselves?'

Another kick, well-placed in the metaphorical backside. 'Yes, I admit that too, but—'

'Did you wonder how they knew where we were, and who we are?'

'I've had no time to think about it, but—'

'Would it surprise you to know that Mallinna eavesdrops routinely on the Primate's councils?'

I gave up. 'It wouldn't surprise me at all.'

'That her information is then smuggled from the archives to the Primate's opponents?'

'Enough said.'

'That Mallinna's gleanings have more than once prevented bloodshed—'

'I understand.'

'—and warned innocents who were doomed to the Moss-lines to drop out of sight before the troopers came for them.'

'I understand, Tig.'

'You should also know that misinformation passed from the archives kept the Primate from finding and plundering the secret holies of the Plaviset—'

'I honestly do understand.'

'—and allowed several small mid-kingdoms to sue for better surrender terms, which saved the Omelian silk groves and the oyster communes around Glishor from the Primate's punitive torch—'

'Mallinna, I was wrong,' I said loudly. 'Revered Angel, forgive me for my foolish doubts. Father, you can stop talking now.'

At last I knew why Tigrallef had spent so much time grinning at the ceiling of our well-upholstered prison, and who besides the First Flamen had visited us while I snored in drunken slumber. The Temple Palace had no between-ways, but it was wormholed with air ducts and light wells to supply the large inner warren that was carved into the Gilgard rock, and Angel had learned every twist and turn of them while the Sherank still occupied the castle. Although Tig and Shree had patiently trained him to use the corridors after the liberation, he slipped back into his old habits not long after they left him behind. Eventually he grew too frail and too brittle in his bones to pull himself through the ducts, but by then Mallinna was the heretrix of his knowledge. And a good thing for us that she was, too.

Breakfast over, indeed, and Angel having gone into the stacks to supervise the apprentices, it was almost time for Mallinna to pay her daily informal visit to the Primate's council chamber. Still chastened, I helped her pile the trenchers and empty bowls outside the door of the private work-room for the skivvies to pick up. While being fairly handy with the dishes, I fumbled clumsily with more words of apology. Mallinna said with genuine sweetness, 'Your assessment was based on incomplete information,' and left it at that, smiling at me as if everything was now explained and excused. I suddenly perceived that a child raised by Angel in the archives from the age of five was bound to have some odd ways of looking at human behaviour. My own upbringing began to look relatively normal.

Back in the workroom, where Tig was sitting at a work table poring over some papers, Mallinna abruptly pulled her robe off over her head and stretched to hang it on a hook. My father did not even look up. I gasped. Swallowed. Sat down, grabbed a book and opened it in my lap. Pretended to read the book. Began to mutter the Zelfic Mathematical Protocols under my breath. I was not being prudish. She was not even naked underneath the robe – there was a garment that might have been a loincloth or else very brief under-britches, and she was wearing ankle-high socks as well. Anyway she was not the first woman I'd ever seen without her clothes on. Clothing was considered a perversion among the sea savages of Itsant; in the hotlands of Storica it was a rarity; in some islands of the Ronchar Sea, all sartorial effort was lavished on astonishing hats.

No, her near nakedness in itself did not shock or embarrass me, but I was well into the Third Protocol before I felt safe in putting the book aside. Then I saw what she was doing; back went the book; I moved on to the Fourth Protocol. She had pinned her plait into a tight knot at the back of her head, and was rubbing oil on to her bare shoulders and hips and . . .

'Perhaps you'd like to come,' she said brightly. 'Stand up, let me see how big you are.'

I groaned. Fifth Protocol. Warily I stood up, keeping the book in a strategic defensive placement. She hovered in front of me, almost pressing against my body – after a delirious few moments, I realized she was directly comparing the breadth of my shoulders against her own.

109

'No,' she said, disappointed, 'you're far too large. You'd get stuck.'

While I choked back another groan, she called out a farewell to Tigrallef and climbed the shelves of a pier of books as if it were a ladder, to a wooden screen inset into the ceiling above it. This screen she pushed up and aside, leaving a square hole just large enough for her to wriggle through. Sixth Protocol. I looked away, then back again just in time to see her feet disappear.

I was glad she was gone. I wanted her out of my sight before I ran out of Zelfic Protocols. And I very much wanted to have a firm talk with my father, alone.

It was not easy to start. Tig remained stubbornly absorbed in the papers on Angel's work table, even when I shook his shoulder and tried to catch his attention. Rescue plans, none of them much good, were filling my head: stealing a ship, pirating a ship, even bloody well buying a ship if we could scrape up enough palots with Angel's help. I had little hope of getting the *Fifth* back.

'Tig,' I said decisively, 'we have to go after them. We must get a ship somehow.'

He bent over the work table, ignoring me as he'd been doing all morning.

'Look at me, Father, we have to talk about what we're going to do. Think about Calla. Think about Kat.'

He gave no indication that he even knew I was there. I hovered behind him for a moment or two – until I noticed the splashes of bright red on the papers in front of him. Then I took him by the shoulders and forcibly rotated him on the stool until he was facing me.

Trouble, and not just the blood on his chin. Where he wasn't bloody he was slick with sweat, a shining sheet of it that was far more profuse than the warmth in the workroom justified. His eyes, too lambent, were fixed on the neck of my tunic, his lower lip was nearly healed from being bitten through. I sighed and wiped the blood from his chin, but

110

just as I was launching into the Lucian proverbs, his eyelids flickered.

'Oh please,' he said faintly, 'not the Lucian proverbs.'

I hesitated. 'Are you all right? This is the Pain, isn't it?'

'It is, but don't bother. I'm afraid we've moved beyond that form of helpfulness. Don't bore us both by trying.' He even managed to laugh, a ghastly little cackle with no mirth in it. I was not fooled. Any thoughts of Mallinna fled my mind – even my mother and the rest were pushed into the background. As always, the Pain took precedence. I sat down heavily on the edge of the work table and tilted Tigrallef's head until he was looking into my eyes.

'Deep breaths, Father.'

He laughed again. 'How much better it would be if I could stop breathing altogether.'

'Don't talk like that. How can I help you? Is it like that time in Amballa?'

'It's like nothing we've ever seen. No, Vero, I believe the Harashil and the Naar turned a corner together last night. I doubt the old rules and remedies apply any more.'

'Just keep hold.' Pretty feeble, but there was nothing much I could say.

His eyes drifted down to the table top. Mine followed. His right hand was in a claw palm-down on the granite veneer, with the fingers bent so the knuckles of the first joints formed a prominent ridge; but the whole hand was slowly and effortlessly sinking into the granite surface. The fingertips vanished first, then the back of his hand, leaving the knuckles standing proud like islands in a sea of reddish stone; then they sank as well, clean out of sight, prompting a vagrant thought of Iklankish. Tigrallef wore an expression of extreme interest. From my angle, he gave the illusion of a one-handed man pushing the stump of his wrist against the edge of the table. Then he twisted the stump and lifted; the hand began to emerge from the granite, fingertips first, the stone dripping out of his palm like water.

'That was interesting. Would you like to see it again?' His hand was poised over the table top.

'No. Stop it. What's happened to you? Is it because Calla's been taken? We'll get her back, Tig, I promise you, we'll—'

'I could get her back at once if I was willing to pay the price; but don't worry, I'm not that far gone. There has been no act of will as yet.' His lip visibly finished healing as he spoke, his hand descended as gently as floating thistledown – to the top of the table this time, not through it; but the granite rippled, the books and papers on it rocked gently like fallen leaves on the surface of a lapping tide. A moment later, when I touched the table with great caution, it was solid again.

I tried to think of something sensible to say.

'I have an idea,' Tig said.

'What is it?'

'Watch this.' Without further warning, he flung himself off the stool and charged straight at the stone wall, leading with the crown of his head. I threw myself after him a broken second too late. His head encountered the wall with a crash that felled him flat, jolted the dust out of the chinks in the masonry, toppled a book or two and would have staved in the skull of any normal man – I fell gasping to my knees beside him as he rolled over on to his back.

I discovered later that a rash of strange incidents were reported all over Gil City at about the same time as my father tried to batter his brains out against the wall of Angel's workroom. The three that were best supported by the evidence were these: first, the Great Head of the Scion that overlooked the inner harbour blinked its stone eyes, opened its mouth and sang a snatch of song in a strange tongue, which I tentatively identified from garbled eyewitness accounts as the primary dialect of Gafrin-Gammanthan. The song itself was probably indecent. Second, the four life-size idols of Tigrallef in the Great Garden, ranged protectively around the base of the almost immemorial statue of the Lady in Gil, spun around to stare accusingly at the stone woman in their midst and turned their backs on her again. Third, the remaining portions of the Sherkin bastion crumbled into a drift of dust and rubble, fortunately with no loss of life; the adjacent shrine dedicated to the Scion Tigrallef, Ark and Sceptre of the Lady in Gil, an ostentatious structure in the style of Tallislef Second, slumped on its foundations but did not fall.

Other reported miracles – such as the dog who proclaimed the Scion's return in fluent Gillish with a marked Zainoi accent, the seventy-foot sea-eel sighted weeping in the outer harbour, the flock of birds that spelled out Tigrallef's name-glyph as they flew over the roofs of the Lower Palace – all these I considered to be signs of the people's thirst for wonders, mere superstition, a kind of mass madness fuelled by the fear that hung over the Primate's domain.

Back in the archives, I knew nothing about the antics of statues and bastions, but I could see Tig actually felt better for that crushing blow to the head. If anything, he seemed less dazed than before. I climbed to my feet again and helped him to his.

'What was that, your new revised emergency procedure?' I asked disapprovingly, brushing the dust off his tunic.

'You'd be surprised,' he said in a perfectly normal voice, 'how much better it made me feel. And I'll wager it shook *you* up, you cursed old sow,' he added with satisfaction, fingering the point of impact on the top of his head. By rights a lump the size of a maiden's fist should have been pushing up under his hair, but there was not even any blood. He looked weary but unusually sane.

'What brought this on?' I asked, guiding him back to the stool.

'Am I acting strangely?'

'You always act strangely, Da, but lately you've found a few new ways of doing it. It's because the others have been carried away to the Mosslines, right? Which reminds me—'

He performed a half-twirl on the round stool. 'I wish it were that simple. Everything has changed, Vero, and it changed well before this morning – it changed when we set our course for Gil, though I didn't know it until last night, which is of course the whole point.'

I surveyed him with great care. There was no sign that the Pain was going to retaliate for the knock on his head. Yet. 'I understand you somewhat less than usual,' I said diplomatically.

'It's not that difficult, Vero. All this time, I've been so sure I understood what passes for the old sow's intelligence. All these years, I've been faithfully following the line of most resistance. The harder the Harashil fought me, the more clearly she marked my path.'

'I understand: like two meshed gears. If she spun one way, you spun the other. If she said yea, you said nay. If she said stay, you said go. If—'

'Exactly. When we returned to the known world, she said: *Don't sail to Gil.* So we sailed to Gil. When the inspection party came on board, she said: *Don't let them see you.* So I rushed on deck. When the troopers came to capture the ship, she said: *Don't be captured, resist the troopers; let the others fight to the death.* You know how badly that came out.'

'We were doomed either way.'

'Yes, but the point is, this time I read the old sow all wrong. I let her manoeuvre me straight into disaster.' With one fingernail, he scraped at the dried bloodspots on Angel's paperwork.

I held myself ready in case he made another assault upon the wall, but I did think I had spotted a flaw in his logic. 'Are you certain your decision was the wrong one?' I asked.

'Yes,' he answered positively. 'By the fact that, owing to my stupidity and overconfidence, your mother and sister and our good comrades have been snatched off to a living death on the Mosslines; by the fact that we are almost certainly unable to go after them unless I surrender and use the Harashil's power by my own choosing; by the fact that I have detected a certain smug satisfaction in the old sow's emanations—'

'But,' I insisted, feeling subtle, 'what if the Pain wasn't

misleading you then, but is misleading you now? Maybe we're *meant* to follow the others to the Mosslines for some purpose that we don't know yet, and things are actually turning out as they should . . .'

'Alas, Vero, this is not a Calloonic farce. As far as the Old Ones are concerned, all that's *meant* to happen is for me to build the Great Nameless Last and then bring the world to an end. If we want to follow a different script, we have to think it up as we go.'

He broke off and frowned at the ceiling, tilting his head to listen. 'Raksh take it, but she's in a hurry.'

'Mallinna?' I strained my ears but could hear nothing.

'Who else do we know that pops in and out of ceilings?' He took his eyes off the wooden screen above the bookshelves long enough to glance at me. 'She's a fine woman, Vero.'

'I'm aware of that,' I said coolly.

'She'll make a grand colleague – ah, here she comes.'

The skittering and slithering noises overhead were so subtle I would have missed them if Tig hadn't been there to point them out. The wooden screen slid aside, bare brown feet emerged followed by remarkably long brown legs and – and I bent over the work table and pretended *very hard* to be reading. I heard her agile descent of the bookshelves, her breathless greeting to my father, the rustle of cloth . . .

'Hurry, help me get the oil off.'

When I turned around, she was sponging at her bare shoulders with a wet rag, and she seemed to be in a great hurry. Tigrallef, working industriously on her back with another rag, flung me yet another. Averting my eyes, I moved as close as I dared and scrubbed away at whatever came to hand, fumbling under my breath for the Lucian proverbs.

'Quickly, no time to tell you now, the Flamens are coming.'

She danced out of reach; the next sounds I heard implied the brown robe was being pulled on over her head, a comb was attacking the thick, dark hair, Tigrallef was helping her on with her slippers. 'Wait here,' she said hastily, and then she was gone. I felt as if a whirlwind had passed through the room and out again.

'You can look now,' said Tigrallef. He seemed amused.

An hour passed. A brittle edge developed to Tigrallef's behaviour that I had never seen before, but otherwise he seemed to be in control of himself. I tried once more to get him to make plans, perhaps to discuss our chances of acquiring a boat without raising too much suspicion among the brokers, but it was impossible to hold his interest. At times I thought he was listening with close attention to something that was happening in the stacks or the main workroom, at times he simply stared into space. His eyes were bright but not particularly mad.

'They're going,' he said at last, followed immediately by 'they're coming.' For once I did not care about his maddening imprecision with pronouns. We both looked expectantly at the door as it opened.

Angel hobbled in leaning on Mallinna's arm. An odd couple they made in their matching brown robes, she so tall and straight, Angel so bent and shrunken, but they wore identical expressions of being terribly pleased with themselves.

'Well?' I asked, taking Angel's other arm. Tigrallef kept silent.

'Kesi. Good news,' Angel said as we conducted him between us to a comfortable chair.

'He means, Kesi the First Flamen came to the archives to give us some excellent news – though, of course, I knew it already because I'd listened to the Council's deliberations, and I can tell you it was all the First Flamen's idea anyway.'

'What was?' I asked.

'Requisition,' Angel remarked, nodding significantly.

'He means, some time ago we put in a requisition for a small ocean-going windcatcher to be attached to the archives, for a survey we'd proposed of the Sherkin Sea—'

'A ship!' I cried. Tigrallef was still silent.

'Yours,' Angel said modestly.

'That's generous of you—' I began.

'He means,' Mallinna interrupted, 'that the Primate has been persuaded to give us *your* ship.'

This was stunning luck, and it very nearly didn't happen. In the debate regarding the disposal of the *Fifth*, the Primate's first impulse had been to fire it and scuttle the hulk in deep water south of Malvi Point, thus erasing the evidence of a sensitive and disappointing matter. It was Kesi, the First Flamen, who timidly suggested such a boat might just suit the needs of the First Memorian for his expedition to the Sherkin Sea; a great pity, he said, to scuttle such a sleek-looking little windcatcher when it could be put to good use. And, of course, it would save the expense of building another to give to the First Memorian, which was exactly the sort of argument to impress the Primate. The decision was made in minutes, and the First Flamen was delegated to inform the memorians that they now owned a boat. Mallinna had raced him back to the archives.

'There was something else you should hear about the captain's report,' she said when our jubilation had died down to the point where she didn't have to shout to be heard.

'More good news, I hope,' said Tigrallef.

'Good and bad,' she answered. 'Officially, the two of you are dead. The Council accepted Captain Abro's conclusion that you foolishly tried to escape through the window and fell to your deaths. No further search will be ordered for you. That's the good news.' She paused. 'The bad news is, they recovered your bodies from the beach.'

Tig and I exchanged puzzled looks, followed by a moment of trying to work out whether Mallinna was joking, and then the rapid disappearance of elation.

'Unrecognizable, naturally,' Mallinna added. 'You more or less exploded when you hit the ground – bits of flesh all over, Captain Abro said, and enough blood to redden the tide along quite a stretch of beach. He wasn't exaggerating, either, he brought along a representative sample of body parts. He said the rock-pool crabs were already—'

'Enough, Mallinna,' Tig said, not happy. 'Poor sods, I wonder who they were.'

'Whereas *I* wonder who threw them out the window,' I said.

We thought it over in silence. It was an excellent question, because whoever had arranged our unfortunate replacements knew perfectly well we weren't dead. On reflection, I didn't believe the Primate had anything to do with it. Mallinna said he had been severely displeased at the news of our deaths – yes, it was true he had ordered the Flamens' Corps to murder us, but he did not like his wishes to be anticipated. Jumping out the window was bad form, an outrageous gaffe, the sort of disrespect that would be punishable by death if we weren't thought to be scattered over an acre or so of beach already. Perhaps it was fortunate for my mother and the rest that the *Dowager Dazeene* had already upped her anchor by then, with them safely aboard and out of reach of immediate retribution – as if anybody on their way to the Mosslines could be considered lucky.

'It can only have been the captain of the Flamens' Corps,' said Tigrallef.

'Or Kesi,' Angel put in, surprising us.

'Or Kesi,' Tigrallef agreed. 'Yes, or even a collaboration between Kesi and your Captain – Abro, was it?'

Mallinna looked pensive; Angel shook his head. 'They are not friends,' he said positively. For once Mallinna did not bother to interpret for him.

'Bear in mind,' I said, 'that two innocents were pitched out of a wickedly high window to support the deception. We know Captain Abro, killer of scribes, would be capable of that – but would the First Flamen?'

Angel and Mallinna looked at each other, and Angel shrugged rather expressively. 'He means maybe, if the reasons were good enough,' Mallinna answered, 'though Kesi's a very nice old man.' She tapped her forehead suddenly, as if just remembering something. 'There is another matter,' she said, fishing something out of her pocket. She unwrapped and held up a small object on a broken string of leather. 'I would guess it's from a marine predator, like a large shark, but I can't place the species.'

I didn't need to look at it.

'You're right,' I said, 'but you wouldn't know the species because it's not indigenous to these oceans. We saw sharks like these near Itsant, in one of the unknown worlds. The savages called them the Bloody Spirits of the Sea. Where did you get it?'

'From the First Flamen,' she said slowly, 'as he was leaving the archives. He put it into my hand. He often donates odd items to the natural history collection. Is it yours? Would you like it back?'

'No,' I said, 'you keep it. It was the First Flamen's gift to you.'

There was another long silence while I, and presumably the others, devoted some solid thinking to the motives of the First Flamen. Angel surprised me again by eventually giving voice to my own thoughts, in what was for him a veritable spate of words.

'Maybe not a gift,' he said. 'Maybe a *message*.'

PART TWO

The Benthonic Survey Expedition

Vero sighted the seafolk from the moorage about half an hour before sunset: three barges, seven war-skiffs, minimum three hundred spearmen. Tig and Katla were besieged in the Eighth Mamelon. When we arrived in the Third to take them off, Katla had a slight head injury and Tig was gripped by the worst attack of the Pain we've ever seen. Confirmed destroyed: three barges, six war-skiffs and eleven mysteriously exploded Mamelons. Presumed destroyed: the seventh war-skiff. As for the spearmen, the Bloody Spirits of the Sea should be thanking Tig for the feast. No damage to the Third. Bless the Old Ones, Katla will be fine.

Much to our surprise, this does not seem to have constituted an act of Will. If it had, Tig would be busy with the Great Nameless Last now instead of the same old struggle with the Harashil. If he ever wakes up, we'll ask him.

We were pretty much finished at Itsant anyway.

Excerpt from Chasco's Journal Vol. 3, 'Itsant and
the South Ronchar Sea', in the Archives of the
College of the Second Coming

7

And so, the memorians had a ship — not just any ship, but our own beautiful *Fifth*, and there had never been a vessel like her in the known and unknown worlds. In designing her, Chasco and my father and I had collected bright ideas from a dozen or more shipbuilding traditions, ancient and modern, and profited from mistakes made with the ill-fated *Fourth*. According to the state of the sea, she could cut the waves with the tirelessness of a Bloody Spirit, skim them with the swiftness and grace of a Bauli cormorant, or resist them with the stability of the ice mountains in the waters off Myr. The Sherkin Sea Benthonic Survey Expedition — as Angel's project was called in the account ledgers and year-end fiscal statements of the Flamens' treasury in Gil — was fortunate to get her.

Furthermore, if one happened to be planning, say, a potentially suicidal excursion to a remote deathtrap across a sea bristling with large naval windcatchers armed to the mast-tops with spearchuckers, flame-slings and bouldershots, she'd be just the sort of vessel one would choose.

Roughly speaking, that was the plan. We would set off as the Benthonic Survey and cross the Sherkin Sea as our most direct route to the continent shared by Grisot, Miishel and Fathan. At that point we would be transformed into the Mosslines Rescue Mission; we would head south around the coast of the great landmass to where the blasted wilderness of ancient Fathan began, bypassing the Mosslines port of Deppowe before coming ashore at a site carefully chosen by my father. Our success after that would depend on whether the ancient maps bore any useful resemblance to the post-apocalyptic topography of the ruined land — too many changes, and we would be up a mountain pass without a rope, almost literally. Our plans for returning Angel and Mallinna to Gil were equally vague, another bridge we'd build when we reached the river.

Crew: the *Fifth*'s rigging was designed to let her sail with a minimum of hands, but Angel was too old, Mallinna had never set foot on a deckboard, my father could be knocked askew by the Pain at any moment, and I would have to catch the odd hour of sleep now and then. We calculated two experienced sailors would be necessary and sufficient to round out the ship's complement, but how could we find even one trustworthy citizen in Gil? Someone who would willingly go to the Mosslines with us – someone who would not start blathering about the Primate's stupid prophecy the moment he saw Tigrallef's face?

No problem, Mallinna declared, we could leave it to her; she had contacts outside the archives who could pretty much tell the difference between a bollard and a highsheet, had no great love for the Flamens, and would fancy a tour of the Mosslines. She would ask the Opposition to recruit two seamen, subject to our approval. What could we say? We said thank you.

But the thought of Mallinna's contacts with an anti-Flamen faction of rebels and spies kept me awake at nights. I was certain I could trust Mallinna and Angel, but I knew nothing about the Opposition except that we shared a common enemy, which was no guarantee of anything. What were their motives? What were their aims? What were their own plans for Gil? How large was the lunatic element that always exists in these organizations?

I tried to learn more from Mallinna, but I could have saved my breath. She became a deaf-mute when I tried to raise the subject. She had been risking herself for them for the better part of a decade and I think she was firmly in the habit of secrecy where they were concerned. She would not even tell me how she passed her intelligence to them, though it did not take a genius or a mind-reader to work out that a small packet left the archives every few days in a basket of dirty laundry.

Of course she might have been more forthcoming if my father had asked her, but Tigrallef took astoundingly little interest in the Opposition. I could not understand this. It was not just that our safety, at one remove, was in the hands of these strangers; the Tigrallef that I knew would have been fascinated, keen to trace their history and compare them point by point with the Web in Gil, the Silver Ghosts in Gafrin-Gammanthan, and similar underground movements. Back in one of the *Fifth*'s hidden holds was a thick file of raw research gathered over the years on just this subject, but Tigrallef never even picked up his pen on the Opposition's account. It was not like him, and it worried me.

For the next two weeks, the time it took to prepare for the so-called survey, Tigrallef and I were confined to the inner workroom at the archives. We were, after all, supposed to be dead. We saw nobody but Angel and Mallinna and each other, and any one of those three could independently have driven me mad in his or her own way. It was therefore fortunate that we had little time to contemplate our situation or the plight of our family. There were all the details of the expedition to be worked out, the lists of supplies to be drawn up, whole shelves of reports from the Mosslines to be culled for useful information or copied to be taken on the voyage. The memorians had virtually been given a key to the treasury to equip this survey, the best of everything, excellent wines, many leathers of smoke-cured meat and pressed fruit essence, star charts and sea charts, sounding and sighting tools based on the most advanced Zelfic designs. A crate of weapons and climbing gear was purchased through Mallinna's shadowy contacts and listed on the manifest as STATIONERY SUPPLIES.

The *Fifth*, which was moored in the imperial boatyard in the inner harbour, was not only overhauled but tarted up – we were entertained by it being at the Primate's expense – with fresh paint, shining new galley arrangements and floor-matting throughout the cabins. The sailors designated by the

Opposition, subversive fishermen named Malso and Entiso, moved on board when the work was about half done, largely to ensure no supplies or fittings were pilfered in harbour. We planned to sail on the evening of the very day the ship was ready and all the supplies were loaded.

The Pain was not much of an overt nuisance during that period of waiting – that is, my father neither complained of it nor undertook any drastic remedies, such as self-induced concussion. If anything, he seemed to sleep more peacefully than he had for years; and if sometimes he had to set aside what he was doing and hunker down on the pallet with his arms wrapped around his knees, eyes closed, lips moving silently, at least he was not getting into worse mischief. That's what I thought at first. It was only gradually I became aware that the knife's edge he was treading was even sharper than before.

For example, there was the affair of the painted wooden fishes. All the personal effects found on the *Fifth* made their way to the archives, conveniently enough, for the memorians to study at the Primate's request – not just Tigrallef's effects and mine, but those of the others as well, and the task of sorting and repacking them was heartbreaking. Tigrallef started the job with me, but retired mumbling to the pallet after a few minutes, leaving me to suffer through the job alone. My mother's sandals and boots were all accounted for – the vermin must have carried her off to the Mosslines in her bare feet. On the other hand, the chest holding her priceless collection of silk-brocade robes from Gafrin-Gammanthan was missing, presumed stolen. Shree's journal was there, plus all of Chasco's logs except the current one, which I remember he had on his person that morning; and I found Kat's girlish treasures, her alchemy kit, the twenty painted wooden fishes Chasco made for her long ago, the shells and bones harvested from dozens of farflung beaches, her collection of knives and swords . . .

On second thoughts, I went back and counted the items in her personal armoury; looked vainly for her box of hoarded palots and exotic coinage from the unknown world;

126

rechecked the chest of old wooden playthings; and did an inventory of her footwear and clothing, as far as I could remember. Then I slammed my fist on the table. Tigrallef, who had apparently recovered but was still slouching idly on the pallet, gave me a startled look.

'The bastards,' I spat, 'it's not enough they dragged the poor child off to some hell of a work camp, they also had to steal her pathetic bits and pieces. Look what they've taken! The rippercat I carved for her; the stuffed bat; her boots and sandals and some of her clothing; her writing kit and journal; her Gafrin-Gammanthan belt; her throwing disks, the ones specially made for small hands; at least three of her blades, including the scimitar from Itsant – you know how she loves that scimitar . . .'

I had to stop there and bite my lip. It was I who had taught Kat how to clean her blades without losing any fingers; my memory presented me with an image of her as a small child on the foredeck of the *Third*, her little face stern with concentration as she ashed and polished the scimitar's blood-runnels and tested the edge with a hair pulled from her own curly head – all the sorrow I was holding back struggled to break through. With shaking hands, I began to repack her prized rubbish into a crate labelled SOUNDING WEIGHTS, in which it would be smuggled back on to the *Fifth*.

'Is it only Kat's things that are missing?' Tigrallef asked.

'Those, and the chest of silks,' I snapped, 'but I don't keep a complete inventory of everyone's cabin in my head. What does it matter?'

'It's just – interesting.' His tone was light. I glanced over at him and saw he was smiling vaguely into the distance, and my irritation turned to real anger.

'You don't give a tupping toss what they're going through, do you? All that concerns you, now and ever, is the Pain.'

He stopped smiling and sat up straight. 'That may be true, Vero, but it certainly isn't fair.'

'Oh, it's fair. I think you hardly notice they're gone.' I turned my back on him.

Silence from the pallet; but the painted wooden fish I was

holding wriggled in my hand, leapt free and landed gasping on the Flamen-green carpet. I stooped grimly to pick it up, only to have it slip through my fingers again. Vigorous flopping noises inside the box suggested that the nineteen fishes I had already repacked were also being unduly lively, lively enough to start jackknifing out of the box faster than I could retrieve them. When seven or eight of them were writhing and heaving their sides on different parts of the table, I gave up and went to sit on the pallet beside my father. A large greasefish, Chasco's masterwork, flung itself through the air in a magnificent arc and landed in my lap. I shoved it off – was walloped in the face by a flying lacefin – tossed it overhand in a perfect trajectory into the crate. Seconds later it bounded out again.

'Is there a point to this?' I asked.

'Of course.'

I waited. 'Well?'

'It's absurd.'

'Tell me anyway.'

'I just did. It's *absurd*.'

'I don't understand.'

'Too bad. I don't want to talk about it.'

Which was all Tigrallef would say, and I had no real understanding of what he meant until much later, when his illness had moved on a few phases, though it should have been clear enough on this occasion. A few minutes later, when the fishes returned to their more tractable wooden state, he helped me pick them up and pack them tenderly away.

Mallinna's tendency to drive me mad was of a different order, and was not her fault. Confined to the workroom, I could not arrange to be absent when she stripped down for the air ducts; averting my eyes was much, much worse than useless. Reminding myself that the Pain left no room for a woman in my life just made me irritable, usually with Tigrallef.

And yet, when I could forget about the lust for a few

minutes, I liked Mallinna. I was amused by the way she and Angel conversed in tandem, touched by her protective concern for him. I was impressed by the breadth of her knowledge and often left behind by the speed of her thought processes – apart from my father, she was probably the brightest person I had ever met. She was sweet of temper, unaffected, honest; courageous and spirited enough to spy on the Council at great personal risk. Her automatic acceptance of our cause as her cause moved me to gratitude. When she dropped my title and began calling me Vero, I was warm inside for two full days.

The problem was, it was unfair of her to look the way she did; and it didn't help, either, that she was unaware of how she looked. She seemed to think of her body as a useful device for getting her head from place to place, nothing more. She had all the worldliness of a hermit in a cave, all the self-consciousness of a marble statue, all the flirtatiousness of a Lucian temple virgin. As a scholar she had a huge stock of knowledge about love and lust as abstract concepts, but she had never connected them with herself. It annoyed me to catch myself wondering whether she would ever connect them with me.

The third of my tormentors, Angel, did not mean to madden me either. In his case, it came down to the sheer energy and patience one needed in order to converse with him, except when an idea excited him to the point where one couldn't shut him up. I first saw that side of him on our third night in the archives, when he cleared away a few layers of papers from his work table so we could see what he and Mallinna had been doing with the Fathidiic and Vassashin texts.

The Fathidiic texts were from the selfsame archive that the Bequiin Ardin of Miishel had carried off from the ruins of Cansh Fathan twenty-five years before, thus giving the first turn to the wheel of events that led to my father marrying the Princess Rinn. No more than a quarter of what the Bequiin had pilfered was still in existence, some having been burned and some scattered to the five winds during the civil wars in Miishel; the remainder had been 'donated' to Gil. Even that small residue was enough to render Angel temporarily eloquent.

He and Mallinna had found that the term *Naar* referred mostly to a people but occasionally to an individual, which confirmed what we had seen in the texts from Khamanthana and Nkalvi. There was a fragmentary mention of 'the guileless, the brave and the [wrathful?] . . .' which seemed to parallel some end-times passages recovered in Khamanthana and Myr. But most exciting of all were fragments of illuminated manuscripts with fine drawings of seven figures, presumably divine: three human, two reptilian, a cat-creature and something like a wolf or dog.

Now, we had seen something like that before, etched on a wall in Nkalvi, and we had reconstructed exactly such a heptad from the sherds of narrative vases dredged out of the seabed at Itsant. On the one hand, they appeared to tie in with the widespread tradition of the Old Ones; on the other, with the previous manifestations of the Harashil – the Myrwolf, the Master of Hands, the White Dragon and so forth. An eighth figure occasionally intruded on the narrative vases, always a human male wearing a circlet and a square breastplate. Mallinna whooped when Tig mentioned that, and leapt across the workroom to fetch us a few scraps of a Vassashin scroll showing a similar octad.

'But what there is not,' Angel said decisively, 'is any foreshadowing of the form the Harashil took in Gil, that is to say, the Lady. You found seven named empires of the Harashil, and we know there was a Great Nameless First as well – and there is a matching heptad of 'Old Ones' plus the man in the breastplate. Highly suggestive. But there is nothing about the Lady – where does the Lady fit in?'

'Maybe she doesn't.' Tig sounded far too bright and happy. I looked at him sharply. The sweat was already rolling down his forebrow and his eyes were glassing over. I got to him just as the little faces carved in the cornice of the bookcase opened their tiny mouths and broke into 'So Little Time', a Tatakil tavern song about a man with seventeen wives.

Evidently the Harashil did not like the way this conversation was going. I was only surprised the old sow had let it go on so long.

One morning, two long weeks and three days after our first sighting of the Gilgard, we were about forty hours away from leaving. Mallinna had gone to the harbour to supervise the loading of several crates from the archives, taking all the assistant and apprentice memorians with her as pressed labour. This meant that for the first time since we arrived, Tig and I could emerge from Angel's windowless inner studio and walk freely through the stacks to the main workroom with its broad view of the harbour, the brilliance of real sunlight, the holiday treat of air that hadn't already been through several pairs of lungs on its way to ours. We stood at the open window, breathing it in. Angel, hunched over a work table, was just finishing another thick sheaf of instructions for the Second Memorian, to add to a stack of similar sheaves on the shelf behind him. I wondered, from the sheer bulk of the paperwork he was producing, if he feared he might never return from this journey.

The harbour was so full of ships of all sizes and designs that I gave up trying to pick out the *Fifth* and turned my eyes to the shore. It was now high summer, and the city below us was tessellated with lush gardens among the grey-tiled roofs, brilliant awnings striped in all colours, the polished-lapis shapes of a hundred pools and fountains. Some festival was evidently approaching. Strings of thousands of green and gold banners flashed in the sun along every street and byway, a shining net laid with great precision over the grid of the city. In a shaded roof-pleasance almost directly below us, nestled in the terraces of the Middle Palace, a band of hornists was making an almighty but fairly melodious racket.

'That sounds like the old Gillish Paean of Praise,' Tig said, frowning. 'The last time I heard it was at my marriage to the Princess Rinn—' He broke off and cocked his ear towards the door.

I listened too. Nothing much. 'What do you hear?'

'Feet. Lots of feet.' He grabbed my arm and pulled me away from the window, casting eagerly about the room, then dragged me into the shadowed alcove behind a pier of bookshelves, not far from the table where Angel was now working on the expedition's accounts. Still frowning, Tigrallef dropped to his knees on the green carpet and pulled me down beside him. Over the tops of the books on the second shelf up, we had a restricted but reasonable view of much of the room, including Angel at his table. Angel lifted his head to peer at us inscrutably through the chink.

'Be ready, Angel, they're almost here. Remember what I told you.'

Angel nodded without expression and returned to his work. I sighed and made myself more comfortable.

'What can you hear, Tig? How many?'

'Hard to tell,' Tigrallef whispered, 'but I don't believe it's an arrest party. Arrest parties generally thud along in lockstep – there's a certain grim rhythm that signals their intentions. This group isn't doing that.' He concentrated again, then broke into a smile. 'Furthermore, arrest parties don't habitually transport items of comfortable furniture around with them. Vero, I think we might enjoy this. I've long wanted to hear the two of them in conversation.'

A few seconds later there was a clatter of feet and a low buzz of voices in the corridor, and I heard the door swing open. I craned to see who came into the visible patch of the workroom. Nobody I knew at first: a young man in a green tunic with a burden on his shoulders, rapidly identified as the forward shafts of a chair-litter. He eased the burden down with great care and stepped out of sight. Soft shuffling noises, and two other young men in green pushed a large padded armchair into a position directly across the table from Angel, who continued to scratch busily at the paper in front of him. The first lad reappeared with a different burden in his arms and tenderly transferred it into the armchair. Angel looked up at last with his customary air of bewilderment.

'Memorian,' said the Primate Mycri, sitting forward rather menacingly in the armchair, 'we have some matters to discuss before you depart.'

Angel regarded him benignly. 'Twice six plus seven,' he remarked.

'What?'

'Nineteen.' His pen scratched at the paper.

'Memorian, I said—'

Angel frowned at the column of figures. 'And three more.' He added a scribble, looked up and smiled shyly at the Primate. 'Twenty-two,' he announced.

'*Hopeless.* Where's that damned woman?'

'Damned woman?' Angel repeated wonderingly. 'Damned woman?'

'The damned woman,' said the Primate through tight lips, 'who usually speaks for you.'

'Not here.' Angel's eyes drifted back to his accounts.

The Primate glared at him with an intensity that would have withered a less worthy opponent; he growled, 'There are times I wish I had not made that bargain with the Dowager Dazeene. This is one of them. Kesi, you try.'

The First Flamen moved into our field of view and bent over the table. 'Angel,' he said gently, 'where is Mallinna?'

Angel glanced at him and placed his pen carefully on the rack. 'She's out,' he said. He picked up the blotter.

Kesi sighed patiently. 'Yes, Angel, but where is she?'

'Harbour?' Angel suggested, staring hard into space. He put the blotter back and picked up the pen. He squinted at the paper.

'She's gone to the harbour?' Kesi persisted.

Angel nodded vaguely. 'Yes, harbour. Eight times eight palots?'

'Sixty-four palots. Will she be back soon?'

'Plus twenty.'

'Eighty-four,' the Primate broke in shrilly. 'Listen to me, Memorian—'

'And six makes ninety-two.'

'*Ninety*. Eighty-four plus six makes *ninety*. Sainted Scion, Kesi, can't you do something?'

Kesi glanced nervously aside at the Primate and reached across the table to lift the pen out of Angel's hand. 'Please, Angel, the Most Revered One wants to talk with you for a little while. It will be all right.'

Angel's ancient face split in a brilliant smile. 'Of course, Kesi Flamen.' He folded his hands on the tabletop in front of him and looked attentive.

It was fortunate for us that the First Flamen took charge at that point. My sides were already aching with suppressed mirth; more arithmetic might have finished me. Tig was crouching beside me in the same friable state. All that sobered me was the thought of how awkward life would become if the Pain chose one of these moments to attack.

Strange as it may seem, this was the Primate's idea of a goodwill visit. He was just not very good at goodwill. He glowered at Angel from the armchair, his whiskered old goatface in profile to us, often hidden by the intervening bulk of the First Flamen. Kesi, in his anxious and timorous way, was in fact an effective medium, but he had obdurate material to work with on both sides. Slowly and painfully, the goodwill visit dragged on.

But once the pleasantries had been dispensed with, and the administrative details to do with the expedition disposed of, the Primate's other reasons for visiting the archives became apparent. So did the Council's motive in throwing the treasury wide open to outfit the Benthonic Survey so lavishly. The Primate's questions were illuminating, far more illuminating than Angel's answers. It seemed that Mycri was not interested in Sher's drowned ruins simply for reasons of scholarship, nor to extend the boundaries of knowledge; he expected and demanded that Angel should search for Sherkin ruins lying in water shallow enough so they could be mined for salvage, for resources, or simply for treasure.

He mentioned the chalcedony and lapis quarries in the northern hills of Sher as desirable subjects for research, also the tar-wells in the east; he stressed the value of locating the site of the legendary Stronghouse of the Warcourt, filled to bursting with gold and copper looted from Sher's slave nations, notably Gil; he spoke of the Northern Stronghouse in Krin, and the salvageable goods that might still be recovered from the grand warehouses of Kishti in the far south. Through Kesi, Angel happily agreed to everything.

The next item on the agenda concerned the mysterious previous owners who – in the old deceiver's words – had *abandoned* the fine little ship which had been granted to the memorians. The Primate was guardedly anxious to know: had Angel discovered any clues to their identity in the effects taken from the ship? Had their story been confirmed? Angel brought forth the keywords Tigrallef had primed him with, Gilborn, Calloon, copper. The Primate seemed satisfied, as far as could be told from a face capable of two basic expressions, annoyed and very annoyed.

The final item raised by the Primate was a shock, though it was intended to be a favour and an honour. With great pleasure, the First Flamen informed the First Memorian that the Most Revered Primate had detailed a Warrior-grade windcatcher, the *Scion Cirallef*, to escort the Benthonic Survey Expedition on its important journey around the Sherkin Sea. Even better – worse – a guardsman seconded from the Flamens' Corps would sail with the survey ship as the First Memorian's personal bodyguard, also as flagman in communications with the *Cirallef*. Indeed, he was already on his way to the harbour, to take up his guard duties that very afternoon. No seawolves or fishmen, no pirates or monsters of the deep were going to interfere with the safety of an enterprise blessed by the Most Revered Primate in Gil.

What could Angel say? He said thank you.

The Primate and his damned armchair and most of his retinue bustled out of the archives a few minutes later, but Tigrallef put a restraining hand on my arm. Someone had remained behind. We could see Angel, still seated at the table, staring in the direction of the door with bemusement in his face and a wary tension in the way he held his shoulders. His hand moved in the fingerspeech.

Don't even breathe.

Soft footsteps hissed across the carpet but the visitor remained outside our field of view. 'First Memorian, accept my apologies for continuing to disturb you.' The voice was smooth and hard-edged, also familiar. Its associations were not happy ones. 'May I leave a message with you?' he went on. 'I've long been meaning to visit you again.'

'She's not here,' Angel mumbled.

'I know where she is, First Memorian, I heard you tell the Most Revered Primate.' The tone was hardening. 'You know, I've never believed you to be as thick or as tonguebound as you make out. I'm sure you can converse like a perfectly normal person when you feel like it. Am I right?'

Angel sank a little deeper into his chair. 'Normal,' he said thoughtfully.

The unknown sighed. 'Never mind,' he said, 'You'll be more open with me someday, I'm sure. Why, we'll be practically family soon! Keep that in mind, First Memorian.'

Angel said nothing, but by this point I had placed the visitor's voice: Lestri, Second Flamen, great-grandspawn and probable successor to the Primate. No redeeming features. From the sound of his feet I gathered he was already moving towards the door, but he stopped before opening it. 'Don't forget to tell her I was here, First Memorian; remind her I'll be finishing my time by midwinter. She'll understand. And if your work in the Sherkin Sea is not finished by then, you will send her back on the *Scion Cirallef*. I hope that's clear.'

A sullen expression was working its way across Angel's face. Pointedly, he took his pen from the rack and looked down at the accounts in front of him. 'Nineteen palots and fourteen,' he muttered.

'Thirty-three palots,' came Lestri's voice. 'Don't forget to tell her.' The door closed softly behind him.

Tigrallef and I emerged from our hiding place in a mood rather less than cheerful. Angel was no happier, nor was he in one of his rare loquacious moods. Showing every minute of his eighty-odd years, he threw down his pen and looked up at us dolefully. 'Bad,' he said.

'Bad,' Tig agreed, 'but not fatal. We'll find some way to slip the windcatcher's chain, don't worry. At worst we'll need to do a few days of genuine surveying until we can lose them, but wait till you see how fast the *Fifth* can cover those waves. And once we've lost the windcatcher, we'll put the Primate's guardsman ashore on some deserted island—'

'Lestri,' Angel interrupted.

'So?'

'Lestri Flamen was here.'

'We know, Angel. What about him?'

Angel slumped in his chair. 'He wants Mallinna.'

'*What*?' That was me being outraged.

'What for?' That was my father being obtuse.

Angel gave him an eloquent look.

'Oh,' said my father.

'You can't be serious,' I protested, 'not Mallinna and the Second Flamen, that – that—'

'Devious power-crazed conniver at abduction and murder?' Tig suggested, being helpful. 'That truthless underhanded scribe-slayer and thief of ships?'

'Yes,' I said.

'You're quite right, he wouldn't do at all for a scholar of Mallinna's fibre,' Tig said decisively. 'He used to cheat in his writing exercises, and once he defaced a scroll. I caught him with the pen in his hand.'

The Second Flamen's childish sins in the archives, twenty years past, did not distract me. I was seething with indignation. 'The idea's obscene. She could never marry that—'

'Not marriage.' Angel shook his head sadly. 'Not offered.'

'*What*?' That was me being outraged again, this time to sputtering point. 'You don't mean – not *marry* her – you mean, as a – as a—'

Tig patted my shoulder. 'Calm down, Vero. How could he marry her? He's going to succeed the Primate someday. He needs to make a brilliant marriage, preferably royal, a Satheli

137

peeress, a Plaviset *imbash*, a Frath's daughter from Miishel. He can't father a new dynasty on the child of a dead doxy and a nameless Storican, now can he? Whereas he can look anywhere he likes for a concubine.'

'I'll kill him.'

Tig looked at me curiously. 'Perhaps you should consult with Mallinna first.'

Angel stood up so quickly that his chair toppled, and the clatter it made stopped me short. 'Mallinna,' he said, faltering and starting again with greater force, 'Mallinna will do what is best.' After this exhausting burst of loquacity, he looked lingeringly, regretfully and very significantly around him at the massed treasures of the archives. Then he sank his chin on to his chest and gazed with sorrow at the accounts on the table. Silently I righted his chair for him and helped him into it. Perhaps I should have thanked him for the warning, but the meaning I perceived behind his words was depressing me beyond speech.

Mallinna will do what is best. Best for the tupping archives, was what he meant.

Tigrallef was watching me too closely and with far too much interest. I tightened my mouth and wandered off to the window in silence, bleak with jealousy. Not of Lestri, the Primate's pet parth-asp; Mallinna might let him bed her and keep her someday for the good of the archives, just as my father had accepted the dubious blessing of marriage with the Princess Rinn, but it would not be because Mallinna fancied the little toad. She might even let him sire the customary brood of bastard brats on her – the Flamens tended to be relentlessly prolific with both wives and concubines, as if to make up for the statutory decade of celibacy – but I could not imagine her smiling at the oily smooth-voiced road-rubbish over breakfast. No, I could not be jealous of Lestri Flamen.

I was jealous of a collection of paper, inscribed clay and associated materials. It appeared the archives was to Mallinna what the Pain was to me: a responsibility that was unsought but inescapable, a responsibility we had each been reared and shaped to assume. It was fortunate, I told myself bitterly, that I had decided very early on not to become too attached to her.

My eyes moved blindly across the harbour. Slowly I became aware that I was staring at the clean lines and peculiar rigging of the *Fifth*, tiny with distance; more than that, I discerned a cluster of gnats moving shorewards along the jetty where the ship was moored. The object of my thoughts was on her way home, complete with workparty.

I stalked past Angel and my father to the stacks, grabbed a book at random from the shelves, and took it into Angel's workroom to read. There was no point in torturing myself by talking with Mallinna, and it would be good to forget about lustworthy females altogether for a while. How unfortunate, then, that the book I chose at random should be the second and more explicit volume of the *Erotic Mistifalia*.

Early next morning, in the cool hour just around dawn, two archival assistants in hooded cloaks accompanied Mallinna to the harbour with a surprisingly large wainload of personal luggage, mostly hers and the First Memorian's. These assistants were Tigrallef and myself, sporting two weeks' growth of beard in case anyone manning the gate bothered to look at us closely. Nobody did. Mallinna was well known. So, apparently, was her status as mistress-elect of the Second Flamen. We were waved through the gate without even having to show the identity seals that Mallinna's anonymous friends had acquired for us.

The wain trundled through the peaceful streets at a strolling pace, Mallinna at the reins, Tigrallef next to her, while I walked morosely beside the horse's blinkered head. Banners flapped in green and gold along both sides of the remarkably clean street, ribbons in the same colours bedizened the house fronts and the shrubbery, streamed from the window sills, wound in elaborate patterns around the signposts and the trunks of the few trees. I wondered about it all, but I was too depressed by Mallinna's presence to ask her. From the time

139

she got back to the archives the afternoon before, I had managed to address not more than a dozen words to her.

But with Tigrallef around, I did not need to ask. 'About six weeks,' Mallinna was explaining behind me. 'The banners go up before the Day of the Lady, which is next week – we'll miss it – and come down in the autumn, after the Day of the Scion.'

'What a waste. They'll fade long before then,' Tigrallef said disapprovingly.

Mallinna laughed. 'There's a patrol of street cleaners who spend their nights changing faded banners for fresh ones. It's the greatest festival of the year – pilgrims have been pouring into Gil City from all over the Empire for the last week. By tomorrow there won't be an empty bed in any hostel closer than Malvi. Do you feel honoured, Lord Tigrallef?'

'Not especially,' he answered, with a hollowness in his voice that caused me to snap my head around to check on him. I hoped the pale glimmer on his face was from the sunrise. The beard paradoxically made him look even younger than usual. Otherwise he appeared about normal, but I was not convinced. I plodded along grimly beside the horse, straining my ears for any note of danger in his voice, the subtlest whisper of the Pain.

Mallinna had not noticed. 'A few more miracles than usual this year, though,' she went on. She chuckled. 'You've been sighted every night this week, Lord Tigrallef, somewhere or other in the city – did you know, last night you were seen in a cloud of fire hovering over the Great Garden?'

'Oh?' said Tig. He sounded uncomfortable.

'Reflections off the clouds, I suppose, my lord. These omens and wonders spring up like mushrooms around festival time. Ludicrous, isn't it? Two nights ago, a hundred people swear you walked into a tavern on the Thread-of-Gold, spilled somebody's drink, and walked right out again. When they hurried out to the street to look for you, you were gone.'

'Well, well,' said Tig.

'You were described as ten feet tall, though, and lighted up like a giant glowfly. You had to bend double to get through the door.'

'How amusing.' His voice was not quite right.

Mallinna shook the reins. 'And the Great Head at the harbour is reported to have spoken again.'

'Really?'

'So it's said. It lectured briefly on botany to a watchman on the midnight round. The watchman was very surprised.'

'I should imagine so.'

I glanced back again. Tig was hunched stiffly on the box of the wain with a starched smile on his face. Mallinna, I saw at once, was not innocently passing the time with amusing snippets of rumour. She knew exactly what she was doing. She had the look of a cat following a trail of spilled cream – thirsty, eager, and full of hope that she'd find the jug itself just around the next turn. She was working her way up to a more dangerous question.

Out it came. 'I was just wondering, Lord Tigrallef – did you and the Harashil have anything to do with those appearances?'

Tig did not hesitate for a moment. 'I have not set foot outside the archives for the last two weeks,' he answered firmly and truthfully; but the timbre I was listening for was present in his voice, and the strength of attack it portended was not the sort of thing I wanted to deal with in a public roadway.

'Tig! Mallinna!' I broke in with desperate cheerfulness, 'look at that sunrise! Wonderful colours! The painting palette of the gods!'

Silence behind me.

'I don't think so,' Mallinna said, surprised.

'And look at the sea! Like a pond! Not a ripple!'

'Is something the matter with you, Vero?' my father asked. 'It's a pallid and unexciting sunrise, and the sea is choppy outside the breakwater.'

'I think he's just trying to change the subject,' Mallinna said with her lethal directness. 'Why don't you want me to ask Lord Tigrallef about the miracles, Vero?'

'He's afraid it will upset me,' my father answered on my behalf, 'and bring on an attack of the Pain.'

'Is he always so protective of you?'

'Yes, bless him, and with good reason.'

'But were you upset, Lord Tigrallef?'

'I was getting close. Events like those miracles, as you call them, have been in my dreams every night this week, and all the while my body has been snoring in the archives. And it wasn't a lecture on botany, by the way, it was Curallef the Versifier's *Enumeration of the Flowers*.'

'Much the same thing,' Mallinna said judiciously. 'I can understand the watchman's mistake. Most of the verses of Curallef's middle period aren't so much poetry as natural history.'

'I think that's grossly overstated. He may not have returned to the classic themes until after *Treefall*, but he always kept to the classic forms.'

'You're forgetting the *Verses of Intent*,' said Mallinna.

'I'm not, actually . . .'

I left them to it and turned my attention to guiding the horse with a hand on its bridle, Mallinna becoming far too involved in the debate to remember she was holding the reins. On several scores, I was almost giddy with relief. Tigrallef's voice had lost its Painful undertones, an imminent attack had been averted, and the two of them were distracting each other from sensitive subjects far better than I could. By the time we pulled level with the Great Head, they were too busy speculating about who really wrote the plays of Addeni Clanseri to notice it was there.

In fact, relief at the Pain's ebbing had made me unbelievably slow. It took me several minutes to think over the import of my father's words and to realize what he had actually admitted.

Too often over the years, our departures had been dramatic, hurried, bloody, awkward, fiery, unplanned, or straight into the jaws of something. Our departure from the harbour of Gil City that night, none of those things, was in fact the dullest of my life. That alone made it remarkable. Thank the Old Ones, the Primate did not make good his threat to come down and wave goodbye, though he sent a small guard of honour from the Flamens' Corps to usher the First Memorian to his ship just after sunset. He also sent his apologies: he had urgent business concerned with the upcoming Day of the Lady. To my surprise and bitter pleasure, the Second Flamen Lestri did not come down either, to wish his future mistress a good journey.

Tigrallef, who turned strangely sombre as we approached the *Fifth* along the quay, went straight to his cabin as soon as we boarded and did not leave it until after we sailed. The sombreness worried me, but the side effect was that he ran no danger of being seen by the guardsman from the Flamens' Corps, a sensible precaution while we were still trapped in the inner harbour. There was less peril of me being recognized through my beard, since few people remembered what my uncle Arkolef looked like anyway – Mallinna said there were only three portrait statues of him in the entire city of Gil, all of them tucked away in inconspicuous places, whereas Tigrallef stared at the populace from every street corner, shop wall and public façade in the empire.

And so, while Tigrallef skulked in his cabin, I worked like a serf all morning, unpacking and stowing the last of the supplies as they came on board, going over the rigging with our new crewmen Malso and Entiso, firing up the galley for our first meal of the journey. I was doing everything possible to keep my mind off Katla and the others, when the *Fifth* was so full of cruel reminders of them. In the afternoon I slept, knowing I would take a double watch that night.

Without really intending to, I also managed to avoid our resident guardsman. His very presence was an irritant, though. I was also annoyed to find that he had set up his quarters in the middle hold, precisely where the hatch to the secret holds was hidden. As long as he remained on board, I could not even risk checking that our valuables and research papers were safe, nor fetch the drawings of the Itsant vases and rubbings of the Nkalvi texts that Angel and Mallinna were so anxious to see. Getting rid of him moved very high on my list of priorities.

By the time Angel was ushered on board and tucked into bed by Mallinna, there was nothing more to wait for except the turn of the tide. At midnight, just after the hour bells rang in the city, the ropes were cast off at last, Malso and Entiso raised the sails, and I steered the *Fifth* into the track of clear water outlined by the fire buoys. The quay was almost deserted by then. There was nobody to see us off except the guard of honour, who did not even wave. When they were behind us, the only human figures I could see were the dark shapes of Mallinna and the guardsman in the bow. A few lights burned on the ships around us, but nothing else was moving, and the waterfront was held by as deathly a hush as on our first fateful night in Gil. Since then I had learned why it was so quiet. An anti-noise ordinance was in force, not to be relaxed until the eve of the Day of the Ladys, which was nearly a week off.

We glided ghostlike through the outer harbour. As the twin watchtowers guarding the entrance rode past us on their own reflections, the larger spectre of the *Scion Cirallef* slipped into line a short way behind us. I muttered a curse in its direction. Then it was time for the turn, the tight curve that would swing us around the flank of the Gilgard and on course for the east. As I spun the wheel over, Tigrallef came softly up the aft companionway and fastened himself into his restraining chair. He said nothing to me, nor did I have anything to say to him.

The silent city, plated with moonlight, lay to starboard. Above it glimmered the thousand windows of Gilgard Castle, where the cost of lamp oil was obviously not of great concern. I left the wheel long enough to spit Itsant-style over the side. The Gilgard was beautiful: my ancestor Oballef had built it, my Scion forebears had ruled in it, my father had liberated it, and I, Verolef, hoped I would never have to look at it again.

*

Two hours later, when we were well out on the eastern sea, Tigrallef silently released himself from the chair and vanished into his cabin, Shree's cabin in happier times. Mallinna, yawning, stopped by the wheel not much later and stood beside me for a while, looking astern to the dark hulking shadow of the *Cirallef*. The seaman Entiso, another dark hulking shadow, mumbled a greeting as he passed by us on his way to his quarters in the hold, followed a few moments later by the guardsman. He wished Mallinna good dreams in a fashion that I thought was a little too friendly.

'Have you spoken with Jonno yet?' Mallinna asked when he was gone.

'Who's Jonno?'

'He is, the guardsman from the Flamens' Corps. I had a long talk with him in the bow, and he's not at all what I expected. He's – sweet.'

I snorted. 'That's an extraordinary word to apply to one of the Primate's hand-picked wolves. He'd probably be offended.'

'No, Vero, he's not like that. He's hiding something, though.'

'Aren't we all?' I asked bitterly.

'Of course we are – but he isn't hiding what we thought he'd be hiding.'

'He's the Primate's spy, Mallinna.'

She edged closer and spoke in a whisper. 'That's what I'm not sure about. I've seen enough of the Primate's spies in my life to recognize the mould, and he simply doesn't fit. For example, he was asking a lot of questions about you and Lord Tigrallef—'

'Well, there you are.'

'—but they were clumsy questions, far too obvious, put to me with no subtlety at all. He's terrible at it, whereas the Primate's spies are taught to pick your mind like a dip would pick your pocket. And he's *sweet*.'

Sweet, was he? The sod. The last thing I needed was to listen to Mallinna, whose courtship I was nobly and dutifully forswearing in deference to the needs of my father and the

145

archives, prattle on to me about some other man being *sweet*. Especially when she was standing close enough to make me willing to forget all about my resolve.

'Mallinna,' I said wearily, 'go to bed.'

The glow from the mast lamp sidelighted her cloud of dark hair, but her face was invisible. That was unfortunate at a time when I was particularly eager to see her expression, because she put her hand on my shoulder a moment later and said in a normal non-flirtatious voice, 'Don't get me wrong, Vero. I think you're sweet, too.' A swift pat on the shoulder, and she was gone.

'I am not sweet,' I told her, but only when I was sure she was out of hearing.

8

When Malso took the wheel about two hours before dawn, I wrapped myself in a fleece and stretched out on the deck beside Tigrallef's chair, instructing Malso to waken me if he had problems. He did not, and I slept better on the deckboards than I had on dry land in the Gilgard, rocked by the ship and dreaming of happier times in Gafrin-Gammanthan. When I finally turned over and opened my eyes, the morning chill was already off and the sun was a third of the way to the zenith of a hazy blue sky. Malso called a greeting from behind the wheel. A few feet away, a shapely young face was regarding me over a steaming beaker.

'I brought you some breakfast.'

Sweet of him. 'You must be Jonno.'

'Yes, memorian.' He sat down beside me and handed me the beaker with a ravishing smile. His bright hair was pulled back in a neat queue. He had the kind of staggering blue-eyed long-lashed beauty that would have sent him straight into the catamite division of a seraglio in certain parts of the world. I calculated that, as a guardsman of the Flamens' Corps, he could be no more than four or five years younger than I, but one look at him made me feel faded and world-weary, a sour old man with tough skin and a blunted spirit. It was almost impossible to believe he was a member of the Primate's crack private bullies.

'You're Vilno, aren't you? One of the First Memorian's assistants?'

I sipped. 'I am.' In fact, I was taking his word for it, because my current name had slipped my mind. After another few time-gaining sips, it came back to me. Yes, I was Vilno; Tig was Talno for the moment. I silently thanked the young man for reminding me.

'I saw you yesterday when you came on board,' he went on, 'but I didn't want to disturb you while you were so busy.'

'That was good of you.' And highly unlikely; when had a guardsman ever consulted a target's convenience, unless it was with hidden motives? And yet this Jonno hardly looked like a devious character.

He watched me eagerly as I drank down the broth, as anxious for approbation as if he had cooked it himself. He gave the impression of a pup ready to wag his tail at the first pat on the head; he was sweet. To restore my balance, I pondered the very real possibility we would have to throw him overboard sometime in the next few days. I smiled back at him.

He was sitting in the same place when I returned a few minutes later from washing, changing, and checking that Tigrallef and the others were still asleep. Malso was laughing as I approached, but Jonno did not look as if he appreciated the joke.

'Ho, Memorian,' the seaman said, 'the Primate's man has a few questions for you.'

Sighing, I lowered myself on to the deck and leaned my back against the side of the chair. 'I'm sure he does. Well?'

The guardsman, with a badgered glance at Malso, inched

closer. 'You're a memorian, yes? And you studied the records of this ship?'

Unsubtle, all right. 'The logs and journals belonging to the previous owners were examined in the archives, that is correct,' I said carefully.

'That's just what Mistress Mallinna said. She told me you'd know, if anyone did.'

'Know what?'

He hesitated and dropped his voice. 'Whether there was anything – *strange* – recorded in the logbooks.'

'Strange?'

He frowned most decoratively as he searched for words. 'Peculiar happenings – things out of the ordinary, notable events . . .'

Behind the wheel, the smile broadened and became nastier on Malso's weatherworn face. 'What the lad means is, could this ship be haunted?' he called out. The guardsman flinched, but he looked at me expectantly. I was surprised. It was not at all the kind of question I was anticipating.

'Haunted?'

'Please don't think I'm mad,' the guardsman hurried to say, 'I'm not the first to wonder about this. The shipyard workers thought there was something strange about the ship too, some kind of invisible *presence*. And then I saw – well – I feel foolish about this, Memorian.'

'No need for that,' I said cautiously. 'No, there was nothing in the previous shipmaster's records to suggest a history of revenant visitations.' Malso's mention of haunting was allowing me to be honest without exactly telling the truth. You could wager your permanent teeth that strange things had happened on the *Fifth*, but hauntings in the traditional sense had never been one of our problems. 'What was it you saw, Jonno Guardsman?' I added, out of a sense that I might as well confirm the worst.

I waited with resignation to hear what Jonno thought he had seen, but I was fairly sure it would involve a phantom figure of the Scion Tigrallef approximately ten feet tall and shining from the inside like a frosted lamp glass. Chances were good that this figure would be declaiming Old High Gillish poetry or seeing how long it could stand on one foot.

But I was wrong.

'He thought he saw the phantom of a pretty girl, that last night we spent in harbour,' Malso informed me in a voice that was unduly loud, seeing as the guardsman and I were only about five feet away from him. Much louder, and the crew of the *Scion Cirallef*, a few hundred feet to port of us, would be able to enjoy the jest as well. The guardsman's smooth cheeks flushed to the colour of a vicious sunburn.

'The phantom of a girl?' I murmured. 'What did she look like?'

He shot an embattled glance at Malso. 'I didn't see much, I was half-asleep and the only light was the moon through the companion. All I remember is that she appeared suddenly out of the darkness and stood by my pallet looking down at me – her face was clear for a moment or two – and then she floated back into the shadows and vanished.'

'Floated?'

'Her feet didn't seem to touch the floor – that's why I thought she was a phantom. Otherwise,' he looked resentfully at the man at the wheel, 'I might have thought she was some doxy that sinner smuggled on board.'

'At least,' Malso said cheerfully, 'all the women that come to *my* bed are real flesh, and when I say flesh—'

'Dark hair,' said Jonno loudly, 'a little wavy, clipped fairly short around her head; straight eyebrows like yours, Memorian, except dark instead of fair. A lovely face she had, slender with high cheekbones and – what's wrong?'

'Nothing. Did you notice what your phantom was wearing?'

'I don't remember. Wait.' He shut his eyes. 'Yes I do. Her robe was pale-coloured; it looked white in the moonlight, but it might have been yellow or even grey. Yes, and there was a darker band at the neckline, black or purple.' He opened his eyes and looked at me anxiously. 'That's all I can remember. Are you sure there's nothing wrong? You look—'

'Nothing's wrong. And I think you must have been dreaming.'

The guardsman's face fell; then he lifted it again and smiled. 'If she was a dream, then she must have come as a portent,' he said. 'She came on the very eve of the voyage – that's a good time for portents. Perhaps it was the Lady in Gil herself, come to give us her blessing. Don't you agree, Memorian? Wouldn't you think she was a portent of good fortune?'

Malso snorted, but I responded with a smile that did its best to look genuine. Inside, I was reeling with shock, fear, and the beginnings of grief. 'Let's hope so,' I agreed pleasantly.

That morning's work consisted of sitting in the shade of the midsail explaining to Mallinna's hired seamen the remaining technicalities of the rigging and the double rudder system, and the special steps to be taken in storms or high seas. Luckily this was a task I could do without thinking, because my mind was on other things.

I was asking myself some terrible questions; my head ached with them as I explained the function of the demi-lateens on the foremast and the unique configuration of the buntlines. Was the guardsman's phantom visitor the wraith of our Kat? Did this mean she was already dead? Had she been broken on the Mosslines before we were even clear of Gil City?

Or, I asked myself, was the Pain beginning to expand its repertoire? (I sketched out the freakish arrangement of the upper yards, the flexible bracing of the crosstrees.) As far as I knew, it was nowhere ordained that the Harashil could only wear my father's face. I wondered how I could ask Tigrallef – tactfully – what his dreams had been like the night before last; whether, perhaps, they had involved the Harashil sleepwalking around the *Fifth* dressed in Katlefiya's second-best robe, the grey one from Amballa with the purple braid at the neck.

*

150

We were lucky in the weather for the first week of our journey. I calculated we had a nine-day sail to the sunken coastline of Sher, but two days before that we would put in at the island port of Beriss, and it was there that I planned to lose the *Scion Cirallef*. Until then, it was actually useful to have that threatening mass sailing just downwind of us, a shark shepherding a minnow. Patrol ships never challenged us, merchant ships gave way to us, the only pirate convoy we sighted turned tail and fled. For the first six days of the journey, we amicably threaded the maze of navigation points together.

Angel was prostrated, partly with seasickness, but partly (Mallinna and I suspected) with sheer terror at being so far outside the walls of the Gilgard for the first time in his life. We carried his pallet out on to the open deck every afternoon; by the third day he was taking an intelligent, if somewhat wan, interest in the flight patterns of the seabirds, and we figured he was on the mend. By the fifth day he was making copious notes and sketches when he wasn't throwing up.

Tigrallef was a different matter. The gloom that descended on him as we came on board the *Fifth* in Gil harbour became even darker during those first days. He never left his cabin, he neither read nor wrote, and he refused to talk about what was troubling him. It was true there were no attacks of the Pain that followed the old familiar pattern, nor any of the lambent new ten-foot manifestations, but there were other developments that I found about equally disturbing.

On the fifth day, with his dinner tray in my hands, I stopped outside his cabin door at the sound of voices inside and ended up eavesdropping on a lively debate of which I understood hardly a word, since it was carried out in Naarhil, the secret tongue of Oballef and the Harashil. Both sides were using Tig's normal voice; it was impossible to tell which one was Tig and which, presumably, the Pain. A pity, because one of them was clearly losing the argument, and I would have liked to know who. As soon as I touched the door, however, my father's voice fell silent. He was standing stiffly in the middle of the floor when I entered, and the glow I had been prepared to see was not shining through his skin, as it had before, but was an aura the thickness of a finger that enwrapped him and reproduced him in meticulous detail, down to the neckstring of his tunic and a shimmering patch on his knee.

'It was just about here,' he said darkly.

I set his tray down and gave him a gentle push towards the chair. 'What was?'

'It was here that we came out of hiding,' he explained.

'Oh?' I shook out a napkin.

'Yes, child of the Naar. It was on this sea, in a great Miisheli ship, that we made our presence known to us, and we – she – raised a storm. He did not mean to, he was sorry afterwards.'

'I've brought you some nice lentils.'

'We are not hungry.'

'At least one of you must be,' I said lightly. 'Eat, Father, or I'll start quoting you the Collected Wit and Wisdom of the Patriarch Firopos of Granze.'

That was just about the most powerful weapon in my memorized armoury – Firopos was to the Lucian proverbs as, say, a bouldershot is to a sling – but Tigrallef continued to regard the bowl of hotty with obvious contempt.

'Not-clean wet-rot of the world.'

'You love lentils,' I said.

His face twisted. 'If you could see it as we do – maggot-riddled humus of dead vermin . . .'

'It's very tasty.'

'. . . and this body disgusts us – loathsome dung-factory compounded of foulness and small daily corruptions . . .'

'The unknowable,' I began, 'known only through those verities which are, firstly, either known or not known but knowable, and secondly, which are not knowable but not yet known as being either knowable or known or not known, and thirdly, which were thought to be not known or unknowable but are now known to be both knowable and known, and fourthly—'

'It does smell good,' said Tig.

I handed him the napkin. 'That was suspiciously easy.'

'The balance is delicate these days. Anyhow, I had the old sow on the run before you came in. This needs salt.'

'It's on the tray.'

I sat down on the pallet to watch him eat. The food did not visibly cheer him, but the vestiges of his aura gradually faded away. When he was finished, he put his head down on the table and fell immediately into a sleep as deep and silent as a temporary death. That also worried me. I moved him on to the pallet and then left, taking the tray with me. Halfway to the galley, I finally let go of the forced calm and surrendered to the trembling. I sat down on the Primate's new matting with my back against the wall and took deep breaths until I could control my knees again. At least part of that conversation had been with the Harashil.

When I was not too worried about my father, mother, sister and honorary uncles to take notice, this period of the journey gave me a useful opportunity to observe our fellow travellers. The fishermen Malso and Entiso were brothers of around my father's actual age, whereas the guardsman Jonno was perhaps a little younger than the age my father looked. That was all we knew about them when we came on board, except that the former were vouched for by Mallinna's dissident contacts, and the latter was almost certainly a spy for the Primate. Perversely, I warmed to our enemy Jonno and not to the other two, who were on our side.

Everything they knew about us was a lie. The Primate thought that the Calloonic coppermonger's sons were dead; the Primate's spy, in theory, would be under the impression that Talno and Vilno were ordinary memorians from the archives. That was fine with me as long as I could remember our official names. As for Malso and Entiso, we had decided from the beginning not to tell the opposition the awkward fact that my father was exactly who he looked like. The risk was too great that one rebellious faction or another would want to use a genuine Scion Tigrallef for their own purposes, with results that did not bear thinking about.

All that Mallinna's contacts had been told, therefore, was an extended version of our old Storyline Two, the one about Gilborn copper traders from Calloon on a pilgrimage gone horribly wrong. The extension was a scenario that fitted one version of the facts well enough: the extraordinary resemblance Tig and I bore to the last of the Scions, the Primate's decision to destroy us and exile the others to the Mosslines, our lucky rescue by the memorians. It was a version of the facts the dissidents could sympathize with, since many of them had suffered losses of a similar kind at the Flamens' hands.

Malso told me, in bits and pieces through the first few days of the journey, that he and his brother had been fishermen under the Sherank, under Arko's rule, and under the Primate's regency. For many years after the wrack of Sher they had taken no interest in who governed Gil, just so long as they could mend their nets in peace, catch a few fish and have themselves a woman now and then. Malso was anything but taciturn, a boastful sun-leathered bear of a man full of fairly dubious stories; his brother Entiso was perhaps a couple of years younger, several degrees quieter, and even larger, with arms and legs like hairy meaty tree trunks. There was one subject that never seemed to come up – the events that led them into the ranks of the Opposition. They neither looked nor talked like men with a tragic injustice in their past, but Mallinna warned me it would be impolitic to ask.

Jonno was a different kind of mystery. He was obviously educated and of good family, bright as well as ornamental, full of good spirits and an endearing desire to please, and he carried out his signalling duties to the *Scion Cirallef* with cheerful efficiency. Despite the hated black uniform he wore, I found him impossible to dislike. The thought of setting him adrift, marooning him or throwing him overboard became increasingly repugnant as the week passed.

What I could not understand was how a lad so fresh, dewy

and essentially *sweet* had come to be numbered among the Primate's most vicious and fanatical enforcers; but when he mentioned one day that his late father had been in the Flamens' Corps before him, I reckoned I understood – Jonno was a second-generation guardsman, raised in loyalty to the Flamens as my mother had been raised in the Web. It was even harder to condemn him after that. I began to think of kinder ways to get rid of him.

I was resigned to getting rid of him somehow, even though he was not a great threat, being a clear disaster as a spy. More than once I caught him hovering in the upper passage close to Tigrallef's door, in full view of anyone on deck; out of every two of his ingenuous questions, one or both would concern my father. Was Talno ill? Was he never going to leave his cabin? Had I known him long? Had he ever been aboard ship before? Could he, Jonno, meet with him? And an assortment of other questions, of a type that any decent spy would find answers to without having to ask. How could the Primate have sent this child? After a few days his persistence stopped being a worry and became something of a private joke.

And then there was Mallinna. Beautiful Mallinna. Incomprehensible Mallinna, the greatest mystery of all. My life was a little easier now that she was keeping her clothes on, but I wondered as I watched her spoon-feeding Angel, cleaning up his sick, standing in the stern gazing at the horizon where the Gilgard had vanished, whether she regretted committing herself to this mad venture. What if Angel weakened and died? What if they were never able to return to the archives, or what if the Primate discovered how his own tame memorians had tricked him? Would she begin to resent sacrificing her quiet scholarly life? Would she hate me?

I finally got up the courage to ask her. She had formed the habit of sitting with me as I took the evening watch at the wheel, neither of us speaking very much – nothing romantic, more like two weary old-marrieds being cabbages together after a hard day's work. I would not have had the energy to spare for courtship even if Mallinna had shown the inclination. Both Tigrallef and Angel had become heavy burdens, on top of the burden of the expedition, the dangers ahead, the constant background of fear for those imprisoned on the Mosslines.

On the evening before landfall in Beriss, we were sitting together watching the ritual of shift-change on the fighting deck of the *Scion Cirallef* across the water, followed by as fine a sunset as I had ever seen. The evening was a little too warm, the air sultry with a strong but unsteady breeze, and I'd had to alter the sails twice in two hours. Somewhere, a storm was gathering. Tired out, and still deeply uneasy about my brush with the Harashil the day before, I was probably quieter than usual. Mallinna lounged with unconscious elegance on a pile of fleeces paid for by the Primate, looking, I thought, gently melancholic. After a long silence she sighed heavily. The sound brought all my guilt clawing to the surface.

'I'm sorry, Mallinna,' I said abruptly.

She looked in all directions as if seeking a tangible reason for my sorriness, and then she yawned. 'Sorry, Vero? What are you sorry for?'

'For dragging you and Angel into this. We should never have brought you with us. We should have – I don't know – found some other ship, some way of getting to the Mosslines that didn't involve you in our danger. If anything happens to you because you helped us—'

'That makes absolutely no sense, Vero.' She yawned again, sat up and sighed. The last blush of sunset was spreading a copper-coloured light over the sea and the high masts of the *Cirallef*, giving Mallinna's dusky skin a glow that rivalled Tig's at his shiniest. 'We wanted to help you. The First Memorian worships Lord Tigrallef, always has, and so have I, ever since he was my first teacher in the archives. We'd never forgive him if he sailed off without us a second time.'

Long pause. 'Fine, I can see that Angel might want to come along, even if it kills him – but what about you, Mallinna? I thought your heart was in the archives, that you'd be miserable without your work.'

She stretched disturbingly. 'I've never had a better time in my life. As for the archives, I'm a scholar, not just a keeper of books and scrolls and mouldy old pieces of tortoiseshell, and it's about time I did some primary research, don't you think?' She reached back with one long brown arm to loosen the clasp that secured her hair in a knot, and shook her head until the mass of black waves tumbled down and pooled on the surface of the fleece. With a stab of desire, I wondered exactly what kind of primary research she had in mind. 'For example, the official reports on the Mosslines are deficient in so many respects,' she went on, 'no account of natural history beyond what is germane to the moss itself and a few off-hand mentions of birds nesting seasonally in the highlands, very few descriptions of visible ruins or the nature and distribution of the slag, no—'

'Yes, I see.' That kind of primary research.

'There are so many questions I can answer only by going and looking for myself. I know we'll be busy rescuing your mother and so forth, but I plan to make observations as we go.'

'Yes, of course.' I had not told her yet she would be staying in the presumed safety of the *Fifth*, even if I had to lock her in her cabin when the time came.

'But I was thinking, Vero.'

'Yes?'

She sat up straight and piled her hair on top of her head, then let it fall. 'When we've rescued your family and you set off again to search for the Will of Banishment, would you mind if Angel and I came with you?'

I half choked. 'What did you say?'

'Well, if there's enough room. I wouldn't mind sharing a cabin with someone.'

With whom? I strangled that question. 'But what – what about the archives?'

'Costi, the Second Memorian, isn't brilliant but he's competent. He's better prepared to take over than Angel was when Lord Tigrallef left him in charge, believe me. In fact, Angel and I – no, never mind.'

'And the Second Flamen? What about him? I thought you were – Angel implied he was – that is—'

'I don't want to talk about Lestri Flamen,' she said, a little tartly for her.

I sighed. Part of me wanted to offer her a half-share in my cabin for the next sixty-odd years, but part of me was honest and well-meaning. 'You have no idea what you'd be getting into. Life with Tigrallef is – not easy.' A masterful understatement. I was on the edge of telling her what I had seen and heard the day before and blurting out my fears about the tightening hold of the Harashil, but I strangled those words as well.

'At least you've always been free,' she said.

'I don't think you quite understand. We've never been free. We've spent our lives as prisoners of the Pain, and that's only part of it. In the last twenty years we've hit every pisspit blightspot we could find, looking for clues to that damned Will. We've been battered by storms and bombarded by volcanoes. Four ships have sunk under us. We've gone from bloody hot to bloody cold. Sometimes we've nearly starved. Unfriendly people have tried to kill us in a number of horrible ways. Friendly people have been almost as bad. Some battlechief in the Ronchar Sea once *honoured* us with a casserole of human ears—'

'Did you eat it?'

'It would have been rude not to. Possibly fatal.'

'It sounds wonderful.'

'Rather tough, actually; tasted like chicken.'

'Not the casserole, the life you've led. You see, I've read about so many things and places, but I've never been anywhere—'

'Look, Mallinna,' I began.

'—and I want to stay with you for ever.'

That silenced me. The pronoun she used was indeterminate. Singular or plural? Me in particular or us in general? I was trying to decide whether I should ask her to clarify, when a slender shadow fell across the deckboards between us.

'A lovely warm evening, Vilno, Mistress Mallinna. I'd be most grateful if you'd let me join you.'

Jonno would never know how close he came to being thrown overboard then and there. Mallinna offered him a couple of fleeces while I sulked at the wheel. He was depressed, poor lad; it was the Lady's Eve – feasts, processions, family vigils – and here he was, far away from his widowed mother and two beloved sisters and the bright streets of Gil City, on a ship in the middle of the Great Known Sea. The most pathetic part was how brave he was trying to be about it. Within minutes I was doing my best to cheer him up. By the time he went more happily off to bed, about an hour after Mallinna retired, I had almost forgiven him. Which did not change the fact that I planned to get rid of him the very next day.

The port of Beriss, on the west coast of Canton Ber about two days' sail west from the site of lost Iklankish, suffered badly in the barrage of waves that followed Sher's sinking. During the Last Dance, much of the surviving town was turned into smoking rubble by a fire that the people were too weak or too dead to fight. Twenty years later, one would never know by looking at it. Rebuilt, it had all the characteristics that I would come to realize were typical of a city in the Primate's empire: orderly, terrifyingly clean for the most part, well regulated to the point of being smothered, littered with busts, statues and street murals of the divine Scion Tigrallef. At least we did not have to contend with the usual bureaucratic procedures, though, sliding into the harbour in the middle of the morning in convoy with the *Scion Cirallef*.

The *Cirallef*, too large for the quays, dropped her anchors just inside the breakwater at the mouth of the harbour. The *Fifth* was directed to the main quay, where a rather harried-looking courtesy party was waiting for us. We had inconveniently arrived on the Day of the Lady, which meant the local officials had much better things to do, but they would not dare give less than full honours to a ship flying the Most

159

Revered Primate's colours. To keep out of sight, I joined my silent and restless father in his cabin.

We were still there when the captain of the *Cirallef* was rowed over in a smallboat to consult with the *Fifth*. Mallinna and I had spent hours drilling Angel for this encounter, and our efforts paid off brilliantly. There was no great rush to be over the ruins of Iklankish, Angel told the captain. A couple of nights in this pleasant harbour to let the *Cirallef*'s crew participate in the festivities of the Lady would not come amiss. Anyway, there was a look to the sky and a heaviness in the air that suggested a stormbowl might be building up over the Sherkin Sea; better to wait and watch, and if it came, to ride it out in the shelter of the breakwater. Mallinna reported the captain was visibly relieved to hear that. He said he had also noticed the weight of the air, and remarked on how richly the Sherkin Sea deserved its reputation for evil storms.

When I heard the captain's smallboat pulling away, I turned uneasily to Tig. He had spent the whole time staring into space and saying nothing. I did not know whether to be grateful to him for behaving himself or terrified about what unspeakable strangeness might be taking place inside his head. His face had never been so blank and pale.

'Tig? Tig, look at me. I have to go now, but I'll be back soon. Do you need anything? Will you be all right?'

He raised his head slowly. His face took on a bit of colour and relaxed into fairly amiable lines. 'You're planning on leaving this harbour tonight.'

'If we can,' I said, taken aback, 'unless the stormbowl forms too fast. A good chance to lose the *Cirallef*, I hope.'

'You're thinking of heading east, aren't you?'

'That's right,' I said, sitting down next to him on the pallet. This was the first interest he had taken in any aspect of the voyage since we came aboard, and I wanted to fan the flames a little. 'I plan to swing to the northeast just past the Tooth of Raksh and head for a point close to the mouth of the Deppowe Strait. That will keep us off the main shipping lanes for most of the journey, but won't take us too far out of our way.'

'And you want to leave tonight.'

'Yes, before this stormbowl passes over. I'm reckoning it'll come its closest early tomorrow afternoon, late enough so we'll be skirting its edges, nicely timed to keep the wind-catcher from pursuing us very far.'

'You're right and you're wrong. I have to tell you, Vero, this stormbowl is a big one. Not our handiwork, by the way, but we've been watching it build with a great deal of aesthetic admiration. Very big, very powerful.' He smiled dreamily. 'And very fast.'

'When do you reckon, then?'

'It will be here much sooner than you think. Now listen carefully. The centre of the stormbowl will pass to the south of Canton Ber by the breakfast hour at the latest. If you must leave harbour tonight, leave no later than midnight and make a dash for the north-northeast with every rag of sail you can safely hoist – you'll be running with both the wind and the tide at that point. If you manage to make it through the channel, you'll find yourself in the Pilazhet Basin, which is as good a place as any to ride out the storm. Nothing much in the way of land to get wrecked on, but there's a solid string of skerries to the east between you and the Sherkin Sea, and that will break the swell. The Sherkin Sea has the longest fetch inside the boundaries of the known world, did you know that?'

The question sounded rhetorical, but he paused for me to answer. 'No,' I said, 'I didn't know that.'

'Well, it has. But – pay special attention, Vero, this is a warning – if you head too far east, or founder on the shoals, or get driven on to the skerries, it's quite likely I'll have to use the old sow's power in a deliberate act of Will to save your skins. And then where will I be?'

'You talk almost as if you won't be with us.'

'Oh, we'll be with you,' he said gently, 'alas for you. You'd better go now, the timing is very important. As I said, if you leave this port much after midnight, the old sow will be licking her ugly chops at the prospect of an act of Will, and I'm not sure I'd be able to hold back.'

So now we had a deadline of sorts. The first thing I did was go to Angel's cabin and get out the expensive sea-charts and tidal almanacs which the Gillish treasury had so obligingly bought for the expedition. I looked for the Pilazhet Basin and the skerries, checked the tides in the Canton Ber channel, memorized the dangerous shoals that infested the northern approach to Beriss, noting with reluctant gratitude that the Primate had caused all-weather lighthouses to be set up at intervals all along the way. When I was confident I could steer us along the course my father recommended, I went out on deck.

It was already late afternoon, dismally hot and heavy, though the light was oddly clear. One or more processions were winding through the streets of the town, the music of pipes and horns and chanters being now muffled, now magnified, by the vagaries of the unstable air. Festive crowds surged along the banner-brightened corniche, and I could see the *Cirallef*'s smallboats setting out for the quays with loads of grinning dun-shirted troopers. Mallinna emerged from the main cabin and joined me at the bowrail.

'I've put the First Memorian down for a nap,' she explained. 'He did very well with the *Cirallef*'s captain, but all that coherency with a stranger wore him out. What now, Vero?'

I told her about Tig's warning, then called Malso over and repeated it to him. 'So I want to leave before midnight,' I finished. 'You and Entiso get the smallboat lashed down. I'll leave instructions about the rigging before I go ashore.'

'You're going ashore?' Mallinna asked.

'I have an errand to do — a package to deliver.'

'Jonno?'

'Exactly.'

Her face fell. 'You're not planning to hurt him, I hope.'

'As little as possible,' I said hurriedly. I had given a lot of thought to this. My first plan had been to take him ashore,

162

get him blind drunk and leave him to sleep it off in a dark alley. By the time he stumbled back within signalling range of the *Cirallef*, bleary and hung over, we'd be long gone. Talking it over with Malso, however, the fisherman pointed out gleefully that if the lad managed not to be murdered in the dark alley, he would almost certainly be handed a death sentence by the Flamens' Corps for drunkenness on duty – either way, Malso added with great relish, there'd be one less black-tunic bastard stinking up the world.

So much for that plan, I'd said to myself. It would be not much kinder than just throwing him to the sharks. The best alternative I could think of was to take him ashore but keep him sober, hit him very carefully on the head, and leave him to sleep it off in a reasonably well-lighted alley.

Early evening. Jonno was standing solitary by the bowrail watching the jovial uproar of the crowds ashore. The sunset was a strange one, still with that ominous clarity of light, but a front of high fibrous clouds was advancing steadily from the east, messenger clouds bearing news of the approaching storm. Several breadths of sky behind them there would be the thicker mats of cloud, blue-grey and darkening, that would deepen rapidly to a black ragged-based mass of rain and thunder and killing winds. Meantime the swell was already slightly up outside the breakwater, running ahead of the worst of the winds. Tig's time estimate began to look too optimistic.

Aware that Mallinna was watching from the cabin, I went to Jonno and touched him on the elbow. He started and looked at me with desolate eyes.

'Looks quite festive in the town, doesn't it?' I said amiably.

'Yes, very much so.' He sighed.

'There's no curfew tonight, is there?'

'Of course not – the celebrations will go on until dawn, just as they will in Gil City. It's the same all over the empire. Didn't you know that?'

'I've never spent the Lady's day in the provinces before,' I said truthfully.

'Neither have I.' He propped his elbow on the bowrail and his chin on his palm, the very picture of wistfulness.

'Like to go ashore?' I asked. Casual but friendly – I'd practised on my father.

He straightened and looked at me with brighter eyes. 'Could we? Could we really?'

'I don't see why not. We wouldn't be ashore for very long – we'll have to be back before that storm breaks, anyhow. What do you say?'

His delight was wrenching. At the dawn of pleasure in his face, I had to armour myself with annoyance – a sudden impulse to shake him hard and say, *look here, you young idiot, by the Eight Rages of Raksh, what are you doing working for a stone-hearted tyrant like the Primate? Why don't you go home to your widowed mam and your two adoring sisters?* Instead I said, 'Might be a bit of fun, eh?'

'Yes, oh yes! Wait here while I get my money belt.' He practically flew towards the aft companionway; following him guiltily with my eyes, I was waylaid by Mallinna's mournful face in the half-open cabin door. I spread my hands helplessly: *it's for his own good.* With a definitive click, she shut the door.

9

Our holiday excursion began to go wrong from the moment we stepped off the quay, with the problem residing wholly in Jonno's smart black tunic and green armband. True, his uniform got us plenty of respect. Crowds parted to let us pass. Chanters broke off singing at the sight of us. Laughter died within a wide radius. Pretty girls shrank or were pushed behind their mams. Little children were called to heel. Men's flushed faces turned guarded and pale. Even the dun-tunics from the *Scion Cirallef* gave us a wide berth. One would have thought poor Jonno carried a deadly contagion.

The town itself was potentially quite pleasant. Most of the buildings were newish and neatly put together, dating from after the great fire twenty years past and built to survive the stormbowls that regularly swept in off the Sherkin Sea. The main streets were broad and well paved, with covered drains down the centre, and the street decorations, though not as elaborate as those in Gil City, added a gleaming element of gaiety to a scene that was already lively. A well-fed populace shone under the lamplight in bright festival silks and fine cottons – clearly, although the Primate was a tyrant and a murderer, he was very good at organizing empires. If not for the reaction to poor Jonno's uniform, I might have been impressed by the Most Revered Primate's achievement. As we walked on through the streets, however, preceded by a bow-wave of sullenness and suspicion, trailed by a wake of whispers, Jonno's excited chatter grew more sporadic and eventually stopped altogether. When I stole a glance at him, his face was set in an expression of careful nonchalance.

We came to a small market, a double row of brick stalls set well apart, festooned with banners and presided over by a life-sized statue of my da on a high pedestal – the Blessed Scion Tigrallef, that is, the Ark and Sceptre himself, brandishing the Lady in Gil over his head. The Lady was represented by a gilded figurine, and the Scion's robe was also gilded, and both were dazzling in the unsteady flare of hundreds of candles crowded around the base of the pedestal. Beyond it was a small but ornate stone building, also gilded over much of its surface, that could only be the local shrine to the Scion. Its arched doorway was reached by a flight of broad black-stone steps, up and down which flowed constant streams of worshippers. Two Flamens were at the portal accepting offerings, flanked by two hard-faced guardsmen of the Flamens' Corps. I pointed them out to Jonno.

'Anyone you know?' I asked.

'No.'

'Don't you want to greet them? Maybe you could drop in

on the local Corps barracks.' I was hoping he would want to, because I needed a good excuse to find out where it was. After seeing how the Berissu viewed men in Corps uniforms, I had a bad feeling about Jonno's life expectancy if I left him unconscious and helpless almost anywhere in that town; but if I could drop him at a carefully calculated distance from the Corps barracks, say, close enough to be safe until found by the guardsmen, far enough not to be found too soon . . .

'I want to buy a present for my mother,' he said flatly. He headed straight towards one of the stalls. I sighed and followed.

The counter was laid out with dozens of terracotta reproductions of the Lady in Gil — what the damned thing was supposed to look like, anyhow, nothing to do with the plain glass tube my father had shattered with such good intentions and disastrous results. These examples were mostly crude, stylized and fairly hideous, cheap mass-moulded obvious females stamped MADE IN GIL on the bottom. But on a shelf at the rear of the stall, behind the proprietor, was a row of hand-carved wooden Ladies of much better quality, brightly painted and picked out with real gilding. Jonno surveyed the terracotta abominations on the counter with tactfully disguised distaste, then pointed at the shelf.

'How much are those?' he asked in Gillish.

The stall-keeper had drawn back out of the lamplight as Jonno approached. Without a word, he lifted one of the wooden figurines down from the shelf and put it into Jonno's hand. He turned away.

'How much?' Jonno repeated in a louder voice.

The proprietor shook his head sullenly.

'Two palots? Three palots?'

Berissbal is part of the Miisheli/Grisotin/Fathidiic language family, and also incorporates large numbers of Sheranik loanwords. I could thus pick up the gist of what the stall-keeper said in carefully humble tones: 'Just take it, thou whoreson, thou [thief?], thou tupper of [unknown], thou [unknown] assassin of [innocents?], and leave my family alone. Just [unknown] take it and go away.'

Uncertainly, Jonno balanced the object in his hand. 'I'm sorry, I don't understand. Do you speak any Gillish?'

The stall-keeper gave us both a long resentful stare. 'Take,' he muttered in Gillish. 'Is yours. Not palots. Only but take.'

'But I can't accept—' Jonno began. He stopped suddenly. 'Oh,' he said. Very gently, he placed the figurine on the counter among its terracotta cousins and walked away.

I turned to the stall-keeper, finding him in the last phase of an obscene gesture at Jonno's retreating back. First I caught his eye. Then I leaned over the counter and grabbed his throat. 'Thou whoreson dog's-behind,' I hope I said, 'that young one *wanted* to pay.' I squeezed very briefly, then released him and strode after Jonno.

By the time I caught up with him, he had cut through the middle of the market and into the mouth of the least salubrious street I'd seen so far in Beriss. He was very much on his dignity, ploughing through the crowds with a determined smile on his face. We walked along without talking for a short stretch. Some of the looks he was getting worried me; I was also unhappy to notice how the long banners billowed and snapped in sudden gusts of wind. I was about to bring up the subject of the Corps barracks again when he stopped and touched my arm. 'Come along, Memorian, let's have a drink,' he said brightly.

My heart dropped. If he smelled at all of booze when they found him . . . 'Oh, no,' I said hastily, 'not just now, thank you. But I'll wager you could get a dram and maybe a drop of food and some good company down at the Corps barracks—'

'That may be so,' he said thoughtfully.

Relief. A sense that I could still get rid of him without danger to himself. '*Well* then, good. I'm sure we can ask directions from the Flamens at the shrine—'

'But, no, I think I'd rather go to a tavern,' he interrupted. 'This place looks all right.'

He dived into the entrance of the first tavern I'd seen in Beriss that wasn't bright, clean, neatly painted and thronged with jovial faces. No, young Jonno had to pick a dingy little pothouse with a villainous smell oozing out of its dim interior and a pool of sick beside the door. Grumbling, I shook my fist after him and followed him in. This was not going as I had planned.

The inside was worse than the outside. The only light came from a few smoky lanterns spaced along the crossbeam of the ceiling. The thronging faces were not jovial. The room was quite full when we came in, and thick with a low growl of voices, but voice by voice it fell silent until the only sound was a scuffling of feet as the patrons slunk past us out the door. Jonno took no notice.

'So you changed your mind, Vilno? Oh, look, we can have a bench to ourselves.'

By that point we could have had twenty benches to ourselves. The only other patrons left were the handful of sots who had already passed out. Jonno marched over to a bench in the centre of the drinking hall and pulled up a table. I dusted off the bench and sat down beside him.

'Just a small one, Jonno, and then I think we should—'

'Tapman! A small one for my friend here, and a very large one for me!'

'Oh, gods,' I said faintly.

Unfortunately, the landlord appeared to understand Gillish. He sent a tapman like a lard barrel with a scowl to set two beakers in front of us. Jonno's was big enough to boil whole spud-roots in. 'How much?' he said to the tapman, who only shrugged and began to turn away.

'I said, *how much?*'

The tapman stared at him with wonder and disapproval and said nothing. Snarling, Jonno pulled his money belt into the open, reached in and pulled out two golden palots, which he slammed down on the table. He glared at the tapman until the latter reached out and scooped them up.

I waited while the tapman stumped away. 'Guardsman, don't you know you should never show your money belt in a pothouse?'

Jonno switched his glare to me. 'Tup that.'

'Did you know you paid him enough to keep us both drunk for a month?'

He lifted his beaker with both hands in a defiant salute. 'Good. To the Blessed Scion's return, Vilno!'

'Oh, surely.' I sniffed mine while Jonno choked on his first swallow. It was the real old rotbelly, I could tell that from the sickly vapour curling off its surface. After a couple of discriminating sips, I decided it was not the worst I had ever tasted; probably the fourth worst. Still, it was so bad that I saw no danger Jonno would drink too much of it. 'Jonno, we'd get much better brew at the Corps—' I began, turning back to him.

His face was entirely hidden by the kettle-sized beaker, which was tilted at an angle suggesting most of the contents had already vanished down his throat.

'Jonno!'

He set the beaker tenderly but a little unsteadily on the table. By my estimate, somewhat more than two-thirds of it was gone. Looking slightly dazed, Jonno rubbed his hand across his mouth and wiped it on his heretofore spotless black tunic.

'S'good,' he said thickly. 'You don't get brew like that in Gil City.' He gulped.

'I'm sure you're right.' The time for heroic measures had arrived. I swept my hand out in a gesture that culminated in slapping Jonno on the back, but succeeded on the way in knocking his beaker off the table. 'Oh, *sorry*,' I said.

'Wha'? Never mind. Tapman! Tapman! Another enormous one for me, good tapman, and one for my dear friend here.'

'No! Jonno, I really think we should find the Corps barracks, but first we should find an eating den and get some food and root-tea down you, because—'

'But whass – what's wrong with this place, Vilno? I like this place. I think we should have juss another little—'

'*No!*' I frightened off the hovering tapman with one very black look. Meantime, Jonno picked up my beaker and almost drained it before I noticed what he was doing and wrested it away from him. Then he nestled his head on his arms, which were folded on the table in front of him. That fiendish brew had hit him fast and hard. What I could see of his face was an exemplar of tragedy.

'Memorian, I've never been hated before.'

I sighed and patted his shoulder. 'You probably have, lad, you just never noticed it before.'

'Really? Do you really think so? Honestly? Thank you, Vilno, you're a great comfort.'

I ground my teeth together when I realized he was being sincere. 'Now, guardsman, about the Corps barracks—'

I broke off. The tapman, just visible in the shadows of a smoky alcove behind the counter, was looking intently towards the door, which was latched open. I was almost certain he had signalled to someone in the street. When he caught my eye on him, he started and moved further back into the darkness. The landlord was not visible at all.

'See, Vilno, you're a good – a good man, but the trouble is – the trouble is—' Jonno hiccoughed.

'Tell me about the trouble, Jonno.' I kept my eyes on the door. I could not see outside from that angle, but a lantern in the street was casting a useful rectangle of light on the floor just inside the threshold. To our left, one of the sleeping sots made munching noises and turned over. A squall of wind clattered the door in its socket and sent a devil of dust swirling across the room.

'See, the trouble is, you're just – *urp* – a memorian, Vilno. Nothing wrong with memorians, but you could never understand a man of – *urp* – a man of action, like me . . .'

'No doubt you're right.' I lost track of his babbling for a bit – two shadows, three, five, were gathering in outline in the patch of light at the threshold.

'—great p-poets on my da's side – did I tell you I write p-poems? Would you like to hear—?'

'Maybe later.' I scanned the pothouse for other exits. The few windows were small and high; there were no other doors unless the alcove led to one, but I had a feeling the tapman and the landlord would have their own small armoury back there. I loosened the Gafrin-Gammanthan belt and pulled the fighting chain out of its compartment; that was for the left hand. The cosh I had brought for Jonno's benefit went on the table by my right hand, along with the two knives from the chest scabbard. The knives in my boots would be left hidden until I needed them. Outside, the wind shrieked again.

I did a quick survey of the sots snoring the rotbelly off in various corners of the drinking hall. Five were visible, and there might have been any number sleeping under the tables, but none of them looked like an immediate threat. I glanced at Jonno in passing, but took a second to register what I'd seen; then I swung round on the bench to stare at him with horror. Sitting up again, he had gathered six or seven abandoned beakers from the adjacent table and was systematically finishing them off. I grabbed the one he had just emptied and sniffed it. 'Great balls of Oballef, Jonno, that's rakk. You should never mix rakk with brew.'

'Thirsty.' His head drooped. He dribbled some more on what was already a large damp spot on the front of his tunic. He looked very young and sleepy, *sweet*, a frayed angel from the Lucian tradition. Fiercely, I punched his shoulder to keep him awake.

'Tell me the truth, guardsman,' I demanded, 'how old are you?'

'Thirty-two,' he said vaguely. 'No, wait. Twenny – twenty-three.'

I glared at him. 'How old are you really?'

'Nineteen,' he mumbled, ashamed, 'nearly.'

'So you're eighteen.'

His eyes grew distant as he worked it out. 'Yes,' he said.

'Oh, gods.' I leaned my elbows on the table and propped my miserable forehead against my cold hands. 'Eighteen. Oh, lords of Fathan. How could the Primate send a cub like you on a mission like this?'

'Not him,' Jonno said, 'Grandda.'

'Hush!' From the street came the distinctive clash of a knife being withdrawn clumsily from its sheath.

'S'Grandda – but Great-uncle—' He gulped, turned green and cupped his hand over his mouth.

Out of the corner of my eye, I saw the shadows change again at the doorway. At least one scragger out there had nearly got his courage up. *Come on, come on.* I wished they would hurry; I wanted the first rush to happen inside the pothouse, where the chain would be at its most effective, but waiting was not easy. Jonno moaned softly behind his hand.

'Last time this happened, I was with Chasco in Uagolo,' I muttered bitterly. 'Between us, Chasco and I wiped the streets with those bastards.'

Jonno let his hand fall away. 'Uncle,' he said faintly.

'Shut up about your tupping relatives,' I snapped. 'We're about to be attacked – do you understand? Listen carefully: no matter what happens, you must stay close to me. Jonno, do you understand?'

'Attacked, did you say? Ah, damn.' His voice turned tragic again. 'It's because I'm in the C-C-Corps, isn't it? Everybody hates me . . .'

'It's the money belt as well, but yes, if you must know, the Primate is not popular, and neither is the Flamens' Corps. Be quiet.'

'But I told you, s'not the Primate, s'*Grandda*.'

'Tell me later.'

'He said – he said to ask a *question* . . .'

'Ask me later.'

'No, no, no, no, not you. You're *tall* . . . s'posed to ask the *short* one . . .'

'Shut up, Jonno.'

'S'about the cook.'

'*We don't have a cook.*'

Offended, he subsided into hiccoughs. Now I could hear a murmur of voices in the street. In the alcove, suddenly, lamplight flashed on something too large to be a knife, more likely a cleaver, rising for an overhand pitch. I estimated the distance and shook out a length of chain. The glittering filament of it snaked across the room and retracted itself red-tipped; the shadows gurgled, the cleaver clattered on the

172

flagstones. Lardbarrel sagged into the light and fell half across the counter with his head and arms dangling and his hair hanging straight down. Below him, a dark puddle began to collect on the floor. A ghastly burbling noise deep in the darkness of the alcove suggested the landlord had got in the way of the same stroke. Jonno squinted at the body of the tapman.

'Wha'?'

'No, don't get up yet.' I pulled him back on to the bench. 'Don't move until I tell you.'

'But tha' was – thass *magic*.'

'It's wrist action.'

'Can I t-try?' He reached towards the shining coil on the table.

'No! Don't touch it.' I swatted his hand away before he could lose his fingertips. There was a flurry of clatters in the street, just audible over the rising howl of the wind, and the telltale rectangle was empty for the moment – the scraggers outside may also have thought the tapman's fate was magical. I remember thinking something of the sort myself, the first time I saw the chain in action. Quick change of plan: it could well be a good moment to move, while the object lesson was still fresh in the scraggers' minds. I stood up and quickly redistributed the weapons, cosh and one knife handy in my belt, one knife in the right hand, chain fully retracted in the left.

'Come on, Jonno. Wake up. Stay with me.' I hoisted him up, keeping my chain-hand free, and dragged him a few steps before his own feet swung into action. His head lolled against my shoulder and then forward on to his chest. He completed the ruination of his black tunic by vomiting a mixture of second-hand liquor over it.

'Why am I doing this?' I hissed. 'Why don't I just leave you, like I meant to in the first place?'

The boy was beyond answering. Cursing him, I hauled his dead weight as far as the door and peered into the wild night. The scraggers were still there, a cluster of six standing across the narrow street out of the wind, whispering heatedly among themselves. At the sight of me, they looked startled and flattened their bodies against the wall. There was a sharp incongruity between the holiday colours they wore and the knives and clubs they carried in their hands. I assumed my most menacing face and pulled Jonno across the threshold into the street.

I suppose they could not be blamed for relaxing a bit. At rest, the chain does not look like a weapon. They could see the knife, but it was held awkwardly at the end of the arm burdened with the guardsman. They looked at each other and began to fan out in a semicircle around us.

'Get thou gone,' I snarled.

One of them laughed. 'Or what?' he shouted in Gillish. 'Or you'll have the Primate's bastard there throw up on us? *Kashkibal*, we've been waiting a long time to have one of his kind in our hands.' He moved a step closer and feinted with his knife.

I dodged a club thrown from the left. 'I'm warning you, friend. I do not want to hurt you. Leave the boy alone, and we'll have no quarrel, you and I. Otherwise, I'll kill you.'

He laughed again. 'We want his belt and his balls, that's all. You can have the rest of him. Just drop him, friend, and move out of the way.'

'All right.' I let Jonno slump to the ground, freeing my knife hand. That gave them a broken second's pause, but at a cry from the leader they advanced on all sides, and I had to short-chain three of them with one swing and slice with the knife at one coming in from the right. By the time the chain was retracted, only the two hindmost were left standing. They looked at me stupidly.

'*Witchcraft!*'

'Would you like to see it again?' I gave them a demonic smile and raised my left hand. When they were gone, I sighed and pried Jonno out of a puddle of new vomit and set off hauling him down the street.

We attracted less attention this time, mostly because the worsening weather had driven many of the merrymakers indoors. It was about two hours short of midnight on a night when the streets should have bustled right through until dawn, but the great stormbowl had other plans for Beriss.

The marketplace we had passed through little more than an hour before was now almost deserted except for merchants cursing the loss of business as they secured the storm shutters on their stalls. Of the hundreds of bright banners, many were reduced to tatters clinging to their fastenings. The figure of the Scion Tigrallef, lonely and unlighted, stood on its pedestal amid a great mob of dead candles. The shrine was still open but the Flamens had obviously taken refuge inside, leaving the two black-clad guardsmen to keep watch on the nearly empty stairs.

Studying the guardsmen from the shadows between two boarded-up stalls, I spent a few precious moments reviewing the facts.

Jonno was a spy.

I had brought him ashore with the intention of leaving him here. This was my chance.

It was his own choice to pickle himself in rotbelly brew; I had tried very hard to stop him.

I had already saved his miserable life once that night.

I owed him nothing.

He was getting heavy.

He stank.

My most sensible course would be to drop him as close as possible to the foot of the stairs and run like a rippercat . . .

. . . and then, of course, to wonder for the rest of my life whether he got his hands and his head chopped off, in that order, for losing us while drunk. I sighed.

Earlier in the evening, Jonno and I had found the market-place to be a gentle fifteen-minute stroll from the waterfront. Going in the reverse direction took almost an hour.

Jonno's dead weight was only one of the retarding factors. Occasionally his feet even worked properly, and I could tow him along as a welcome rest from dragging him. Every so often he would whimper and make noises about wanting to lie down; he called me Uncle and carried on wild dialogues with Grandda, to the point where I seriously felt like dumping him after all.

The greatest delay was the frequent need to make detours. Four were to avoid patrols of the Flamens' Corps or of ordinary troopers out to round up drunkards, one was to avoid a knot of revellers who might have recognized Jonno's uniform through its surface layer of mud and vomit, but the worst was when I realized we were being followed, and pulled Jonno into somebody's slop pile to hide. When our pursuers slunk past a few moments later, I saw it was the two surviving scraggers from the pothouse with an indeterminate number of their friends. I waited until the furtive scraping of their sandals had faded away into the next street, then pulled both of us, reeking, out of the slop pile and down the nearest dark alley. Two streets later we were lost, and it took a while to find our bearings again. The only comfort – a mixed one – was that advance rain-squalls of ferocious power and wetness swept over us every so often, washing the puke off Jonno and the slop off us both. At the same time, they soaked us to the skin.

At last, by sheer chance, we hit the corniche about a hundred yards from the main quay. Now all that lay between us and safety was the guardpost at the head of the quay, manned by a troop of dun-tunics under the harbour master's command. Pulling a semi-comatose Jonno along to a sheltered spot across the corniche from the guardpost, I could see no way past them that did not involve more bloodshed, of which I had already done more than I liked for one evening. But we were just over an hour from midnight by then – Tigrallef's deadline – and my scruples were beginning to feel like a luxury the expedition could ill afford.

Beside me, Jonno stirred and sat up. He sank down again immediately, clutching his head. I explained the situation to him in a savage whisper, including the information that it was all his fault.

He moaned and opened his eyes a crack. 'We d-don't need

to hide from them, Memorian. We have clearance to go on the quay.'

I banged my head against the wall a couple of times at the magnitude of my own stupidity. That's what being pursued and then attacked for much of an evening will do to one. I pulled Jonno up – 'All right then, laddie, you've got to walk and talk for about five minutes, and then you can lie down, Vilno promises' – and led him confidently across the corniche to the head of the quay. He walked like one of the undead of Satheli demonology, but at least he was upright.

The two troopers in the outer guardpost, stepping out to challenge us, held their hands up in a Gillish salute at the sight of Jonno's rain-washed uniform. To me, a mere civilian but a memorian under the Primate's flag, they accorded a respectful nod. Jonno returned the salute creditably, though he made an asinine comment about the lovely evening just as another rain-squall bucketed down on us; and then we were past them, and I was frogmarching a rapidly fading young guardsman along the wave-washed quay. Twice before we came level with the *Fifth*, I saved him from stumbling to a watery death. I had to carry him the last few yards. Altogether, I'd had about as much of Jonno as I could bear for one day.

I dumped him at the foot of the gangplank. The *Fifth* looked properly battened down, with the storm fenders in good order and a storm lantern burning at the bow, and I could see Malso and Entiso had followed my instructions about the rigging. What I could not see was any sign of the crew. The gangplank was still holding, loosely secured at the top end, but with the tide in and the water so high in the harbour, it was dauntingly steep. It was also slick with spray and sliding up and down like a hand saw against the edge of the deck in the still moderate swell.

'Hoy! Malso! Put out the boarding net! Malso! Malso! Entiso! Mallinna! Raksh take you, where is everybody?'

No reply. Cursing, I grabbed Jonno and threw both of us flat against the gangplank. It was very like crawling up a rockface hauling a dead deer with me for supper; but the last time I did that, it was not raining and the rockface stayed put. Furthermore, the dead deer did not groan, tremble, sneeze and try to struggle free in a panic when it realized where it was. Jonno did all those things before passing out and becoming a dead weight again. A couple of centuries later I managed to push him over the top of the gangplank and roll after him on to the deck.

Lying flat on my face on the sopping deckboards, gasping for breath, muscles on fire, fingernails bristling with splinters from clinging to the rough wood of the gangplank, I made myself a solemn promise: that I would never, never, *never* again take young Jonno out for the evening.

In fact, given recent disasters, it hardly surprised me at that point to discover a thin cold object was pressing into the back of my neck.

'Keep very still, Master Vero, for your own sake.'

'Oh Raksh,' I groaned, 'Malso, what do you think you're doing?' I started to flip over. Sharp metal bit into my neck on three sides.

'Keep still, I'm warning you. There's a new moon at your neck. Anything too energetic, you could take your own head off.'

A new moon. I had never heard the phrase used that way before, but the concept was clear enough. I kept very still, apart from trying hard to push my neck into the deckboards, as far as possible from the razor-edged metal crescent arching over it. 'Why are you doing this, Malso? What have you done with the others?'

'They're safe, all three of them – be patient. Hurry it up, Entiso, I hate getting wet.'

Entiso hurried it up. Arms trussed behind my back, legs forcibly bent back at the knees, ankles bound together and connected to wrists with a short cord in such a way as to give me the shape of an archer's bow. All this in under a minute. Entiso had done this kind of thing before.

10

Malso lugged me across the deck into the main cabin, now Angel's quarters. When my eyes adjusted to the storm-mantled lamp in its clamps on the wall, I saw that everyone was accounted for. Angel was propped up on cushions on the big pallet; beside him on a wooden stool was Mallinna, pale and angry, with her hands tied behind her. Beside her, Tigrallef was bound to another chair but otherwise looked alarmingly at ease with himself, with his eyes cast down and a half-smile on his lips. Mallinna made up for his silence and Angel's by cursing Malso and Entiso fluently in about eight languages while they carried me in, dumped me on my side on the smaller pallet and swabbed the blood off my neck.

'What have you done to him, you *pillak briin koshu*?' She had finished on an impressively filthy note. This was new light on Mallinna's character. 'Vero, how bad is it?'

'Just a few scratches,' I said sourly. I tried to move my legs, found that any serious effort threatened to dislocate my shoulders, and compromised by lying still.

'Don't worry, Mistress Mallinna, it looks much worse than it is. Anyway it's his own fault, I warned him not to move.' Malso got up and propped the new moon against the wall next to the door – a wicked oxbow of metal, now I could see it from a safe distance, trimmed darkly with my blood along its inner edge, fitted to a sturdy wooden handle like a broomstick. He nodded to Entiso, who silently left the cabin. 'Are you comfortable, Master Vero? Shall I get you a pillow? I've got some very good ointment for those scratches down in my quarters, I'll fetch it when I have a moment.'

'Don't bother.'

'No, I must. Even scratches can fester.'

'You show a surprising regard for my health.'

179

'You will see—' he began; but the door opened again with a gust of wind and rain, and Entiso dragged in an object that I figured had to be poor Jonno. He lay where Entiso dropped him, a bedraggled black heap in the unsteady shadows on the floor. I saw Mallinna frown as she tried to figure out what he was, then she gasped with outrage.

'You *pillak*, Malso.'

He spread his hands innocently. 'None of my doing, Mistress, he was like that when Master Vero brought him aboard.'

'Vero! You said you wouldn't hurt him!'

'I didn't hurt him. He's blind drunk.'

'You said you wouldn't get him drunk!'

'I also said I wouldn't bring him back. Next time *you* can take him ashore.'

'I doubt there will be a next time,' Malso said.

'What do you mean?' she flared at him. 'Are you going to murder us, you ferret, you traitorous shull, you *pillak*, you great pile of—'

'I'm not a traitor, Mistress Mallinna,' Malso said firmly, 'I'm a loyal soldier of the Opposition, and I would not think of killing you unless the good of the cause made it necessary – and then, believe me, I would find it a terribly sad duty. No, you and the First Memorian are quite safe. As for Masters Vero and Tilgo, we offer them something better than a hopeless fool's errand that would get them slain for nothing – we offer them vengeance against the murderers of their loved ones, may their bones bring forth flowers.'

'They haven't been murdered yet.' Tig lifted his head and smiled dreamily at the so-called fisherman.

'Oh, lad. Once they've been sent to the Mosslines, you have to consider them dead; and then you pray it comes true as quickly and painlessly as it can. No, Master Tilgo, you can't bring them back from the Mosslines any more than you can bring them back from the dead. We can't let you waste your precious gift in the attempt, not while the cause of freedom needs you.'

'Precious gift?' I asked with terrible foreboding. 'What

180

precious gift do you mean?' Mallinna sat up straighter on her stool. Angel laid his arm over his eyes. Tig did nothing.

'Precious gift, yes. Your face, Master Vero, and your brother's, the faces of the Priest-King Arkolef and the Divine Scion Tigrallef.'

'Oh, that gift,' I said, relieved. Mallinna relaxed. Angel sighed. Tig did nothing.

'A precious resource which the Primate, may he rot, was willing to throw away, but the Opposition is less wasteful. We are also your truest friends.'

'If we're such friends,' I asked, 'why are we tied up?'

'We'll untie you when we're sure you understand your own best interests.'

'What about the guardsman?'

Malso looked regretfully at the crumpled figure on the floor. 'Poor lad. Let me say it this way – he may never have to suffer the hangover he deserves.'

'You bastard, Malso!' Mallinna shouted. 'You touch a hair of his head and I'll make damned sure the Truant hears about it!'

'I am the Truant.'

Mallinna's jaw dropped.

'Who's the Truant?' I asked.

'He is, obviously,' said Tigrallef, raising his head.

'No, I don't believe it,' Mallinna cried. 'The Truant is the great hero and war chief of the Opposition, the one I've been sending information to all these years. I do not believe the Truant would betray us and then threaten to murder a helpless prisoner. I do not believe you, fisherman. The Truant is an honourable man, a fighter for justice and freedom, and you're a – a—'

'*Pillak*,' I supplied. 'Anyway, why would the great war chief of the Opposition be honouring us with his personal attention? I don't believe you either.'

Malso turned wearily to Entiso. 'Who am I, partisan?'

'You're the Truant, sir.'

'Why should we believe *him*?' I said.

'Because, Vero, he's telling the truth.' That was my father, and his tone worried me far more than just being trussed up like a roasting chicken in the hands of armed maniacs, which was at least something I had experienced before. Tigrallef's voice was *different*.

Malso said, 'Thank you, Master Tilgo. There's no need just now to convince the rest of you, but I promise when we get to Pilazhet—' He broke off as another rain-squall pounded the roof of the cabin and the *Fifth* ground her storm fenders lightly against the quay.

'What's it to be, sir?' Entiso said impatiently. 'Enough talking! If we don't leave in the next half hour or so, we shouldn't leave at all.'

'And yet leave we must. We're committed now. Let me think a moment.' Malso narrowed his eyes and took a deep breath. 'Dead, this poor young guardsman would be a fan to the flames. Quite useful. Alive, he'd be a hostage, possibly a valuable one, and we could certainly use the funds. That is, if the Most Revered Primate values his brother's progeny as highly as his own.'

My jaw fell open. *Great-uncle.*

'Don't forget the Rolso case, sir. All the trouble we went to, and in the end we had to cut his throat anyway. Of course he'd only married into the Primate's line, but still . . .'

Grandda sent me.

'Yes, I see your point. His own great-granddaughter's husband, the mean-minded old palot-pincher. Whereas if the Most Revered Primate's great-nephew, a promising young guardsman of the Flamens' Corps no less, were to be found viciously murdered in Beriss, I can see all manner of positive effects.'

'Beriss will be blamed,' said Entiso.

'And brutal reprisals will follow. Entiso, you've swept away my doubts. The Opposition in Beriss needs an imperial atrocity or two to focus their minds, they've been getting too comfortable of late. A shame, though, because he's a nice lad.'

'He won't suffer,' Entiso said.

At that moment Mallinna did what I was longing to do

and couldn't – launched herself at Malso with her head at his gut level, connecting with a good solid thud before Entiso caught her by her hair, swung her around and flung her against the wall beside my pallet. Angel cried out. I grunted as she thumped down more or less on top of me. It flashed into my mind that this was a ruse on her part – she had engineered being thrown on to me, she had a blade concealed in her hand, she would take this chance to cut through my bonds, I would leap up and overwhelm the two fraudulent fishermen, we would save the life of the guardsman, sail off, conquer the Mosslines, free the family, find the Banishment, get married . . .

Entiso dragged her off me. There was no knife, alas, and she'd have been too dazed to use one anyway. He conducted her firmly to her stool and set her down, draping her over the side of the pallet. Malso, winded by the belly blow, straightened himself with gratifying difficulty.

'You shouldn't have thrown her so hard, Entiso. Remember her long and valuable service to the Opposition. Go deal with the guardsman now, and call me when you're done – I want to be off the quay within the next quarter hour.'

'Malso!' I don't know what my voice sounded like, but it got his startled attention and Entiso's as well. 'I'm warning you – don't you harm the boy. If you kill him, I swear you'll get no help me, or from any of us; and I also swear, by the Old Ones, that I will make you bleed for it someday—'

'Master Vero, be reasonable. He's the vicious bloody-handed lackey of an imperial despot. You'll forget all about him in a day or two. Just remember that *we* are your true friends.'

'Friends? Not likely.'

'We have ways of making friends,' he said vaguely, 'and five weeks to do it in.' Less vaguely: 'Get moving, Entiso.'

With the toe of his boot, Entiso flipped Jonno on to his back and straightened the boy's neck relative to his shoulders; at the same time, he reached for the new moon leaning against the wall. Without waking up, Jonno groaned and trembled in his sodden tunic.

Malso made an impatient noise in his throat. 'Not in here, Entiso. Messy. Take him on deck.'

'Of course, Truant. And then?'

'Dump him on the quay – but you'd better nail him down or the storm will wash him away. He's no good to us if they don't find the body.'

Entiso nodded impassively, grabbed Jonno by the ankles and dragged him to the door. 'You'll find the mallet in the bow locker,' Malso called as the door shut behind them. All that time I had been feverishly experimenting with dislocating my shoulders and seeing how much skin I could scrape off my wrists and ankles; Mallinna, looking as if she would gut-charge Malso again if she could figure out where her feet had gone, was groggily trying to get herself upright on the stool; Angel was lying back on his pillows with his eyes wet and closed.

Tigrallef was smiling at the floor.

After a minute or two, the sound I had been dreading came to our ears over the keening of the wind. A terrible sound – a sustained shriek of pain and terror, that rose higher and went on longer than I had expected or could bear. The death we were listening to was not being an easy one, nor particularly quick. Even hearing it was agony. At last, mercifully, the death-cry either faded away or mingled with the wind.

'May his bones bring forth flowers,' said Malso piously.

I loathed him too much to bother cursing him. Since there was no immediate point left in struggling, I lay still. Poor little Jonno, I thought tight-lipped, with his golden hair and his beauty, his grandda, his two loving sisters and his rather endearing ineptitude as a spy. I wondered what his poems might have been like.

The minutes passed. Malso essayed a bit of light conversation, sitting companionably on the end of Angel's pallet, but the rest of us did not respond very well.

Perhaps I should have been paying more attention to the strange state Tigrallef was in, but his symptoms had shifted so rapidly recently that it was hard for me to keep up. For twenty years, one of our fundamental rules had been: when he was able to sit still, he was fine; when he began to fidget, it was time to brush up on the Zelfic Protocols. How was I to know what to watch for when the Pain kept changing the rules? Anyway, I was distracted, raging inside over Jonno's murder, straining my ears for any echo of Entiso and his damned mallet. Every muscle in my body, moreover, was starting to complain about being pulled out of shape.

More minutes passed. Presently, it was Malso who began to fidget as he watched the door and waited vainly for Entiso's signal. The swell was on the rise, putting the deck through a complex dance of pitches, yaws and rolls – much longer, and the *Fifth* would have trouble clearing the quay, not to mention the breakwater. The wind rattled the door between its hinges and its latch.

'Perhaps Entiso can't find the nails,' I suggested.

'They were with the mallet.' Malso refused to be goaded. 'Ah, there he is!' He rose expectantly, but the thump outside was not repeated; the door shook in the wind but remained stubbornly closed.

'Messy,' said my father.

'Your pardon, Master Tilgo?'

'The blood coming under the door. Messy.'

I could not see it, myself; but Malso swore softly and squatted down by the door. After a moment he pulled off his tunic, revealing a body scabbard strapped across his hairy chest, with slots for four blades, all full, and a broad belt medallioned with throwing disks. Crouching beside the door with his back against the jamb, he reached up cautiously with one of the knives and lifted the latch. The wind caught the door and crashed it open, spraying rain inside; even protected by its mantle, the lamp's flame flickered.

'Entiso!' he shouted, 'what are you playing at?'

No answer came to him over the wind. By craning my neck I could see a watery dark stain diffusing along the drenched deck and into the cabin; the origin of it was in darkness, beyond the edge of the lamplight that fluttered across the threshold. Another swell tilted the *Fifth* to star-board – I glimpsed a round object about the size of a head rolling downslope past the door.

'Entiso, answer me!'

Reverse tilt. The head-sized object tumbled back again. This time as it passed the door it bounced with a soft thump on the outer jamb, hesitated, and – responding to a slight lifting of the bow – wobbled inside to come to rest very briefly in the middle of the room. Even Angel sat up to see it better. Then the stern lifted and the object rolled straight to Malso's feet, ricocheted gently, and continued past him out the door. Malso watched its progress, inwards and outwards, with an air of stupefied interest.

'Was that Entiso?' asked Mallinna. 'I couldn't quite see.'

'Only part of him,' my father said drowsily.

'*Hush!*' Malso was breathing hard. Keeping his body in the shelter of the jamb, he darted his arm out to grab the edge of the door and drag it shut against the wind; but in the broken second that it resisted his efforts, a thread of silver light whipped out of the darkness, curled around his hand, and was gone. With a scream, he jerked his arm back.

'Did you see something just then?' asked Mallinna.

I had seen something, all right. I even knew what it was. I was not surprised, therefore, that the hand Malso was exam-ining with such bewilderment was missing the top halves of all three middle fingers. In every other respect, I was a solid mass of astonishment.

Who was out there?

The second time, I missed it by blinking. I did hear the click as the last link made contact with the floor, though, and then of course there was Malso's roar of rage and pain. Incautious enough to expose the edge of one bare shoulder to the view of whatever was outside, he had paid with a long slice of meat from the upper arm.

I lifted my head and filled my lungs. 'Shorten by three spans,' I bellowed in Gafrin-Gammanthan. 'Korfin's Lateral Twist! Six spans up for the throat!'

Malso threw himself sideways – in time, unfortunately.

186

Like a snake's tongue, the silver thread lashed through the door, seemed to hang motionless for a broken moment, then curled back in a sinuous shimmy that sliced the air where Malso's throat had been.

Apparently, Malso was a man who knew when he was beaten. The big square port, barred and shuttered, was just above his head. With amazing quickness for such a ponderous body, he knocked the bar away with his good hand, smashed the shutters open and vaulted out, leaving a fair amount of blood in a trail behind him. The stormwind howled through the cabin and deadened all other noises, all except a muffled crash a moment later and another a few seconds after that.

'Gangplank,' Tigrallef shouted over the wind. 'He's gone now.' His chin dropped towards his chest.

'Father – who's out there? *Which one? Or all of them?*'

He shrugged, and the ropes fell away. He wandered over to close and bar the shutters, which improved the noise level in the cabin; he picked up the knife Malso had abandoned on the floor, frowned at it, looked thoughtfully at me, wandered over and hacked through the ropes that were holding me in a semicircular shape. The sudden release of tension was a new kind of torture. My joints flatly refused to straighten, my muscles shrieked at me for even trying, but I managed to catch at his arm before falling off the side of the pallet.

'*Who's out there?*'

'See for yourself, Vero. They're just coming.' He drifted over to cut Mallinna's bindings.

They?

I was on the floor trying to get my arms to work, but I had a clear view of the deck through the door. I was looking for four figures; all I saw was two – both slight, one somewhat taller than the other, the shorter one supporting the taller as they limped out of the shadows and rain into the wavering light at the threshold. I forgot about my muscles and stared as the lamplight fell on her face. Cheeks too thin, eyes too big, burden too heavy; the guardsman, just barely on his own feet, was held up largely by her too-thin arms around his middle.

Kat was home.

She let Jonno sag to the floor and wrestled the door shut behind her. Then she slid towards our father on a slick of rainwater and Malso's blood, but skidded to a halt a couple of spans short. I saw the eagerness in her face turn to horror, and the horror vanish in turn behind a mask of gravity.

'Father,' she breathed, 'what's happened to you?' He said nothing.

They regarded each other solemnly. I forgot the howling chorus from my body, grew deaf to the urgency of the storm – I was absorbed in watching an eerie convergence take place. Kat was said to favour our mother in looks, but in those few moments she might have been our father's image in a pool of still water. Then Tigrallef reached out and embraced her as sadly as if he held her lifeless corpse instead of her living body.

'Kat, Kat, I'm happy you're safe, but I wish you were anywhere but here.'

She put her arms around him, also sadly. It occurred to me as I sat on the floor, watching them while I tried to massage my knees into working order, that my little sister already knew far more than I did about what was going on in our father's head. Then she backed away, snapping the thread between them, and suddenly I found I could speak again.

'Kat – beloved little sister – happy to see you – sorry I can't get up—'

'Oh, *Vero!*'

She burst into tears and threw herself into my lap, landing with considerable force on the one leg that was responding to treatment. I didn't mind.

'How did you get here, flower? Where are the others?' Me, to Kat.

At the same time: 'Where's Mother and Shree and Chasco?

Who's she?' Kat surveyed Mallinna suspiciously and wiped her wet face with an equally wet sleeve.

At the same time: 'Was it you with that silver whip thing? What was that?' Mallinna held out a nose-rag and regarded Kat with interest and sympathy, in that order.

At the same time: 'What was the cook called?' That was a feeble voice near the door which none of us heeded because we were all too busy asking more sensible questions; too busy, indeed, to give sensible answers. I held up my hand with an audible creaking of joints.

'I've got a thousand questions for you, little Kat, and a thousand things to tell you, but now is not the time. We're not safe yet.'

'Just tell me one thing,' she said forcefully. 'Where's Mother?'

I hesitated. 'I thought you were with her and the others. Enough now, Katla. We're on our way to them, but we have to cast off now, right away, and make a run for the Pilazhet Basin while we still can.'

Kat gasped. 'In this weather? Your cargo must have shifted, Vero.'

'What cargo?' Mallinna again.

'It's a metaphor, Mallinna. Kat, I'll explain later. Take Mallinna out, get the two of you secured, show her what to do. And get ready to cast off.'

A mournful cry from the door: 'The name of the cook . . .'

'Oh, gods. I'll be out in a minute – go!'

Kat trumpeted into Mallinna's nose-rag. She rose, giving Mallinna an appraising look, and motioned for her to follow. I noticed she avoided glancing at Tigrallef, who was sitting quietly on the end of Angel's pallet with a vacant look on his face.

When they were gone, I limped over to Jonno, joints shrieking, hoisted him off the floor and walked him over to the pallet I had recently occupied. There was no longer any question of leaving him behind. I only wished, a little sourly, that he was in good enough condition to be put to work in the rigging. As he was just barely conscious, I tied him down

189

on the pallet, less to keep him out of mischief than to make sure his neck did not get broken in the next few storm-tossed hours. He was still mumbling something about the cook. I covered him with a blanket.

It was clear Tigrallef was not fit to work either, so I left him and Angel in the cabin to keep an eye on each other. The best luck we had was that Malso and Entiso had already done all the hard labour of storm-rigging the *Fifth*. By the time I left the devastated cabin for the windy spray-ridden chaos on deck, Kat had helped Mallinna harness herself to one of the safety lines and was giving her a quick lesson in which sheet was which.

One last job before casting off: Entiso. The Truant Malso had evidently departed the *Fifth* via the gangplank, and might even have survived his departure; but the significantly shortened (and, I discovered, one-armed) body of his henchman had not been obliging enough to walk off, and was very much in the way. I dragged most of him to the port side and heaved him into the water. When that was done I spent a few moments searching for the head and the missing arm; stumbled over the latter and slung it overboard; located the head and had a rapid but thoughtful survey of the mincemeat Kat's chain had made of the neck. Then I chucked it overboard as well.

I do not know whether we left harbour by Tigrallef's deadline; if the houring bells were rung in Beriss at midnight, we could not hear them over the fury of the wind. All I can say is, the next hour or so was much too exciting, to the point where I nearly decided to abandon the attempt and take our chances on losing the *Cirallef* another day. In theory, we could still cover up the evening's events. It was improbable that Jonno had heard much, or would remember anything, of what took place in the cabin; perhaps we could concoct some story to explain Kat's advent and the fishermen's disappearance, a credible lie that would not spark the suspicions of the *Cirallef*'s captain. Malso, even then perhaps bumping about at the bottom of the harbour with his colleague Entiso, was unlikely to return as a threat.

But I still wanted to put Beriss and the *Cirallef* far behind us, bad weather, high seas and all. What swayed me in the end was a vague instinct that the Pain was becoming more dangerous than any trivial stormbowl. We could run before the wind once we were safely past the breakwater – I'd been through enough stormbowls in the Ronchar Sea and even the Deeps to have a fine feel for these things – but I had no such confidence about Tigrallef's state of mind. The sooner we got him away from the Primate's forces, from populous places and unpredictable human factors, the better would be his chances of riding out the Pain.

Casting off and manoeuvring away from the quay were not impossibly daunting, since the swell was still moderate inside the breakwater; the nightmare consisted of picking a perilous way through the other boats pitching at anchor in the harbour, with particular reference to the looming obstacle of the *Scion Cirallef*. Moreover, the storm's outermost rainbands were already relieving themselves over Beriss, such that we seemed to be breathing just as much water as air, and the wind was a crazed howl. I was strapped to the wheel, shouting orders to Kat – Mallinna, for all her inexperience and the sedentary life she'd led in the archives, was quick to learn and strong as a man. Between the shortened foresail and the demi-lateens, we tacked downharbour through the rolling targets of the moored ships without grazing more than two, at the cost of some minor damage to the Primate's paint job. As far as I know, we did not sink anything.

At last we were far enough upwind of the gap in the breakwater that we could go about and make a run for it. The prospect was not hopeless, but it was not very cheering, either. The great lanterns that normally flared on both sides of the opening were not showing, but the far edge of the gap was obvious as a churn of white water where the storm-waves were throwing themselves against the masonry and its foundation fringe of boulders. I selected a few sea gods to pray to on a more or less random basis and assessed my angle of approach. It was a tighter angle than I liked – an unintended jibe could lose us the masts and perhaps kill us, while any slackening of wind or loss of way could end with us shattered between the masonry and the breakers. The track leading to it, however, seemed clear. Blessing the double rudders, I aimed for a point well to the left of where we needed to go and shouted to Kat to watch the foresail.

She was at that moment watching something else, or so it seemed, and Mallinna was doing the same. I could see them braced together by the foremast, staring up into the open sluice gates of the sky. I screamed at Kat again as the foresail shivered, and she heard me and caught the sheets and hung on with all her weight; but Mallinna stayed where she was, staring first up at the sky, then to starboard and back again. Odd, I thought, there was nothing to see, even the few lights still showing along the Beriss waterfront had vanished behind scudding blots of rain. I risked an upward glance of my own, glimpsed lights slipping past us at some height on the right, went back to concentrating on the gap in the breakwater while I puzzled over it; then had a small seizure without losing hold of the wheel. I had completely forgotten the *Cirallef* was there.

The windcatcher was a great black wall looming above us to starboard, sliding sternwards; she was perhaps twelve or fourteen feet away at the waterline, but our mast-tops must have been grazing the rail of her overhanging fighting deck. Too close, inescapably convergent. I could see her prow now by the waves boiling around it, and heeled the wheel over. The *Fifth* shuddered without responding; if anything, her nose moved a point or two closer to disaster, only moments away. Shouting to the women, I braced myself.

A black wave rose between us and the windcatcher.

We were under water – confusing, because as far as I knew the crash hadn't happened yet. Then I was in air again, water was pouring off the decks on all sides, the *Fifth* was wallowing and recovering and miraculously still on course, and I looked around just in time to see our stern in the process of shaving past the windcatcher's high prow, and the lights of Beriss reappearing from their eclipse. A dripping Kat was already hauling herself back to the foresail sheets along her safety line. Mallinna was unpeeling herself from the foremast. Whatever had just happened, we had come through it in the original number of pieces.

All that was ahead of us now was the frothing mouth of the harbour, armed with its deadly stone teeth. Our angle was almost right – a little more to port to compensate for the wind, a signal to Kat about the demi-lateens – and suddenly we were in the delta of violent turbulence that marked the meeting of harbour and channel, and the sea was doing its best to suck the stern towards the lethal ferment at the rocks even as it shoved the bow away with the backwash.

I held my breath, leaned on the wheel and prayed. The *Fifth* lurched and straightened, the sails rippled but did not split, and a broken second later they steadied; through the wheel, I felt the tension on the rudders as the tide caught the keel. Then the froth was receding to starboard, and the few lights of Beriss vanished – Kat shot past me to the bow, trailing her safety line, to release the drag anchor. I took a breath and gave my aching shoulders a holiday for a few seconds. We still had to pass through the perils of the channel of Canton Ber, but the worst dangers from the sea and the stormbowl were already behind us. Now I could go back to worrying about Tigrallef and the Pain.

11

Morning in the Pilazhet Basin. The wind, still strong but well below storm force, had swung around through the night until by dawn it was coming fitfully out of the west. The sea was a rough blue-black, stitched all over with whitecaps, and the sky was pallid with a veil of thin high mist that was mainly visible by the halo it made around the sun. I had let myself fall asleep sometime after dawn, still strapped to the wheel, with Katla and Mallinna slumped in a single heap on the deck at my feet and the drag anchor keeping us to the wind. When I awoke not long before midday, I was on the deck with a fleece over me, Kat was at the wheel and Mallinna was somewhere else entirely. Aching in every muscle, I sat up.

'Mallinna's just gone down to get the fire going so she can heat up some gruel,' Kat said. 'She'll bring us our breakfast when it's ready. We had a long talk, Vero. I like her. She told me about the Mosslines and all, and about Angel and the archives.'

'What have you told her?'

'Nearly everything.'

'Then you can start all over again and tell me. You have a lot of explaining to do, little Kat.' Actually, some of it was already clear to me. All through the long tempest-driven night, as I wrestled with the wheel, my mind was busy putting pieces together: Jonno's vision of the Lady, the rumours of haunting in the shipyard, the supposed theft of Kat's blades and clothing, the overnight disappearance of leftovers from the *Fifth*'s galley now and then, which I had attributed to Malso or Entiso getting hungry in the middle of the night watch. 'You were on the *Fifth* all along, weren't you, Katla? Those bastards never even carried you ashore. You got yourself to the hidden holds when the Flamens' Corps attacked—'

'Wrong,' she replied, a little sullenly. 'I did go ashore, that first night in Gil – by myself. I didn't think I'd ever come back, either.'

'What do you mean?'

'I ran away, Vero.'

'Ran away?' I started to laugh, but caught myself when I saw her face darken, and bit my lip. 'How could you run away, Katla? How would you have survived on your own? Where would you have run to?'

'*Away*,' she said coldly, 'just *away*. I didn't care where.'

'But why?'

She glared at the distant line of breakers that marked the skerries, far ahead on the eastern horizon. 'Because nobody understood.'

Idiot that I can be at times, I did laugh at that. 'Oh Katla, I remember feeling misunderstood at your age. You were too young to notice, probably, but there was one time in Gafrin-Gammanthan when I was about fifteen—'

'I kept trying to warn you, all of you, about what was happening to him, but nobody listened to me,' she broke in impatiently, 'and it's probably too late now. I saw what he was like last night, he's worse than ever.'

There was no doubt whom she was talking about, and I could not argue with her there. 'I know, I know. You don't know the half of it, Katla. To be honest, the last few weeks have been difficult altogether.'

'More than difficult, by the looks of him! I had to get away, Vero. I'd had enough of the Pain, couldn't bear it any more; watching Father get stranger by the day, watching the rest of you fool yourselves that you could help him. I didn't care where I jumped ship, and I didn't care what the rest of you thought, so long as I didn't have to be around the Pain any more. I didn't want to become like *you*.'

'Thanks.'

'You still don't understand.' Frowning, she gave the wheel a corrective nudge and looked up appraisingly as the foresail bellied.

'I understand better than you might think,' I said, pulling the fleece up around my shoulders. 'Never mind, flower, just tell me what happened when you ran away.'

Kat leant back in the wheelman's chair with her hands lightly on the wheel, instinctively tracking the feel of the rudders. 'It was at the end of your watch, when you were waking Chasco to take over. Maybe you need to sharpen up a little, you and Chasco. I put a line over the stern while you were distracted, and swam along under the lip of the moorage until I could climb out without the troopers seeing me. Then I took that walkway that runs along the top of the breakwater

– there were a couple of patrols to avoid but they were no problem, they just slowed me down a little.'

'Of course,' I said. No problem for a child of our mother's anyway. For long stretches of our wanderings, four bored grown-ups had nothing much to do with their time except teach us things. Calla made sure we grew up with all the wisdom she had acquired in her own childhood in the Web: dirty fighting and inaudible sneaking, to name but two. Chasco made us into sailors. Shree passed on many useful soldiering skills from our Sherkin heritage, notably dozens of techniques of being deadly, maintaining our weapons and mending our own clothes. Tigrallef's curriculum was too varied and comprehensive to list. Watching Kat's ease behind the wheel, remembering how decisively she had dealt with Entiso and Malso, I began to realize that our little flower would probably have survived very well on her own.

'What happened in Gil City? Why did you come back?'

She sighed, looking years older than fifteen, in fact looking very like our mother on one of Tigrallef's bad days. 'Because in the end I couldn't leave. It was too late for me, I'm already like the rest of you. We'll need to tack soon, Vero.'

'There's plenty of time for that. Don't change the subject, tell me what happened ashore.'

'Nothing much, I didn't get far and I was only there about half an hour. It took me a long time to work my way along the breakwater, and I reckon it was about an hour and a half before dawn when I finally got to the waterfront. The walkway comes ashore on to a kind of landing plaza, with a lot of jetties coming off it – did you see that part of the waterfront?'

'Oh, yes,' I said.

'Well, there was a thick fog in the inner harbour that morning, and it was still dark, and I got turned around a little on the landing stage – I couldn't even tell which way the water was, because the fog spread the sound of the ripples out and muddled the direction. I cast around for a while, and at last I saw a huge dark shape through the fog that I thought must be a house, or at any rate something larger than a guardpost and on dry land, so I went towards it; but when I got close enough, I saw it wasn't a house at all.'

I nodded sagely. 'Was it by any chance a very large bust of our da?'

'You saw it too?' She frowned. 'Well, it was our da and it wasn't, if you know what I mean. I had to work the face out feature by feature because of the fog, and I was just deciding it *wasn't* Father when a watchman came up and grabbed me and demanded to know what I was doing there, and why wasn't I showing proper respect for the Divine Scion Tigrallef, and where was my identity seal, and maybe if I was very, very nice to him he'd let me go, and so on.'

'What did you do?'

'Sherkin half-trip and a toss.'

'Break any legs this time?'

She shrugged. 'I don't think so. They weren't bent oddly when I left him.'

'Good girl.' I reached up and patted her knee approvingly. 'You know what Shree always says — fit the force to the occasion. And then?'

'I started back for the *Fifth*. That bust of our da changed everything — I thought there was still a chance we could get the *Fifth* out of the harbour. But there were already hordes of troopers at the moorage when I got back, and I was just in time to see you and Father carried off — that was a great fight you put up, Vero.'

'Thank you.' As I recalled, it had been the thought of her threatened innocence and presumed helplessness that lent me strength and fury, but I was not about to tell her that. 'Where were you?'

'There was a good covert on the roof of the customs shed. Mother and the rest were dragged away a little while later, and then the ship was sealed off and a guard was posted. I had to wait all day until after dark to get back on board,' she added indignantly, 'and then I just had time to gather up some supplies and some things from my cabin before I heard feet thumping on deck again, and I locked myself into the hidden holds. And that's it.'

'Not quite,' I said. 'We've been on board for over a week now – why didn't you let us know you were here? I've been worried about you. I was afraid you were dead.'

Her chin rose defensively. 'I didn't know you were on board, did I? All I knew was the *Fifth* spent weeks in a shipyard with workmen swarming over her night and day; and then she was sailed somewhere else, and I came out to see where, and found a trooper in uniform had set up housekeeping in the entry hold and was fast asleep in front of the hatch. How was I to know he was a friend of yours? Anyway, I don't understand why Father didn't know I was there. He can hear a dust mote land on a pillow.'

Revelation hit me very hard on the head. I gasped and tried to cover it with a cough. 'Only if the old sow lets him,' I said quickly. A thin excuse – of course Tigrallef had known all along she was aboard. He had known from the time we were coming along the quay with Mallinna, back in Gil harbour, when his mood had suddenly plummeted; and for reasons known only to himself and the Pain, he had not told the rest of us. I shelved this to beat him over the head with later, and tried to move on. 'So this whole time,' I said, 'you've been hiding in the holds, afraid to come out except to raid the galley.'

She gave me a hard look. '*The fool jabs at the armour, not waiting to glimpse the throat,*' she quoted in Sheranik.

'Meaning?'

'Meaning I was not afraid, Vero, I was just watching for the right moment to take the ship back. Pretty stupid to try anything while that big black warship was sitting on the *Fifth*'s tail, don't you think? Meantime I had plenty to do, assembling the beartraps and working out where I'd put them, and clearing the main weapons locker, and making up some of that Amballan sleeping-poison to put in the soup, and—'

'Never mind, I see. And last night you got a *glimpse of throat*?'

'Not really. I was planning to wait until the *Fifth* was alone on the open sea. But last night, while you were ashore, those

198

two pirates were in the entry hold going through the guards-man's things, and I heard them talking about you and Father. That's the first sign I had that you were aboard.'

'A good thing you didn't reveal yourself to them.'

'I'm not stupid, Vero. You should have heard what they were saying. They had plans for you and Father, you know, something about the Day of the Scion. And they were weighing the idea of killing the guardsman . . .' She trailed off and indulged in one of her rare blushes.

I carefully did not smile. 'I suppose you didn't like that idea.'

'I had no feelings either way,' she said with dignity. 'He was wearing an enemy's uniform, but I could see those two pirates were enemies as well, which maybe meant he was a friend, unless – anyway, I decided to watch and see. I was hiding on deck when they hustled Father and Mallinna into the cabin, and also when you came aboard with the guards-man, and I saw what they did to the two of you then; when the big fat one came out to kill the guardsman, I was ready with the chain. That's all – now you know everything.'

'You made quite a mess of the big fat one,' I said, not meaning to sound chiding, but she took it the wrong way.

'I wasn't aiming for the neck, Vero! He stooped down just as I let fly, with one of his arms raised above his head, and that's how the chain caught him. And then he tried to free himself, and the chain got tangled and wouldn't release, and—'

Abruptly, Kat let go of the wheel, slid off the wheelman's chair and bent herself double. I took over the wheel until she finished retching, then lifted her up on to my knee and held her while she shivered with reaction. The chain was designed to be swift and clean; botched, it could be horrible. I was glad I had not been obliged to watch Entiso struggle himself to death. Keeping one hand on the wheel, I patted her shoulder with the other, and after a while she stopped shaking.

'His name is Jonno,' I said.

'Who?' She wiped her face with her sleeve.

'The guardsman whose life you saved. The one with the eyelashes. His name is Jonno.'

'Why should I care what his name is?'

'No special reason.' I made the mistake of grinning over the top of her head. She lifted her wet face in time to catch me.

'Mallinna's very pretty,' she said pointedly.

'Is she?' I patted Katla on the shoulder again and closed the subject by pushing her gently off my lap. Conveniently, there was work to do. We were close enough to the skerries to turn north and make for the least perilous crossing marked on the chart, and it was time to haul in the drag anchor and start tacking.

This was not a normal nor even a very safe place to cross the skerries marking the eastern edge of the Pilazhet Basin, which suited me very well. The skerries were the salient points of a great granite ridge arching from Canton Ber on the south to Canton Pilazh on the north, and our lovely new sea charts marked them as exceptionally dangerous to shipping of any significant size.

The *Fifth* was small and agile, however, and built to slip through passages too shallow or turbulent for ordinary wind-catchers to challenge. We were already well off the main shipping routes, which also suited me, and I had seen no other ships apart from the mast-lights of a large windcatcher to the north of us, some time before dawn; she was probably riding out the storm in the safe waters of the Basin, just as we were, and she was out of sight by the time the sun came up. Therefore I was a little surprised to see a wind-galley of middling length, at least fifteen oars to the side, standing precariously off the high-humped skerry we were passing, about two miles south of the gap I was tacking for.

Kat was managing aloft while I worked the wheel and the buntlines in turn. I shouted to catch her attention and jabbed my arm towards the wind-galley. She stood up on the cross-trees to get a better view.

'They're looking over at us,' she screamed down to me.

'Now they're waving at us – there's a banner going up – two banners – red on black – they don't look like pirates to me.'

Absorbed in watching her, the wind-galley, the buntlines, the wind and the wheel all at once, I did not hear the footstep behind me until a beaker of gruel was thrust into my hand. Without pausing to wonder, I took a grateful swallow.

Mallinna, beside me, suddenly clutched my shoulder. She was staring wide-eyed at the wind-galley. 'Vero, those banners. They're red and black.'

'That's what Kat said.'

'*Hoy Vero!*' Kat shouted down from her vantage point high in the rigging. 'They're putting the sea ladders over the side now. A bunch of them are lining up on deck. It looks like a guard of honour or something.'

'They're expecting us,' Mallinna said suddenly.

'How could they be expecting us? We didn't know ourselves that we'd be here.'

'Vero, red and black are the Opposition's colours when they care to use them. That's the Truant's banner. That ship is here to meet Malso – I'll wager you anything you like that it's so.'

I had a sudden inappropriate thought about possible wagers with Mallinna, and cursed the distraction. It was not the time to think about such things. We were already about even with the wind-galley, close enough so we could see the ovals of faces turned expectantly towards us, the double row of figures forming an aisle along the deck. Somebody in the bow waved his arms over his head. The sound of massed cheering came faintly across the water.

Mallinna was frowning, chasing her idea. 'Didn't Malso say something about coming to the Pilazhet Basin?'

'Of course he did. You could hardly sail anywhere else in the teeth of that stormbowl.'

'There was more to it than that, Vero, I'm sure there was. He had plans for you and Lord Tigrallef, that's what your sister overheard. If you were Malso, sailing out of Canton Ber and wanting a lonely place to rendezvous with a ship-full of confederates, this part of the Pilazhet Basin would be the logical choice, even without the stormbowl. I think that galley's been waiting here for some time to meet Malso – and you and Lord Tigrallef.'

She was making sense. 'If you're right,' I said thoughtfully, 'they'll be displeased to find nothing of Malso on board but his fingertips and a slice of his arm.'

'I tidied up, Vero. But – can we go any faster?'

I was already trying to work that out. 'Not safely. But they'll be expecting us to come to them; we can hope it takes them a while to realize we aren't going about, and a while longer to decide what to do about it. *Kat! Keep an eye on them!*'

We were past them a few moments later. They were still watching us uncertainly, but then a panic of activity broke out on deck; almost at once, the sea-ladders were hauled up. Kat shouted down: '*Hoy Vero!* They're going to the oars!' Someone on the wind-galley had faster reflexes than was good for us. I shut my eyes to visualize the charts . . .

'When you have a moment,' Mallinna said, 'Jonno wants to see you urgently.'

'Oh, Raksh! I suppose he wants to ask me the bleeding name of the poxy cook again. I don't have time right now.' The channel where I was intending to cross the skerries was almost two miles to the north – the wind-galley might not catch us up in that distance, but it would be able to follow us through into the Sherkin Sea. On the other hand . . .

'No, that's all right now, Lord Tigrallef has already told him the cook's name. Jonno wants to see you about something else, he says, something extremely important.'

. . . there was an ugly little fang of rock about twice the size of the *Fifth* just north of the humpback where the Opposition's ship was anchored, separated from its brother skerries by narrow channels of white water. It was risky, but I was pretty sure we could make it through; the captain of the wind-galley would be a tupping fool if he tried to follow. And by the time he could beat north to the safer passage, we would be long gone into the wastes of the Sherkin Sea.

'Vero? What shall I tell him?'

'Who?'

'Jonno. He's very anxious . . .'

'So am I.' I waved Kat down from the rigging; said, 'Kat will show you what to do,' to Mallinna; gulped my gruel and dropped the beaker on the deck. By then it was time to turn with the wind, which put us on a course that would cross the wind-galley's bow at dangerously close quarters – and when we were committed to that course, and the cries of the oarsmen on the wind-galley were audible and approaching even faster than I had feared, and I was in a position to see that the channel was narrower, shallower and more ragingly vicious than I had hoped, one thought came to lodge itself unshakably inside my head: *What did she mean, Tigrallef told Jonno the cook's name?*

Of course we got through, though it was a near thing. How could I have faced Chasco if I let anything happen to his beloved *Fifth*? The last I saw of the wind-galley, she was making valiant efforts to row, sail and warp herself out of trouble on the Basin-side of the passage, and seemed to be succeeding; she was out of sight behind the skerries before I could see whether she turned north to find another passage or sodded off altogether, and I really did not care which.

The sea on the other side of the skerries was moving in a classic pattern of smooth swells, high in the crest and low in the trough, but spaced so considerately that the ship skimmed up and down them like a seabird on an air current. According to the charts, this was the broad Gulf of Krakash, which once lay west of the continent of Sher; now it was effectively the western portion of the Sherkin Sea, the selvedge of the emptiest body of water in the known world. Nothing much lay between us and the Mosslines now except a great expanse of ocean and up to a quarter of the Gillish navy.

When we were well away from the skerries and settled comfortably on a northeastern course, I turned the wheel over to Kat and beckoned to Mallinna. Outside the door of the main cabin, I stopped and faced her. 'What did you mean when you said Tigrallef knew the cook's name?'

'Just that. Poor Jonno kept on about it until Lord Tigrallef finally told him.'

'But how, by the Eight Rages, did Tig know? What cook? We've never even had a cook. How could he know the name of a cook who doesn't exist?'

'I have no theory to offer, Vero. Why don't you ask him?'

'I'm just about to.' I stopped with my hand on the door. 'One more thing – did you get around to telling Jonno he's a prisoner?'

'I thought we should wait until he feels better.'

'Oh, *Raksh*.' I pushed the door open firmly, grimacing at the air that wafted out. Poor old Angel, wheezing in his sleep on his pallet, had been seasick again, whereas Jonno was paying the price for too much bad Berissan rotbelly brew – was it really only the night before? He lay on the pallet where I had placed him, wan and shadowy eyed and more beautiful than ever except for the crust of sick around his mouth. Tigrallef was in the shadows of the far corner, in a chair; it took me a few seconds to realize he was trussed to it with many rounds of rope and several interesting knots.

Leaning my back against the door, I heaved a sigh. 'Who tied him up, Mallinna? It wasn't Jonno, was it?'

'Don't laugh, but I think Lord Tigrallef tied himself up.'

I sighed again. 'That's all right then. How are you, Tig?'

He seemed to be dozing on the chair, but I could see a glitter under his half-closed eyelids. He raised his head when I knelt down beside him. 'We have been better,' he said. His head drooped again.

Wearily, I turned my attention to Jonno, who was awake and making a brave effort to focus on me, though he was distinctly wall-eyed. He sat up and fell back again, clutching his belly. He said faintly, 'About last night – I'm sorry about the trouble I gave you, Memorian. I've never done anything like that before. I feel so foolish.'

'I should think you do. Is that all? You wanted to apologize? Is that the terribly important matter you wanted to see me about?'

'No . . .' He interrupted himself with a groan.

'Well, then?' I said impatiently. 'What is it?'

'In my quarters – there's a wooden chest with my glyph burned on the lid . . .'

'What about it?'

'Can you bring it to me?'

I had not been blessed with much sleep-time last night. 'You want me to fetch your tupping box for you? Well, guardsman, I can see you need to change your tunic, but I'm not your valet. If you want fresh clothes, you can trot down and get them yourself.'

'It's not about the clothes,' Jonno moaned. 'A compartment in the lid – there's a letter . . .'

'I'm sure it can wait.'

He lifted his head feebly in protest; the effort turned him green. 'But the letter's from Grandda – I mean the First Flamen – it's a letter from the Revered First Flamen . . . it's for *him* . . .' He waved his hand weakly in Tigrallef's direction.

Three minutes later I was back with the box. Jonno had used that time profitably to throw up into the slop bucket Mallinna had put by his pallet, and looked much better. Angel having awakened, Mallinna had propped him up with cushions and was holding a beaker of gruel to his lips. Tigrallef raised his head again as I came in the door.

'It's in the lid,' said Jonno in a less miserable voice, 'there's a spring in the top left corner that you have to press – that's it – and then you just slide the inlay back – that's right.'

It was a scroll of several papers tied with green ribbon; I prised it out of the compartment and held it out to Tigrallef. His face did not change, and he kept his eyes cast down.

'You read it, Vero. Read it out loud. No secrets here, you old sow – I don't mean you, Vero.' His voice worried me – too much echo. Watching him anxiously out of the corner of my eye, I worked the ribbon off, flattened the scroll and scanned the first few lines of quite a lengthy message on the first sheet. The salutation nearly knocked me off my chair.

'You've gained a few titles, Da,' I said, 'including one of mine.'

'Just read it, please,' said my father; so I read it.

Under the seal of Kesi, First Flamen in Gil.

Lord Tigrallef of Gil, Scion of the Line of Oballef, Son of Cirallef, Grandson of Arrislef, Prince Royal of the Gillish Empire, King Consort of the Court of Miishel, Patron of Malvi, Exalted Patron of Plav, High Peer of Sathelforn, Lord Kalkissann of the Daughters of Fire in Vass, Blessed Heritor of the Old Ones, Singular Touchstone of Prophecy, Conqueror of Iklankish, Dread Scourge of Sher, Divine Ark and Sceptre of the Lady in Gil: Greetings.

Forgive me, Lord Scion. I knew you almost at once, from the moment when we were taking you to Mycri and you turned off into the passage that leads to the archives. Were you giving me a sign? I think you were. Then I saw the others from your ship and recognized the Sherkin Lord Shree and Chasco of the Clanseri, missing these many years, and my best hopes and prayers for your return were confirmed.

It does not matter how I discovered you had taken refuge with the First Memorian; but I can assure you that I have told no one, not even my grandson Jonno of the Flamens' Corps, in whose hands I shall place this message. Since you have chosen for the moment to veil your powers and manifest yourself only in your physical body, I shall not presume to tear the veil away.

I have, however, presumed to do you some small services in token of my worship and respect, the simplest of which was yielding up your ship to you. As for Lord Shree, Chasco Clanseri and the woman, I had no choice but to send them hastily away from the Gilgard for their own safety, but I arranged that they should be well fed and gently treated on their journey, and that your woman's treasures be restored to her. You need fear nothing on their behalf. When the *Dowager Dazeene* reaches Deppowe, they will be taken to the beacon-house at Faddelin to await your coming. Attached to this letter are the documents for their release, issued under my authority. Jonno will know how to present them.

I have failed you in three respects, Lord Scion. I am unable to tell you where your esteemed mother and revered brother are now lodged, only that they will be brought to the Gilgard for the rites of the Day of the Scion. The young girl Katla (mentioned in the report from the customs scribes) is also missing, though Gil has been scoured for her. I know only that she was never taken prisoner by the Flamens' Corps, and that the Primate was most severely displeased thereat. I shall continue my efforts to trace her, and if she should fall into the Primate's hands, be assured that I shall do my best to protect her.

Lastly, I was unable to give the Primate a good reason not to send the windcatcher *Scion Cirallef* with you, and I can only pray that you will not be inconvenienced by it. I have faith that, in your merciful divinity, you will find some bloodless way to leave it far behind you.

I beg you two favours in return, Lord Scion, one small and one great. First: I commend to you my beloved grandson Jonno, a pious and clean-hearted youth of temperate habits who will serve you well if you accept him into your retinue. Please take note that he is my daughter's son by the late Bresno of the Clanseri, brother to Chasco.

Second: I beg you to forgive the blasphemies of my brother Mycri, whose worst sins have always been committed with the best intentions. When the great day comes that you return to Gil in glory, infused with the ineffable powers of the Lady, I pray you will show him the mercy that he himself often left by the wayside in his zeal for the larger good.

Permit me to say this, Lord Scion: you were an interesting child, and I always liked you. Do you remember the time in Exile when I stopped Nanzid Cook from dealing you an undeserved beating? It was perhaps unwise of you to store your grub collection in his herb-pantry, but I could see you were innocent of both mischief and malice. I think you will indeed remember that event, which is why I chose Nanzid's name to be the password to this letter – a precaution, in case you really are a coppermonger's son from Calloon, and I am a fanciful old fool after all.

My regardful greetings to the First Memorian, Mistress Mallinna and your companion Vero; and, in due course, to Lord Shree and my kinsman-by-marriage, Chasco Clanseri. May your Will be done.

I finished reading in a rush and burst out, 'By gods, what astonishing news! Did you hear that, Tig? We won't have to fight our way through the Mosslines to find Mother and the rest, we can pick them up as easy as windfalls under a tree! Blessings on the First Flamen, they're safe!'

'Strange sort of safety,' Tigrallef mumbled.

'What do you mean?' A damp weight descended on my elation.

He did not answer. Jonno meantime was struggling off his pallet with fear and wonder on his face. Once off, he successfully staggered across to Tig's chair and dropped flat on the floor at his feet – by intention, it seemed, not hungover dizziness. With his face pressed to the deck, he said, 'Lord Scion, Ark and Sceptre of the Lady in Gil, forgive me for not worshipping you from the first, but your glory was hidden from me. I beg to renew my sacred oath as a guardsman of the Flamens' Corps, to be the humblest and least worthy of your servitors.'

Tig looked at him impassively. 'I don't mind.'

'Get up, Jonno, by the Eight Rages of Raksh,' I snapped. 'It isn't like that at all. This Ark and Sceptre business is just something the Primate made up.'

The boy lifted his head off the deckboards. 'Is my grandda's letter mistaken, then? Isn't this the real Scion Tigrallef?'

'Yes, it's the real Tig, all right, but––'

He sat up, anxious questions written all over his face. 'And did he break the divine talisman that was known as the Lady in Gil, as the Flamens taught us?'

'Yes, yes, damn it, that's true as well.'

'And did the power of the Lady in Gil enter his body at the moment the glass was broken?'

'Unfortunately,' I admitted.

'Then it's all true.'

'*No!* Well – in a way. But not the way you think.'

Jonno stared at me with pitying incomprehension. Poor old infidel, he was almost certainly saying to himself; won't accept the truth when it's staring him right in the face. He shook his head sadly and prostrated himself again before Tigrallef.

'Don't you dare start enjoying this kind of thing,' I told Tig severely. I picked Jonno off the floor by the scruff of his soiled black tunic and marched him over to Angel and Mallinna. 'Give the young fool a history lesson,' I said. Then I went outside to tell Kat the good news.

12

'This is wonderful. I never want to go home.' Mallinna was supposedly going through the reports that dealt with the old Fathidiic port of Faddelin, where we would be landing; but she had chosen to do it while lounging on her belly in the shade of the sternsail, about five spans from where I was sitting in the wheelman's chair. Naturally I had been watching her out of the corner of my eyes the whole time, and for the last quarter-hour I had not once seen her glance at the thick volume of bound reports lying open in front of her. She yawned and stretched in a way that did amazing tricks with the lines of her body. I turned my eyes quickly to the horizon.

Everybody was on deck that tranquil afternoon, even Angel, who had found his sea-belly at last. I honestly feared he would die of seasickness during the stormbowl or on the long rolling billows of the wake-sea that followed the storm

– instead, the sea cured him. On this day, the sixth since crossing the skerries, he had colour in his cheeks, strength in his legs, and an enormous appetite. I could see him in the bow with Jonno and Kat, to both of whom he had taken a great fancy. This was the wonder: Angel was talking to them with animation, and they were listening spellbound.

'He always liked children and young people,' said my father from his chair beside me. 'I think it's because he didn't know any when he was a child himself.'

'He's having a slice of his childhood now, I'd say,' Mallinna put in.

'How did you know I was thinking about Angel?' I demanded of both of them. 'Is my mind so easy to read?'

'Your face is, Vero. I try to leave your mind alone. Mallinna, dear girl, one of the knots behind my chair is uncomfortably loose. Would you be kind enough . . . ?'

Mallinna climbed to her feet and tested the knots. There was a separate rope for each of his limbs, plus the leather straps that were built in to the chair and some iron fetters he had recently added; one of the spare hawsers was coiled round and round his torso, binding him to the chairback. None of which had stopped him from appearing promptly for lunch when I shouted from the galley earlier, though he had been identically trussed and alone on the afterdeck at the time. I really did not know why he bothered with the ropes, unless they made him feel more secure.

Those were the golden days of our journey, that week and a bit of crossing the northern quarters of the Sherkin Sea. The storm wake had been succeeded by fair winds, easy seas and a perfect cotton-wool sky. The urgency, the corrosive anxiety about our people's supposed sufferings on the Mosslines, the dread of their deaths before we could reach them, had all been exorcised by the First Flamen's letter. Until that weight was lifted, I hardly realized how heavy it had been.

Of course we were not entirely without worries, even apart from the Pain: there was still the *Scion Cirallef*. If we had known about Kesi's letter sooner, we might have handled the parting differently. All the advantages, however, were on our side. The *Cirallef* would probably waste a day or two making sure the *Fifth* had not sunk in Beriss harbour during the storm, and another day waiting for the wake-sea to subside – those fighting windcatchers were top-heavy and not very stable. Moreover, if her captain sent to the Gilgard for instructions, he could well wait ten days for a reply; if he set off to search on his own initiative, he would have no idea we were heading for the Mosslines. Even in the worst case – the *Cirallef* making straight for Deppowe in our very track – we could be in and out of Faddelin before the lumbering windcatcher was halfway across the Sherkin Sea.

Meantime, our blessed Kat was safe, Jonno had recovered from acute alcohol poisoning and an excess of piety, and Tig was giving me less cause for worry as the Pain appeared to recede. Even though the sunken wastes of Sher lay far below our hull for much of that week, a circumstance I thought might distress him, we were treated to no great absurdities except for the business with the ropes, no auras, no eerie slumped silences and no undue echoes when he spoke. I foolishly put this down to his anticipation of being reunited with my mother, who had always been the anchor of his sanity. As I have said, the warning signs had changed so completely that I cannot blame myself for missing them; but even I could not miss seeing how assiduously he and poor little Katla avoided each other.

That perfect and rather drowsy afternoon, however, all our problems seemed far away as I watched Mallinna tighten Tig's knots and then stretch herself out again on the deck beside the wheelman's chair. We were silent for a while, though I could hear peal after peal of laughter in the bow. I tried to remember when I had last heard Kat laughing so freely.

'So what have you found out about Faddelin?' I asked idly after a few minutes, mainly to keep from dozing off.

Mallinna yawned behind her hand and flipped a few pages. 'It's on the extreme eastern edge of the Mosslines – the slag

211

is everywhere across Old Fathan, of course, but the moss only grows between Faddelin on the east and Mashakel on the west, which is not far from the border with Miishel. Deppowe is about midway between. No one knows why the moss won't grow elsewhere in Fathan – that's one of the mysteries I'd like to investigate.' She sat up, looking more lively. 'I think it might be something to do with the prevailing winds, or the ambient humidity on the south coast of the continent, or the differing composition of the slag from place to place—'

'What about Faddelin?'

'Sorry, yes, Faddelin, let me see.' She flipped another page. 'Nowadays it's just an outpost – supplies the workcrews in the far eastern sector of the Mosslines, sends galley-loads of the moss to Deppowe for shipment to Gil. The quay was rebuilt five years ago, but it's not large enough to take the big windcatchers. It should be fine for the *Fifth*, though.' Another page. 'Now that's interesting – pity it's so sketchy – an account of the inshore ruins.'

Tigrallef twitched; I caught it, Mallinna didn't. From the bow, I heard more laughter.

Mallinna perused the page thoughtfully before speaking again. 'I remember something about this now. Strong indications that Faddelin was on a river delta before the Fathidiic collapse, the river having cut a pass through the mountain range about two days' march inland. No water runs there now, but the old river bed can be traced pretty well.'

'Faddelin was the port for Cansh Fathan,' Tigrallef said suddenly.

'Was it?' Mallinna scanned the rest of the page, turned over to look at the next. 'There's nothing about that in here. What's your source, Lord Tigrallef?'

I gave Mallinna a warning look. Tigrallef had gone rigid inside his cocoon of ropes and fetters; a fine film of sweat was breaking out on his forehead. I looked for any tremor in his hands, but they were stiff claws on the armrests of his chair. I considered that just as ominous.

'Father, would it help if I—'

'No thank you, Verolef.'

Mallinna noticed nothing. Frowning, she looked up from the open volume of reports. 'Nothing here about Cansh Fathan, Lord Tigrallef – mind you, the Primate's surveyors didn't go into the mountains where the capital appears on the ancient maps. They were only interested in the moss.'

'None of them went inland?'

She shrugged. 'Not very far. There were two men lost while surveying for the new road in the foothills – they're presumed to have fallen into a crevasse – but they were still a fair way from the mountains, according to the report.'

'No historical notes?' I put in.

'Nothing that goes very far back. Faddelin appears as a name on some pre-collapse Grisotin charts, but the first stories are less than two hundred years old. A tribe of the legendary gilled fishmen, apparently, haunting the ruins and preying on the fishermen who downed their nets in the Deppowe Strait.'

'Complete nonsense,' Tig snapped without warning, 'no species of gilled fishmen has ever existed in the known world.'

'I'm only telling you what the report says,' Mallinna said mildly. She seemed very slightly taken aback, but I was astonished. I had at various times seen Tig bitter, anguished, pointed, vehement and even angry, but I had never seen him *rude*.

'Father?'

'Why do people always get things wrong? Sloppy thinking, sloppy observation, fishmen in the wrong place—'

'Father, calm down. What's the matter with you?'

'Stop fussing at me, Vero, nothing's the matter. I'm better than I've ever been. Carry on, Mallinna.'

'If you're quite sure,' she said, looking dubiously from Tig's expressionless face to mine and back again. Then she shrugged and turned her attention back to the report. 'The legends were collected by Miisheli scholars: the Bequiin Siffer originally, that was two hundred years ago, and then they were rechecked by the Bequiin Ardin in this century. We have Siffer's surviving papers as well as Ardin's in the archives, of course. I brought copies of some of them. In fact, I see this addendum was written by Angel on the basis of the Bequiins' notes.'

Tig twitched more violently.

Mallinna turned over another page. 'That's the end of the report – nothing about Faddelin being the port for Cansh Fathan, Lord Tigrallef. Do you remember where you read it?'

He looked down at her inscrutably. Perhaps it was my imagination, but I thought he was growing taller and broader in the chair, as if inflating himself like a pufferfish from the Ronchar Sea. I also noticed a few wisps of smoke rising from the ropes.

'Father,' I said, 'I'm worried you're going to damage that hawser. We only have one other spare.'

He turned his inscrutable look on me. The knots abruptly unravelled themselves, the lightly charred ropes fell away. 'Have your damned hawser,' he said. The straps and fetters parted as he stood up. Without another word he stalked to the companionway and started below deck. Perhaps I imagined this too: although the sun still shone brightly among the fairweather clouds, and the sound of laughter still rang from the bow, here on the afterdeck the day turned darker, colder and chokingly oppressive.

'That was sudden. What's wrong with him? I didn't offend him, did I?' Mallinna sat up and watched curiously as he vanished down the companionway. 'I wasn't questioning his scholarship, just asking about his sources.'

'Quite right, too. Don't worry, Mallinna. Perhaps the Pain was bothering him.'

'Are you going after him?'

'Raksh, no.'

She gave me an inscrutable look of her own. 'You know more than you're telling me.'

'I don't *know* anything, I'm only guessing. I have no idea why the mention of the fishmen upset him so much, since he usually loves folklore. But this matter of Faddelin being the port for Cansh Fathan – I would guess it's not something he read, but a detail the Pain remembers. After all, the old sow was there when Fathan was in its prime.'

'So she was,' Mallinna said thoughtfully. 'I wonder – does Lord Tigrallef share all the Harashil's memories?'

I glanced at her with suspicion; her eyes were preoccupied but bright, a look I'd seen more than once in my father's eyes. Rampant scholarly thirst, that was.

'No,' I said, 'he blinds and deafens himself to the old sow as much as he can; the few things he would like to learn from her, she conceals from him, like the Will of Banishment we've spent twenty years searching for, the location of the Great Nameless First, the truth about Oballef ... but you listen to me, Mallinna. My father is not well – I hope you're not thinking of asking him to settle a few historical controversies for you with the Pain's first-hand observations.'

Her face filled with surprise. 'What a shocking thought, Vero. I would never dream of such a thing. Although,' she added, 'when this is finished, we should encourage him to write down all he can of the Harashil's memories. It would be a priceless historical document.'

'*If* this is ever finished,' I muttered ungraciously, 'there may be nothing left of him to hold a pen.'

The next day, an equally perfect midsummer confection of blue skies and fair winds, our course was due to take us across the northern highlands of the continent of Sher not long after midday. Our complement had split itself into groupings that were starting to become habitual, a riotous assembly of youth and old age in the bow, the rest of us being more sedate on the afterdeck. I had the early afternoon watch again, but Mallinna was in the chair getting some experience in wheelmanship under my guidance, while we passed the time discussing the evidence for and against the existence of gilled fishmen. When we saw Tigrallef emerging from the companionway, we tactfully dropped the subject.

He had not joined us at any time since our little misunderstanding over Faddelin and the fishmen the day before, though the trays of food I left outside his cabin door had been healthily depleted. It was, therefore, a surprise when he greeted Mallinna and me in a manner that suggested no unpleasantness had ever taken place; even more of a surprise when he grinned at us and lounged sideways in his chair with one knee hooked over the armrest, without resorting to straps, fetters or ropes. More surprises: he had exchanged his beloved but patched and threadbare tunic for a spotless new one, shaved off the not-very-impressive beard he had started in the archives, and trimmed his hair into the basin shape that Kat's hair was just growing out of.

Indeed, he looked so much like a normal uncomplicated human being – say, a jaunty young rakehell all spruced up for courting – that he made me very, very nervous. Normality did not become him; I preferred it when he was abnormal in ways I was familiar with. He accepted our slightly startled compliments with a wide smile and a modest shrug, then stared off towards the north and began to hum a little Gafrin-Gammanthan tune that was so blithesome it set my teeth on edge.

No, I did not like this development at all.

'It's almost a pity we're not the Benthonic Expedition any more,' Tig said after a while. 'There's a chalcedony quarry under our keel now, which would please our revered patron no end. Though he'd need to enslave a tribe of gilled fishmen to work it for him.'

I caught Mallinna's eye; she looked as uncomfortable as I felt. Walking to the rail, I peered down into the sea – nothing was visible in the murky waters below, but I called forward to Kat anyway on the assumption we were nearing the sunken highlands. She scrambled up to the crosstrees of the foremast, leaving Jonno and Angel to keep watch from the bow. When I got back to the wheelman's chair, Mallinna and my father had begun an amiable comparison of Calloonic and Satheli weather-control rituals, and seemed quite happy.

Although these waters were largely uncharted, the maps of Sher were still of some use to us. The crags and alpine meadows of the old highlands were in many places close enough to the surface to endanger deep-draughted wind-catchers, and to raise the Primate's hopes that some portions of Sher's sea-bloated cadaver might still be pillaged. If we had truly been the Benthonic Expedition, that afternoon alone would have justified our existence.

Less than an hour after I sent her aloft, Kat sang out from the rigging, '*Hoy, Vero!* Shoals ahead! You'd better take a look!'

I dashed to the bow where Angel, already busy with a notebook, looked up long enough to give me a brilliant smile. Nothing was breaking the surface ahead of us, but Jonno grabbed my shoulder and pointed excitedly into the depths. The bottom was visible, all right, rising towards the northeast in great irregular hillsides of blurred terraces and bald out-crops of rock, falling away to the southwest into deep impenetrable shadow. Waving seagrasses grew in what must once have been cultivated fields; a stroke of paler green snaking up the hillside in a series of switchbacks may once have been a road. Otherwise there was no sign of human workmanship in all that rich and faintly sinister underwater landscape.

'Ridgetop ahead, Vero!' Kat shouted down.

Peering past the end of the bowsprit, I could tell I was about to be needed at the wheel. The slope I was looking at crested in a toothy line of crags running roughly east to west directly athwart our course, and some of them appeared close enough to the surface to endanger the *Fifth*'s long keelboard and rudderstocks. 'You'll need to guide me,' I called back to Kat. I stayed in the bow only long enough to see that the supposed road was winding upwards to a broad cleft in the ridge, and then I was scrambling back to the afterdeck to reclaim the wheelman's chair from Mallinna.

We were never in any peril. The sea was calm; there were no great wave-troughs to carry us down and impale us on the sharp needles of those Sherkin crags. The ridge we were approaching was only the first of a series of parallel sawbacks, each with its own set of teeth, but there was plenty of room to manoeuvre and only a few places where we needed to go

217

about. Kat stayed on the foremast, calling out directions – 'Two points to the east, Vero!' – but Mallinna deserted the afterdeck fairly quickly to go to the bow, where all the fun was. The dark arch of a bridge still spanning the chasm between two sawbacks, with a school of fish flowing under it like a river; stone ruins of watchtowers and of several small castellated structures that could have been hunting lodges or even follies of a peculiarly Sherkin variety; the scars of at least five quarries, lapis and marble according to Tigrallef, so high on their ridges that they were within diving distance of the surface. The Primate would have been pleased to hear about those, but we hoped we would never have the chance to tell him.

Unfortunately I got to see very little of this scenery because I did not dare leave the wheel throughout most of the traverse. All I had was the mixed pleasure of looking through Angel's notebook later, to find out what I missed. I should have been grateful to Tig for staying aft to keep me company rather than running to the bow to gawk with the others, but that jaunty new persona of his was too unsettling.

'Tig,' I asked hesitantly after a while, because I really had to know, 'is it bothering you to be passing over the ruins of Sher? I know you used to feel—' I cut myself off.

He was sprawled at ease in the chair where always before he had sat self-bound in a stiff, upright position. 'I suppose you mean *guilty*, don't you? I've gone well past that by now, my son. Remember, Sher was only one of many.'

In response to a call from Katla, I shifted the rudders. 'What do you mean, one of many?'

'Nkalvi, Baul, Khamanthana,' he chanted, 'Itsant, Myr, Vizzath—'

'Nonsense, Da,' I said, 'you were as unborn as I was when those empires fell.'

He did not answer. He started to hum that sprightly Gafrin-Gammanthan tune again. It was very hard to choke back my irritation.

'Father, I wish—'

'Don't wish, Vero,' he interrupted. '*Never* wish. It's dangerous. I know.'

'I was going to say, I wish you'd stop talking in puzzles. I used to think I could help you, now you won't even let me try. It was bad enough in the archives in Gil, with the painted fishes and the singing statue at the harbour and all your other little absurdities, but ever since we came back aboard the *Fifth* – wait a minute, by Raksh, that reminds me. Why didn't you tell me Kat was in the hidden hold? You must have known all along.'

'Of course I knew, I could hear her breathing.' Another snatch of the damned tune.

'Stop that! Why didn't you tell me? Why did you leave the poor child to live all that time in the dark, and me in agonies of worry—'

'Enough, Vero, please. I had good reason, and let's leave it at that.'

I was moving from irritation to real anger. 'Not this time, Tigrallef. I think you should tell me the reason, and I hope it's a good one. And I also want to know why you've been avoiding her ever since. Don't imagine I didn't notice. Your own daughter! Anyone would think you didn't care about her. What would Mother say?'

He whistled the same tune; it was at least a welcome change from his humming. Then he said, 'You seem determined to make me feel guilty, Vero – if not about Sher, then about Kat. Is this your idea of being helpful?'

'I have no idea how to help you now, except by getting you to Mother. Tell me why you had to keep Kat's presence a secret.'

After giving me a long appraising look, he pulled himself smoothly out of the chair. 'Better you should talk to Katlefiya about that. I'll take the wheel – you go aloft and ask her to tell you in detail what she sees when she looks at me. Perhaps it's better that you know. Go on, Vero, I promise to behave.'

I hesitated, not being very eager to give him the wheel. It was no insult to his seamanship, which was at least as good as my own, but in all the years of our wanderings he had never been able to take a watch at the wheel without somebody else nearby, to take over if he was suddenly distracted by the Pain.

'Go on,' he said, motioning with his head towards the foremast, 'you can trust me for a few minutes, can't you?'

Laden with misgivings, I slid out of the wheelman's chair and galloped to the foremast. Seconds later I was up on the crosstrees with Kat, with the broad vista of the Sherkin Sea all around us. So hurried was I that I no more than scanned the sweeping stripes of the ridges below the surface, the crags highlighted by the sun striking down through the water, divided by the fathomless shadows of the valleys. All I wanted was to carry out the farcical mission Tig had sent me on, and then get back to the wheel.

Kat, comfortably braced where the crosstrees met the mast, was surprised to see me. 'What is it, Vero? We're doing fine, nearly through. It looks like the next ridge is the last one we have to worry about.'

'Good.' I scanned ahead, saw she was right; beyond the last ridge lay waters that always had been waters, the old Kild Sea that used to embrace the cliffbound north coast of Sher. The shipping lanes were perhaps a day to the north; there was ample time to indulge my father's fancy. 'Do something for me, Kat. Take a look at Tig and tell me what you see.'

She gazed at me very strangely. 'Why?'

'How should I know? He's the one who said I should ask you — I gather there's a revelation in there somewhere. Quickly, Kat, please.'

'Oh, all right.' With apparent reluctance, she twisted around to glance very briefly at the afterdeck. 'About the same.' She looked to the bow again, shading her eyes with one hand.

'About the same as what? No, Katla, give me details.'

'All right, maybe he's a little changed.' She twisted for another look, and her face hardened. 'The old sow. To be truthful, Vero, he looks much worse. If we don't get Mother back soon—'

'Details, Kat, I need details. When you say worse, I get the feeling you're not talking about the shave, the haircut and the new tunic.'

'Shave? Haircut? I didn't notice. It's the glow that's become worse, and that face-shifting trick is new, and the awful thing that happens under his skin; not to mention his eyes . . .' She shuddered. 'When I first saw him like that, that terrible night in Beriss, I couldn't believe the rest of you were taking it so lightly. I'm willing to go along with it, Vero, but I really can't bear to look at him for very long, especially when I'm eating. I suppose he's upset that I'm avoiding him, and I'm sorry about that, but I just can't help it.'

I was starting to lose my breath. 'If you're avoiding him, you may not have realized that he's also avoiding you. Kat, please, by the Eight Rages, describe in detail what you see when you look at our father.'

'If I must.' First she scanned ahead – we were on a course that would take us neatly between two crags of the final ridge. Then she glanced back towards the afterdeck. 'Let's see – the glow is dimmer at the moment, probably because he's in direct sunlight. He's being the wolf, see? That's not so bad. Last time I looked he was being either the snake or the dragon, it was hard to tell from this distance – it's easier to distinguish up close because you can smell the fire on his breath when he's being the dragon. Do you find the snake and the dragon hard to tell apart, Vero?'

I gulped. 'Not really.'

'No? Though I suppose that's not surprising, since you've had longer to get used to it.'

'Well . . .'

She looked back again, shuddered, fixed her eyes on the unthreatening alternative of the landscape beneath the sea. I glanced back too; Tigrallef, lounging in the wheelman's chair with one hand on the wheel, saw me looking and smiled up at us.

'What would you say he's – being – at the moment? Are you still seeing him as the wolf?' I asked.

'No.' A single tear escaped from each of her eyes and ran

down her cheeks. 'He's being nothing right now. Just himself.'

'And that's the worst of all,' I guessed.

'Don't you find it so?' Another brace of tears began to work their way towards her chin. 'The skin – the face is his, yes, but I can't bear seeing all the layers at once, and the blood, and the voids behind his eyes – just *look* at him, Vero! I don't know how you can stand it.'

I squinted obligingly through the bright air and took a long hard look at Tig. This time he gave us a cheerful wave, which Katla did not see. She was wiping the tears away as fast as they came, but the tears were winning. With a sigh, I stretched around the foremast to pat her shoulder, which was all I could reach.

'Don't worry, Katla,' I said, 'he'll be all right. All of us will be, you'll see.'

I climbed heavily down the foremast and dragged my feet back to the afterdeck, where Tigrallef was humming that detestable little tune again as he kept the wheel steady with one hand and combed his hair with the fingers of the other. He rose out of the wheelman's chair as I approached, and he looked normal, even good: skin a little tanned, eyes bright, and he'd done quite a competent job on the haircut.

'So, Vero, did you ask her?'

'I did.'

'What did she tell you?'

'I think you already know.'

'And what did you tell her?'

'You mean, did I tell her you look reasonably normal and human to everyone but her? Certainly not.'

He nodded. 'Yes, good, it's better that she isn't told just yet, if ever.'

I slid into the chair, took the wheel, felt the steadiness of the rudders. 'I get the feeling there are several things she hasn't been told, along with all the rest of us.'

'Not even Calla knows. I've always hoped I'd never need to tell her.' He lowered himself into his own chair, not lounging now, but as stiff and straight as if all the ropes on the *Fifth* were bound around him. He had lost the over-cheerful smile.

'Tell me, Tig. Who is seeing you more accurately, Kat or the rest of us?'

'Katlefiya, of course.' The tone was bleak. For a broken second, I could see what Kat meant about the voids behind his eyes; I blinked and the illusion vanished.

'Raksh. If her description does you justice, it's no wonder she's been avoiding you. But why is it just poor Kat? Why not me too? Last week, as we were approaching Beriss, I could see the Pain as an aura around your body, and now I see nothing. Why am I blind to what Kat can see?'

'Partly because every day the old sow moves on a pace or two,' Tig said tonelessly, 'and every day I push her back again, but not always far enough. Every day the old sow changes her tactics, and I'm forced to change my defence. Channelling her into absurdities worked for a while – now it doesn't. I'm losing ground, Vero.'

'That doesn't explain why Kat sees you differently and I don't.'

He shook his head with impatience. 'Think, Verolef, think. There's a crucial difference between you and Katlefiya. Primarily, she should never have been born.'

'How can you say that'?'

'Oh, I don't wish her unborn – but if I had realized what would happen to her, I might not have—' He stopped.

The first stirrings of comprehension; a lump of ice began to take on solid substance inside me. 'You fathered me before you broke the Harashil,' I said flatly.

'That's so.'

'And you fathered Katlefiya after you broke the Harashil. Is that the crucial difference?'

'Right again,' he began, but Katla's voice rang out from the foremast.

'*Hoy Vero!* We're clear of the last ridge!'

I started, and waved in acknowledgement. Tig also started, and momentarily his skin flamed with the kind of fire that burns in a thin layer of lamp oil floating on water. He smiled with what looked like bitterness when I instinctively pulled away.

'I've had to do double duty for years; I've had to keep hold, and I've had to keep a barrier up between the old sow and Katla. Protecting her from the Pain, and the knowledge of the Pain, has not been easy. It seems, though, that the farther away from me she keeps, the better I can keep hold, and the safer she is.'

'Which is why you were not overjoyed to find her on board,' I said slowly.

Tig nodded, watching Kat swing herself down from the foremast, look towards us, hesitate so briefly it was almost an insult, and drift away from us towards the happy sightseers in the bow.

'Does Kat have any idea about this? That for all the years of her life—'

'She knows nothing. But it's only been twelve years, not fifteen; I had no inkling of it myself when she was born, not until the first time she got truly frightened and upset. She was not quite three years old.'

I counted back. 'Year Eight. But that was the year when – oh, Raksh . . . that was the year we left Itsant . . .'

'If you jerk at the wheel like that, Vero, you'll damage the rudderstocks.'

'Oh, Great Raksh . . .'

'I see you've made the connection. Yes, it was a terrible thing, a brutal and bloody tragedy, three hundred or more killed, much worse by far than Amballa or Nkalvi; but the poor child didn't know what she was doing.'

Feeling giddy, I leant my forehead on the wheel. 'We all thought it was you.'

'I encouraged you to think that. Katla was not much more than a baby at the time. How could I burden her mother, or any of you, with such sorrowful knowledge? Anyway, I was sure I could bar the old sow from feeding on Katla – I was sure I could prevent it from happening again.'

'And could you? Did she – was she the one—?'

'Who did the others? No. The massacres at Amballa and Nkalvi were both done through me. Itsant was another matter. Itsant was done through Katla.'

I did not sleep very well that night, nor for many nights thereafter; but whenever I did manage to exhaust myself into a state of unconsciousness, I was haunted by dreams, all of them concerning dread manifestations of my little sister.

There was the full-grown Kat with light shining under her skin, herding the Bloody Spirits of the Sea along the sunken roadways of Sher; there was Kat as a small child weeping with fear at the Mamelons of Itsant, those summits of drowned towers thrusting above the surface from the coral-grown ruins of a great city; there was Kat standing on the grim iron ramparts of a city I had never seen, with lightning flickering around her short brown hair. I always wakened from these dreams drowning in sweat.

I never dreamt about Tig; perhaps I didn't dare to.

PART THREE

Second Comings

. . . and all but [the?] Naar shall perish . . .

Naarhil text fragment, wall text, Nkalvi; copy in
the Archives of the College of the Second Coming

*Vase 12. Recovered from the interior of Mamelon Four.
Upper register: Seven figures (three human, one snake, one
snake/dragon, one feline, one dog/wolf) enthroned in separate panels. Tentatively interpreted as assembly of gods.
Lower register: Same seven gods(?) facing human male
with square chestplate, as seen on Vases 4 and 11. Tentatively interpreted as king (or high priest?). Beside king is
unique ninth figure, heavily robed. A broad red stripe,
originally gilded, links robed figure's face with king's chestplate. Tentative interpretation: ritual transfer of kingship
from incumbent to successor, in the presence of the gods.*

Excerpted from the Joint Field Report on the
Narrative Vases of Itsant, in the Archives of
the College of the Second Coming

13

Jonno was the one sitting in the wheelman's chair when the *Image of Oballef* raced towards us out of the east just outside the Deppowe Strait, with the Flamens' banner and a whole laundry line of signal flags streaming from her masthead. The wind had freshened and the sea had roughened in the three days since we left the Sherkin Sea behind us, and the great black wind-galley was not only showing more yardage of sail than I thought was wise, but also had the oars fully manned. Her speed was impressive but dangerous. I hovered by the wheel while I made sure there was no risk of a collision or an attack, and that Jonno knew what he was doing.

'Remember what I told you yesterday, guardsman? Now, can you point out to me anything that her captain may be doing wrong?' I was speaking in my role as instructor of seamanship.

Jonno's eyes narrowed as he studied the big wind-galley, approaching rapidly about ten lengths off our port side. Just half an hour before, she had been a black smudge on the horizon. 'Yes, Lord Verolef,' Jonno said, 'he's going the wrong way.'

I shook my head chidingly. 'That's not the sort of answer I had in mind. Anyway, how would you know?'

'Well, sir, that's the *Image of Oballef*. The *Image* is supposed to patrol between Deppowe and Zaine, but she's headed west towards Sathelforn and Gil.'

'Maybe her orders have changed. Look, Jonno, I'll give you a hint. It's something about the rigging.'

'The fighting deck would never pass inspection either, I can tell you that,' Jonno answered. 'Her captain would be busted down to an oarsman in his own galley-well if he sailed into Gil City in that condition, unless—'

He stopped and squinted, shading his eyes with one hand. The big ship was level with us now, as close to the *Fifth* as she was ever going to be.

'Yes, but what about the sails?' I demanded wearily. 'Remember what I told you about the Myrene wind/wave/canvas ratios and—'

Jonno, against all my patient instructions, let go of the wheel, jumped out of the chair and bounded to the portside railing. Sighing, I slid into his place and grimly rehearsed what I would say to him when he returned. Kat and Mallinna, I could see, were just drifting towards the afterdeck from the bow.

Jonno got back to me first. 'Something's happened,' he said breathlessly.

'You're damned right, something's happened. You've deserted your post without securing the wheel. If you did a stupid thing like that in a rough sea, my lad, or with the wind in an awkward direction, you'd risk the ship turning broadside—'

'Something's happened in the *Mosslines*,' he broke in, eyes wide. 'The signal flags: they're a fourth-level warning to avoid Deppowe – that means all ships – and a second-level instruction to certain ships of the fleet to divert to Mashakel and wait for orders.'

Mallinna and Kat were in time to catch his words. 'Fourth-level,' Mallinna said gravely. 'That one isn't often used. I think the last time was about seven years ago, during a resurgence of the Last Dance in southern Kuttumm. The blockade lasted for six months, and ended with three port cities being cauterized by flame bolts fired from the sea.'

I abandoned for the moment all thoughts of teaching. 'Did the signal flags mention anything about a plague, Jonno?'

'No, sir.'

'Did they say anything useful about the trouble at Deppowe?'

'No, Lord Verolef, not much information at all, just orders.'

'Like so many of the Most Revered Primate's arrangements,' Mallinna put in wryly.

I glanced over my shoulder at the receding stern of the *Image of Oballef*, at the pale blots of a few faces staring at us from the big ship's fighting deck; which did, now that I focused on it rather than the rigging, appear to be damaged and in disarray.

'Jonno – was Deppowe the only port mentioned in the warning signal?'

'Yes, Lord Verolef; though Mashakel was in the order to divert.'

'Was there any mention of Faddelin?'

'No, sir.'

'Thank the Old Ones for that. Is there nothing else you can tell me?'

Jonno shook his head, but he was looking thoughtful. 'I doubt that it's a plague, Lord Verolef. If it were, they wouldn't be ordering some of the fleet to gather at Mashakel, they'd be blockading the coast all the way to Cansh Miishel. My great-uncle the Primate is very particular about plagues.'

'So I've noticed. It doesn't matter; plague or not, blockade or not, we still have to go to Faddelin. We'll just hope we can get there before the trouble spreads, whatever it is. Which means that now we're going to make exactly the same mistake as the captain of the – what name did you give it? – the *Image of Oballef* made. I don't imagine, Jonno, you can tell me what mistake we're going to make?'

'I think I can, Lord Verolef. I would guess we're going to raise more canvas than we should, and sail too close to the wind.' Suddenly and rather cheekily, Jonno grinned.

I was pleased, but not really surprised. Jonno had been making great progress in the theory of seamanship since I took over his training. Kat was his instructress while we were crossing the Sherkin Sea, but the two of them spent far too much of their wheel time locked in earnest conversation – largely on the meanings of life, so far as I could tell, though inevitably Jonno's poetry came into it.

This had a good side — Katla had never had a friend so near her own age before, and it distracted her from the chronic alarm about our father — but I badly needed Jonno and Mallinna to be useful members of the crew in case anything happened to Kat or me. For obvious reasons I thought Jonno's training might proceed faster if his instructor was neither so keen to discuss the great verities of life nor so distractingly pretty as Kat was becoming, and so I elected myself to be Kat's replacement. The seamanship lessons I was giving Mallinna were also strictly businesslike, of course.

The Deppowe Strait, a deep-water channel more than fifty miles long but less than three miles wide at its broadest, lay between the coast of Fathan and the hazardous Kerriin Shoals that ran parallel to it on the south. I had planned to sail well outside the Shoals so as to enter the strait at its eastern mouth, thus avoiding the well-patrolled waters around Deppowe at the western end, at the cost of two or three extra sailing days. Two factors changed my plans.

First, if Jonno had read those signal flags correctly, the strait would be virtually empty of ships — Mashakel was a good way west around the coast. Second, I could feel time pressing at us again, a desperate urgency to reach Faddelin and take our people off before the emergency that had arisen at Deppowe had time to affect the outlying settlements; if, indeed, it was not already too late. The lengthy detour skirting the Kerriin Shoals was no longer an option.

And so, it was just at dawn of the next morning, the morning after the *Image of Oballef* sped past us, that we entered the western mouth of the strait with the reasonable expectation of mooring in Faddelin by nightfall. Kat was beside me, ready to begin her watch, but I was in no great hurry to give up the wheel. Kat's waking company was preferable to the fearsome versions of her that haunted my dreams; and anyway, the entrance to the Deppowe Strait at sunrise was like nothing I had ever seen before.

On my left hand, across a stretch of dawn-gilded water, was the legendary slag-land of Fathan: an astonishing tumble of broken peaks and unnatural flats, of smooth, glassy sweeps and tormented angularities, in more shades and textures of black than I knew existed – here absorbing the light like the deepest velvet ever woven in Glishor, there reflecting it with the sheen of the finest Omelian silk. On my right hand, the Kerriin Shoals dappled the sea with a hundred thousand silver sandbars, most of them smaller than the afterdeck of the *Fifth*, but a few of them stretching for hundreds of feet in both dimensions, like small sea-locked deserts. At high tide they would all vanish under a few inches or feet of salt water; at mid-tide, as it was then, they were a busy little world of rock pools, resting sea-pups, flapping fish and seabirds on the hunt, marked here and there by the skeletons of unlucky ships. Kat and I watched in wonder.

'Perhaps I should wake Tig up to see this,' I murmured.

'Don't bother – he's up on the crosstrees already.'

'Is he? I didn't see him come up.'

'Neither did I,' Kat whispered grimly, 'but he's there now.'

I glanced at her, winced and kept silent.

In due course, within the next half-hour, the rest of our crew drifted on deck, Mallinna helping Angel to his favourite spot in the bow, the invaluable Jonno arriving from the galley with a tray full of steaming mugs. There was little conversation and no laughter that morning, however; the appalling beauty of the Fathidiic barrens stunned our faculties and stifled our tongues. The stillness was a contagion spreading from the shore. We spoke in whispers when we spoke at all, and I even found myself tiptoeing when at last I yielded up the wheel to Kat and Jonno and joined the others in the bow.

Sitting down opposite Angel and Mallinna, I peered up at the foremast to check on my father. He looked normal, even a little better than normal, with a touch of colour in his newly shaven cheeks, and he was gazing at the shore of Fathan with an air of impersonal interest. Angel, I noticed, was spending as much time watching Tig as watching the Fathidiic landscape unscroll silently before us.

There was no question of going below deck to my pallet. I curled up in the bow and fell into a doze on the bare boards, and was immediately assaulted by dreams. Katla was in one of her younger manifestations that morning, a small child with a painted wooden fish in her hand, wearing a tunic Shree had sewn for her from one I had outgrown. She smiled at me most affectionately, but I could not bring myself to embrace her because she was on fire, her smooth babyish skin charring and sloughing off to reveal an identical face underneath, which then caught fire –

'Vero, wake up. You have to see this.' Mallinna's voice; and it was probably her finger that was poking me in the ribs.

I had done eight watches out of twelve in the previous three days and I was in no mood to have my ribs abused, even by the most beautiful woman in the known world, after whom I hopelessly lusted.

'Go rot, Mallinna. Leave me alone, let me sleep.'

'Vero, no, wake up. I tell you, you have to see this.'

Groaning, I sat up and blinked around me. I had been asleep longer than I thought, at least an hour judging by how far the sun had moved up in the heavens. Katla had struck some sail but raised the demi-lateens, and we were scudding along at a very decent pace with hopeful seabirds circling over our mast-tops. Tigrallef was still in the rigging, now wearing an expression of faint boredom; but it was over the bowrail that Mallinna was pointing, and she looked anything but bored.

The channel had narrowed, and Kat was keeping well to the centre. We were less than half a mile from the black shore of Fathan, close enough to see the fused sand and heaped black boulders of what might have been a long stretch of beach a thousand years ago. Radiating from it were networks of grey lines, pale and distinct against the dark slag, branching and branching again like a child's drawing of a row of trees until I lost them far inland in the confusion of broken black hills.

'What are those grey tracks? Dry river beds? Old roads?'

'No, they're just the Mosslines, the cracks in the surface where the moss grows; except I don't understand why they're grey, they should be a nasty kind of pale green. But that's not why I woke you – look further east, over that way. Do you see it?'

'I see it.' Dark smoke: three separate columns of it, close together and still some way ahead.

Angel said flatly, 'Deppowe is burning.'

Mallinna added, also flatly, 'That's not all. We've seen two bodies in the water already, and look – here comes the third.'

We passed the ruins of Deppowe just over an hour later. Long before then, the seabirds deserted our mast-tops for reasons that were not too hard to understand. I suppose it was a grand and memorable time if one happened to be a carrion-eater. We gave up keeping track of the corpses in the strait when the count reached forty; after that, as we neared the last small headland before Deppowe, the bodies were too thick in the water for us to keep a reliable tally. Many were naked. We estimated, however, that about a quarter of those still clothed wore shreds of the dun-coloured uniforms of ordinary troopers, about half were in the rags and tatters of civilian garb, and a very few were in remains of the smart black tunics of the Flamens' Corps. The remainder were unclassifiable.

'They've been in the water for a few days,' Mallinna said sombrely. 'See how bloated they are.'

I could not bring myself to comment. The implications were too disturbing. If catastrophe had hit Deppowe as long as several days ago, there was plenty of time for it to have spread out along the Mosslines. What, then, could we expect to find at Faddelin?

Deppowe itself was even worse than we feared. As we rounded the last headland, the scene that met our eyes was devastation piled on devastation: a town recently shattered and still smouldering, at the edge of a great slag-field from a destruction more than a millennium old. It was an extensive and well-planned town, the Primate's Deppowe, purpose-built for efficiency and good order; I had seen a map of its layout in the Mosslines reports, a neat grid centred around the guardtroops' barracks and the governor's residence, and fortified on three sides with a solid masonry barricade at least ten feet tall. This had been designed as much to keep the Mosslines slaves in at night as to keep attackers out, but it would have failed signally on both scores in its present condition, having been breached in so many places. The town plans also showed a gate midway along the wall's northern stretch; now there was not much left of either the gate or the north fortification, as if some terrible wavefront of destruction had swept down from the hills, razing everything in its path.

Inside the line of the wall, not a building remained standing. The columns of smoke we'd seen from far away were rising from three enormous ruins, the largest of them close to the waterfront, the second in the centre, the third filling most of the northwest quadrant of the shattered townsite. Respectively, these were the great warehouse, the barracks and the main lockup for the Mosslines slaves, all three of them large and ambitious enough to have smouldered on for days. The rest of the enclosure was a trackless litter of charred wreckage, as black as the slag that lay under it, with here and there on the ground a dark, log-shaped bundle that I strongly doubted was a log. Among the stumps of the ruined quays, the blackened hulks of two great windcatchers and uncountable smaller ships were rocking gently in the tide. Nothing else moved, neither ashore nor on the water.

Nobody said anything about stopping. The *Fifth* pushed on through the mat of corpses until we reached clearer water, and then Kat shouted to me to run up some more sail. Not one of us, except perhaps Tigrallef, had the stomach to look back.

We were halfway to Faddelin before the wind stopped bringing the stench of the Deppowe shambles to our nostrils. To our right, the Kerriin Shoals gradually vanished beneath the sea as the tide rose; to our left, the smoked-glass landscape of Fathan rolled on and on, devoid of sound, colour, movement; devoid of everything except an unpleasant atmosphere of menace. What had seemed so beautiful to us only hours before – a shining faceted jewel of jet one-third the size of a continent – had become hateful, hideous, and above all strangely *boring*. Even the branched grey scars that occasionally cut across the glaring plains did little to relieve the sameness.

Tigrallef had not moved from the rigging all day, nor had he eaten. The mug of gruel Jonno brought for his breakfast (with an air of making an offering at an altar – habits of worship die hard) was still sitting on the deck at the foot of the mast, along with the bread and cheese I had less ceremoniously tried to give him at midday. He had not seemed overly disturbed by the horrific sights at Deppowe, nor was he peering ahead towards Faddelin with any sign of anticipation, anxiety or even mild interest. And all the while the rest of us were straining our eyes to the east, long before there was any point in doing so, peering through the hot haze of our own sweat and the blinding glare off the slag, searching for the first glimpse of Faddelin – or the first far-off columns of smoke that would mark the well-roasted ruins of Faddelin and anyone with the bad timing to have been there.

He took notice of us only once. Kat had left Jonno at the wheel and come up to the bow; she took pains to keep her eyes well below the level of the rigging where our father was perched. 'What could have happened back there?' she asked. 'Who could have destroyed a town so completely, and killed all those people? I don't understand.'

Obviously, that question had been bothering me too. 'Miishel?' I suggested. 'Or Grisot? Or one of the client states that doesn't appreciate the privilege of being part of the Gillish empire? Or even,' I glanced at Mallinna, 'I was wondering if the Opposition might be involved?'

Mallinna flushed, rather becomingly. 'Ten days ago, Vero, I would have said no. Ten days ago, I'd have said the Opposition would happily slaughter troopers and guardsmen as legitimate enemies, but they would free the prisoners on the Mosslines. Now I'm not so sure. Whoever crushed

Deppowe killed everybody – *everybody*...' Distressed, she paused.

'And you think your former hero, the Tru nt Malso, would be capable of ordering such an atrocity if he thought the Opposition would benefit. A terrible thought, Mallinna, but I would have to agree.'

Angel spoke up, in a return to his normal cryptic style. 'The moss,' he said, lifting his eyes significantly to Mallinna's.

She nodded. 'He means, whether it's the Opposition or a rebel state in the empire, the moss itself would be a powerful motive. The Flamens maintain an insanely lucrative monopoly – if it were knocked out from under them, they'd have to impose a heavier burden of taxes and tributes to keep up the Order's income—'

'—which would mean more disaffection among the people and a stronger common cause against the Primate; yes, yes, that makes good sense.' I was actually getting excited, partly with rage, partly with a twisted sense of hope and relief. 'If that's anywhere close to the truth, then Deppowe and all those poor sods in the water should be enough of a demonstration – the point's been made, they wouldn't need to destroy Faddelin, in fact they'd want to preserve Faddelin and Mashakel against the time that *they* control the Mosslines and the moss trade, and—'

'Stop, Vero,' Katla said quietly. 'This all sounds pretty thin to me. You're working yourself into a lather over a mere supposition. And you're one of the people who taught me about reserving judgement until the evidence is in.'

Rapid snapping of fingers from above us, from high up in the rigging; Tig was applauding. 'Nicely put, Katla, poppet. You'll be teaching your brother before long.'

Kat glanced up at him very briefly and then dropped her eyes to the deck, a sudden pallor making her few freckles stand out. I took a longer look at Tig, wondering what my sister had seen: wolf, snake, dragon, some other horror entirely? All *I* could see was an unwontedly well-groomed young man without a care in the world, sitting comfortably on the crosstrees like a paying customer on a tour – a customer, moreover, who considered the tour to be not quite worth his while. That was based on the sulky little smile I thought I saw on his lips.

I was, of course, very tired. Twenty years tired.

'You're among us again, are you?' I shouted up at him. 'You've chosen to honour us with your attention, have you? Then perhaps you'd honour us with your opinion as well. Maybe you can illuminate this disaster at Deppowe for us. Or maybe you can tell us if we'll have to sort through a crowd of bloated corpses in the waters at Faddelin—'

'Stop it, Vero, stop it.' Katla pulled at my arm.

'—or if we'll need to sift through the ashes to find their bones—'

'Stop it, Vero!' This time Katla punched me, a thoroughly competent blow that called on all the training Shree and I had ever given her. Taken off guard, I only just caught myself from lashing back.

Without a word, Tig stood up and stepped off the crosstrees; only Angel managed to let out a cry. The fall was about fifteen feet, but Tigrallef landed as lightly as if he had stepped off the bottom stair of a short staircase. The rest of us stood frozen where we were, dumbly looking at Tig's face and then down at his feet. I cleared my throat with difficulty.

'Anything broken, Tig? Sprained ankle, sore knee . . . ?'

'What does it matter? The old sow would only fix it again.'

'I know, but—'

'Never mind that now, Verolef. Katlefiya, I know you can't bear to look at me, but you must listen. *It is very important that you keep calm.* Do you understand? When you're excited, it's harder for me to keep hold, and that ends up as dangerous for everybody. I can't tell you why, flower, but it's so. That's all.'

She nodded without raising her eyes, and turned back towards Jonno and the wheel. I put out my hand to delay her, but Tigrallef shook his head. 'Let her go.' He waited until she was out of earshot then turned to me again, gave Mallinna and Angel an apologetic smile, and pulled me a short distance away from them.

239

'Vero,' he said quietly, 'there's something I have to tell you, for your ears only, something you must be prepared for.'

Although there was nothing very tragic or portentous in his tone, I felt my body go cold with a terrible premonition. He was going to say that he had seen Faddelin with the Harashil's eyes; that he had seen the charred and bloody corpses of Chasco, Shree, Calla and a hundred others scattered carelessly among the ruins; that he had seen them floating in the water, naked and swollen, ripped by sharp predatory beaks, impaled on the blackened spars of a smouldering hulk, contorted among the ashes with hands curled in black talons on their bony black chests . . .

'By Raksh, Vero, you've got a grisly imagination.' Tigrallef viewed me with apparent horror.

I closed my eyes and took a few deep breaths. 'All right, Father, just get it over with.'

He looked around carefully to check that the others could not hear, and leant forward to whisper into my ear: '*None of this is important; none of this matters.*' With a quick shushing gesture, a finger tapped against his lips, he turned away and began walking back to the foremast.

I stood stupidly on the spot for a moment and then, furious, leapt after him to seize the shoulder of his immaculate tunic. He did not resist as I swung him around. 'Is that all you have to say?'

He made no attempt to shake my hand off. 'That is all we need to say. We just want to help you prepare for what lies ahead.' Tig had picked up a bit of an echo in the last few seconds, as well as the plural pronoun, but he was still trying to keep his voice down. 'Here – we will explain, listen carefully because we do not like repeating ourself: the Primate, the Opposition, the Empire, all those trivialities you were speculating about – they do not matter. They are not important. Just remember that.'

He made another move to go, and sighed when I tightened my death-grip on his shoulder. I said nothing, because I was too choked with rage.

'Vero, what is this about? Was there something else you wanted to know?'

Through gritted teeth, I forced the words out. '*Are they dead?*'

He disengaged himself gently. 'Not yet. Some day. But Verolef, you have not been listening.'

Something happened then, either to him or to my eyes – the effect was a momentary shimmering of his form, a blurring and wavering of his outlines, like a wax figure when it first comes to the heart of a fire – and then I was flat on my back on the deckboards, looking a few hundred feet straight up through closed eyelids as solid as iron doors, to where my father's face, enormous, was flaming brighter than the sun. His voice boomed around me, shaking the sky.

'*NOTHING THAT IS HAPPENING HERE HAS THE WEIGHT OF A VERY SMALL HEADLOUSE ON THE GREAT BODY OF HISTORY. REMEMBER THAT WHEN THE TIME COMES, CHILD OF THE NAAR.*' And he added, 'Have some water and a little rest, Vero, you'll feel much better.'

I opened my eyes. Something odd was happening with the speed of time. My head was cradled in Mallinna's lap, and Angel was taking for ever to bring a beaker to my lips. Jonno and Kat were inching towards us across the deck in a strange leisurely fashion that looked like a run but was taking far too long, as if they were trying to move under water. Mallinna's voice was a deep slow rumble.

'Yoooooooooo . . .'

Tig turned away and walked to the foremast. In this slow-time world, he was the only object moving at a normal pace.

'Faaaaaiiiii . . .'

He climbed up into the rigging and out of my sight.

'. . . nted, but you'll be fine, Vero.' Mallinna dipped her clean nose-rag into the beaker and swabbed my forehead with it, with a tenderness that I only recognized when I had a chance to think it over. At the time, I was too shaken to think at all. I struggled to sit up, fell back again under a fresh wave of dizziness, fought hard to refocus my eyes. Four anxious faces formed a square above me, but Mallinna's was the closest.

Another sip from Angel's beaker and I was able to talk. 'What just happened?'

'You fainted, Vero – too much sun and worry, too little sleep and water. You'll be fine.'

'That's absurd, I didn't faint. Surely you saw what happened?'

Mallinna shook her head soothingly. 'Nothing happened. Lord Tigrallef is right, Vero, you need to rest. We can wake you up when we reach Faddelin.'

'But didn't you see my father?'

Three of them traded puzzled looks; the fourth just watched me. 'Yes,' Mallinna said, 'of course we saw him. He's gone back up the mast, though. Shall I call him down?'

'No!' I shut my eyes, reviewed the sight of my father rearing up against the dark background of my closed eyelids. 'Just tell me something: what did he do when I – what did he do just before he went up the mast?'

'He caught you as you fell, and stopped you from cracking your head open on the deck.'

'Is that all? You're sure he didn't—'

Multiply his height a hundredfold? Speak like an earth-quake? Shine like two suns?

'—do anything else?' I finished weakly.

Three pairs of eyes said no, nothing to speak of; the fourth refused to comment. Katla abruptly abandoned the square and strode away. I closed my eyes and let my head fall back into Mallinna's lap.

14

They rolled me on to a fleece on the foredeck and let me sleep most of the way to Faddelin. Soundly and dreamlessly, I snored through the first sighting of a haze of smoke overhanging the shore a few miles ahead, and the nasty surprise of the first face-down cadaver bumping tentatively against the hull of the *Fifth*, and the sight of the mast-tops of a ship about the size of ours thrusting up at a tilt from the waters near the shore. Mallinna only shook me awake when the site of Faddelin was actually in view, about a mile away at the far end of a sweeping bight backed by a gentle roll of hills. She did not say anything – her face was enough. Yawning and stretching, I sat up and surveyed the distant billows of yellow-grey smoke, which hid the townsite even as they marked its location.

Mallinna cleared her throat uneasily. 'How do you feel?'

'Fine. Best sleep I've had in weeks.' It was true. I felt stronger and fresher, less gloomy about Tigrallef's thunderous pronouncements, more sanguine about his others. I scanned inshore from the townsite for any sign of movement. Nothing stirred, but I was still hopeful.

Mallinna, following the direction of my eyes, laid her long hand on my shoulder. 'I'm sorry, Vero.'

'Sorry? What for?'

She hesitated. 'Because it looks like we're too late. Whatever hit Deppowe also hit Faddelin, and hit it just as hard. I'm so sorry.'

'Thanks, but it's too early for sorrow.' I put my hand over hers and flashed her a quick smile. 'They're not dead, you know. I have that on my father's authority. He said it very clearly.'

She favoured me with a long dubious look before turning

her eyes back to the townsite, via another sunken hulk and a scatter of floating corpses. After a while I remembered my manners and let go of her hand.

Kat brought the *Fifth* in as close as she dared to the naked pilings of the quay before we dropped anchor. A few minutes later, with the sun already sliding down to the western horizon, we began to gather on the port side of the foredeck to stare in shock over the wrack of Faddelin. Tigrallef came down the foremast in a more conventional manner this time and stood close to the railing with a supportive arm around Angel. Kat stood a little apart, but otherwise the discomfort we might have felt in Tigrallef's presence was swallowed up by the unrelieved grimness of the prospect before us.

As for my hopes, they had died as abruptly and violently as the trooper I could see lying half out of the water on the black shingle beach, the one without a head. My father had sounded so sure they weren't dead; I had half-expected to see the figures of Calla, Chasco and Shree waiting patiently for us in the very epicentre of the devastation, or leaping up to wave at the *Fifth* from the ruined landing stage as we sailed into the tiny harbour. I felt betrayed.

Jonno, detailed by Kat to secure the buntlines, was the last to join us on the foredeck. Shaking his head, he whistled in awe. 'What in the known world could have done that?' he exclaimed. 'By the Divine Scion Tigrallef – oh – I'm sorry, my lord, I meant no disrespect.' Blushing, he shut up before I could tell him to. For what seemed like a long time after that, we stood in silence trying to make sense of the picture puzzle which was all that was left of Faddelin.

The town had been a fraction the size of Deppowe, a rough rectangle of an outpost without fortifications, amenities or the smallest element of grace in its surroundings. In addition to the two wrecks we had passed further out, the remains of a little galley and a somewhat larger windcatcher were hard up against the stumps of the pilings, apparently torched at their moorings. The windcatcher, built for cargo, had burned with special ferocity, and I recalled that the moss was said to be almost explosively flammable.

The smoke was still rising from what had been the largest structure in the outpost, the warehouse for the moss, which fronted directly on the quay in the centre of the rectangle. Around it were grouped some rather interesting sculptural arrangements of burnt beams and flame-cracked stones that no doubt represented barracks, lockups, storehouses, clerks' quarters; but so completely had the recent fires destroyed them that there was no telling which was which. Aside from the smoke and a few ash devils raised by the breeze, nothing moved on shore.

Mallinna broke the silence. 'How long do you suppose—?'

'Two days ago at least,' said Tigrallef, 'so we shouldn't delay our departure if we want to catch up.'

'Catch up?' I looked at him sharply. As the numbing effects of the shock wore off, I could feel my anger beginning to build. 'You said they were still alive, Tig. So where are they? Faddelin's been wiped out. Everybody's dead. Where are they?'

'Oh, they're not *here*,' he said. His look told me I was mad to suggest such a thing.

'Do you mean to say they didn't come to Faddelin after all?' Wild flare of hope.

Tigrallef immediately threw cold sand on it. 'Oh yes, they were here. That's where they were housed.' He pointed to a tall finger of scorched masonry poking out of a pile of rubble near the warehouse. 'But they're not here now, and that's why we need to get going.'

I sighed; unclenched my fists with great effort. 'Where, Father? Back to Deppowe? To Mashakel? All the way to Gil? Where's the old sow going to drag us this time?'

'At the moment, Verolef, insofar as I am able to tell, I still appear to be dragging the old sow. I think.'

'But where? Where?'

'There.' He pointed in the direction of the hills behind Faddelin. Beyond the hills were starker uplands. Beyond the uplands were mountains. Puzzled, we all stared along the line of his finger and then around at each other.

'Are you telling us they escaped into the hills?' I asked hopefully.

'No, my son. I'm telling you they were taken into the mountains.'

'Taken? Who—?'

Tigrallef waved rather too cheerfully at the devastation that used to be Faddelin, the blackened bundles that used to be citizens of the glorious Gillish Empire. 'Whoever it was that did all that.'

This was already a horribly memorable moment; we did not need a spectacular sunset to mark it, but we got one anyway. Long streamers of light stabbed out from the dying sun and strewed reflections across Fathan's broken surface like a scatter of overblown jewels, painted the clouds with an unnecessary range of golds and lilacs, ignited the glossy black peaks of the mountains. My eyes were drawn to the highlands again, along with everybody else's.

'Cansh Fathan,' Angel said suddenly.

'That's right,' said my father, 'that's where we're going. And I think we're going to find some old friends there, too.'

At the time, I thought he was only talking about Chasco, Calla and Shree.

Tigrallef's intention was completely mad. It involved six people – one of them a girl of fifteen years, another a bent old man of eighty-one who refused to be left behind – blithely setting off over fiendish terrain into what could very well be the mouth of a dragon, metaphorical or real. It meant the same tiny crew of six challenging the might of a blood-hungry horde of indeterminate size, on the horde's home ground.

It meant leaving our beautiful *Fifth* unguarded near a charnel-ground that used to be a prison camp, for anyone who came along to seize or sink as they pleased. It meant a camping trip – a camping trip, by Raksh! – into the dark heart of a cursed land, the very name of which gave goose-flesh to half the known world.

Maddest of all, Tigrallef proposed to make this journey at a time of vicious massacres, apparently perpetrated by the very group of unknowns whose footsteps we would be following into the interior of Fathan. It was madness for him to suggest it, and worse madness for the rest of us to agree. We set off in the morning.

The *Fifth* could not be camouflaged. The best we could do for her, after using the smallboat to ferry people and supplies to the shingle beach, was to sail her around the point just east of Faddelin and leave her anchored in the shelter of a small cove, visible to any ship coming along the strait from the east, but not visible from west or from the townsite. Kat sailed over with me to help in the melancholy task of battening the ship down and doing whatever else we could to secure her, which was not a great deal. When we finished, it was only about two hours past dawn.

Neither of us said very much until we were in the small-boat again, rowing away from the *Fifth*'s shining sides towards the cove's tiny beach. I rowed, Kat made wake patterns in the water with her fingers, just as Tigrallef was fond of doing. I watched her covertly, thinking of Tig's revel-ation about her birth. Certainly she was not your standard-issue young girl trembling on the brink of womanhood – as I understood it, few young girls had mastered eighteen languages, ten weapons and the art of Sherkin trip-fighting by her age – but she still seemed fairly normal for a child born with the Harashil's poison in her veins. Then I won-dered how much Tig might have suffered over the last twelve years to keep her that normal.

She shook the water from her fingers and gazed sadly back at the ship. 'I hate to leave the *Fifth* on her own like this,' she said.

'So do I; but unfortunately she's a ship, little Katla,' I answered, 'and not much use in the mountains.'

'You know what I mean. Look at her – she looks lonely

247

and vulnerable. What if something happens to her while we're gone? Or what if we don't come back at all?'

'Oh, we'll come back, flower, all of us will. Mother as well, and Chasco and Shree. And when we do, the *Fifth* will be waiting for us, pretty as ever.'

'Who made you a prophet?' She took hold of the painter as the smallboat's keel crunched against the shingle.

'It's something called optimism, little Kat. Look it up in Angel's lexicon when we get home again.'

She hopped over the smallboat's nose to the shore. 'So who made you an optimist?'

That was impossible to answer, so I didn't try. Kat was too bright to fob off with easy answers, hollow comfort or counterfeit confidence. I busied myself with hauling most of the smallboat's weight while she struggled with the stern, and together we moved it above the tideline and hid it between two boulders. Then we set off to climb the low ridge that divided the cove from the broad bay of Faddelin, a pathless slope of dark scoria and sharp black pebbles, fortunately not too steep. An odd cheerfulness crept up on us as we climbed – though I hate to say this, I think it was because we had managed to put a little distance between us and our poor father for even a few short hours. It was a guilty relief.

'All right, Vero,' Kat said, 'as long as you're playing at being an optimist, let's assume we get back safely from Cansh Fathan with Mother and the rest and find the *Fifth* in one piece. What then?'

I grinned; *what then* had been a favourite game of Katla's from the time she learned to talk. 'What then? We sail away, I suppose, and try to pick up the trail of the Great Nameless First. Though we'll have to find some way of getting Jonno and the memorians safely back to Gil before we do anything else.'

She glanced up at me. 'I don't know about Jonno, but Mallinna and Angel aren't going back to the Gilgard. Didn't you know?'

'Who told you that?'

'Mallinna did.'

I kicked a chunk of slag out of my way. 'Oh, Kat, she wasn't serious. She once told me something like that too, but it was clearly the enthusiasm of the moment. Pleasant sailing, a sort of holiday for her, a rest from her routine, the illusion of freedom; I think she fancied it would always be like that, but I set her straight.'

'Did you kiss her?'

'What?'

'Did you kiss her?'

'No!' I kicked at another chunk of slag, which proved to be more solidly connected to the ground than the first one.

'People who wear sandals should not kick rocks,' Katla quoted smugly. 'You haven't broken a toe, have you? And you should try kissing her, Vero, I've seen her face when she looks at you.'

'That is none of your damned business, Katlefiya.'

Just then reaching the crest of the ridge, we stopped to catch our breath. Kat turned around for a last glimpse of the lonely little windcatcher in the cove, while I sat down on the ground and made sure the toe wasn't broken. Down in Faddelin, the others were visible in the shade of the ruined warehouse, knocking together the sledge we would use to transport Angel when he was no longer able to walk. I could clearly hear the intrusive clack-clack of the hammer Mallinna was wielding. Even at that distance, insect-sized, she looked enticing – the man-style tunic and britches suited her long Storican frame. After an awkward few moments I coughed for Kat's attention and asked, 'So tell me: what about her face when she looks at me?'

'It's none of my damned business,' Kat said in a cool voice.

I thought that over and decided I deserved it. Silently, I got to my feet and began to limp down the slope. Kat's feet grated on the pebbles behind me.

'It's true about the archives, though, Vero,' she said, catching up. 'Angel and Mallinna were looking for ways to leave the Gilgard long before you and Tig came along. That's why they made up the idea of the Benthonic Survey

249

Expedition in the first place and asked the Flamens for a ship.'

I scraped to a halt and swung around to face her. 'That's nonsense!'

'It is not nonsense, Vero. Mallinna told me herself. There was some high official, one of the Flamens with a lot of power, who wanted to have her as soon as his celibacy expired—'

'Lestri? The Second Flamen?'

'Could be.'

'But she was going to accept his offer—'

'That's unlikely. She described him as a smelly little turd-for-brains.'

'—for the good of the archives . . .'

'No, you're thinking of Poor Tigrallef and the Wicked Princess Rinn.' This had always been one of Kat's favourite bedtime stories. 'Anyway, this Flamen was going to remove Mallinna from the archives at midwinter, so she had nothing to lose by running away. She and Angel were planning to fake a shipwreck in the Sherkin Sea and then take refuge outside the Gillish Empire, but when you and Father came along . . .'

Still chattering, she started down the slope. I turned again and limped along by her side, rearranging my ideas instead of listening. I had been so sure about what Angel meant – that Mallinna would willingly move into Lestri's bed for the sake of a few rooms of spotty books and tortoise plastrons; but now that I tried to recall the old memorian's exact words, his meaning was not so clear. *Mallinna will do what is best.* Best in what sense? And there were other oddities to fit into the picture: Angel's many stacks of instructions for the Second Memorian, his careful attention to accounts, the regret in his face as his eyes tracked slowly around the workroom. He had been a man setting his affairs in order before leaving them behind him for ever. I thought it was because he expected to die on our journey, but he had brought along an extraordinary amount of baggage for a man who intended to be buried at sea.

Mallinna, come to think of it, had brought a great deal of baggage along as well – from the look of it, just about everything she owned . . .

'. . . foot feels better, does it?'

'What? I'm sorry?'

'You've stopped limping,' Kat said, 'and you've got a funny smile on your face.'

'I'm fine.' I was better than fine. Yes, we were walking downhill into a scene of horror, fiery destruction and bloody death. Yes, we were about to embark on an uphill trudge of unknown duration into dangers I could hardly imagine. Yes, my mother was still missing, possibly dead, my sister had a doom hanging over her and my father was still host to a demented cult fetish with a wild agenda for the future of the world. And so on. For just a little while, however, I managed to feel good. That foolishness did not last long.

The first few hours were not too difficult. We moved inland from Faddelin along a gentle incline where a good Gillish road had been laid over the treacherous ground of glass and clinker, all greyed with a thin powdering of ash. Angel was able to walk this stretch without slowing us down, so we had the luxury of hauling the backsacks on the sledge instead of on our backs. The others had that luxury, anyway. I ended up pulling the sledge.

Not long after we left the smoking ruins of the modern town, we came to traces of the town's reason for being, the first of the Mosslines. It was nothing more than a crack in the slag; but it was a crack a good two spans wide, and it zigzagged away from us until it merged with a broader crack a hundred feet or more away. Instead of moss, it was filled to within a couple of fingers of the top with fine grey ash, and lying across it near the road was a curious faggot of what looked like sticks of charcoal. I recognized the latter, after some study, as a spectacularly incinerated human skeleton. The others did not seem to notice, so I kept my mouth shut.

'Whoever it was that smashed Faddelin,' Mallinna breathed, 'they also fired the Mosslines and destroyed the moss. Thousands of palots-worth, think of it! You could touch a burning brand to one end of a crack, and the fire would race along from branch to branch until a whole Mossline was blazing. It must have been an astonishing sight . . .'

'We should keep moving,' said Tig, 'but don't worry, there will be a hundred astonishing sights to marvel at before we're done. How are you feeling, Angel?'

Angel was well enough to be scribbling in the small notebook he was wearing on a string around his neck. Tig waited patiently until Angel closed the book and let it fall back against his breastbone, and then we moved on, but not very far. Within half an hour we had to stop and gawk again, because the road had wound upwards on to a plateau covered with some of the strangest ruins I had seen in twenty years of tramping around fallen cities and blasted empires – a complete town apparently sheared off at knee height and baked in a thick black glaze. Only the coral-encrusted cadaver of Itsant came close to matching its strangeness; Nkalvi and Khamanthana and the others were hardly in the same contest. The fire that destroyed Fathan had been hot enough to melt this masonry like so much candle wax.

To my eyes, the inshore ruins at Faddelin looked like a full-scale model of a townsite constructed out of large black boxes without lids. We had an excellent view of it from above – the Gillish road, which crossed the perfect grid of streets and avenues at an acute angle, was raised to just above the level of the surviving walls on a bed of black gravel and rubble fill. We walked along the roadway in silence, looking down into plan views of small courtyards and large houses, and vast enclosures that may always have been open to the sky, all with ash piled in drifts in their corners. Down the centre ran a broader avenue where the slag had something of the appearance of lava flows I had seen, billowy here and there, in places lapping up against the vitrified stumps of the structures.

Angel stopped midway through the ruin-field and opened his notebook. Mallinna fumbled to get another out of her backsack on the sledge. Jonno's lips moved silently, and I bet myself that he was working up a poem on this thought-provoking scenery. Tig looked around with great interest, not necessarily at the ruins, but in a way that suggested he was seeing much more than the rest of us, and Kat stared determinedly at the gravel surface of the Gillish roadway as if trying not to see the ruins at all.

On this occasion, Tigrallef gave the note-scribblers considerably less time to fill their notebooks. 'That's enough,' he said, 'and there will be no more stopping to enjoy picturesque views. We have a long journey ahead of us.' We moved on.

Three hours and two hills later, however, it was necessary to halt again. Angel had been hobbling on bravely, but when he stopped abruptly and sat down in the middle of the road, it was obviously time for the sledge. While the others unloaded the backsacks, I followed my father to the brow of the hill and sat down beside him, rubbing at my aching neck. We had a clear view down to the Deppowe Strait past the ancient ruins and the new ruins, and I even thought I could pick out the mast-tops of the *Fifth* in the next cove over. I glanced at Tig, wondering for the fiftieth time that day whether he saw the same view that I did.

He caught my glance and returned it with a high rate of interest. 'You can ask me, I don't mind,' he said.

'Fine, I'll risk it. What do you see?'

He waved his hand at the view, making a prong of two fingers – a highly informal, colloquial and unadmiring gesture from the fingerspeech. 'I see exactly what you do, Vero. The bleakest landscape in the known world.'

I gave him a shrewd look. 'But what does the Pain see?'

'Oh, the Pain. That's a different matter. Alas, I'm not as good as I once was at closing the old sow's eyes.'

'Well then? Tell me what the old sow sees when she looks at Fathan.'

He sighed. 'It would be hard to explain in ways you could understand, Vero. A landscape is a palimpsest with many layers. I could hardly begin to tell you all of them.'

253

I glanced back at the activity around the sledge; Angel was nowhere near to being strapped in. 'We've got a few minutes. Be selective.'

He sighed again, stood up and moved dangerously close to the edge of a steep slope, almost as if he perceived an unseen barrier there – a decorative railing, a rustic fence. 'I'm looking at a river that runs into the sea just a little west of where the harbour will stand someday. On its banks there's a cluster of huts – hovels, really – with mud walls and thatched roofs, and there are fishing boats pulled up on the beach. The beach is broad and covered with clean white sand, and a ship of light is just sliding into the bay.' He paused, with his eyes following something across the water far below.

'Carry on, Tig.'

He glanced at me. 'You're sitting in a garden – this is centuries on, of course, the huts are gone and there's a tidy little harbour built astride the river's mouth where the ship of light came in. The town on the plateau is – beautiful. Shining white walls; the roofs are terracotta, but they're painted in stunning patterns and a few are even gilded, and there's a great gilded skull in low relief above the temple door.'

'Beautiful,' I said wryly.

'You have no idea. Pity the garden didn't last. It's long gone, and the town is not so pretty now. There's also a pain-wheel above you, and somebody's in it. Whereas the gallows block is over there near the stump of a rose tree, about where the arbour used to stand. The gallows block is also in use.'

He looked past me with such conviction that I whirled around, fully expecting to see a corpse leering at me from the end of a rope overhead. Tigrallef had made much stranger things appear in his time. But there was no visible gallows block beyond me, no rose tree nor arbour nor pain-wheel, nothing but a barren hilltop that overlooked an equally barren coastal plain stretching far to the west, webbed all over with the grey scars of the Mosslines.

'You've seen enough, we'd better be going,' I sighed.

'But you haven't heard the most interesting part.' He

swung me around again and pointed down the valley towards Faddelin. 'Look at it now! The melting is happening so rapidly we can hardly take it in; no screams, though, because streaks of soot have no voices to scream with. The sea must be boiling – there's a great bank of steam rolling uphill where the harbour used to be. That salient over there,' he pointed to a broad black depression on the next hill, 'is slumping into the riverbed, and it's already halfway to the town. Impressive. Rather loud.'

All I could hear was the breeze soughing along the hilltop. 'I'm sure the sledge is ready now,' I said nervously. It was the echoing timbre and the scintillant pupils that were getting to me, plus another disturbing element in his voice – a detached kind of pleasure. I was sorry I'd asked.

'*We have not finished looking.*' Again he pointed towards the harbour. The echo was stronger. 'We are watching a rowboat.'

I was not sure I'd heard him correctly. 'A rowboat,' I repeated.

'Yes and no. We can't explain what it truly is – the rowboat is more than a metaphor and less than a rowboat, with a few other aspects on the side. But we will call it a rowboat.'

'It's a rowboat,' I agreed.

'There is one man in it, who is something more than a man; and there is a crowd on the shore. Shouting, waving, weeping.'

'They've come to see him off?'

'You're guessing, Verolef, child of the Naar. No, they're imploring him to return. The shouting and waving are for him, the tears are for themselves. He's turning his face to the west and weeping loudly enough to block the others out of his own ears. There is a bundle in the bow, a small thing wrapped in an old blanket.'

'I think I see where this vision is going,' I said.

'You see nothing, seed of the seed of the Excommunicant.'

'Oh come on, Father. The rowboat and the bundle make it fairly obvious.' I was getting my nerve back.

'Still you see nothing, *calos masha*. Not even Oballef can

see now where it will end; poor man, to be carrying such vain and useless hopes in his heart. We, on the other hand, know very well what we are doing. Of course it has all been foretold.'

I risked a glance at his face. 'You can't tell me Oballef went all the way to Gil in that rowboat.'

'As I told you, Scion of the Great Tree, it is not exactly a rowboat.'

Footsteps crushed the cinder surface behind us. Mallinna said, 'Vero, Lord Tigrallef, we're ready to move.'

'Thank you, Mallinna, we're coming,' Tigrallef said; the echo was gone, the timbre was normal, his eyes were blue, but somehow I was not relieved. There was a brief silence behind us, then the sound of Mallinna's feet crunching back towards the sledge. Tigrallef began to rise, but I stopped him by grabbing the front of his tunic.

'Just a moment. There's something that worries me. You enjoyed those visions, Father.'

'Not at all.' He gently brushed my hand away.

'Yes you did. I heard it in your voice, especially while you and the old sow were watching the wrack of Fathan. You enjoyed it. The devastation was a treat.'

He stood up, put his hand under my elbow and pulled me to my feet. 'I won't deny there was a grandeur to it, Vero. The Harashil has a talent for grandeur. It's part of what the old sow tempts me with. Destruction is the other hand of creation and can be just as beautiful in its own way.'

'Was the wrack of Sher beautiful?' I asked bluntly. He did not answer, nor even look at me, and suddenly I lost my desire to pursue the question. I really preferred to remain ignorant of how far the Pain had pulled my father along the road to the Great Nameless Last.

15

We had set off on our journey carrying four leathers of a compressed fishpaste, called *fenset* in the original Satheli, which smelt evil and tasted even worse but had one shining attribute: the amount you could force yourself to choke down your throat was almost enough to keep you going for a full day. In combination with three bags of sea biscuits and a sack of apples divided among four backsacks, the fenset leathers should have sufficed for an expedition of at least four weeks, even taking into account the three extra mouths we hoped to return with. We also brought some waterbags from the *Fifth*, but the heavy dew that collected every morning in the highlands turned out to be sufficient for our needs.

For two days we climbed steadily from the low hills near the shore to the higher foothills behind them, following the Gillish roadway. Every so often we would pass field-camps associated with the Mosslines, ranks and files of crude stone huts erected for the labourers and their guards, but we did not bother to get too close because of the powerful stench of death that hung around them. As on the plains below, every scrap of the moss had been fired, leaving a fine ash that sifted out of the trenches with the prevailing wind and made long grey scars down the hillsides. We saw not one living thing, not so much as a bird or an insect or a blade of grass, all through that portion of the journey.

Our first two nights were spent in the open, curled up in our blankets under a clear, jewelled night sky – at that point, we were still warm enough and well nourished enough to appreciate the stars. We even let Jonno recite some of his poetry for us, and it was not bad at all. The most trenchant criticisms, for some reason, came from Katlefiya.

*

About midway through the third day, we came to the end of the Gillish roadway and found we were right on the edge of the mountains. We detoured silently around the stinking huts at the roadhead and stared at the furrowed peaks looming over us; except for Kat, who rarely moved her eyes from her feet these days, and Tig, who was concentrating on the mountains' lower flanks. He pulled me a little apart from the others.

'How fortunate we are,' he said happily, 'that we won't need to hack our way through thick forests and tangled undergrowth, or encounter small animals that would tempt us to hunt them.'

'That's the bright side, is it? I don't know, Da.' My own feeling was that a forest, any forest, even the Hungry Woods of Nkalvi or the mantrapgroves of the South Ronchar Sea, would have looked benign and welcoming compared with those brooding black mountains straight out of a Lucian hell. This opinion must have been apparent on my face.

'It won't be that hard, Vero. We can follow what used to be the river valley – a few gorges to cross, but the old roads and bridges are still passable. I'd say seven days to Cansh Fathan from here, eight at most, unless something happens to hold us up.'

I tried not to think about the sort of thing that might hold us up. I tried not to think about what or who we'd find at Cansh Fathan besides our loved ones. I asked, 'How do you know all that?'

His face seemed to flicker a little – glimpses of other faces, not all of them human, passed in such rapid succession that I could almost dismiss them as a trick of my eyes. 'I can see the pass, of course. None of this is new to me. We should be able to pick up the old imperial highroad just about a mile from here, beyond that knoll.'

'The old imperial—Isn't that just a trifle indiscreet?'

'Indiscreet? How?'

I wiped a whole new batch of sweat off my forehead. 'Oh, Da. You saw what happened to Deppowe and Faddelin, and yet you want to wander straight into Cansh Fathan along the main road, like a sightseer on a tour – I suppose when we get there you'll want a room in the best tavern.'

'Don't be stupid, Vero, I don't think Cansh Fathan has taverns any more. As for the road, I will know when to leave it. Just wait till you see the bridge at the Carthenten Cleft! One of the wonders of the Fathidiic Empire – the old sow remembers it well. She's not very pleased at the prospect of showing it to you, however.'

'That makes several of us,' I said gloomily. I left him there surveying the mountain peaks with wide bright eyes, and joined the others around an open leather of fenset.

And so, after a brief halt to gag down a half-day's ration, we set off into the mountains which the old Grisotin maps called the Blessed Range, no irony intended. After a difficult first mile of broken ground and irritating crevasses, we did indeed find the old Fathidiic high road, and the going became as relatively easy as Tig had promised. That was enough to get me worried all over again – if the road was passable for us, it was passable for travellers going the other way, and I never rounded a bend without wondering if we were about to meet the demons who smashed Faddelin, off on their merry way to another massacre; but the only sound we heard, apart from the wind, was the echo of our own feet and the scrape of Angel's sledge.

The road was a broad flat ribbon as shiny and slippery as black ice, climbing monotonously along the curves of the mountains above a winding, barren scar of a valley. Tigrallef assured us the latter once held a river of heart-stopping beauty, lined on both sides by graceful trees and artfully wild parklands, plied by boats with multicoloured lateen sails. He was starting to be something of a Pain on his own account. As the rest of us strode grimly along, watching the clefts and ledges above us for suspicious movement, straining under the weight of the backsacks or the sledge, occasionally slipping on the glassy surface, he chattered on unstoppably about the fine inns and gardens that punctuated this road in the early days of the empire, the forbidding gate towers and guardpoints that succeeded them. All gone now, though he seemed to see them as clearly as I saw the bubbled rock, the seared surfaces glaring in the sun, and the ripple marks where the rock had once flowed like a flaming river.

Kat mostly watched her feet. I kept meaning to ask her why.

The first three nights in the mountains were spent in reasonable warmth and even comfort in shallow caves near the road, theoretically defensible in case of attack. On the fourth night, we did not have the same luck. The best shelter that offered itself was in the roofless and largely wall-less remains of a structure on a plateau by the roadside, one of the few identifiable ruins we had seen along the pass. It was not a pleasing spot, even by the standards of a remarkably unattractive landscape. Most of the walls had been burned or melted to the tops of the foundation courses, which were visible in the slag like the ghostly engraving of a full-sized architectural plan; but short stretches of masonry survived here and there to the height of a few spans, and two that were preserved to about chest height formed a rough kind of sheltered corner at one edge of the ruin. About two hundred feet away, the little semicircular plateau it stood upon was bounded by a line of cliffs.

I examined the standing walls without enthusiasm. They would give us some protection from the wind that howled down the valley from sunset to sunrise, but would leave us vulnerable to attack on two sides as well as open to the chilly night air of the mountains. Overall, I did not like the set-up – however, dusk was already falling when Kat and Jonno and I drew even with the ruins, and nothing better was visible on the long curve of road ahead. Moreover, nothing had threatened us for five nights running, and the terrors of Cansh Fathan were still a long way off.

Pale with exhaustion, Katla sealed our choice by dropping her backsack and then herself on to the ground a short distance from the ruins. Jonno sat down beside her and began talking to her in a low voice, in what I assumed was the next round in their ongoing discussion of life, the universe and his poetry. By this point the others had arrived – Mallinna drooping under her backsack, Angel resembling a crumpled heap of blankets on the sledge, Tig ambling along as if he had forgotten the broad leather harness around his chest had a heavy weight attached to the other end. I could see by his eyes that he was not fully with us.

'This appears to be the best we can do for tonight,' I said.

Tig looked straight through me and then up, a fair way up, though not as high as the polished peak of the mountain. 'And a very fine guardpoint it is, too, Vero. Middle-Empire style, we'd say; designed at a time when the Fathids were still building for beauty – out of habit, mainly – but were just beginning to display the more brutally minimalist propensities of the Late Empire. Note the—'

'Do you need any help with the sledge?'

'We'll manage.' He towed it blithely behind him through the ruins, into the lee of the standing walls. I did notice, though, that while most of us simply walked across the foundation traces embedded in the ground as if they weren't there, my father carefully followed the line of the outer wall to the vitrified threshold of a doorway before entering the ruin. Oddly enough, Katla took the same route a few minutes later.

It was just another evening in the mountains as far as routine went. Since we could carry very little fuel and the dead terrain provided nothing to burn, the fire we built was a pathetic affair just sufficient to heat water for a tepid infusion of herbs. We huddled together for warmth as we downed a dismal supper of fenset and biscuit; we went out in pairs for our ablutions, one acting as guard for the other; and finally we cleaned up the camp, a task which consisted of piling the backsacks on the sledge, secure in the shadowed angle where the two walls met. Then, fully dressed, we went straight to bed – that is, we wrapped ourselves in our bedrolls and curled up close together on the cold hard ground, five packages in a row along the base of one wall, with Angel beside the sledge and me at the other end. Jonno, whose watch it was, hunched himself in a blanket near the dying fire. He was too tired and cold to recite any poetry, and the rest of us were too tired and cold to listen. A quarter-moon was expected somewhat later, but it had not yet risen clear of the mountains; the only light was from the embers of the fire, the only sounds were our breathing and the wind. In moments, I was asleep.

We had divided the dark hours into three watches. On that fourth night in the mountains, Jonno had the first watch, Mallinna the second, and it was going to be my turn to enjoy the dawn. I think I slept with the concentrated stillness of a corpse for the first part of the night, but by the time Mallinna shook me awake, I was deep in a dream that for once did not involve awful things happening to Katla – a dream, in fact, in which Mallinna herself figured prominently and delightfully. Confused by the transition, but not so confused that I forgot to keep the blanket around me for warmth, I sat up and yawned – Mallinna put her hand over my mouth before I could make any noise. She brought her lips close to my ear.

'Something's out there,' she breathed.

Three developments within a broken second: I was fully awake, the leather guard of the chain was looped over the fingers of my left hand, and a naked knife was in my right. 'Where?'

'I don't know.'

'How many?'

'I don't know.'

'Only one? More than one? Big? Huge?'

'I don't—'

'How long ago?'

'Just now.'

We peered out of our half-chamber at the phantom outlines of rooms and courtyards gleaming on the silver-washed surface of the slag, the fragments of walls standing in their own shadows among pallid pools of moonlight. Mallinna shivered – her blanket had slipped unnoticed off her shoulders — so I laid my knife down and pulled her inside the warmth of my own blanket with my right arm wrapped around her; the more lethal left hand stayed outside the blanket with the chain at the ready. Her skin was icy, even through the tunic; she put her arms around me gratefully, though she said nothing and never moved her eyes from the cold silver slag-flats stretching between us and the road. Tense and watchful, we sat like that in silence for a good ten minutes, listening to the wind, and nothing happened except Mallinna's teeth stopped chattering as she warmed up. At last I whispered, 'Are you absolutely sure you saw something?'

'Not absolutely sure,' she whispered back. 'Maybe something was moving, I don't know — mostly, I just felt *watched*. Do you know that feeling?'

'Oh, yes.' I knew it well. It was the classic reaction of a neophyte night-guard. I almost whooped with relief and the release of tension. At the same time, it felt quite natural to hold Mallinna closer. 'Don't worry, I think we're safe.'

She peered up me out of our shared blanket, her tilted chin just about touching mine.

'So you don't think there's anything out there?'

'Nothing but the wind, Mallinna. It's easy to start imagining things when you're keeping watch alone — an eerie place like this.'

'But the feeling was so strong.' She shivered again, but her hands felt quite warm against my back. 'I'm sorry I woke you up for nothing, Vero. You're not on watch for another hour yet.'

'You were right to waken me if you had any doubts at all,' I protested, pulling back a little while I tucked the chain away, then using that hand to pat her shoulder comfortingly under the blanket. She gazed back at me from such close range that I could see the separate moonshadow that each eyelash cast on her smooth cheek. We cleared our throats simultaneously.

'Well — so — we're in no danger, then,' she said after a few moments.

'Apparently not.' I turned my head to survey the quiet

camp. Angel was snoring softly at the far end of the row of five shadowy bundles, beside the deeper shadow that concealed the sledge; at this end, the bundle that was Jonno twitched in his sleep. I turned my head back again and was surprised to find my nose and mouth resting comfortably against Mallinna's still fragrant cloud of hair. It was now quite warm inside our blanket.

She had dropped her head against my chest with her lips somewhere in the region of my breastbone, so her voice was muffled. 'Vero – may I ask you something?'

'Of course. Anything you like.'

She moved her cheek against my dusty tunic, just about where my heart would be. 'Did you ever see a work in the archives called the *Erotic Mistifalia*?'

'In two volumes,' I answered breathlessly after a short, stunned pause, 'dating from the reign of Cosillef Third. Profusely illustrated. I may have glanced through it.' One of her hands, I noticed, was slowly tracing a circle between my shoulderblades. Without thinking, I kissed the top of her head. 'Why do you ask?'

Warning! Warning! An alarmed voice in my head.

'It's just that I've always wondered about some of those illustrations,' she whispered, swivelling her face up, somehow managing to brush my collarbone and neck very lightly with her lips on the way.

'What – what about the illustrations?' I asked.

Five shadowy bundles?

'Well, you see – I've often thought some of the acts depicted do not look physically possible—'

'Oh,' I said, 'they're all possible in theory, though some of them would require a great deal of practice—' I broke off.

Five? Five?

'Vero, what's wrong?'

Five!

'Raksh!' I whispered, 'Oh, great gods!'

'Vero?'

I pressed her face into my shoulder to silence her – the tiny scrape of sound I'd heard was not repeated, and I could not tell where it came from. The moon was midway across the sky between the peaks, just beginning its slow slide to the west, changing all the shadows around; one end of the sledge was now visible, and it was empty. Empty. Angel snuffled in his sleep at the far end of a row of four shadowy bundles. Four.

'Stay down,' I hissed, 'keep flat on the ground.'

I pushed her down and dropped to a half-crouch, the chain out and ready in my left hand, trying to watch all the puddles of shade around us at once. Nothing moved. From behind us, there was the subtlest grating of sound; I whirled to find myself facing the blank wall. Something scrabbled again and something else clicked – just the thickness of the wall away. Mallinna drew her breath in sharply.

'Don't move.'

Gradually, still facing the wall, I began to straighten my legs. The wall was about a span away and no higher than my mid-chest; as I inched silently towards it upright, the moon-flooded northern arc of the plateau came slice by slice into view, over the top of the wall: the cliffs at the far rim . . . a segment of the road . . . the open ground behind the ruins . . . the edge of the long shadow cast by the wall . . . the eyes . . .

The next sound I heard was the hissing of my chain.

I must have missed. Seven, eight, nine dark forms streaked into the moonlight and scampered for the cliffs. They ran close to the ground, almost as if on four feet, but straightened when they were midway across the flats. More or less straightened; there was something odd and tilted about them, halfway between man and mantis, a little too long in the legs and a little too short in the body, and when I tried to see them in my mind's eye later I could conjure up no clear picture of the head. And, by Raksh, despite the strangely familiar burdens which four of them were dragging along by the back-straps, they were certainly fast movers, scuttling like woodroaches when a log is thrown on the fire. All in near silence, too; the only sound I remembered later was a tattoo of rapid clicks, which put me in mind of birds' claws scrabbling against a pane of glass. By the time I could draw in the chain and throw myself over the wall, they were already at the foot of the cliffs; and there, they simply vanished.

I could count. I knew nothing would be left on the sledge. All four backsacks had been taken, and with them every scrap of our food and fuel. Jonno and I still had our fire flints but nothing to burn. All of us had our own knives, Kat and I had our chains, Jonno had two swords and five throwing disks, and Angel had his notebook and a writing stick. Tigrallef, meantime, had a damn good sleep. Everyone but him was roused by my roar as I set off after the thiefpack – fortunately Mallinna caught up with me while I was still casting about for a way up the cliffs and Jonno pounded up a moment later, and between them they persuaded me to abandon the almost certainly suicidal pursuit.

I could hardly look at Mallinna as we trudged back to camp in grim silence; shame, mostly, coupled with bitter embarrassment. I was very busy assigning blame, none of it to Mallinna. It was not significant that this disaster had happened on her watch – she had quite properly wakened me, so the responsibility was mine. It was true we had neither heard nor seen anything that would have caused me, say, to ring the *Fifth*'s alarm bell during an ordinary watch – whatever these creatures were, they had made a science and an art out of moving without noise – but Mallinna had been wiser than me in her perception that something was wrong. I could not blame Mallinna.

But I could hotly, vigorously and justly blame myself. I was experienced – how many thousands of hours had I spent on watch in the past fifteen years? – and yet I had made the mistakes of a raw beginner. I had let myself be put off guard by the lifelessness of this landscape and a few uneventful nights; I had allowed myself to dally unforgivably with Mallinna. At one point, I realized with a shudder, I had actually seen one of the mantis-thieves, camouflaged in the guise of a sleeper *right beside Angel*, one body over from my sister, a deadly enemy loose in the very heart of our camp among helpless sleepers who trusted me – and I had been too fuddled by Mallinna's closeness to notice until too late. It was all my fault.

'It's all my fault,' Mallinna whispered.

'It's not your fault, it's mine.'

'It's *my* fault, Vero,' she insisted, 'I started it. If we hadn't – if I hadn't—'

She shut her mouth abruptly.

'If you hadn't what?' Jonno asked.

'If we had not been discussing some works of literature from the archives,' Mallinna said with dignity and truth, 'we might have seen the danger earlier.'

I stopped short; so did Mallinna.

'Jonno,' I said, 'run ahead and make sure the others are all right. Check the sledge, see if those ghouls left anything behind.' He gave me a very interested look, but he ran off without protest. When I judged he was out of earshot, I turned to Mallinna and reached for her hand. 'Flogging yourself with blame is not going to get the supplies back.'

'You should take your own advice.'

'But it was all my – never mind, we won't start that again.'

'Everything's in ruins, isn't it?' she said.

'I suppose you could say that.'

'We're probably going to die in these mountains – yes, Vero, when all factors are taken into account, that seems the most likely outcome. No food, no fire, enemies all around and their stronghold ahead of us; and Lord Tigrallef, who is choosing our path, is digging himself deeper and deeper into insanity every day. Don't deny it,' she insisted when I shook my head, 'by any definition I've ever seen, he's completely mad. I've seen ecstatics from the Niltha dreamflower cult with a firmer hold on reality; I've seen Lucian zealots with a more balanced view of the world.'

You've got it backwards, I wanted to say; he's not mad, he just sees things too clearly and in too many layers. But I said nothing about it, because I knew the effect was identical to madness and just as likely to lead us into disaster. All I said was, 'I'm sorry you were dragged into this, you and Angel and Jonno. Perhaps if we turn back now—'

'I'm not sorry, and I don't think we should turn back. I've told you before, I'd rather be here in the middle of a doomed venture than sitting in the archives waiting for the Second Flamen to work through his decade of celibacy. There's a fine fate worse than death for you! And we both know Angel's happy just being at Lord Tigrallef's side again, even if it means dying there. Jonno, well – if he dies now, he'll die with his soul intact; a life in the Flamens' Corps would murder more than the poetry in him within a few years, trust me. All that I'm sorry about—'

She hesitated, frowning at the ground and shifting from foot to foot. I was still holding her hand; she withdrew it gently and used it to push her hair off her face.

'Well?'

'I'm sorry,' she said firmly, raising her eyes, 'that we didn't get to finish our discussion on the *Erotic Mistifalia* – and it looks like we never will.'

Before I could respond – and I had no idea how to respond – she turned and started for camp with her long confident stride, her boots ringing on the armoured surface. I let her get about ten paces ahead before I followed.

Back in camp, Tigrallef was just sitting up and rubbing the sleep out of his eyes as I stepped around the end of the wall. Angel looked up at me with no expression. Jonno, sitting rather dolefully on the empty sledge beside Katla, shook his head and spread his hands in a gesture of emptiness: nothing left.

Tigrallef yawned. 'Good morning, all. It's a bit early for breakfast, isn't it?'

'What breakfast, Da? We don't have any tupping food.' A small part of my self-reproach shifted in his direction.

'Oh, really?' He yawned again and stretched until I heard his muscles creak. 'They took everything? In that case, as long as we're all awake, we might as well push on, don't you think?'

'It might make more sense to turn back,' I said bitterly; reproach was turning to anger.

'Nonsense, Vero. We're probably fewer nights distant from Cansh Fathan than we are from Faddelin.'

'Probably?' I repeated. The anger was rising, starting to pile up like water behind a dam. 'Don't you know for sure? You and your all-knowing parasite?'

He looked up at me mildly. 'Perhaps we should clarify. We're significantly closer to Cansh Fathan than to Faddelin, but the road is uphill. We cannot accurately estimate our rate of travel from this point, given the incalculable effects of hunger versus stamina. However, Cansh Fathan—'

'—will be expecting us,' I interrupted. 'That's another thing. We've been seen now. They know we're here.'

'You'll wear yourself out with worrying, Vero.'

The dam burst. 'Mighty Raksh, Father! Don't you dare tell me there's nothing to worry about. But do tell me this, Great Ark and Sceptre: why didn't you hear anything with those sensitive ears of yours? If you can see Cansh Fathan, why not a band of thieves in the cliffs right beside the road? And what if they'd killed us all, turned this ruin into a small Faddelin or a little Deppowe—'

'Please don't exaggerate. They wouldn't have hurt us,' Tigrallef broke in calmly. 'Did you get a good look at them?'

'No.' I said this very firmly, because I was trying to convince myself that it was true; the unhappy alternative was believing what I had seen. I was already certain that the odd-shaped eyes in the shadow of the wall had been reflecting the moon, not glowing with their own silver light.

'What a pity,' Tigrallef said. 'As for turning back, the answer is that we must go on. What's happening is not important. How many times do we need to tell you that?'

'You can tell it to our bellies in a day or two.'

Kat's voice emanated from the direction of the sledge: 'Stop it, Verolef.'

I ignored her. 'How will starving to death or getting ripped to pieces in the mountains help Mother and Shree and Chasco? Eh, Da?'

Kat again: 'You must stop it, Vero. You're going too far.'

Tig also ignored her. 'What would you like us to do, Child of the Naar?' There was a slight edge to his voice. 'Would you like us to set up a great banquet for you, over there in the guardsmen's mess? What do you fancy? Tripe and lentils? A haunch of deer? Nine-bird pie?'

He pointed to the southwest corner of the ruin, and suddenly a wavering vision of stone walls sprang up from the foundation courses, lamp brackets and troopers' graffiti and all. A spectral fire glimmered into life on a misty stone hearth; the ghost of a table began to take shape, groaning under high-piled platters, steaming jugs, soup basins, salvers of roast meat.

Kat pushed past me and flung herself to her knees beside our father; Katla, who had not addressed a word to him for days, who could hardly bear to look at him. 'Let it go, Father,' she cried, 'you've got to keep hold! Vero, don't push him! Father, listen to me, we'll be all right, we'll be fine, we'll find Mother and everything, but *just – keep – hold!*'

The vision collapsed in a flare of moonlight.

'Not even tripe?' Tig asked. His eyes were glassy.

'Nothing. Fight the old sow. Keep hold.' She rose from her knees, knocking nonexistent dust off her britches out of habit. With a severely minatory look at me, she stumbled back to the sledge and hid her face on Jonno's shoulder.

It was five days later, and the Myrwolf was prowling along beside me with its tongue hanging out and its golden fur patchy over a washboard of ribs. When I looked again, it was the White Dragon of Khamanthana, which I personally, unlike Katla, had no trouble distinguishing from the Sun Serpent of Vizzath. It was very simple – one of them had wings, the other one was not white. As if to demonstrate the difference, the Sun Serpent slithered into the Dragon's stead while I was wiping the sweat out of my eyes.

'Raksh take it, Father, can't you just *walk*?'

At once he was back to stumbling along on two feet: slim high-arched feet at the end of legs as long as Mallinna's. The

270

Lady's filmy robe was tattered and her hair hung down her back in a greasy tangle of snagglethorns and tiny burrs – which was quite clever of her, because nothing of the sort actually grew in the mountains of Fathan.

'I had your own feet in mind, Father.'

'Of course,' he said, 'sorry.' He was just as frayed and filthy as the old sow's many manifestations, as thin and hollow-eyed as the rest of us. About ten paces ahead, Jonno and Kat were pulling the sledge in tandem – although it weighed hardly more with Angel on it than it did empty, hauling it was now beyond the strength of any one of us on our own, except myself when absolutely necessary. Whenever we stopped, I checked Angel to make sure he was still breathing.

Why were we in such bad shape? An interesting question. As fasts go, five days should hardly have counted. The faithful of Zaine fasted annually for fourteen days, one day in honour of each *etys* of the Pantheon; the Plaviset regarded nine days without food as a health cure; eight days was our own record, set while drifting through the waters of Balqees Hoh in the shattered hulk of the *Fourth*, and we had been in better shape at the end of it than we were now. On the other hand, eight days of enforced leisure at sea level was not as draining as five days of hard hiking in thin mountain air. Indeed, there was something about the air of the Blessed Range that struck up a vicious alliance with the hunger and cold, and altogether the flesh seemed to melt off our bones.

Tig's troubles began on the third day of the fast. More accurately, the third day is when the rest of us began to see what poor Katla had been seeing all along, ever since she emerged from the *Fifth*'s hidden hold. We didn't like to mention it at first. Four of us thought we were lightheaded with hunger and having individualized hallucinations, while Kat didn't realize anything had changed; but that evening, as Jonno and I went out of camp for our ablutions, he asked me shyly if I thought my father was looking quite himself. Somehow it was small comfort to discover there was nothing wrong with our eyes, since it meant my father was getting much worse.

Not surprisingly, I was the one elected to ask him about it. I left it until the next morning and waited for him to be on two feet before I fell into step with him. 'Father . . .' I began hesitantly.

'We know what you're going to say, Vero. The many faces, right?'

I nodded.

'Don't worry about it,' he said testily, 'in fact, ignore it. You'll only encourage her otherwise.'

'You mean the Pain?'

'Of course I mean the Pain. Who else?'

'But why – how?'

The Flaming Skull of Fathan gave me an impatient look. 'We're fighting on other fronts at the moment – the old sow is honestly reluctant to continue on the road to Cansh Fathan, but you don't notice us turning back, do you? And if the core of the Will is Tigrallef's, the Harashil can do what it likes with the façade.'

'Then I don't need to worry? You'll be all right?' I felt absurd saying that – how much farther from all right was it possible to be? But the Itsanti Master of Hands reached out with three of its twenty-odd arms and patted my shoulder.

'We'll be fine,' the Lady in Gil told me.

Towards evening of the fifth day of our fast, when we reached the high pass which Tigrallef and the Grisotin charts called the Carthenten Cleft, we were long past being disconcerted by the Pain's repertoire of shapes. Perhaps our hunger-induced dullness helped; perhaps we were starting to have genuine hallucinations, and could not tell the difference. I had two other obsessions by then anyway, the first one a powerful and persistent feeling that we were being watched on all sides. There was no evidence for it – we sighted nothing and nobody in the high places above the road as we trudged wearily along, and nothing approached our miserable camps during the cold nights – but the feeling only grew stronger.

Something about that instinct of being watched kept

plucking at strings in my memory. It was a sensation similar to the one called *seen-before*, but it appeared to involve a story I had once heard rather than a personal experience. This led by short steps to the second obsession, an unscratchable itch, a terrible desire to remember or reconstruct that particular story, which was teasing at the edges of my mind. The genre was travel, that much I knew, but that knowledge was not very helpful in narrowing down the field. Approximately two-fifths of all literature, by my father's estimate, dealt with getting from one bit of the world to another, usually through bits that were nastier than either of the first two – perilous quests, heroic voyages of exploration and discovery, glorious expeditions of conquest or rescue, traveller's accounts of places any sensible person would avoid like the Storican pox. The story I was trying so hard to remember could be in any one of those categories, coming from any one of several dozen scattered literary traditions.

'We're nearly at the bridge,' Tig said in a voice that mixed excitement with the dreaded timbre of the Harashil.

'Hmm, good,' I replied. A winter's tale, perhaps? A background of snow and ice seemed just about right. Ahead of us, Kat sagged in the leather tow-strap of the sledge and folded at the knees – Jonno caught her as she fell. I sighed. 'Put her on the sledge with Angel, Jonno. I'll take over pulling for a while.' Not a story from the known world, I was thinking as I fitted the tow-strap to my chest; and probably a story I was told rather than one I read, because I seemed to remember it with my ears rather than my eyes. I plodded on with the sledge in tow, Jonno and Mallinna stumbling with hunger and fatigue on either side of me, the Myrwolf loping ahead of us waving its tail like a great golden flag. Though the pass was cold, a constant supply of sweat ran down into my eyes.

Eyes – the eyes were a significant piece of the puzzle. Silver eyes plucked the string quite vigorously; but surely I was thinking of the moon's reflections off the eyes of the mantis men, which could not possibly be right. The mantis men were a distraction, a cold trail – *cold trail*. Snow and ice. I was back to that again, remembering in circles.

'The bridge of the Carthenten Cleft!' Tig cried, 'and just as beautiful as before the great fire!' The Myrwolf bayed with excitement; a moment later the White Dragon lifted a few spans off the ground, brushing me with its great white wings.

'Damn it, Da, keep your wings to yourself,' I mumbled; but it was the Myrwolf that stayed in my mind. Myrwolf. Myr. Ice and snow. It felt like I had the right landmass at last; but we had heard so many stories in Myr . . .

'Look, Vero! Jonno, Mallinna, have you ever seen anything so beautiful?'

'Many times,' Mallinna said in a dull voice.

I lifted my head with great difficulty and squinted through sweaty strands of hair. Myself, I could see nothing of any beauty at all. The roadway here was running along the upper lip of a broad canyon, walled with sheer onyx cliffs falling away beneath us; at the bottom, perhaps two hundred feet below, I could see the dry rivercourse winding serpent-like through a stony black valley. Ahead of us, the road curved to the edge of the abyss and met an arch of gleaming black drawn like an ink stroke across the twilit sky to the other side, where I assumed the road would continue.

Putting my head down, I concentrated on shifting the full-sized windcatcher on the tow-strap behind me, evidently loaded with stone blocks and Storican trunk beasts. Myr, Myr, Myr. Snow and ice . . . the story stubbornly eluded me. Mallinna stumbled several times. Jonno wordlessly joined me in the loop of the leather tow-strap, easing the burden enough to let me start thinking again. Myr, Myr, Myr . . .

Then the road turned and our feet were on a smoother black surface that rose ahead of us like a gentle hill with a fading evening sky at the top. Tigrallef was suddenly there, slipping the leather strap down and helping Jonno and me step clear of it. He was himself for the moment.

'Our turn to pull,' he said. 'Stay near the centre, all of you – much of the parapet was melted away, and it's a long way to the bottom, though we must say . . .

He walked away up the black hill, chattering steadily, with the sledge trailing behind him. Angel had his eyes closed and looked dead, but he had looked that way for three days; Katla's eyes were open. She stirred dazedly on the sledge, lifted her head and let it drop again. Somehow Jonno and Mallinna and I ended up drifting after Tigrallef as a unit, tangled together in mutual support; when we caught up, he was still talking.

'. . . quite an engineering feat, but they wouldn't have been able to build it without our help, just like the Gilgard. Strong enough to withstand the fires which blasted Fathan – fused into a single stone spanning the abyss! Stronger than ever, as far as we can tell. No cracks at all. Astonishing—'

'Eyesuckers,' I said suddenly.

'What was that, Vero?'

'The Eyesuckers of Myr,' I croaked in triumph. 'I've been trying to remember that story for days.'

'Funny you should think of the Eyesuckers now,' he said in an odd voice. He flicked with dizzying speed through the Flaming Skull, the Sun Serpent and the Nkalvi Great-of-Fangs, and became himself again. On the sledge, Katla sat up with her eyes wide and her nostrils flaring.

Her tension was contagious.

I broke free of Jonno and Mallinna. For the first time since Tigrallef took over the sledge, I stood up straight and had a good look around. This black hill was the bridge and we were about halfway across it, on the highest point. Under my feet was a solid surface of black glass, fortunately not transparent; about ten feet away on either side the surface simply ended. Far ahead, just glimpsed through a notch between two crags, was a mirage of high towers and ochre-streaked ramparts catching the late rays of the sun – a clear sign to me that my mind was beginning to go. I recognized them as the grim iron ramparts where Katla sometimes stood in my nightmares. I had a moment of intense vertigo, an almost irresistible impulse to drop to the ground and crawl the rest of the way across the bridge on my belly. Katla's shout snapped me out of it.

'They're coming!'

She rolled off the sledge and leapt to her feet. For a terrible moment I thought she was going to break for the knife-edge of the span and cast herself over – I launched myself at her, grabbed her in my arms, lost my balance and toppled with her to the hard ground.

'Gods' sake, Vero, get off me.'

'They won't hurt us.' Tig's voice was normal, matter-of-fact, without Painful overtones. 'They could if they tried, but they've been waiting for us a long time. The Pain can't hurt them at all. That's just how it is.'

'Who's he babbling about?' Nobody answered. I had to wait for Kat to extricate herself furiously before I was able to sit up and see for myself.

Jonno and Mallinna were standing stiffly side by side looking back at the end of the bridge we had come from. Katla was standing with her hands on her hips glaring at the end we were heading for. At both ends – silver eyes gleaming through the dusk, long misshapen bodies taking every posture from four-legged to upright – the mantis men were gathered to greet us.

'We're dead,' I breathed.

'Not yet,' my father said behind me.

'Then it's only a matter of time. Raksh, Tig, are they even human?'

'Well, you weren't far off thinking about the Eyesuckers,' he said cheerfully. 'It was clever of you to make the connection. And yes, they're more or less human. Vero, put the chain away. Jonno, forget the sword.'

'But who are they?'

Soundless burst of light – I shielded my eyes in the crook of my arm. He was Tigrallef, but he was glowing through his skin with a light as strong as the sun, as pale as the moon. He said, 'They're sort of distant cousins, Vero. Be polite, now.'

276

16

'Distant cousins?' I repeated. 'That's not funny, Tig.'

'Very distant cousins. Collateral descendants of your direct ancestor Oballef. Just as much children of the Naar as you and Katla. Oh, Verolef,' he chided me as I opened my mouth with a dozen panicky questions, 'we'll explain later. They're waiting for us.'

'Do you mean *us* in the sense of you and the Pain?' I was really asking whether the rest of our complement would be cut into stewing-pieces while he and the Harashil were reverentially escorted to the towers of Cansh Fathan. Tig looked thoughtful.

'More precisely, it's probably Oballef they're waiting for; but we suppose we'll have to do. Jonno, Kat, Mallinna – time to move.'

I did not like it, but there were only three ways to go: two of them led straight into the arms of our remote cousins, and the third was a very long drop.

The towers and ramparts had not been a trick of my eyes nor a carry-over from my nightmares; they were the small part of Cansh Fathan that was visible from the summit of the Carthenten Span. We could see much more when we reached the far end of the bridge, where the growing horde of relatives parted to let us pass.

It was a strange parade that set off from the bridgehead: Tigrallef, giving off enough light to read by in the deepening dusk, ambled along in the lead – then came the sledge, sliding effortlessly behind him with a puzzled-looking Angel on board, then the other four of us keeping together in a tight, uneasy cluster, then the multitude. There were no overtly threatening gestures; though I felt herded, it was in the direction we were heading anyway.

Somehow, they were marginally less terrifying now that I could see them up close. Short hunched bodies, scrawny and pot-bellied, with long legs and long curving arms; heads that drooped rather touchingly between their collarbones on the ends of too fragile necks; massive foreheads, receding chins, surprisingly delicate noses with long slanted nostrils – a marked over-abundance of teeth. The eyes, silver-irised and slightly bulging, followed Tigrallef in a unison that was almost comic. Their sartorial taste ran to wrong-sized tunics and britches, many of them the familiar dun or black of Gillish imperial troopers, and a ragged assortment of cloaks and robes. Booty of war, obviously – one could tell by the slashes, rips, bloodstains and bad fit. An altogether dazzling gown of jewelled brocade that hung in tatters on one ugly cousin might well have belonged to the Deppowe governor's lady. I found myself watching for the white-trimmed red tunic Shree was so fond of, the grey one Chasco was wearing when I last saw him. My mother's chest of Amballan silk robes? I didn't dare think about that.

They were everywhere around us. They crept in from the shadows on either side of the road as we passed, to join our growing snake of followers, and they were as silent as the thieves who had left us to starve. I felt a hand slide into mine: Mallinna's. Meantime, the vista of Cansh Fathan broadened and deepened ahead of us until, about a half-mile from the Carthenten Span, we reached the most scenic viewpoint any sightseer could ever wish for. It was on the edge of a precipice sheer enough to convince me I really might be afraid of heights after all.

There it was at last, the fabled lost city of Cansh Fathan. I was no stranger to fabled lost cities, but there was something different about Cansh Fathan. Much of Myr was under ice, Itsant under water and coral, Khamanthana partly under the suburbs of latter-day Gafrin-Gammanthan, Baul many feet deep under Amballa, Nkalvi smothered in creepers and delving roots and poisonous rock-devouring thorn bushes – but Cansh Fathan was a standing ruin where somebody still lived.

The precipice was the curved backdrop to a huge amphitheatre of a valley, its floor a good two hundred feet below where we stood. To our right, the road began a serpentine descent down the cliff wall; to the north across the valley, the open front of the amphitheatre rolled away in smooth black foothills, as glassy and desolate as the plains around the Mosslines; and between the foothills and the cliff was a sprawling walled city whose lowest towers were on a level with our eyes, whose tallest towers thrust as high again above us into the darkening sky. A curtain wall forty or fifty feet high enclosed it. Within it rose level upon level of massive ramparts, each with its own bastions and towers, leading the eyes on and up to a lofty central spire.

Three miracles. First, whereas the rest of Fathan was as barren as a garden where a locust swarm has just had supper, in the valley of Cansh Fathan the greenery sprang wildly and profusely from the crevices of the cliff, the ramparts and the curtain wall. Second, the black-glazed surface covering the valley floor was not stone but water – a still lake that lapped from near the base of the cliff to the curtain wall, and around it to the first rise of the foothills. Third, many of the window squares in the ramparts of Cansh Fathan were already glowing gamely against the approaching darkness; which meant that the scores and scores of mantis-people already gathered behind us were only some of the ancient city's populace.

I edged closer to my father. Without moving his eyes from the city, he said, 'Amazing. Spared by the Harashil for the sake of the Naarlings dwelling inside, but the years have been less kind to Fathan.'

'Never mind that. Did you know all this was going to happen? You said you'd know when to leave the road.'

'It wasn't necessary. The road is still going in the right direction, just as we are.'

'I could wish we were going with a little less company.'

'Vero, we'll say it again – none of this is important.'

'What about Calla and Chasco and Shree? Are they important? Are they somewhere in that great pile of rock?'

'We shall see, Vero. We'd better go down into the valley now, we believe they're anxious to greet us.'

He led us on to the meandering road, conveniently lighting the way with his own internal fire. Night came quickly – before we were halfway down the cliff face, full dark had fallen and the sky was black. When I looked back up the road, all I could see was a throng of shadows pressing close behind us, pierced with hundreds of shining round eyes – like the eyes of wild beasts in the night-time jungles of Nkalvi. It still shocked me that these mantis men could be almost on our heels and still make no sound loud enough for our ears to catch.

Looking ahead, I gradually realized that a constellation of little lights at the bottom of the cliff was not, as I had thought, the reflection of stars on the smooth surface of the lake – it was too active to be that. This was our first hint of another, and larger, welcoming party; and these ones, unlike the crowd we had already collected, did not stand aside to let us pass when we reached the foot of the final switchback. We halted, faced by innumerable shining eyes.

'We wish you'd stop fiddling with that belt buckle, Vero. You weren't planning on swimming across, were you? This lake is very deep in places and stocked with strange fish. This way.'

For all the world as if he'd lived his whole life in the valley and knew it like the lines of his own palm, my father veered to the right on a path that was invisible to the rest of us. Confidently, he led us past the silent watchers, made a couple of mysterious detours, and came at last to a point where the lake water lapped infinitesimally against a muddy beach. Still dragging the sledge, he slogged straight through the mud and set off across the water on foot. Angel, unperturbed, continued to gaze back at us blankly.

The rest of us hesitated on shore. In seconds, a host of shades with lambent eyes pressed around us. They did not touch us, but I could feel – and smell – their breath blowing down my neck.

'Tig? Oh, Tig?'

He stopped and turned around a little wearily. Aspects of the Myrwolf, the Sun Serpent, the Burning Child, the Lady, chased each other across his gleaming face. 'What is it now?'

I ground my teeth together. Mallinna pressed my arm and called out, 'Lord Tigrallef, about this idea of walking on water . . .'

He grinned as he turned his back on us. Even Angel looked amused. 'Try it,' Tig called over his shoulder. 'Your feet might get a little wet, nothing more.'

Jonno, bless him, probably started across the water as a pious act of faith in the Divine Scion Tigrallef – that devout background coming to the fore again, though he had more than once partnered Tigrallef on the evening ablutions and should have known very well my father was not divine. He did not, however, sink; his faith seemed vindicated; but he stopped and looked down at his feet, and called back to us in a voice that had as much chagrin in it as relief, 'It's all right. There's a causeway.'

'Why in the name of Raksh didn't those jokers say so?' I grumbled.

Kat shrugged. We set off – the causeway was covered by only an inch or two of water – and within a few minutes we were climbing the steps of a broad landing stage under the great gate of Cansh Fathan.

Up until this point, not a word had been spoken to or by our mass of followers. If I looked back, I could see them strung out along the causeway in a long patient queue, visible mainly by their glowing eyes, waiting up to their ankles in cold water for us to precede them into the city. Such quiet courtesy bothered me mightily. On the other hand, I reassured myself, they had already passed up numerous chances to tear us to tatters – perhaps I was being too suspicious.

The gateway was a cavern cut through the immense thickness of the wall. Thriving bushes leaned out of cracks in the masonry; twenty feet above our heads, a crust of heavy moss partly obscured a band of Old Fathidiic glyphs, each one the length of my arm. We could see all this partly by Tig's light and partly by torches being held by a semicircle of dignified cousins – our third welcoming party in under two hours – advancing on us from the greater cavern of the city proper. All were naked: three males, two females, two who rather defied classification. About ten feet away from the sledge they stopped and silently abased themselves before my father. He was in no great hurry to respond. He kept them waiting while he finished unstrapping Angel from the sledge and handed him over to Mallinna and me for safe keeping, and only then did he move forward to greet the newcomers and raise them graciously to their feet. They burst into flood tides of speech. At last somebody was talking to us.

The language was a version of Old Fathidiic with a peculiar slurred accent, probably a result of the many teeth they had to speak through and the odd shape of their throats. The phrases I could pick up seemed to indicate the faithful of Cansh Fathan were ecstatic to see my father, whom they called the Returned One and the Excommunicant, which was a fair confirmation they had mistaken him for our ancestor Oballef. They also declared themselves grateful to his prophets for preparing the way, and hopeful the Excommunicant would smile upon the humble arrangements they had made. There was, moreover, some mention of the Food of the [lost?/departed?] Old Ones, which made my ears grow big and my belly churn with a nausea of anticipation. Murderers, arsonists and committers of atrocities though they were, the despoilers of Deppowe and Faddelin, the degenerate heritors of the vicious Fathids, at least it sounded like they were going to feed us.

Katla, whose grasp of Old Fathidiic was better than mine, frowned. She had been translating in whispers for Jonno's benefit – now she leaned over to whisper in my ear, 'Did the fat one just congratulate Father on having the foresight to bring sacrifices?'

'I missed that. Did you catch what they said about food?'

'Forget the food, think about the sacrifices. That's probably *us* they're talking about.'

'Don't worry, Kat, I'm sure Tig would never let it happen.'

'How sure?' Katla said. She was watching Tig dubiously.

Mallinna coughed. 'Look behind us, Vero.'

I looked. I forgot all over again about being hungry.

If the corpses left unburied on a battlefield lay around for a few days to let the rot set in properly, and then were given group rates to rise up and attend the performance of a travelling comedy show, I have a good idea what that audience would look like. It would be like the one behind us now – a solid press of the happy undead, stretching clear across the breadth of the outer gate and back to the edge of the landing stage. The leaping light from the torches hollowed their cheeks, peeled the flesh back from their bulging eyes and brutal teeth, picked out in high relief every knife-slash and bloodstain on their stolen rags. The comedy-show aspect came from how delighted with the proceedings they managed to look. I reached for my chain – Jonno's hand went to his sword. Tigrallef's voice stopped us before we got into any trouble.

'Our hosts call themselves the Afadhnid – note the slight but interesting sound shift in the second consonant. These are their leaders, the Councillors of the Flaming Skull, and they're going to take us to the prophets. Apparently a feast has been prepared. Keep close to our heels, all of you – very, *very* close.'

No doubt we were led through many grandeurs of architecture that night; but any time there was enough light to see, I was too uneasy and sick with hunger to be interested. Our wits, temporarily sharpened by the presence of the mantis men, relapsed into dullness. I have a few hazy general impressions: narrow paths through heaps of rubble and collapsed structures of wood, brick and wattle; great stone courts and corridors, clear of rubble and open to the stars; lighted towers soaring above our heads. Cansh Fathan was much more tumbled and ruinous than it looked from the cliff top, but the destroyers were time and neglect as opposed to fire and fury. I remember wondering how, in the name of Oballef, we were going to find Calla, Chasco and Shree in this dilapidated labyrinth, assuming they were still alive and the natives continued to be friendly.

We halted in front of a well-preserved monumental doorway, double-leaved, three times my height and broad enough for a dozen persons to march through abreast. Heavy, too; a score of our Afadhnid cousins crowded past us to push the thick wooden leaves open, then fell on their faces in reverence as soon as the light hit them. It was a strong golden radiance that was spilling through the open portal – the Councillors of the Flaming Skull dropped to their knees, but I had a feeling they were anxiously watching Tigrallef's reaction, hoping for approval. He was glowing to rival the light from the interior; he stepped forward with an unconcerned air, pausing on the threshold only long enough to raise his hand and motion the rest of us to keep up with him.

The chamber was a vast rectangle of tile and stone, also well preserved. Its height was lost in shadows, but its corners were illuminated by hundreds, perhaps thousands, of grinning lanterns – human and semi-human skulls lit from within, ranged on great racks of shelves that ran the full length of the room on both sides. Midway along one of those walls was an archway leading to a side chamber. At the far end, the floor rose in narrow tiers to a broad stage whereon three tall, fantastical figures stood in masks and garish robes. I presumed these were the prophets mentioned by our hosts. They were praying around an altar draped with a banner, shimmering white on crimson and gold, the device a skull on a background of flame, and they lifted their hands in salute to us as we trooped through the doors.

Tig waved back and strolled down the axis of the chamber, his sandals slapping on the stone. We followed, with the Councillors just behind us and a rapt mob just behind them. Tigrallef turned on the first tier and raised his arms; the light expanded around him. Abruptly, he became the Flaming Skull of Fathan – Katla gasped and hid her face in her hands, the prophets fell to their knees around the altar and the multitude made an actual noise at last, a surf-like chorus of gasps and low wheezings.

'If you don't mind,' my father boomed in Old Fathidiic, in a voice that was nine-tenths Pain, 'we are to be left alone now to commune with our prophets. Go with our blessing, Children of Afadhna, Twigs of the Great Tree, the Abandoned Ones, and feast yourselves in celebration of the Excommunicant's return. Drink an ocean of strong waters in the name of the Excommunicant – that's an order. We'll let you know if we need anything. Now off you go.'

I think the Afadhnid horde withdrew only with the gravest reluctance, worshipful eyes on Tigrallef right up until the moment they pulled the double doors shut behind them. Then we were alone with the mysterious prophets, and my hand strayed back to the buckle of the Gafrin-Gammanthan belt – Katla, however, was already racing past our father and up the lower tiers to the stage, where she flung herself into the arms of the shortest of the prophets, the one in the bright yellow robe.

'Mother!' she cried.

Twenty minutes later we were sitting on a carpet in the side chamber off the main sanctuary of the Flaming Skull, and the first bout of tears, explanations, embraces, incoherency and gruff manly greetings (the latter from Katla to Chasco and Shree, right after she blew her nose) was just about behind us. The promised feast was already in progress, by urgent necessity, though we were finding it easy to restrain ourselves from eating too quickly after our long fast: the Food of the Old Ones turned out to be fenset. In fact, it was *our* fenset, the selfsame supply stolen from us on the trail. It put paid to my theory that anything, no matter how loathsome, will taste good if one is famished enough.

Jonno and his long-lost uncle were sitting side by side on one end of the carpet, talking soberly together. Family matters, I supposed. There was a strange, hungry look on Chasco's face. It was odd to me, because I had never thought of him as having any family except us. On one side of them, Mallinna was tending to Angel. Opposite them was another family grouping, my mother and father and Katla, who was curled up with her head in our mother's lap.

I was keeping clear – I had embraced my mother but I was not yet ready to answer to her. Although Tigrallef had been on his best behaviour and worn his own face exclusively since the doors swung shut behind the Councillors – evidence, or so it seemed, that Calla could still anchor him – she was having great difficulty concealing her dismay. I knew what she was thinking. How long had Tigrallef been glowing like a candle factory on fire? How long since the Painful timbre had taken over his voice? How long had he been *plural*? How far was he from defeat? Deadliest of all – how could I, Vero, have let it happen? How could I have allowed it to go so far?

'The worst part,' Shree was saying beside me, 'is having to wear this tupping silk robe of your mother's the whole time. I can't take a decent breath without risking the seams.'

I dragged my eyes away from Calla. 'It looks good on you,' I said. Straight-faced, too.

'Good enough to impress the locals,' Shree retorted, 'and that's all that matters. You should have seen them in Faddelin, Vero! Like ghosts – no – like plague-demons, just as silent and deadly. Their tactic was to seep into every corner of the town in the middle of the night and quietly start murdering everything in reach. The alarm was never even sounded. What saved us, now I think about it, was the Faddelin governor's suspicion of the papers that arrived with us – he couldn't quite believe what he was being ordered to do. Who did you say issued those orders?'

'The First Flamen, Kesi.'

'I barely remember him.'

'Fortunately he remembers you. Go on with your story.'

Shree took a sip of the wine the Afadhnids had laid out with the fenset. 'As I said, the governor was worried by his orders, not that we were ever told what the orders were, or anything else. We were just shunted from ship to ship, and finally into the old beacon-tower of that slummy little town, where we were locked up in the topmost chamber while the governor sent to Gil for confirmation that he was supposed to release us. And one morning we woke up to a strange silence.'

'Silence?'

'Well, none of the noises we were used to, prisoners being moved around, overseers shouting, crates being loaded on the quay, that kind of noise. Just an odd crackling, like fire, and the occasional thump. And then, still quite early in the morning, the screaming started; they'd taken prisoners, you see. When we looked out the beacon-ports, we saw – well – you saw the aftermath, we saw the sacrifices in progress. These Afadhnids have an unfortunate fascination with fire.'

'Part of the Fathidiic heritage, no doubt.' I put down the bit of fenset I'd been considering putting in my mouth. 'What saved you?'

'Being locked in,' he said. 'They had plenty to do with the targets at hand. They didn't try breaking the lock for two days, and by then the banner was ready.'

I shook my head. 'I still can't believe it. I still can't quite believe you prepared for battle by *sewing a large quilt*.'

'A warrior,' he quoted in Sheranik, 'makes a sword from a silk scarf.'

'You just made that up.'

'No, it's a real proverb, it's just uncannily appropriate. Anyway, it wasn't a quilt, it was a banner. They'd brought out their poor excuse for a ceremonial banner during the sacrifices, and we could tell it was the Flaming Skull. We made a bigger and better Flaming Skull, that's all, using your mam's silk robes. And while we sewed, we cobbled all the Old Fathidiic we could remember into what we hoped was a plausible story – that we were the prophets of the Flaming Skull, come to announce the return of their Promised One. When they finally got around to breaking the lock of the beacon tower, we'd been waiting in costume for hours. The rest was easy.'

'But what if we hadn't come along to fulfill your prophecy?'

'We knew you would,' he said, lifting his beaker to me in a salute. 'And if you hadn't, eventually someone else would have. The Afadhnids are doomed now, you know. The road to Cansh Fathan will be the death of them. They've given themselves away, given up the advantage of being lost and forgotten – a well-organized army with the right defences will be able to wipe them out in no time. I'd give them six months once the Primate – imagine it, old Mycri, still breathing! – tracks them back through the mountains.'

'Why do you sound regretful? Think what they did to the Mosslines ports. They're monstrous.'

'They're your cousins, not mine,' Shree said airily. 'And yes, they're monstrous, but once you get used to the teeth and forget the blood and soot on their hands, they're extraordinarily endearing. We've spent half the time fearing for our lives, the other half trying not to hurt their feelings. Look how anxious they were to give you a good welcome!'

'What, this feast?'

'They worked very hard on it.'

'But they stole our food. We could have starved.'

'True, Vero, but their intentions were good. Where else but in your backsacks could they find the Food of the Old Ones? Look at it from their point of view. To them, Tig is Oballef and Oballef is an Old One. Old Ones have to be given the right kind of food. And since the Bequiin Ardin walked off with their entire archives twenty-five years ago, they've had no way of checking how things should be done. They've been improvising.'

'With your help, of course.'

'On some things, these last few days – but they didn't consult us on the catering. They worked that out on their own.' Shree grinned.

I grinned back, drew a deep breath and offered another small mouthful to my protesting belly. By the time I got it down my throat, Shree was conversing warmly with his old friend and colleague Angel and telling Mallinna what a very bright little child she'd been, as well as damned pretty, and how sorry he was to hear about her mother; and Calla was giving me the occasional glance across the carpet as if she might summon me for a full accounting at any moment. It was obviously a good time to get up and get interested in the things scattered around this very interesting chamber.

Our backsacks, for example. They had been carefully and precisely positioned, one at each corner of the carpet, and they were intact, if rather pawed-over. Nothing was missing from mine as far as I could tell, down to the last tooth-pry and ragged pair of underbritches. The backsacks were not the only souvenirs of visitors to Cansh Fathan, either. The longer wall was taken up with a display of helmets, breastplates and triple-curved swords, all of Miisheli manufacture, centred around a rather clever mosaic of longbones and disarticulated vertebrae. These had to be trophies of the Bequiin Ardin's expedition, which had lost something over half its complement to a never-seen enemy. On either side of the door, the walls were given over to shrines of smaller expeditions – a few single explorers, their travelling cloaks, bedrolls, saddle-packs and even notebooks lovingly embedded in the plaster along with their bones. Two were Gillish, and very recent. The plaster was still slightly damp. A group of five arranged in a tasteful starburst effect was probably a team of noted Zelfic geographers who vanished about three hundred years ago, last seen heading inland from Cansh Miishel. A fresh undercoat of plaster was drying on one of the end walls – a large pile of Gillish Imperial armour and weaponry was gleaming in the corner. A new exhibition of trophies was evidently in preparation.

There remained one wall – the shorter wall at the far end of the chamber. I leaned over Shree and shook his shoulder.

'What's behind the curtain?'

He glanced towards the end of the room. 'I don't know. We never had a chance to look.' As he spoke, he nodded to Angel, got to his feet and walked with me towards the curtain. 'It always happened that either the workmen were in here or we were busy making up rituals to keep the Afadhnid off our throats – a tiring business. We had a chance to look at some of these other relics, though. Quite a museum. I wonder if there'd be time before we escape—'

He fell silent as I drew back the curtain and light fell across the wall.

'Our ancestor was stating his intentions,' said Tigrallef. 'This was written by the Excommunicant himself.' He moved his forefinger shakily along the lines of faded black letters inscribed on the wall. The forms of the glyphs were Old Fathidiïc, but the language was not – after a bit of puzzling I realized it had the sound of Naarhil, the language of Oballef and the Harashil, of which I understood very little. All of us crowded around Tigrallef waiting for his translation, except Calla, who was sitting on the carpet staring grimly at the depleted platter of fenset. Although the curtained alcove had been the only dim corner of the room, we needed no lamp or candle to see the inscription inked with such care upon the time-worn plaster. Tigrallef was shining again, brighter than ever. His finger reached the bottom line and stopped. His hand fell to his side. Thinking back later, I realized that was probably the moment on which subsequent history was hinged.

'Well? What does it say? How much of it can you read?' Shree asked eagerly. My father showed no sign of hearing him. The light was fading under his skin, leaving him pale and tired and very young. He turned around and pushed between Katla and Shree, managing to take a few stumbling steps towards Calla before collapsing. Five of us leapt to catch him – Calla won.

'What is it, dearheart? What did you read there?' Her voice dropped hopefully. 'Is it the Banishment?'

'No, Mother.' Kat alone was still peering at the words on the wall. The other members of our old crew were clustered helplessly around Tigrallef, who was a heap on the floor with his head on my mother's yellow silk knee. Of our new additions, Angel had tottered back to the carpet with Mallinna's help and was gazing pensively into the distance, Mallinna was drifting back towards Kat and the inscription, and Jonno had joined the mother-hen contingent around

Tigrallef. Not an hour had passed since we were reunited, and we had already fallen back into the same old tableaux. I experienced a moment of despair that had nothing to do with the old sow.

'So galling,' Tig whispered. 'So obvious, and we missed it. Cycles upon cycles, but the old sow blinded us to the great cycle that overarched the others.'

'What are you talking about, dearheart? Tell me.'

'Seven empires,' said Angel suddenly.

'Exactly,' said Tig.

'And one to begin with?'

'The Great Nameless First.'

'Plus one more to finish with?'

'The Great Nameless Last.'

'Gil?'

'Yes and no. The Gil that should have been.'

'The vases? The Old Ones?'

'One canine, one feline,' said Tig, 'two reptilian, three anthropomorphic. Too tupping obvious. However, the Lady was Oballef's own invention.'

My mother rebelled at this point. She clapped a hand over Tig's mouth and bent herself at the waist until her nose almost touched his. 'Enough of that. In clear, simple sentences, my beloved, you'll explain to the rest of us what Angel already seems to understand.'

'It's about the Great Nameless First,' Kat broke in without turning around. 'Oballef was the Child of Naar chosen to return there, only he wasn't supposed to go alone. And that's not all.'

'It's funny.' Tig gently pushed Calla away and sat up slowly, giving the impression that his body was too heavy for his own strength to move, or perhaps that the old sow was determined to stop him. 'All these years,' he said, 'we thought it was Oballef who was excommunicated, but it was the other way round – he left the others behind to suffer the fate of all the Naar's discards.'

'The Afadhnids,' I said.

'And the Myrene Eyesuckers, Vero, rapidly becoming

extinct. Yes, they're your cousins too. The demons of Gafrin-Gammanthan mythology, wiped out by the invading Gafrind. The fishmen of Itsant, food for the Bloody Spirits. The ape tribe of Nkalvi, massacred by the descendants of their surviving subjects. The Vizzathan – same story, but the canny Heretrixes twisted it to their own purposes. There have always been some left behind, but Oballef went altogether alone. He never did build his ship of light.'

'Perhaps,' said Calla evenly, 'you could just tell us what the inscription says and let us work it out for ourselves.'

He stared at her with glassy eyes. 'Tricky old sod, Oballef. The Excommunicant. The bargain-breaker. He crossed the Old Ones, well and truly; but, by the balls of – by his own balls, he certainly landed Tigrallef in the quicksand. None of this was meant to happen, *none of it*. And that's our best hope.'

My mother sighed and shook him gently. 'The inscription, dearheart?'

His mouth worked, but any words were caught in his throat.

'*In the destined Year of the Coming of the Great Nameless Last,*' Katla began, '*being chosen by the Wind and the Tree to redeem the pledge—*'

'When did you learn Naarhil?' Calla demanded with panic in her voice.

'I didn't,' Katla said fiercely. 'Do you want to hear this or not? I don't think the old sow will let Father be coherent.'

My mother sank back on her heels and put her face in her hands. I was grateful for that – she was thus spared Tigrallef's silent but quite spectacular struggle with his own repertoire, right there on the floor. Shree and Chasco saw, went pale and looked despairingly at each other, but said nothing. The rest of us had seen it before.

'I'll begin again,' said Katla. 'He says:

In the destined Year of the Coming of the Great Nameless Last, being chosen by the Wind and the Tree to redeem the pledge of our forefather Naar and yield up his seed and his talisman to

*the Old Ones according to the ancient compact between them,
I do hereby defy the Old Ones and repudiate the compact and
declare a new cycle of the world; and in token of defiance I
shall bear the talisman called Harashil to the Great Nameless
First and thus complete the circle; but I shall not complete the
prophecy, nor make the two be one, nor build the Great
Nameless Last, nor yield up the Harashil and the seed of Naar;
for I shall build according to a new will and a new order, an
empire that shall never fall nor bring the world to an end; and
I do this in repugnance at the works of the Old Ones, and at
the pride of my forefather Naar.*

And that's all.'

'He meant well,' Tig said faintly, 'but he made a big
mistake.' He sighed and seemed to gather strength. 'Ah well,
what's done is done, and we'll just have to deal with it. Come
on, we'd better get moving.' He began to hoist himself off
the floor.

'There's plenty of time, Tig,' I said quickly. 'You need to
rest – we all do. And we need to think about this inscription.'

'No, actually we need to leave, and we need to do it
tonight. As for the inscription, we've already thought about
it.'

'Tonight?' Calla protested, uncovering her wet face.
'You've been starving for days. You have to recover your
strength. You can't possibly ask poor Angel and Katla
and—'

'We have to go tonight. Why else would we have instructed
the Afadhnids to get gloriously drunk? Pack the rest of the
fenset in the backsacks, Vero, and pick up a couple of leathers
of wine – you'll need it for the journey.'

'Tigrallef, dearheart—'

'Did we mention the sacrifices have been scheduled for
tomorrow morning?'

'Sacrifices?'

'Jonno, Katla, Mallinna and Vero. They assumed Angel
was our priest. Did we forget to tell you? A symbolic re-
enactment of the immolation of Fathan, using real fire.'

Shree was already stripping off the silken gown. 'Vero, can you spare me some clothes? Thanks. Tig, I assume we're going to Gil.'

'That's right. Where it all began,' Tig affirmed dazedly, 'and where the Excommunicant was meant to finish it.'

'And what happens when we get to Gil?' Chasco asked as he caught the tunic and trousers Jonno tossed to him. 'Last time we got no farther than the outer harbour. What if the Primate captures us again?'

'That,' said Tigrallef, 'is not important. Nothing that is happening here and now is important. All the important things should have happened a thousand years ago. Katla, keep hold. Come along, our beloved.'

The Afadhnids were an obedient people. It was not yet midnight, barely two hours since my father told them to hoist a few drinks in honour of the Excommunicant, and about half of them were already in a stupor. Some of them were weeping quietly into whatever villainous liquid passed for brew in those parts; small groups here and there were crooning mournful melodies in surprisingly tuneful voices and pleasant harmonies. The words I could catch dealt with things like young love, motherhood, dear little babies, moon-light, the wildflowers in the walls of Cansh Fathan, the poignancy of old age, the paradise that would be restored when the Excommunicant returned to his beloved Afadhnids. I began to see what Shree meant when he described them as endearing. I also noticed four iron cages hung over a great heap of firewood in one of the squares.

We did not attempt to move stealthily; the cloaks and the darkness were disguise enough, in combination with the gently contemplative style of drunkenness the Afadhnids went in for. Few of our cousins looked up to watch us pass. No alarm was given, even when Tigrallef led us unerringly to the great gate and took some time strapping Angel on to the sledge, which had not been touched since we left it behind. It was only when we were across the water and nearly to the top of the switchback road that Chasco, sharing the sledge's tow-rope with Shree, looked down and noticed a stream of tiny silver points flowing out of the gate and on to the causeway.

'The Afadhnids are coming,' he said grimly. 'I can see the lights of their eyes.'

'Keep moving,' said Tigrallef.

Shree cleared his throat uncomfortably. 'What I'm hoping, Tig, is that you can just tell them to turn around and go home; is that what you're planning to do? Because otherwise we'll have to stand and fight them at some point, seeing as we can't outrun them all the way to the coast.' By the flashing of starlight on a polished blade, I could see he had armed himself from the Gillish weapons in the museum chamber. 'The thing is,' he went on unhappily, 'it'll be a tragic pity if we do have to fight them. I can't help feeling a little – guilty.'

'Guilty?' said Tig. His cloak had a hood, which had been pulled down over his face to muffle the Pain's light. Now he threw it back and illuminated the roadway with a strong golden radiance. The forefront of the stream of silver points was nearly across the causeway, and moving much faster than we were, tipsy or not.

'Don't laugh,' said Calla, 'I know what Shree means.'

'So do I,' said Mallinna.

'It was that song of joy at the Excommunicant's return that made *my* tunic feel too tight.' I loosened my belt, checked the chain. 'But I can't believe we're getting sentimental over a pack of degenerate murderers. Aren't we forgetting what they did at Faddelin and Deppowe? Did anyone else notice those iron cages?'

Jonno was stalking along beside Katla with a sword in his hand. 'You're right, Lord Verolef. But I keep thinking how disappointed they'll be when they see Lord Tigrallef has – um—'

'Abandoned them, just like our ancestor Oballef?' Tig finished. 'They don't know it yet, guardsman, but we're the last thing they need. We should run now.'

We were at the top of the cliff – glancing down, I could see the Afadhnids were already at the bottom and starting up the switchback road. We ran, all right. The sledge bounced behind Shree and Chasco, the hard black rock rang under our feet. We were not running for our lives – we were running to keep Cansh Fathan from becoming another Itsant or Amballa, to keep my father from toppling off his knife-edge path. Unfortunately we were on the verge of exhaustion before we even started, weak from our long fast; I glanced back again as we reached the bridge and saw the constellation of Afadhnid eyes already well along the road from the cliff top. I tried to think as we ran – what shelter was there on the other side of the Carthenten Cleft? Was there a place where we could turn and make a stand? We had passed that way only a few hours earlier, but I could not remember a thing about it.

Up the hill of the bridge at last: slipping a little on the dew-slick stone, recovering, thinking with a shudder of the long fall if one slid too close to the edge; one arm around my mother, the other around Mallinna; Shree and Chasco pounding along on my heels, Jonno and Katla scampering hand-in-hand a few paces ahead of us – then down the hill of the bridge. It was when our feet were on the solid ground of the other side that I noticed Tigrallef was no longer with us. I spun around.

He had stopped halfway across the bridge. He was shining on the summit of the Carthenten Span, facing away from us towards the silver eyes swarming along the roadway. With a terrible flash of intuition, I saw what he was intending to do. I knew it was too late to anchor him or divert him, but I threw myself anyway towards the foot of the great black arch. Shree and Jonno dragged me back; Calla, cursing, struggled in Chasco's arms.

'Let me go!' I roared. 'He's going to—'

'An act of Will, I know. We can't stop him, Vero.'

As the vanguard of the Afadhnid horde reached the far end of the span, I saw my father raise his arms. That is roughly when I gave up struggling. Shree was right. It was too late, there was no point. The Afadhnids began to collect just short of the bridge, with their feet still on solid ground, and Tigrallef cried out to them in Old Fathidiic.

'Children of Afadhna! Listen carefully.'

The bridge glowed crimson at the Cansh Fathan end; the Afadhnid swarm retreated a few paces in characteristic silence. My mother whispered, 'He swore he wouldn't, you know, he swore on Vero's head. He swore he'd keep hold for ten thousand years and more,' and hid her face for a moment on Chasco's shoulder.

'I'm leaving now. I won't be coming back.'

The dull crimson brightened, turned a hot white, spread up the bridge towards Tigrallef. Somewhere in the Afadhnid horde, a few voices howled. My father spread his arms wider.

'You must make your own future.'

The far half of the span sagged all at once along its whole arc from the bridgehead to the high point where my father stood. Within seconds it was bellying downwards in a lengthening parabola; the bridgehead itself was pulling away from the cliff in strings like taffy candy. A moment later it parted altogether and fell away. Now there was only half a bridge.

My mother broke free from Chasco and planted herself on the very rim of the cliff. I caught at her – just in case – but she snapped at me over her shoulder, 'Don't be a fool, Vero, I won't jump. But after twenty years of fearing this, I have to watch it happen.'

As she spoke, my father turned and set off unhurriedly down the black slope towards us. The tip of the remaining demi-arch turned white and molten even as he left it. The rest of the destruction followed him at an easy walking pace, the deck of the bridge drooping and scrolling down into the abyss behind him almost at his heels. The heat of it blasted our faces as he stepped into our midst on the solid cliff top. He turned to look back just as the last few feet of the bridgehead slumped out of sight below the edge of the precipice. Now there was no bridge at all.

Two, then three, then ten, then hundreds: voice by voice, the Afadhnids proceeded to break our hearts with their grief. A whole people knelt on the other side of the Carthenten

Cleft and wailed for my father to come back. A thousand hairy arms were stretched out to him in piteous supplication. Tigrallef surveyed them dreamily while the glow dimmed under his skin.

'Poor things,' said Jonno.

'Not at all. We gave them the best gift we could, at some cost to ourselves. Did you think we destroyed the bridge to save *you* from *them?*'

He picked up the tow-rope and walked off without glancing again at the Afadhnids. I realized dimly what this must mean; that the Afadhnids weren't important either.

With a half-moon rising above the mountains, we trudged off down the road that would take us eventually to Faddelin and the *Fifth*. It was miles before the massed lamentation of the Afadhnids died away behind us, and we could not stop to rest while it was still in our ears. Four of us were mired in despair, defeat and confusion – the latter because Tig was still walking along on two feet like any ordinary earthbound mortal, when as far as we knew, he could no longer be considered strictly human. Kat should have been upset too, but she seemed quite cheerful. Angel was unreadable. Jonno and Mallinna could not be expected to understand. To them, the destruction of the Carthenten Span was a happy miracle that served both us and the poor old Afadhnids rather well.

We did stop at last for a bite of fenset and a rest. Gods be thanked, Jonno, Kat, Angel and Mallinna were asleep within seconds of shutting their eyes. Tigrallef took maybe a few moments longer. When he was breathing quietly and evenly, my mother rose from his side and tiptoed over to the sombre little clump composed of Shree and Chasco and myself, at a considerate talking-distance from the sleepers. She was oddly serene for a woman whose worst nightmare had probably just come true. She said, 'He's sleeping peacefully. That's new.'

'Not very,' I admitted, 'it's been going on for some time.'

'What else has been going on?'

'Too much.'

'We need to hear it.'

'Oh, Raksh. All right.' I told them all I could remember of the Pain's onslaught since the last time they saw Tigrallef, the day we were captured in Gil, omitting only the revelation concerning Katla. When I was finished, I bowed my head and waited for the reproaches.

'Poor Vero, what a burden. You did well, son. No one could have done better. But I think it's all over now.'

'Are we so sure about that?' said Chasco. 'I'm finding it very hard to believe. Look at him! He isn't even shining now.'

'I think we'll find,' Calla said gently, 'that it means the struggle is over and the Harashil has won.'

'That's how it is in theory,' said Shree, 'but Chasco has a point. I can't believe that after resisting the Harashil for twenty years, Tig would blithely go ahead with an act of Will just to protect the Afadhnids, even if they are his relations.'

'It was nothing to do with the Afadhnids,' I said.

'What, then?'

'I think it was something about Oballef's inscription.'

Shree waved this aside. 'But consider what's happened since the bridge. No fanfare, no shape changes, no rushing off immediately to build the Great Nameless Last. Look here – all these years we've assumed that one good solid act of Will, one conscious and deliberate use of the Pain's power, would complete the melding. What if we were wrong?'

'You're thinking the end should have been noisier?' I asked. 'A little more like Vassashinay? A stone bridge melting like soft wax wasn't dramatic enough for you?'

'Well – not quite, actually.'

'Oh, gods.'

Shree stood up restlessly and paced back and forth. 'What about Itsant, Vero? Amballa? Nkalvi? He used the power then.'

Again, for my mother's sake, I choked back what I now knew about Itsant. 'Those were the Harashil's instinctive acts of defence, not Tigrallef's acts of Will. There's a difference.'

'But this could be construed as defensive. After all, we were being chased by a murderous horde.'

'Perhaps. But it looks to me like a fully conscious act of Will.'

'That's still only a theory, Vero.'

Calla slammed to her feet. 'This is a stupid argument. Why don't we wake him up and ask him?'

So we did.

We crouched around him in a semicircle. He looked perfectly normal and harmless and he was smiling in his sleep; he turned over on to his back and gave a little snort. Calla shook him gently. 'Tig, dearheart—'

His eyelids snapped open. All I could see behind them was blackness and emptiness shot with cold sparks of fire. I had to swallow a couple of times before I could speak.

'Da, we'd like to ask you something. It's about what you did tonight.'

His smile broadened. It was not a smile that I recognized, and I really did not like what it did to his face. 'The two,' he said, 'are one.' His voice contained no echoes.

'Thank you, darling,' said my mother after a short silence. 'That's all we wanted to know. Go back to sleep.'

He shut his eyelids on those terrible voids and turned again on his side.

17

Tigrallef was in no hurry to finish things. He could have spoken his Will at any time in Fathan. He could have abandoned us there as unimportant, or wafted the whole packet of us down from the Carthenten Cleft to the coast, or even to the Gilgard, with a wave of his fingers. Instead, he chose to do a walking tour of the sere beauties of Fathan's

Blessed Range, to contemplate the ruins, to hold his nose at the stink of Faddelin, to pat the hull of the *Fifth* as we pulled alongside her. We had been gone sixteen days – ten uphill to Cansh Fathan, six downhill on the return journey – and there was evidence the townsite had been visited during that time, but our ship had gone unnoticed.

We sailed out the east end of the Deppowe Channel before turning on to the sea lane for Canton Pilazh, carried along by the most unnaturally obliging winds that ever filled a highsail. A great Gillish Imperial fleet was sighted to the north at one point, probably heading for the coast of Fathan to avenge the sack of the Mosslines. Tigrallef said it was not important. Just outside the skerries of the Pilazhet Basin we skimmed blithely through a wolfpack of pirates without any of their bolts even grazing us, to their evident astonishment. Signs of a stormbowl approaching Canton Pilazh from the Sherkin Sea dissipated without fuss. The journey was terrifyingly easy.

Meantime, my father's behaviour on the *Fifth* was so normal that it struck us as bizarre. He smiled too much and strolled about on deck humming little tunes. He gave Jonno helpful comments about his poetry. He did more than his share of the cooking. He played fingersticks with anyone he could talk into it, and didn't even cheat. I believe he was indulging us. When we managed to avoid his eyes, we could almost forget he was the power-deranged avatar whose destruction of the world had been foretold. Calla's assessment was probably right – he was at ease because he was no longer resisting the Harashil. There would be no more attacks of the Pain, no more absurdities or helpless spasms of shape-changing, no more Myrwolves, White Dragons or Ladies in Gil. Katla reported he looked exactly like himself *all the time*. The battle was over, and apparently so was the war.

As for the rest of us, a version of the calm my mother displayed at the Carthenten Span enveloped us all. Not one of us felt inclined to desert Tigrallef, though he would not or could not tell us what his intentions were. We knew we were going to Gil – beyond that, it was impossible to think and useless to plan. Perhaps we would all die in a burst of the Harashil's fire. Perhaps we would witness the raising of the Great Nameless Last, more vicious and barbarous than anything that ever burdened the earth before. In either case the worst had already happened – we had fallen over the edge of the cliff and were just marking time until we hit the bottom. There was no point in screaming all the way down.

I made one concession to the possible existence of a future. Throughout the journey I filled page after page of the Primate's top-quality paper with an account of the events since my father's return to the known world; a memoir which could turn out to be either a valuable historical document – *The Last Empire: the Rise of the Emperor Tigrallef and the Beginning of the End of the World. An Eyewitness Account* – or a complete waste of time. Whatever happened, there was a good chance that nobody would be around afterwards to read it.

Still-life on the afterdeck of the *Fifth*, on the last night of our journey. It was well after nightfall, and the Mors Beacon was gliding past us on the port side. The red star hanging on the western horizon was not a star, according to my father, but a powerful new beaconlight erected by the Primate on the very summit of the Gilgard. Chasco, who was on watch in the rigging, estimated we would swing round the north point of Gil not long past sunrise.

Jonno and Katla were leaning against the taffrail talking with their usual intensity, Kat's shining dark head very close to Jonno's golden one, and their fingers (I noticed) were twined together. I contemplated my role as brother-protector for a few seconds, decided that Jonno would not have time to break Kat's heart before the cataclysm, even if he meant to, which I doubted. As for honour and virtue, our Katlefiya was quite capable of safeguarding her own.

Shree was in the galley making dried-meat pies for our last supper. Tig and Angel were in the comfortable angle of the bow, comparing things on the horizon with things on Angel's chart. My mother was sitting nearby in Tigrallef's chair, and I watched her as she watched everyone else. The sadness in her face was a great giveaway, especially when she looked at the two grave children by the taffrail. But when she looked towards my father, her face was sadder still.

Mallinna was at the wheel, nominally under my supervision, though neither she nor the ship needed much guidance by that point. We had spent most of the voyage in each other's company, talking about hundreds of things without ever saying anything of actual importance. The future, for example, was something we never discussed; likewise the *Erotic Mistifalia*. This was not merely because of the dampening effect of the looming catastrophe, nor yet the inhibitive effect of sharing an overcrowded windcatcher with a parent who could see through walls and hear a flea's footfall. No, I think it was because just being beside Mallinna was comfort enough under the circumstances; and though nothing of any importance was said, many significant matters were quietly understood.

Shree came on deck and passed around his dried-meat pies. Though very good, they seemed a little homely for what was potentially our last meal in the old order of the world. I had a feeling we should be marking the occasion somehow, but none of us had much heart for it. Nor was Tig's offer to make oat pudding for breakfast very well received. Oat pudding felt no more fitting than dried-meat pies, and by breakfast-time we'd be in Gil anyway. I had a wild mental image: Tigrallef making oat pudding, then going off to build the Great Nameless Last with his apron still around his middle. He frequently forgot to take it off.

We spread ourselves around the afterdeck eating our pies and drinking dark wine from an excellent butt the Primate had paid for. Chasco was at the wheel. The Mors Beacon was already about a mile astern, the red star was perceptibly rising above the horizon, and a generally depressed silence had fallen over us all.

'Why are you doing this, Tig?' Shree asked amiably. 'Why

didn't you just go ahead and construct your tupping empire as soon as you took on the power? Did we really need to go through this farce of a voyage?'

'Patience, Shree. It's not important. If the Great Nameless Last rises from the ashes of the First, there will be a place in it for you.'

'I don't want a place in your empire, and I'm not pushing you to build it any time soon. I just want to know why it's so important to do it in Gil.' Shree tapped off another beaker of wine and looked up with a trace of the old Sherkin aggressiveness.

My father's equanimity was undisturbed. He turned instead to my mother.

'There speaks our best and oldest friend. What about you, our beloved? Tomorrow we could make you an empress. Would you like that?'

She swallowed her mouthful of meat pie. 'No thank you,' she said.

'Did you realize there's a degree of immortality attached? You would rule with us to the end of history.'

'I said no, dearheart. I don't want to be an empress.'

He looked at her appraisingly with his whiteless eyes. 'What do you want?'

My mother hesitated. Then she scowled at the remainder of her pie and pitched it overboard. 'Since you're asking, what I'd most like to do is go back to Myr. We were happy there. Do you remember anything at all about being happy, Tig?'

Very long silence, then a puzzled voice: 'He remembers.'

'Bloody right, you *should* remember. It was our first home together. And we might as well have stayed there, for all the good we did in twenty years of questing.'

Another long, thoughtful pause from the avatar. 'He agrees with you on that.'

'Well, then?' my mother said.

'The two are one. There can be no turning back now. We must see this through to the end.'

'Fine.' She got to her feet and headed for the companionway. Tig put up his hand to delay her; I saw he was holding a short sword which had not been there a moment before. What happened then was probably not meant to distress, but it was not pleasant to watch someone attempt to disembowel himself in the middle of dinner, especially when dinner consisted of dried-meat pies. There was no blood. Tig's belly reacted to the knife as a bowlful of warm aspic would, by closing seamlessly together again – but Jonno went so far as to retch over the remains of his pie, confirming that his was an imaginative soul. The rest of us were less squeamish.

'Tig, dearheart, you know that sort of thing doesn't work. All you've done is ruin your tunic.'

'He was giving you a sign.' Tigrallef dropped the sword on the deck; we watched without comment as it turned into a kind of silver snake with legs and scuttled overboard.

My mother sighed deeply. 'I must say, if it's a sign, I don't quite catch the message.'

'It's not important.' He stood quietly for a heartbeat or two, looking ahead at the red spark of light that marked the Gilgard – The Great Ark and Sceptre, the Wind and the Tree, the fusion of Naar and Harashil, the world's bane, a smallish, pale-cheeked young man with a ripped tunic and a glitter in his eyes that was not at all cheerful – and then he vanished. We discovered after a frantic search that he had gone straight to bed.

Calla retired also, to keep an eye on him. The rest of us stayed on deck watching the steady approach of the Gilgard's beaconlight, while a grey line gradually defined itself between the dark sea and sky to the east. Katla and Jonno fell asleep, she with her head on his shoulder, he with his cheek against her hair. Angel and Shree carried on a desultory debate about what would happen if we tried to change course away from Gil – the answer was, nothing would happen. I knew because Mallinna and I had tried it a couple of days ago, and Chasco was trying it again that very moment in a quiet experimental fashion, but the *Fifth* seemed to know very well where she was meant to sail.

Mallinna sat beside me, not saying much. I put my arm around her and after a while she dozed off. Sitting there with her warm body against mine, I had another of those moments of ill-timed, quite inappropriate happiness – it was the thought of spending the rest of my life with her, all four or five hours of it – and then I drifted off as well.

One by one, we shook ourselves awake in the grey minutes just before the sun rose. Tigrallef came back on deck not much later, and placed himself in the angle of the bow. There was a blankness in his face that disturbed me. As Chasco steered us into the tight turn around the sea face of the Gilgard, we passed four of those little black galleys that usually infested the harbour proper, but they did not challenge us. A massive windcatcher flying the Primate's banner was approaching from the direction of the Archipelago, and it looked as if it would pass through the breach just ahead of us. I noticed that Tig was watching it with close attention.

We came in view of the heights of Gilgard Castle, as beautiful and hateful as before. Kat and Shree were working the sails by then – Jonno was hastily trying to polish his boots while sponging a gravy stain off his black uniform tunic. Mallinna, beside me at the rail, silently slid her hand into mine. We watched as the big windcatcher slipped through the breach and turned her nose towards a moorage in the outer harbour.

Then it was our turn to run the gantlet between the watchtowers that flanked the breach. I squinted at the spear-chuckers and the flame bolts, expecting to see them being cranked back for the barrage – but I could make out the crews clearly, also the archers in the towers, and nobody was doing more than watch us in return. Indeed, as we came level with the outer arms of the breach, the crews began to desert their posts, archers threw down their bows, troopers crowded to the edge of the breakwater to watch us sail through. Some of them were cheering.

'This is very strange,' I said to Mallinna. She said nothing, but her grip tightened on my hand.

There were banners everywhere, streaming from the watchtowers, the warships in the outer harbour, the wolf-boats, the banner staffs along the breakwater. Katla called down from the rigging that the inner harbour was one great mass of ships; and a moment later, that the corniche and the streets leading down to the harbour were packed with seething crowds. And there was possible trouble to starboard – a flotilla of wolf-boats escorting a strange shining galley out of the shadow of the big windcatcher that had come in just ahead of us. It was gilded, with two figures in the bow – gold robes, bright white hair under gold headdresses.

Then Mallinna struck her forehead and poked Jonno's shoulder and announced in silly-me tones that she'd realized what the date must be. Damn it, I thought. Just our luck to try sailing into Gil inconspicuously on the Day of the Scion.

We pulled in at the main quay of the landing stage just behind the gilded galley. Out of sight beyond it, a band of hornists was midway through the Gillish Paean of Praise. The great stone bust of the Blessed Scion Tigrallef smiled vaguely over our heads, but the real Scion Tigrallef jumped on to the quay with the bow mooring line as I secured the stern, with Chasco on my heels. Troopers with drawn swords were already racing towards us – but when Tigrallef stood up by the bollard and faced them with his hands on his hips, their ranks broke and they dropped their swords and fell on their faces on the polished flagstones. For a terrible moment, until it was clear they were only grovelling, I thought my father had struck them all dead. Revelation hit me hard.

'Oh gods,' I snarled to Chasco, 'they think the Divine Scion has returned.'

'Well, he has,' said Chasco.

'But—'

'And on the Day of the Scion, too,' said Shree behind us, 'just as the Primate foretold. This'll be a shock for old Mycri.' I heard his sword and Chasco's clatter, one-two, back into their sheaths. By this time Mallinna and Jonno were helping Angel on to the quay, and my mother and sister were flanking

307

Tigrallef protectively up by the bow. Above us on the corniche, the crowds nearest the landing stage were beginning to take notice. I heard a few screams, but they were of the ecstatic variety. *The Scion has returned! The great day has come!*

Tigrallef ignored them. A party of officials with green chestbands, waiting by the galley's gold-draped gangway, were the next to fall to their knees when they saw him coming. He ignored them too, rather coldly. The band faltered to a discordant halt. By the time the rest of us caught up, the two gold-robed figures were just limping together down the gangway, an elderly woman with a lovely calm face, a stately white-haired man, strangely familiar in his features, dribbling out of one corner of his beautiful vacant smile. The old woman held her arms out – Shree leapt to embrace her, she greeted Angel and Mallinna with a gesture signifying long friendship, smiled at Calla and Katla, stared at me with a kind of pleased wonder; but she was silent until Tigrallef permitted her to put her arms around him. Then she said, 'Didn't I tell you, Tig, that we'd see each other again? Arko,' she added, 'say hello to your brother.'

It was obviously not the best time for an undiluted, full-strength reunion. Tigrallef kissed my grandmother, the Dowager Dazeene, gravely on the forehead – she took a good look at his eyes and her face sobered without losing any of its serenity. 'Come, darling, we're going to ride in the pretty carriage,' she said, taking my poor uncle Arkolef by the hand. She smiled at me but said nothing more. We moved in a tight group up the ramp that led to the corniche, unopposed but somewhat hampered by worshippers falling in inconvenient clusters in our path.

'The Scion! The Blessed Scion has returned!'

Tigrallef caught my eye on him and looked me full in the face. His expression chilled me. 'They're not important,' he said.

At the top of the ramp was an extraordinary and appropriate vehicle, an ornate open carriage shaped like a grandiose rowboat on wheels, pulled by four sorrel horses in gilded harness. A young Flamen who seemed to be the intended driver backed away, awestruck. By the time we had settled Angel, my uncle Arkolef and the Dowager Dazeene on the carriage's silk-lined seats and piled in ourselves, ten of us in a space intended for six, Tigrallef was in the driver's box and ready to go. Ahead of us, straight and clear, stretched the grand avenue to the Gilgard Gate.

The crowds on the corniche had been just a foretaste of the multitudes lining the route. All nations of the Primate's empire were represented – tens of thousands of the faithful in an excellent mood, held back by a double rank of dun tunics. They had come from all over, these multitudes, to honour the Dowager and the Priest-King on the Divine Scion's sacred day – and when the Divine Scion himself passed by, the response was predictably loud. The troopers were as jubilant as the rest, but they fortunately held their lines.

In the front rank of silken seats, Calla and the Dowager Dazeene talked intently with their heads close together. My uncle Arkolef whimpered beside me at the tumult of the crowd and clutched my hand tightly. Angel was trying to disappear into the upholstery, the rest of us were trying to look as if we rode in religious processions all the time. Tigrallef looked nowhere but directly ahead.

The Gilgard Gate, festooned and embellished, was already wide open. Tigrallef drove straight through it, past the astonished faces of a double guard of honour in the uniforms of the Flamens' Corps. Nobody tried to stop us. I saw that a massive dais had been erected on the portico overlooking the great flagged steppeland of the forecourt, draped in Scion's gold and Flamens' green, forested with banners in the same colours. A green-carpeted grand stairway led up to it, every tread flanked with black-tunicked guardsmen, gold banner-staffs in their hands, green plumes tossing in their helmets – a stirring sight. On the dais, three green figures sat in state on three low thrones: the Primate in the centre, Kesi First

Flamen on the right, and the dreaded Lestri on the left. Directly behind them were three higher thrones, empty and glittering: one each for the Dowager and the Priest-King, the third and highest to be left empty in token of the Divine Scion's eventual return. Well, they had him now.

The Primate was not the only person present whom I would rather have avoided. Though the forecourt was packed solid with people, one face near the gate caught my eye as we rode very slowly past him. He was standing in the front rank, a large man and richly dressed, made even more conspicuous by a high-piled crimson-cloth headdress pinned with a bar of white brilliants. His amazement when he saw me was the sort that everyone else was reserving for my father; then, as our eyes locked, his face grew as red as his headdress with rage. It took me a moment to place him, probably because I'd never seen him dressed as a prosperous burgher before – to be honest, the fisherman's garb had suited him better. But there was no doubt about the face, and I did not need to count his remaining fingers to be sure who he was. I leaned across several bodies to catch Mallinna's attention.

'Malso's here – the Truant.'

'I saw him too,' she shot back. 'He – wait. That's odd . . .'

'What?'

'They're shutting the gate. They don't usually—'

'That's true, they don't,' said the Dowager Dazeene, twisting around in the seat ahead of us. She had a high clear voice with overtones of my father's. 'Mallinna, my dear, perhaps you'd remember from past Days of the Scion: are there usually so many black tunics on the dais?'

'Never half as many, Lady,' said Mallinna after a moment. 'And there are more than usual in the forecourt as well, and in the towers. I didn't know the Flamens' Corps had so many men in the whole empire.'

'Yes, well. And is it my imagination, or are the crowds outside the gate even noisier than before?'

We listened. She was probably right, though any noise from outside the Gilgard gate had serious competition from inside the forecourt.

'Where's Shree? Shree – such a wonder to see you with a grizzled beard, my dear, and streaks of white in your mane, you who became as my third son – Shree, does that sound to you like the beginning of a battle outside the gate? What do the instincts of your father's people tell you?'

'They tell me yes, it sounds like a battle; and they add that more trouble is about five minutes away, but it may not be the kind of trouble you're thinking of, Lady Dazeene.'

'I'm thinking of several kinds of trouble – I saw my son Tigrallef's eyes. I suppose he'll be wanting to go down into the maze under the rock next. Verolef,' she addressed me for the first time, 'you will look after him down there, won't you, my dear? I imagine you've been looking after him all your life, but now is the time when he needs you the most.'

Maze under the rock? That was news to me, and sounded highly unlikely. If I had any prediction at all about Tig's forthcoming behaviour, it was that he'd stand up on the dais, pronounce all present to be not-Naar vermin, and proceed to raise the cruel empire of the Great Nameless Last. Either that or let loose a flaming cataclysm, which in some ways would be faster, cleaner and less painful. As for looking after him, a godman who could boil the seas dry if ever he felt like it could in theory look after himself. But I made a gesture of willing agreement.

'Good man. And you, Katlefiya – what a lovely child you are – you must help your father as well, and look after your poor uncle. Don't let go of his hand, and remember he's frightened of the dark.'

'Yes, ma'am,' said Katla.

'Be careful if there are any stairs – he's got one wooden leg.'

'Yes, ma'am.'

'Do you swear to it?'

'Yes, ma'am.'

Tigrallef was just pulling back on the reins as the Dowager Dazeene extracted these mystifying promises from us. At that moment, I thought my poor old granna's cargo must have shifted. A few minutes later, however, I remembered what my father used to say: that his mother Dazeene could be right about the damnedest things.

The Primate was already halfway down the stairs as the carriage pulled up at the bottom. His back was bent in the shape of a fish-hook, and he was on his feet only because Kesi and Lestri were supporting him on either side. Nobody had yet made to stop us, not even the great army of black tunics ornamenting the grand stairway like rows of wooden statues. The forecourt was in uproar, and so was the stand filled with foreign dignitaries, where a raddled woman with a crown of blue and silver twined in her thick blue hair was contributing more than her share to the overall tumult. The Primate seemed divided between annoyance at her and rage at my father.

'Somebody shut that damned woman up! As for you, young man,' as my father stopped a few stairs below him to look around the forecourt with an abstracted air, 'I don't know how you escaped the Gilgard, but it's fatally stupid of you to come back.'

Tig was frowning over his shoulder at the closed gateway. 'We're not interested, Most Revered Primate, we're on our way to see someone important.'

The Primate was too outraged to speak for a few moments. By now the able-bodied among us had unloaded the others feverishly from the carriage; I tucked my arm under the Dowager's elbow and began to help her up the stairs. The Primate glared from her to my father to the raddled woman in the stand, who was now trying to climb along the shoulders of the Plaviset delegation; he recovered his voice and snarled at the captain of the black tunics, hovering at the top of the stairs.

'You know who this is, Abro. He's not the Scion – he's that lad you *told* me threw himself out the window, and we'll need to have a talk about that later, won't we? Kill him.'

Captain Abro looked uncertain but did not move. Kesi, distressed, whispered in the Primate's ear.

'There's already a riot, you fool. Dazeene, I'm shocked at

312

you for taking up with this ragtag. Think how confusing it is for Arko.'

My grandmother chuckled and pressed my arm; the Primate seemed to shed about twenty years in his fury. He sputtered a moment, then turned to shake his fist at the woman still screeching among the foreign dignitaries.

'By Oballef, won't somebody cut that woman's throat? Listen to me, you witless doxy,' he shouted at her in his still-powerful voice, a shock from that withered body, 'this is not your long-lost husband. Understand? Listen to me, all of you! This man is an impostor – he is not the Divine Scion, may he soon return, he's the son of an exiled coppermonger and a woman who whored for the Sherank. He brutally abducted the Dowager and the Priest-King and the First Memorian – yes, you ungrateful old loony, I see you there – but he will die for his blasphemies. Have no doubt about that! Oh, gods,' he grated as the noise level increased in the stand, 'Abro, tell Rinn of Miishel I'll have that pocketing crown back if she can't control herself, and I'll want her head to be still inside it.'

'You always did believe in a direct approach, Mycri.' Tig turned on the stairs to face the trio of High Flamens. The Primate drew himself almost straight.

'You dare address me like that? Knowing who I am?'

'Of course we know you. You cuffed our ears often enough when we were a child. And now you're the tyrant who holds the puppet strings of a great empire – admirable except for a few murders and more than a few injustices. Truthfully, Most Revered Primate, we admire what you've done.'

'Captain Abro, kill this lunatic *now*.'

'You were angry with us when we destroyed the Lady – Gil was ruined, you said, doomed to obscurity; we could never rebuild the old glory. The joke is, you conquered more of the known world at one go than she ever did. We congratulate you, Mycri.'

'Abro! He is not the Scion, I tell you! Kill him!'

'Actually,' said Tig, 'good Captain Abro doesn't think we're the Scion anyway. He's just wondering if it's too late to fit us

313

into his plans or whether he'd better run a sword through us. We'd invite him to try it, but it's really not important.'

'Plans?' repeated the Primate.

'Listen to those shrieks outside the gate. Yes, Mycri, plans. He's subverted about half the Flamens' Corps – the other half may protect you, but how will you know whom to trust? The duns would support you, but they've been locked out *and* they've got their hands full with the Opposition.'

'The Opposition?' thundered the Primate.

'Oh yes. In fact the Truant himself is here in the forecourt. His agreement with Captain Abro—'

Abro howled a battle-cry and leapt down the stairs with his sword aimed at Tigrallef's heart. A few stairs short, he did a convincing impression of a man running into an invisible stone wall; he followed this up with an even better impression of a man slumped unconscious and bleeding on the stairs.

'—was that the Opposition forces would take over the city,' Tig continued calmly, 'while Abro secured the Gilgard and deposed the Flamens with a directness that you, Mycri, should properly admire. And when you were all dead, Abro was to install the Truant as Protector in the name of the Divine Scion and in the presence of these dignitaries – our mother and brother were to be respectfully preserved, of course, because any competent usurper takes pains to legitimize his claim. But something tells us the Truant was destined to be martyred in the fighting; and when the Gilgard gate was flung open again, Abro himself would inform the Opposition of their Truant's heroic death and humbly offer himself as leader—'

'Madman!' snapped the Primate.

'Abro or us? Oh well, have it your way. But look around at your picked pack of wolves, Mycri, and try to guess which of them were ready to cut your heart out.'

From the abrupt explosion of activity in the forecourt at that precise moment, one would think my father's words had been a signal. At least four of the black tunics on the stairway drew swords and converged on the High Flamens. Jonno

314

leapt past me to their defence, Katla leapt past me to *his* defence, the Wicked Princess Rinn of Miishel, bogeywoman of our bedtime tales, marched up the stairs towards Tigrallef shrieking, 'How dare you leave me, you [several words not in my Miisheli lexicon]' – and some kind of hell erupted at the end of the forecourt where the Truant was, but by then I was too busy to analyse it because someone in a black tunic was trying to snatch my grandmother. Sherkin full-trip and a toss – it was the stairs that broke his neck, not me; and then Tigrallef was hustling us up the steps and around the back of the dais, through a vast double-leafed doorway into an echoing foyer. The heavy doors silenced the racket from the forecourt. By now we were quite a crowd.

There was the Primate propped against a wall looking thoughtfully at my father; Lestri glowering at Mallinna; Kesi embracing Jonno; the Dowager comforting the Priest-King; Rinn of Miishel, considerably more subdued – either because she was staring at Tigrallef's unnatural eyes, or because the thick blue hair had vanished along with the viper crown, and the greying wisps left on her scalp were hardly enough to cover a pikcherry. There were also five guardsmen of the Flamens' Corps who had been defending the Primate loyally, and a sixth who, at a sharp glance from my father, tottered glassy-eyed over to open the great door and pulled it shut behind him.

'Scion,' said the Primate flatly.

'Yes, Mycri.'

'You really are the Scion Tigrallef.'

'Yes and no,' said the Wind and the Tree.

The Primate shrugged off the ambiguity. 'But – did you indeed take on the Lady's powers, as I – as we – as the people have been told?'

'Oh yes.'

A shock-wave passed over the Primate's ancient face; the shock, perhaps, of being caught out in a truth. His recovery was astonishing, though. 'If you have such power,' he said commandingly, 'then you can—'

'No,' said my father. 'No. It matters little or nothing who

315

wins this battle. We will not interfere. We have important things to do.'

'But—'

'We have to leave you now, anyway,' said my father.

I saw the old guard, Shree and Chasco and Calla, individually set their chins and prepare to be stubborn. 'You're not going anywhere on your own,' my mother said firmly.

'Of course not. Vero, Kat, help your uncle Arkolef.'

My mother stiffened. 'I'm coming too.'

'Not possible.'

'Tigrallef—'

His look stopped her, and I can understand why. It was not my father standing there. The strangeness in his face was almost a deformity. She stepped backwards, bumped up against Shree. For the first time in my life, I saw Shree looking genuinely afraid.

'Where are you going?' Calla whispered. 'Why are you taking my son and daughter?'

'We're going where only the Children of Naar can safely go. They'll come to no harm, woman, the Harashil can do nothing to hurt them. Remember this is woven into the fabric of things.'

'Will you come back?' Her voice was anguished.

'Maybe, maybe not. Verolef, Katlefiya, are you ready?'

I glanced at the Dowager Dazeene. She murmured into the Priest-King's ear and gave him a gentle shove towards Katla, who took him by the hand.

'We're ready.'

18

We said no goodbyes, nor did we risk any final embraces – leaving was hard enough already. The only truly single-minded attempt to follow us was made by Angel, and it took both Mallinna and Jonno to hold him back, with Kesi as the voice of reason in the background. The last we saw, Shree was hustling everyone into a more easily defensible position at the far end of the foyer. After that, we didn't look back.

Tigrallef led us through some fine corridors and cloistered gardens, wonderfully adorned, mostly deserted. On the Day of the Scion, it appeared, the entire population gathered in the streets and shrines of the city. The major exception was around the kitchens, where a massive ceremonial banquet was in production – I suppose nobody had thought to inform the chefs that a civil war was getting nicely started outside. We skimmed past the sculleries and along a hallway, around a corner and through an unassuming door; and there Tigrallef stopped on the edge of a vast room, high-vaulted and glittering, furnished with enough costly clutter to finance the archives for a century. The huge expanse of floor was a mosaic of tiles that were no larger than a nail head, gold, silver and copper, depicting the adventures of an obviously brainless hero with a strong facial resemblance to my father. The Priest-King raised his head and looked around dreamily.

'The Hall of Harps,' Tig said. 'This floor is new – scenes from the life of the Divine Scion Tigrallef. Notice the—'

'We don't need a guided tour,' I broke in. 'Where are you taking us?'

Tig drifted to the centre of the Hall, examining the mosaics. 'We're taking you to the place where the bargain was made.'

'What bargain?'

'Naar's bargain.' It was Kat who answered me. I examined her warily, fearing to find the marks of the Harashil on her as well; but she was wearing her what-a-dump face, as seen in filthy little ports and smelly little towns across the known and unknown worlds – who would have thought to see it here? She tugged Arkolef patiently along behind her. He came willingly enough but slowly, like an obedient child with its mind on other things.

'We're going to the maze under the rock, aren't we?' Kat said. If anything, she sounded faintly interested now. 'Is it far down? I suppose we'll use the between-ways to get to the caves, won't we, like you did before, and the caves to get to the maze. How difficult is the maze?'

'It's not important. We are the Wind and the Tree, and we do not need to play that game.' Tigrallef frowned at one of the mosaic scenes on the floor. The large-muscled hero, a sword in one hand and a blurred figurine of the Lady in the other, was beating off a well-rendered caricature of a Sherkin horde. 'Why,' he added, 'do they insist on getting things wrong?'

The tiles in that scene took on a faint glow – 'best to keep our brother well back' – then quivered and abruptly puddled together, gold running into silver running into copper, pouring away together at last into a great black cavity that opened up below them. A sound like hissing steam, a blast of heat; when it was over, there was a square hole measuring about six feet across in the place where the offending scene had been. I approached it cautiously and peered down. It was a pit cut through the solid rock on which this hall was founded; well-cut stairs began at a landing a few feet below the opening and descended steeply into the darkness.

'Was this here before?' I asked my father, 'or did you just make it?'

'It's not important,' said Kat.

'Don't *you* start.' I helped her sit Arkolef on the edge of the cavity, then jumped in to guide his one foot and his wooden leg down to the landing. He came down docilely enough, but promptly did his best to climb back out again, which suggested to me that my poor uncle was not so crazy after all. After a brief struggle on the landing, I patted his back soothingly while he clung to me and whimpered deep in his magnificent throat. I sighed. This was not going to be easy.

Tigrallef had gone ahead, glowing with a white radiance so powerful that it lit the staircase for a dozen feet in both directions, even around its numerous twists and corners. Kat and I started down after him with the Priest-King between us, and from the beginning I made a point of counting the

318

stairs. For most of the first three hundred, I fumed at my father for dragging poor Arkolef along; from about three hundred to four hundred, I suffered vivid images of those we'd left behind, notably Mallinna and my mother; towards five hundred I became furious with Tigrallef for making us do this journey the difficult way, when we really didn't want to do it at all. It struck me that Katla and I were having to work far too hard for the dubious privilege of witnessing the world's doom. Why trudge down to Faddelin? Why sail to Gil in the *Fifth*? Why plod down miles of stairway? Why couldn't he just lift his little finger and take us straight to – wherever it was we were going. Why not—'

It hit me just after seven hundred. It took my breath away, to the point where I had to sit down on the stair for a moment while Kat moved on alone with Arkolef. I examined the idea critically and still found it credible. It had struck me that our father was doing the equivalent of leaving doors ajar behind him – return-trails clearly blazed, escape routes laid down and ready for use. It could only mean, I told myself, that he thought he had a chance of returning from this confrontation with the unknown. Perhaps the outcome was not quite as fired-in-the-kiln as I'd been assuming. I thought of his sign to my mother the night before, the ineffectual blade drawn through his own gut. The two were one, all right, the Wind and the Tree and all that; but perhaps he had been trying to tell her that something of himself survived and was exercising his old contrarian talents. For the first time since the night of the Carthenten Span, I felt a stirring of genuine hope.

By the thousandth step, I decided I was wrong. It was foolish to hope. Tig was lost to us and the world was doomed. Moreover a phrase of Oballef's inscription in Fathan came back to haunt me, the bit about yielding up the seed of Naar to the Old Ones. It suddenly appeared suspicious to me that Tigrallef had brought the entire surviving seed of Naar down those stairs with him, Oballef's branch anyway, ripe to be yielded up. Wondering if a betrayal was in the wind kept me occupied well past twelve hundred, after which I didn't feel very much of anything except the ache in my legs and a vague longing to be back aboard the *Fifth* with Mallinna and far away from Gil . . .

The end came after fourteen hundred and thirty-seven steps. By then I was supporting our uncle on my own, while Kat stumbled along behind us in a dizziness of exhaustion and sore knees. I reached out my foot to take another step and nearly fell over, because my boot met a solid surface it was not expecting. We had come to the bottom of the stairs. I caught my balance just in time for Kat to stagger out of the stairwell and knock me forwards a step or two. The three of us, Arkolef and Katla and I, clung together to stay upright. I shook my head to clear the clouds out of it.

About ten feet ahead of us, Tigrallef was the only source of light. The chamber was probably large – his light did not touch any wall nor reach as high as the ceiling. The air was dry but thick, much warmer than I thought it would be, this deep in the bowels of the Gilgard rock. Breathing it was like trying to draw air through the folds of a heavy woollen blanket. The only sound was the tip of Arkolef's wooden leg scraping against the flagstones.

'Just a little farther,' Tig said. He walked away from us carrying his hemisphere of light with him, and I hooked an arm around my uncle's middle to encourage him along while Katla held his hand and murmured soothingly to him, as promised. I was looking at the floor – well-cut flags, not very worn and with only a thin coating of dust – when Katla stopped her murmuring with a gasp. The light brightened.

I looked up. Perhaps Tigrallef was tired of carrying the light around with him; the walls were now glowing in a great circle around us, along with the white-plastered dome of the ceiling. Seven arched doorways broke the circle at regular intervals, perhaps the entrances to the maze we had started to hear so much about. The stairwell we had arrived by was cut rudely between two of these, an obvious intrusion – the Wind and the Tree's own version of a direct approach.

He was standing meditatively beside a table or perhaps a

bier with something lumpy on it, shrouded under a tapestry woven with unfamiliar glyphs – gold on crimson, picked out here and there with silver. Beyond him, forming a semicircle along the curve of the wall, were seven of the least prepossessing statues I had ever seen, not forgetting my previous benchmarks of iconic ugliness, the cult fetishes of Uagolo and the lantern-jawed Master of Gafrin-Gammanthan. They were just over life-size and seemed to be formed out of dry mud, sculpted with a tool as sensitive and precise as a trench-digger's shovel; one was roughly doglike, one catlike, two vaguely reptilian . . .

'And three in human form,' I finished out loud. I would have slapped my forehead with recognition but I was too frightened to move. Arkolef sensibly sank down on the floor wrapped in his own arms and began to rock back and forth. Katla absent-mindedly patted his shoulder.

'Things of legend,' Tigrallef intoned in a mocking voice, 'terrible creatures of the dark, things older than Fathan, older than Vizzath, older than everything on earth – how often, it seems, the myths have it half right.'

You're late.

I could not tell who said that – one of them, none of them, all seven of them at once; but as I climbed back into my skin and stuffed my heart back down my throat, Tigrallef addressed himself to the dog-like one with a weary kind of courtesy. 'No, Great Fierceness, we are not late. We are not even the one you're expecting.'

A heavy pause.

But we know the Empire of First-Fire was brought to a close. Are you not the heritor, come to build the Last Empire?

Tigrallef swivelled to face one of the human-like figures. 'We are not, Flaming One.' Another heavy pause. 'The heritor in question died a thousand years ago, near enough. His ashes were scattered from the summit of the Great Nameless First.' And after a pause that was long enough to become socially awkward, he added, 'He broke the bargain which our forefather Naar struck with you long ago. We are the unwilling result, and we have come to reason with you, perhaps to plead.'

Seven motionless mud idols mulled this over.

You say the chosen heritor did not fulfill the prophecy.

'That is correct, Fangs-As-Daggers-Swift-To-Rend.'

The chosen heritor did not free our power from the vessel nor build the Great Nameless Last.

'Correct again. He built a kingdom under another name. He defied you, Old Ones. He abandoned the others of the Children of the Naar. He built his kingdom right over your heads, in the place of the Great Nameless First. He used the Harashil, but he gave it a face and form that was none of yours, and he did not open a way to your eyes and ears. He was prepared to leave you in darkness for ever. He let the empires of the Harashil be forgotten. He hid Naarhil from the ears of the faithful. The prophecy has thus been nullified, and the compact has already been broken. Therefore, we ask to be released from its terms. Let the Great Nameless Last remain unbuilt, and the world be left to go its own way.'

Strong disapproval filled the chamber. It smelt something like hot pitch and felt like a wave of icy water slapping across me. Kat flinched. The Priest-King reached up and found my hand. My eyes ached from watching those lumpen figures for any sign of life or movement, even any hint of where the damn voices were coming from; but the figures were dry mud, plain and simple, and they behaved like it. If these were the Old Ones who created our world, I would not have given a quarter-palot piece for the lack-talent who created *them*.

My father, waiting patiently for the Old Ones to respond to his plea, which even I could tell was hopeless, laid his hands on the tapestry covering the bier. What he felt there seemed to interest him. Gently, he grasped one edge of the tapestry and began to draw it down.

We have conferred. You are a twig of the Great Tree.

'Yes, First-Fire.'

And you have broken the vessel of the Harashil.

'We have, Icedrake.'

And the Tree has moved in the Wind, and the Wind has shaped itself to the Tree.

'We suppose so, Many-Handed. The two have become one, if that's what you're trying to say.'

Then the prophecy is well enough fulfilled, though you are not the intended one. The compact stands. You shall build the Last Empire.

Tigrallef's face hardened. 'And then, Shining-of-Scales?'

And then you shall yield up the Harashil and the seed of Naar, the innocent, the brave and the vessel of wrath, to be consumed; and we shall destroy this creation, as it was agreed in the beginning. There was a touch of impatience in the snake-thing's voice; the Old Ones were getting bored with stating the obvious. Tigrallef, however, had already returned to examining the object partially uncovered on the bier. Without looking up, he asked, 'What does this one get out of it?'

He shall join us in a new creation, and live for ever.

'Yes,' said my father, 'that's what we thought. And it's exactly why he brought you from the void, isn't it?' With a sudden powerful movement, he jerked the tapestry off the bier and flung it across the chamber. 'Come here,' he rasped at us over his shoulder, 'and bring your uncle with you. Come pay your respects to our forefather, the wise and mighty Naar.'

I suppose he had been tall and broad, an imposing man, well fleshed with healthy muscle and with a full head of hair, which was long and loose and still a glossy yellow. But the moisture had deserted his body; his lips had thinned and drawn away from his teeth; the fine muscles had shrivelled to strings under his skin, which itself was puckered and a dull blue-grey; his eyes had withered into hard little nuts under leathery eyelids.

The tapestry had been his only covering aside from a silver loin plate and a square golden pectoral that reached from his collarbone to just above his navel. With morbid interest I noted his internal organs had not been removed, as they would have been in all six traditions I knew of that liked to mummify dead dignitaries. Where the arched ribcage ended, the skin was drawn tight over a coiled and petrified serpent, presumably his gut; there were a few other bumps and bulges I did not try to interpret.

Katla asked, 'Is he dead?'

I stared at her in surprise – stupid questions were not Kat's style – but Tigrallef said, 'Not in any ordinary sense.'

Five thousand years. It was getting easier to tell which of the Old Ones was speaking. This time it was the cat-thing with the long name. *He has been waiting five thousand years, since the falling of the Great Nameless First, for the fulfillment and the yielding up.*

'Don't rush us,' said my father. 'After all that time, he can wait a few minutes longer. Kat, Vero, look at him!'

We looked. I felt sick; no breakfast and too many stairs, and on top of it all a desiccated ancestor resembling an anatomy drawing from a Zelfic medical treatise, all bones and bits in place. Kat said, 'I suppose you know all about him, Da.'

'His name is Naar. Six thousand years ago he was a great magician, and he opened a gate that would have been better left closed. Except it wasn't really anything like a gate.'

There was a compact made.

'There was indeed, Shining-of-Scales. He gave you the forms of the Old Ones, didn't he, and fed you on worship; you lent him the powers each of you came with, bundled altogether in the composite persona called Harashil. Together you built great empires, and then you tore them down.'

'Why?' Katla broke in.

Long silence.

'Why?' she insisted. 'What was the point of doing all that?'

The answer came loftily from one of the human-likes. *Eternity is very long.*

'Is that all?' Katla demanded, outraged. 'You left a trail of shattered empires all around the world just to pass the time?'

Empires always fall, Naarling child. We did nothing to the not-Naar that they would not do to themselves, were they able.

'Shul]shit,' she said, 'you played with us. You used us.'

We have an agreement. They were not talking to Kat any more – that was addressed to the Wind/Tree himself, still examining our distant forebear with what looked like impersonal distaste.

'We were not party to the contract, Old Ones.'

Nevertheless, we have an agreement.

'We were not even born at the time, Old Ones.'

Nevertheless, we have an agreement.

'Yes,' said my father sadly after a long silence, 'we suppose we do. But there's still no hurry, is there?'

He picked up the golden pectoral and held it close to his eyes, baring the magician's perfectly delineated breastbone and ribs, the colourless knots of his nipples. From where I stood I saw Tigrallef's strange eyes widen as he studied the metal square.

'Tig?' I whispered. No reply. 'Father? What is it?'

He chuckled. 'Twenty years we hunted for this. What a joke. What a pity. See this part here – it's where the Divinatrix went wrong – the structure's similar to the Greater Will, just a reverse twist in alternate lines. It's a good thing we didn't try out the partial copy we found in Khamanthana, there's no telling what we might have summoned from the void.'

My breath came back at last. 'You're telling me it's the Will of Banishment?'

'Yes.' He smiled at me with great good humour. 'So many things are clear to us now. Long ago, the first reading of this Will invited the powers to come through the – oh, let's go on calling it a gate. The second reading, were it ever to take place, would banish them and slam the gate in their – let's call them faces . . .'

'Never mind the tupping terminology. What are you waiting for? Use the Will!'

He laughed out loud. 'It's too late, Child of the Naar. We're going to build our empire. Shall we tell you an interesting fact? It will be just as terrible as the Harashil foretold.'

'No, Father—'

'Yes.' The black night in his eyes took on a reddish glow, faint at first. 'We cannot stop ourself now. We'll take the entire world for our gallows block – no such empire will ever have existed, in history or before it. Our iron legions will raise the torture frames in Gafrin-Gammanthan and the whipping posts in Amballa, the Pleasure in Vassashinay, and the sharpened stakes in the fields of Calloon. Myr will be a desert of frozen bones, the sea around Itsant will be awash with rotting flesh. We will loose the Afadhnids on to Miishel and Grisot, Zaine will be a barren rock in the sea. The blood will run—'

'Enough, Father, enough.'

'—torrents in the riverbeds of Canzitar, and—'

'*Enough!* I do, I really do, have some picture of what you're planning.'

'You cannot begin to imagine,' he said gently. 'But if you know how to stop us, now would be the time.'

'Stop you? How could we possibly know how to stop you?' I demanded, almost indignantly.

'Why do you think we brought you down here?' His lips were drawn back in a broad death's-head grin, like the rictus on the dead face of Naar. 'Help us if you can, or else watch the fulfillment take shape. At this point we don't care. We – I – I – can hold out no longer.'

It is beginning. That was the cat-thing.

It shall be terrible beyond measure. That was the dragon.

It shall be the last. That was the one with lots of hands.

Tigrallef's eyes shone red, holes into a Lucian hell. 'Help me,' he said. I jerked the golden pectoral out of his hands and scanned it desperately – gibberish. I'd never even seen the glyphs before. 'How can we help you?' I shouted, but I could hardly hear myself in the rising shriek of a wind around the person of my father.

Katla knocked the pectoral out of my hands. Her voice howled in my ear: 'It's not time for that yet. Here!' I found one of my hands suddenly in Arkolef's trusting grip, the other being thrust towards Tigrallef by small iron fingers

326

clamped around my wrist. 'Take his hand,' she screamed over the wind. 'The innocent, the brave and the vessel of wrath, remember? Uncle's innocent, you're brave, and I'm bloody angry. Take Father's hand!'

I groped for it and missed. Tigrallef was farther away than my senses told me. 'What are we doing?'

'We're yielding up the Harashil.'

'What?'

'We're giving them back the powers!'

'Are you insane?'

'We can save him, Vero. Hurry—'

Born of the Harashil. Yes, Katla would know. I had Tig's right hand by then, burning hot but unresisting, and Katla was reaching for the left. Arkolef stood between us, his noble brow lightly furrowed with perplexity, which I shared. I watched Katla's hand complete the circle—

—and I was on a great sliding slope of time, where all directions were up and stars hung like black spiders against a blinding white wall, or perhaps the other way around; and also in a room like half a globe, where seven bright shadows stood in a semicircle and an incandescent river flowed from a spring beside me, a pulsing stream of red flame like blood pumping from a fire-dragon's heart. Too bright, too searing. I turned my eyes through solid rock to the skin of the planet, found it swarming with uncleanness – *not-Naar, none of our kind*, a firm voice told me, *filthy squalling rabble of world-lice, not important, crush them all* – and when I realized it was my own voice, I retreated in terror to the extremes of vision, the curve of time and the curved room, where now the river of red fire was slowing to a trickle and now to nothing. I had hands again, and other hands were holding them, one burning, one cool. The stars flamed more darkly and then not at all.

I opened my eyes. My headache was fit to be stuffed and mounted and exhibited to a wondering public. From the feel of my limbs, my muscles had dissolved clean away. At least

327

the wind had died, so the chamber was a little quieter. I groaned and raised myself on bruised elbows; collapsed again. Lifting my head on a neck that felt splintered, I saw Kat sprawled nearby, her hand still clasped in our father's hand, both of them apparently dead. Beside me, the Priest-King lay peacefully on his back staring at the domed ceiling. I thought he was dead too, until he sat up and looked around with an air of benign curiosity. A half-moment later, Katla stirred.

'Vero,' she gasped, 'the Will of Banishment. It's time now.'

'What?'

'Find it. Read it. Do it *fast*.'

'What? Oh, yes.' I was beyond thinking, but I could still take orders. I groped around on the floor close to me, then saw the golden plate near the bier, many feet away, just beyond the Priest-King. I began to crawl in that direction; collapsed yet again. When I made the next effort to raise my head, I noticed the shrunken corpse on the bier was somehow sitting up. It was already less shrunken.

I saw Katla was also making a pathetic effort to crawl towards the pectoral. 'Faster, Vero,' she said thickly, 'there's no more covenant. They can hurt us now.' She sank down again, her head on her outstretched arm and her eyes shut.

They? *They?* Pivoting my head the other way, I saw what she meant – the looming death of all our hopes. Those crude mud figures were not so crude now, and they were touched with colour; they had eyes as well, glittering at us hungrily. Still rigid, carved out of fine marble by master craftsmen, hand-painted by dedicated artists, every scale of the snake-thing and the dragon, every hair of the cat-thing and the wolf—

'Vero . . . hurry . . .'

Kat's eyes were open again. Tigrallef was blinking feebly beside her. I managed to crawl another few inches, every movement pushing another hot spike through my temples and thousands of tiny needles into every joint, but the weakness sickened me more than the pain.

328

From the direction of the bier, I heard someone take a shuddering breath. The Naar-thing, it must have been, drawing the first air in five thousand years into its lungs.

The golden plate looked so close, so close – I reached out to grasp it. It taunted me by being at least two feet past the full stretch of my arm, while being teasingly close to my useless uncle's right hand. I looked up at him in despair, found he was watching the transformation of the Old Ones with an idiotic smile on his face; might as well ask a newborn baby for help. But he did seem less physically shattered than the rest of us; he was sitting up, and he had considerately pulled his leg out of my way.

'Arkolef,' I croaked, 'Arkolef, Son of Cirallef!' With all the strength I could pull together, I reached out and tugged at the hem of his robe. 'Arkolef, please! If you can hear me – *please* hear me – that golden square by your hand—'

He looked down at me and smiled pleasantly.

'Why, certainly,' he said, 'here you go. Tell me something, young man, what play is this? Those costumes are awfully good.'

There was no time to marvel. I fumbled with the pectoral he handed me (the arms of the Many-Handed trembled into life) and saw that the writing on the pectoral now made sense (the snake-thing falteringly lowered its great flat head) but my eyes would not work and the glyphs danced maddeningly in and out of focus. I tried closing first one eye, then the other. The dragon's tail twitched.

'You know, you don't look at all well. Shall I?'

The pectoral was removed from my hand. Something thudded on the floor not far from my nose – I squinted at it, saw a bare foot, well-formed and rather dusty, attached to an ankle, attached to (I twisted my neck to see upwards) the towering naked figure of our forefather Naar, who was looking down at me with not a trace of family feeling in his strikingly handsome face. Elsewhere claws clicked, scales scratched, robes whispered across the flagstones – I closed my eyes. It seemed we were now going to find out how literally the text about consuming the innocent, the brave and the angry was meant to be taken.

The Priest-King cleared his throat and began to read.

First came the screams: fury rather than fear or pain. I opened my eyes in time to see Naar's foot abruptly leave my field of vision as he staggered backwards and cannoned off the bier to join the Old Ones. The light was already gathering around them, a cold light, strong and white, streaked with the deep blues and purples of the ice-cliffs of Myr. Where the seven graceless idols had stood a few minutes before, there were now eight figures, all of them shimmering with a beauty that the world will never see again, with any luck: dragon, serpent, wolf, cat, and four in the shape of men. The light whirled and tightened around them. Shrieking, they drew together.

Apparently elocution is one of the heroic arts. My uncle read the Banishment beautifully, in a fine deep voice, though I noticed he kept his place by following along with a fingertip. Thus I could see when he had only one quatrain left, then three lines, then two. There was silence just before the end, as if the Old Ones themselves stopped screaming so as to appreciate Arkolef's dramatic final flourish. Then the cold cone of light around them shrank to a streak like a short segment of lightning, which compressed in turn to an unendurable point of light; which in turn compressed to nothing at all.

'My, it's gone dark,' said my uncle.

There was a small gourd of water attached to my belt, and a candle and flint in Kat's belt pouch. The Priest-King chattered affably while he got a candle going and poured a little water down each of our throats. He was still under the impression we'd been involved in an ingenious performance of some new play; he especially liked the concept of audience participation. When he recognized Tig, he was delighted – 'Mother always said you'd come back' – but he wept a little on reflecting that his nephew and niece would never know their cousins.

While Kat began the arduous task of explaining to him where we'd been for twenty years and why no marriage had been arranged for her yet, I crept closer to Tig. Though a headache was still pounding inside my temples, the water had helped and my muscles seemed to be properly connected again. Tig looked far better in the candlelight than I felt, though he had hardly moved. He sat up and frowned at me as I dropped down beside him.

'How do you feel?' I asked.

'Empty.'

'That's to be expected after no breakfast.'

'Not that kind of empty, Verolef. Empty.'

'I was trying to make a joke.'

'Sorry,' he said crossly, 'it's just – I never thought I'd miss the old sow like this. I hardly feel like myself.'

'You'll get over it. What now?'

He brightened a little. 'Well – I was thinking we might take up your mother's suggestion.'

'I meant, what will happen to the world now that we've saved it?'

'Saved it?' That made him laugh out loud. 'Never mind, Vero, the answer's not important.'

'I'm starting to hate those two words.'

'I always did. All right, I'll tell you what I think. Nothing very different will happen. The nations will never even know they've been reprieved. They'll go on much as before, but none of their disasters will be part of some demented divine plan.'

'Will that be an improvement?'

'In practice, it will look very similar.' He laughed again, but this time the bitterness was more apparent. 'The same old cycles will continue. Kingdoms and empires will continue to rise and fall. The difference is, we've cut the puppet strings and left the nations to make up their own dance steps. It was Oballef's foolishness, you know, to think his good intentions justified keeping the strings in place. Well, we learned from

331

his mistake. Now the nations have a chance of learning from theirs.'

'And will they?'

'How would I know? Prophecy just became a lost art.'

'You must have an opinion.'

He hesitated. 'In my opinion, the Second Gillish Empire has already made an interesting start. You may take that however you like. Up we get, Vero.'

He stood up and gave me his arm. I staggered a bit but managed to stay on my feet. 'And what about us?' I asked.

'I foresee a long climb,' he said darkly, staring at the jagged hole of the stairway.

My memories of the departure from Gil are irritatingly patchy. Kat and I were drained by those moments of full-flood exposure to the Harashil; by the time we reached the top of Tigrallef's impromptu staircase, Tig was carrying Katla slung over his shoulder, and I was stumbling along drunkenly with Arkolef taking most of my weight, and his constant sunny chatter in my ear. I suppose he was making up for twenty years of silence. There was a bloody chaos in the Hall of Harps, which died away at the sight of the Divine Scion and the Priest-King; it's hard to keep a good battle going when all parties to it are grovelling on the floor. We walked right through the thick of them.

I do not remember getting from the Hall of Harps to the foyer, nor the foyer to the forecourt; the next memory I have is a blurred vision of the streets of Gil jouncing past, buildings burning and flame-bolts flying overhead, me slumped half in Kesi's lap and half in Mallinna's, her sweaty arms wrapped around me and keeping my neck from breaking when the carriage shuddered over obstacles in the street. I remember Tig saying, 'Look, Calla, I'm bleeding,' in delighted tones. Then the harbour: being dumped out of the carriage and hauled on to the deck of the *Fifth* between Mallinna and my uncle; recovering enough to watch Jonno carry Katla aboard and lay her tenderly down; then a blank spot, and then opening my eyes again to see Jonno and

Chasco looking up at us *from the quay* as the windcatcher pulled into the channel.

'Look after Grandda! Tell Katla we have to find—' They were hidden by a rolling black cloud of smoke before Jonno could finish; when it thinned, they were gone. My memory blanks out for a while after that. The next thing I knew, the *Fifth* was well out in the open sea and Tig was at the taffrail wearing a bloodstained white bandage around his arm with the air of a man sporting a prized trophy. Calla was beside him, and he was in the act of throwing something into the sea. I pulled myself up and leaned over the taffrail to watch it sink. Square, golden, glittering. The pectoral of Naar. It planed down into the green shadows, dimmed and diminished, until darkness closed over it and it was gone.

Epilogue

Our house would win no awards from the Lucian Clerisy's Directorate of Harmonious Design: from one side, a pastiche of an Amballan pirate cruiser, one of the most graceful shipforms ever to terrify an honest seaman; from the other side, a large two-tiered box with a tower of sorts stuck on the front. We have not been able to decide what the privy used to be – Shree swears it's the deckhouse of a Ronchar Sea pearler, whereas my father holds out for the mast-top lookout from a Kerassoc windcatcher. To me, it looks very like a privy.

Across from the house is our cornfield, where my mother puts each of us to work on a rotating basis. Our second harvest is not far off. On the far side of the field, with a sweeping view of the icepack, is the first rough embodiment of the College of the Second Coming, the name of which began as my mother's idea of a joke. As she put it, the Myrenes had the refreshing distinction of predicting Tig would *never* return, all those years ago when they waved us off gloomily in the long-lost *Second*. Furthermore, the fact that we were the first crew ever known to have survived, or even attempted, a second passage through the icepack demanded some sort of commemoration. The name took hold.

Most of the college, built of timber culled from the beach, is taken up by a suite of workrooms and a temporary home for the archives. Shree and Angel have been cataloguing the materials gathered on our twenty-year search for the Banishment – the rubbings and drawings, texts and maps, the language lists, records of oral tradition and observations of natural history. Mallinna and Kat are gradually sorting out the crates of books and scrolls from the archives in Gil, packed for the Benthonic Expedition. Just outside their workroom is the heap of stones we have been gradually compiling, against the time we can lay the foundations of a grander and more lasting structure.

Inland from the rock pile is the new realm of the former Priest-King of the Second Empire of Gil. He's growing vegetables, and tending the piglets we bought in Vassashinay before turning south, which have become pigs of respectable size. The former First Flamen helps him with the gardening, does odd jobs in the archives or sits in the watery sun. I suspect he is courting my grandmother, the former Dowager Empress, though she is very busy these days expanding her woollens business. She is not the descendant of hard-headed Satheli merchant-princes for nothing.

We keep busy. Yesterday I carried a few rocks up from the quarry, weeded in the cornfield with Chasolef slung on my back, contributed two hours of labour to the township and worked with Angel in the College. Today is my day to keep watch across the icepack, and I believe what we've been waiting for has finally come.

Tig had brought me my lunch and was still sitting with me when I sighted the ship, about an hour ago. He could not see it himself for quite a while – he's getting increasingly short-sighted – but at last we were able to agree that it was a small Gillish trawler, and the intelligent setting of the sails indicated somebody must be alive on board. Then we saw it was tacking, using the wind to fight the current for a better approach to the icepack, and Tig said, 'I'd know that hand on the wheel anywhere. Take your baby back, Vero, I'll tell the others.'

I took Chasolef from him, and he loped off towards the College of the Second Coming. Seconds after he disappeared inside, Katla tore out of the doorway and raced for the road that winds down the side of the cliff. Kesi was not far behind her, moving remarkably quickly for a man of his years. I will follow them in a few minutes – all of us will except Arkolef, who finds the road difficult with his wooden leg, and Angel, who hates open spaces.

Meantime the trawler has begun her dance with the ice-islands. She is naturally in some danger, but I think Chasco will bring her through intact, just as I did the *Fifth*; more of her will come to shore, anyway, than a few shattered boards and the good-looking golden-haired corpses of Jonno and his sisters.

Chasco himself will no doubt bring news of the Second Empire of Gil. It will be interesting to see who, if anyone, triumphed in the civil war – the Primate, the Captain, the Truant, someone else entirely. It will be interesting to see what the current victors are doing with the malleable stuff of history. It will be interesting to see whether the cult of the Divine Scion survived Tig's rather off-handed fulfillment of its central prophecy. Interesting, but not important.

I had a nightmare a few nights ago. Many ages had passed; mountains had been levelled to plains, plains uplifted to mountains, deserts had sunk beneath seas, seabeds had risen and dried to deserts. I saw a man turn over an ancient slab of shellstone and be caught by a gleam of gold; he pried at the stone, flake by flake, until a square shape emerged from its nest of antique coral, untarnishable metal figured with strange glyphs. Frowning, he began to read them aloud – sweating, I woke up and shook Mallinna out of her own dreams. 'Realistically speaking,' she said when I told her what I'd seen, 'if all that time had passed, he wouldn't be able to read the glyphs anyway. All this would be long forgotten, and so would we. But since you're awake, you can see to the baby.'

The important things these days are all small: the archives; the cornfield; the white hair Tigrallef found on his head last week, and his not-completely-mad idea of a peace mission to the Eyesuckers; Chasolef, who is a very small thing indeed; our lives. The eventual crumbling of the College of the Second Coming is no reason not to gather the stones.

Katla is already a tiny figure on the beach, having broken all speed records getting down there. The trawler has woven its way to the clear water inside the line of the icepack; my wife and parents, Shree and my grandmother, are on the road waving at me to join them. I'll sling Chasolef on my back and we'll all go down together, four generations, for a reunion that is important at least to us. For the moment, history and the future can look after themselves.